Forever Chance

Also by CJ Murphy

frame by frame

The Bucket List

Five Point Series
Gold Star Chance

Forever Chance

CJ Murphy

Desert Palm Press

Forever Chance
(Five Point Series – Book 2)

By CJ Murphy

©2019 CJ Murphy

ISBN (book) 9781948327565
ISBN (epub) 9781948327572
ISBN (pdf): 9781948327589

Desert Palm Press
1961 Main Street, Suite 220
Watsonville, California 95076
www.desertpalmpress.com

Editor: CK King
Cover Design: TreeHouse Studio, Winston-Salem, NC

Printed in the United States of America
First Edition December 2019

Acknowledgments

I have amazing people in my life who constantly encourage me to keep writing, keep doing, keep moving forward. These incredible people are family to me even if we aren't related. I'm also incredibly grateful to my friends and fans who constantly reassure me I'm getting it right with their reviews, their social media comments, and their emails. There are days when I think everything I write needs to be deleted and started all over again. One kind note about how much they enjoyed the story is all it takes to keep my hands on the keyboard. So, for all of you who tell me to keep writing, I thank you more than I can say.

To my incredible editor CK King, thank God Lee put us together. I am forever grateful for your guidance, your enjoyment of the culinary moments in my books, and your honesty when something isn't working. I truly appreciate you channeling your inner Edward Scissorhands when needed.

To my publisher Lee Fitzsimmons at Desert Palm Press, may we see many books with the character to which I gave your last name to. I can never thank you enough for accepting that first manuscript.

Oh, my beta readers, how do I thank you? I'm continually grateful for your candid comments about the storyline and its characters. You help me keep them alive and relevant. I can't say how much you do in helping me make sure these books are worth reading.

AJ Adaire, my Yoda. What more can I say beyond how valuable you are to me? I learn so much from you and will always consider meeting you in person a true highlight of my literary career. Irene Our Queen rocks as well! I could never have been half the author I am without your patience and sharp wit.

Lastly, to my wife, Darla. You make all the good things in my life possible. Though you're now raising two children, our puppy Jaxx, and me, you manage to keep it all together. I thank you for stepping out of your comfort zone and 'peopling' with me at GCLS Pittsburgh. You are the reason I write and the inspiration for all things in my life. Thank you for giving me my 'Forever Chance' with you.

Dedication

To Darla,
Tha Gaol Agam Ort. Agus Bithidh Gu Brath.-Scottish Gaelic
'I love you. I always will.'

Chapter One

SHERIFF CHANCE FITZSIMMONS SAT on the desk in the front of the auditorium-style classroom at West Virginia University. Her good friend, Professor Scott Ross, had recruited her to speak on rural law enforcement challenges. She looked over her audience, the number of male students far outweighing the females by nearly three to one. She was proud to see that one of those females was her little sister, Kendra. Her near carbon copy sat front and center, a miracle of anything but genetics.

"Rural law enforcement differs a great deal from being an officer in a municipal setting. For instance, in a municipality, the distance between where you are and where you're dispatched to can be a matter of a few minutes or blocks. In my jurisdiction, it could take twenty to forty minutes for me to reach a call location, more if its bad weather. What's worse is your available backup could be on the other side of the county. That reality can have deadly consequences." Chance used her clicker to advance her presentation. A large picture of her father in his uniform appeared on the screen. "This officer died in the line of duty on a domestic call. His backup was very far away when an enraged husband threatened his wife with a gun." She turned to the audience again. "Deputy Ray Fitzsimmons died when he shielded the female victim from gunfire. That deputy was my father, and he died on the scene from a gunshot wound to the head. He was doing all the things he'd been taught, including wearing a vest and using caution. Unfortunately, humans rarely survive gunshot wounds to the head. My dad saved a life that day. It cost him his."

Chance watched as the students stared at the screen. She could see that Kendra's eyes were directed firmly at her. "Firefighters have a saying. You risk a lot to save a lot. You risk little to save little. I spent many years jumping out of a perfectly good airplane into wildfires. I know what that means. I also know the cost of putting your body between an innocent and a bullet. It's one of the reasons all of my road deputies have a K9 unit with them. They are never alone."

A hand went up in the back of the room. Chance nodded to acknowledge the request. A young man, who couldn't have been more

1

than nineteen, stood to ask his question. "Didn't it worry you, when you became an officer, that you might face that same fate as your father?"

Chance gripped the edge of the desk, her chest tightening at the question. She thought about her father every day she put on her badge. It was a part of her morning ritual, as she stretched her scar tissue and repeated something Maggie had said to her when she'd been in the burn ward. *Steel is tempered by fire, and gold is refined by it.* How could she explain what she felt about being an officer? "My dad was my hero. Every day, I watched him put on his uniform and pin his badge over his heart. Ray Fitzsimmons believed in honor and duty, and he taught me those same values. In life, you have to find something you believe in from inside the marrow of your bones, something that's elemental." Her hands reached up and unpinned her badge. "My dad told me there are five points to this badge." She placed her finger on one of them and touched the next point with each word she spoke. "Honor, duty, courage, integrity, and empathy. He believed that the empathy part is the hardest for an officer because it requires finding balance. He said I'd clearly understand that when I was wearing the badge. His words hold even greater truth today."

Chance made eye contact with the students in the room before stopping at Kendra. "Some of you will become officers, some lawyers, and maybe some will find this field isn't for you at all. What I can tell you is, the day you decide to enforce the laws of our land, you will use each of these five points in the performance of your duties."

She touched one of the points again. "Some of you will rely on your courage, and some will rely heavily on duty. I encourage you to lean on the one my father said would be the most difficult, empathy. When you've dealt with the same addict for the third time in as many days, when you've arrested the same abusive partner over and over only to have the other party rescind a domestic violence petition again, when you've put the same thief in jail for the fifth time, you'll find that empathy is the most tenuous to achieve. You'll feel like you're getting nowhere more often than you'll feel like you've made a difference."

Chance held her badge in the air. "I can only hope that one day, someone will walk up to you and say you've been their role model and their reason for choosing this profession." She let her eyes settle on Kendra for only a moment. It was enough to feel the connection she and her adopted sister shared. She fastened the badge back on her uniform. "You'll remember why you pin the badge on every day and stand as the thin blue line between order and anarchy." Zeus barked his approval and the class released a small laugh. Chance reached down to pet him. "He's listened to this speech enough he could give it himself. Thank you for your attention today. I'll leave a stack of business cards with Professor Ross if you have any other questions."

A round of applause came from those in attendance, as chairs shuffled, and backpacks were hefted. Scott Ross stepped to her side and held out his hand. "Thanks, Chance. Having you come in and talk with them, as a current law enforcement officer, really makes an impact."

Chance pulled on his hand and embraced him in a hug. "It's always a pleasure." She pushed him back but held him by his shoulder. "What makes an impact is having a professor like you who's been neck deep in the trenches. You can tell them the truth beyond what the recruiting posters portray."

Scott chuckled softly. "It does differ slightly. Regardless, I am in your debt for so many reasons."

Chance shook her head. "Scott, there's no debt between us, ever. I mean that. I enjoy coming down here. Gives me a chance to take Kendra to lunch and get an eyes-on report for the moms-squared. Isn't that right, pain in my ass?"

"You're buying, so I'll agree." Kendra smiled with a look of genuine mirth.

Chance pointed to her. "See what having a kid sister thirty years younger gets you? An empty wallet and a truckload of sarcasm." She playfully shoved Kendra.

Scott's laughter was contagious. "Hell, having a brother two years younger gets you the same thing."

Chance was aware of Scott's brother, Miles, who'd been in and out of rehab several times. Scott's parents had died over a dozen years ago, and he'd taken it upon himself to try and keep his younger brother on the straight and narrow. "I have no doubt."

Scott put his foot up on a chair and leaned forward, exposing the ankle section of his prosthesis. "The debt goes beyond your guest lecture and you know it."

Chance lowered her gaze for a fraction of a second before meeting his eyes. "We'll have to continue to agree to disagree on that point, my friend. Any time you need a lecturer for a day, give me a call." She snickered when Kendra's stomach growled out a protest. "I need to feed the beast over there. I'm pretty sure that's a lion trying to claw its way out."

Kendra blushed.

Scott shook Chance's hand. "Don't think I won't. I'm glad you're doing all right after this summer. We've both had enough knocks for a lifetime, I think."

"Mags and Dee will certainly agree." Chance nodded her own agreement.

"You'd better include your fiancée. I don't mess with Jax. She's tough." Kendra pointed her finger at Chance.

Scott snapped his fingers. "That's right. You're finally taking the plunge. Congratulations. I hope to meet this miracle worker someday."

"We'll have to do dinner sometime, with you and your wife. I'd venture to say they'd be two peas in a pod. It was great to see you, Scott. Call me anytime, and if I can work it in, I'm there." Chance hugged him again.

"Dr. Ross is busy delivering babies today. I don't know how she does it. She's the most sought after obgyn in the area, and I have no idea what she ever saw in me. Kendra, I'll see you next week."

"Thanks, Professor Ross. I'm looking forward to the session."

Scott pointed to Kendra. "She reminds me so much of you; it's scary. Kendra's going to be a fantastic officer someday. She's got a great role model to follow."

Chance blushed. "I think her professors have a bit to do with that as well."

"You two are embarrassing me, and I'm starving. See you next week, Professor Ross." Kendra hefted her backpack to her shoulder and grabbed Chance's sleeve.

Chance slipped on her Stetson. "I think that's my cue to leave. Call me sometime, Scott."

Once they'd left the classroom, Chance asked the obvious question. "Where do you want to go?"

Kendra didn't even hesitate. "Colasantes."

"Okay, you're on."

"And I have a favor, well more of request." Kendra dropped her eyes.

"I can't say yes or no until you tell me what you want." Chance adjusted the brim of her hat.

"Can I bring a guest?"

"I don't see why not. Who do you want to join us?" Chance watched Kendra. She was sure she was about to learn who her sister had been spending an inordinate amount of time around. Try as she might, she struggled for the name she'd heard Kendra use in one or two

4

of their phone conversations.

"Brandi."

"Do we need to pick her up somewhere, or is she close by?"

Kendra cleared her throat and rubbed a hand across the back of her neck. Chance grinned at the blush her little sister was sporting. Kendra pulled out her phone and tapped the screen a few times, then waited. "She's over at the Mountain Lair. She can meet us at your vehicle in ten minutes."

Chance put a hand on the younger woman's shoulder. "Breathe, Bullseye. I promise I won't interrogate her."

Kendra's nervous laughter made Chance smile. One deep breath later, Kendra met her eyes. "I've wanted to introduce her to everyone for a while. She's...well, special."

"I gathered that."

They started walking toward the parking garage, Zeus on their heels. Hordes of students were rushing from one place to another, earbuds in place while they stared blankly at their phones. It amazed Chance how they were able to navigate without falling over something. One second later, Chance noticed one of the enraptured students walk into traffic. Chance was moving before she could say a word. Her boots gained traction against the blacktop, as she ran toward the oblivious young woman. *Three more feet.* Chance looked at the truck that was barreling down at her. She heard the motor decelerate before she heard the squeal of tires as the brakes were applied. Her arm went around the waist of the unsuspecting student, as she pulled her close and dove for the grassy area on the other side of the street. The two of them tumbled, and Chance wrapped her arms around the woman to protect her from the fall.

The frightened young woman was wide-eyed, as she jerked her earbuds out. "What the hell are you doing?"

"Saving you from becoming a hood ornament." Chance pointed at the truck only feet from them that was now sideways from the force of the sudden need to brake. She winced at a pain in her shoulder from the impact.

Kendra dropped to the ground beside her, as Zeus came to her side. "Chance!"

"I'm fine, Kendra." She turned to the startled young woman who sat beside her shaking. "Another day at the office."

The driver of the truck yelled out the window. "Are you two okay?"

Chance waved him off. "We're good."

A young man in ratty jeans and a WVU T-shirt ran across the street and knelt by the shell-shocked young woman. "Lisha, what the hell happened?"

The young woman shook her head. "I don't know, but I think she just saved my life."

Chance held out her hand. "Sheriff Chance Fitzsimmons. I'm just glad I was here. I hope you'll try and be a little more aware of what's going on around you. If I hadn't been watching, this could have resulted in more than just a skinned knee." Chance pointed to the scrape marks on Lisha's knee.

"I'm Lisha's brother, Ian. I don't know how to thank you. I had her here on campus to visit before she enrolls in the spring. I don't know what I'd have done if something happened to her."

Lisha put a hand on Ian's forearm. "I'm okay; I just wasn't watching. I was texting Jacob."

Chance stood and dusted off the grass clippings from her uniform. "It's really important to keep your eyes on what's going on around you. There are dangers far beyond walking in front of a truck. You two, be careful."

Ian stood and extended his hand to Chance. "Thanks again."

"Anytime." Chance watched the two walk away. She picked up her Stetson from the ground. "Kendra, promise me you'll never be so consumed with your phone, or anything else, that you lose sight of the objects in front of you." She pointed her hat to indicate the student to Kendra. "When you're an officer, that will get you killed." She examined a tear in the shoulder of her uniform shirt. "Damn."

"Looks like you'll have to beg the boss for a new one. I promise, Chance, I try to be aware of what's going on around me all the time. You taught me that. It serves me well with this madhouse down here."

They continued their way through the throng until they reached the open concrete structure. Chance saw a petite girl about Kendra's age pacing near her vehicle. Dark hair cut in a pixie style framed delicate features. "I thought you guys got lost."

Chance grinned and extended her hand. "We had a little delay." Chance pointed to her shoulder where the department patch was hanging by the torn part of her uniform shirt. "I'm Chance, Kendra's sister."

With a voice belying her small stature, Brandi answered in kind. "Brandi, Brandi Antolini. What happened?" Her eyes were an unusual green.

Kendra shook her head and laughed. "Don't mind me. I think I was supposed to make that introduction."

Brandi cocked her head. "Then speak up. You know I don't have a shy bone in my body. If I did, we would still be waving at each other in biology class."

Chance nearly burst out laughing. *She's got Kendra's number.* "How about we make our way to the restaurant and Kendra can tell you about our adventure? We can order while we get better acquainted." Chance pointed a thumb at Kendra. "This one gets hangry if she doesn't eat every two hours."

Brandi looked down at Zeus. "Especially in the morning, she's really cranky before coffee and sustenance."

Kendra cleared her throat and raised her hand. "Kendra here, present and accounted for, don't mind me."

Brandi knelt. "Who is this beautiful creature? And I'll never mind you."

"No, you won't, even when it's in your best interest. Brandi meet Zeus, Chance's K9 partner." Kendra extended her hand and scratched Zeus.

"Is it okay if I pet him?" Brandi asked.

Chance nodded her consent. "I'm sure he'd like that."

Brandi presented the Malinois her hand. Zeus leaned forward and sniffed before looking to Chance, who nodded again. He put his nose under Brandi's hand and bumped it. She stroked over his head and ears. "Wow, he's all muscle."

"He and I spend a lot of time keeping in shape. It's important for our job, and he's all about the job."

Kendra leaned down. "When I go to work for Chance, I'll have a K9 too."

Chance watched a smile light up Brandi's face.

"And I'll take care of it."

Kendra stood. "Brandi's a veterinary medicine student from California."

Chance couldn't help laughing as the irony was not lost on her.

Brandi stood and furrowed her brow. "What's so funny about that?"

"You didn't tell her?" Chance stared gape-mouthed at Kendra.

"Tell me what?"

"That my fiancée is a vet, who moved back to West Virginia after a twenty-year practice in Northern California."

Brandi punched Kendra in the upper arm. "How did you forget to mention that?"

Kendra winced and smiled. "Ow. I didn't think about it."

Brandi put a hand on her hip. "Start using that head for something other than your good looks. You're getting a sister-in-law who's a vet? Kendra, that's pertinent information."

Kendra furrowed her brow. "What's that supposed to mean?"

Chance cleared her throat this time and leaned close to Kendra. "Let me help you out here before you dig that hole so deep you'll need the rope rescue team to get you out." She turned to Brandi. "Let's chalk that up to being starstruck by your charm. I say we go eat."

Kendra shut her eyes and put her head back. "Please, God, save me."

Brandi leaned over and kissed Kendra on the cheek. "I'll let you make it up to me later. Can we go? I'm starving."

Chance hit the locks and opened the rear hatch for Zeus to load. "That we can."

***

Two hours later, Chance was on her way back to Tucker County, a smile playing across her face. She made a call to Jax who answered in the first two rings.

"Hey, you. On your way back yet?"

"I have one more stop, beautiful. Anything you'd like me to bring home for supper, or do you want me to grill?"

"Such a sweet talker. Any chance you're coming home by Clarksburg?"

"Going right through there. I need to stop in at the sheriff's office for some information."

"Then I say you bring home Los Loco's tamales and chips with salsa."

Chance would be happy to stop in and see how Anita was doing. "Your wish is my command."

"Be careful on your way home. I love you. Tell Anita hi for me."

The words Jax spoke never failed to warm Chance from the inside out. How her life had changed. "Will do, and I love you too. See you at home."

It took forty minutes to make it to downtown Clarksburg. Chance wanted to check with her fellow sheriff and friend, William Andrews, about the heroin pipeline that seemed to be streaming into their state. The overdose rate in his county was much higher than in her own. He had a major city in his jurisdiction and the intersection of two major roadways. Interstate 79 traversed the state north and south, and Route 50 east to west.

The natural gas business had brought in more than economic growth with their out-of-state employees. Thousands of gas well workers were staying up to fifty miles away from the well sites. When those workers were present, the opportunity for illicit drug sales and prostitution skyrocketed. She parked her new Suburban in a lot close to the courthouse, where the sheriff's personal office was. The road officers and detectives were in another location.

Chance and Zeus entered the courthouse. An old colleague was acting as security and ushered her through the array of metal detectors and X-ray machines. She stopped at the receptionist's desk and announced herself. Minutes later, Will appeared and invited her into his office.

"How the hell are you, Chance? When we got the word what happened up there, we were all ready to load up and bring in reinforcements." Will sat behind his desk and rocked back in his chair.

Chance pulled off her hat, placed it on her knee, and rubbed a hand through her hair. "I'm doing really well. No lingering injuries from either dustup. We've been back to being a sleepy little county for a few months. With the Leaf Peepers festival coming up, I'll get busier than I'd like to be."

Will reached into his desk and pulled out a pack of nicotine gum.

Chance pointed to the gum he held. "You still trying to quit smoking?"

"Yeah, for the ninety-seventh time. My doctor chews my ass, and my wife threatens pieces of it if I don't. Hard habit to break when you started at sixteen. I'm still not sure how I made it through the academy some days."

"I'm grateful that's one vice I never indulged in. Took in enough of it when I was smoke jumping. Got a few questions for you. Anyone have a bead on the flood of heroin that's floating around? I've got a suspicion mine's coming out of Baltimore, but no real proof."

Will reached for the keyboard of his computer and tapped several keys. He motioned for her to come around. "We've been tracking the overdoses and trying to pinpoint when this shit is coming in for sale. Problem is, these folks are getting it from all over. Gas well workers from out of state with too much money and not enough sense. We've had a few traffic stops with them coming back from Texas or Oklahoma that have yielded some significant product. The bulk is coming out of Pittsburgh by the usual suspects, with a few more heavy hitters pulling the strings. Huntington's pipeline is out of Detroit. Only the low-level guys below the middleman get caught. Our taskforce squeezes them. Unfortunately, they're more afraid of ratting out the kingpins than they are going to jail."

Chance rolled her hat around in her hands. "I'm worried what ski season will bring. We'll have idiots, like your visiting cowboys, crawling over the mountain with too much money and far away from home."

"I think I'd still take your crazy over mine. The view alone is worth it."

"I can't argue with you. I wish I had a better handle on this heroin thing. We've beefed up our emergency medical service with extra Narcan and will have heavy police presence during the festival. No way to keep track of the amount of out-of-state visitors, though I'd really like to put up the license plate reader that came in. I've got the money from a grant; it's the privacy issues I'm tiptoeing around. No matter how many times I explain that this camera won't be used for traffic violations, it's a hard sell. I've explained over and over that the only thing it keys in on is a plate already in the system for a warrant or a be-on-the-lookout. I still have resistance. Hell, I've got sovereign citizens residing in my county, who are calling it unconstitutional even though they don't believe in a single law, constitutional or not."

Will chewed his gum with a furious barrage of pops and cracks. "Those citizens"—he made air quotes—"are nut jobs. Remember that class we took last year at that law enforcement convention? They don't think anyone has rule over them. One of my deputies stopped one a few years ago for having no tags on a vehicle. The guy had no registration and no insurance. I'm still fighting all that in court. The amount of discovery he requested is far outweighing what the fine would have brought. Makes no sense except that they like to fuck with law enforcement. Dangerous as hell too. You be careful."

Chance slipped her hat back on and rose from her seat, as Zeus stepped to her side. She reached out her hand to shake Will's. "I'll do just that. Now, I've got to get out of here and over to Los Loco to pick up dinner, or I may be sleeping on the couch."

Will rose and shook her hand. "I may run over there and do the same. Congratulations, by the way. I thought you'd end up marrying that doctor, but it looks like you found someone who will put up with you and your K9 there." He nodded toward Zeus.

Chance brushed a hand across Zeus' well-healed ear and thought of the care Jax had given them both when they'd been injured. "Sometimes, things work out for the best. Thanks, Will. Keep in touch."

Will waved her out of his office and Chance made her way back to the vehicle. "Let's go make Momma happy."

Chapter Two

JAX TRAILED A HAND down Glenny's flank before reaching up to rub her distinctive dished face. The mare's snow-white coat made her impressive under any circumstances. Her long, arching neck and high tail carriage told anyone who knew horses that she was an Arabian. She was stunning and one of the best endurance horses Jax had ever owned. "Such a sweet girl," Jax crooned as Glenny curled the length of her neck around Jax's shoulder. It was like getting a hug and Jax soaked it up. Mac stood in his stall, stamping his front hoof. Chance's horse, Kelly, nickered softly beside them. "Okay, jealous things. I'll be there in a moment, patience please." Jax chuckled, as she rubbed the curry brush a few more times over Glenny's back. "I'll feed you all in a minute."

"Can I help?" Chance strode into the barn, a warm smile flitting across her face.

Jax patted Glenny and stepped out, closing the stall door behind her. "You most certainly may. First by kissing me senseless."

"Ah, another wish I am more than happy to grant." Chance pulled Jax into her arms.

Their lips met in a symphony of need. Soft skin met warm flesh and a tongue snaked out. When Jax felt it, she granted entrance into the depths of her mouth and reveled at the shiver that ran up her spine with the intimacy. She pulled off Chance's Stetson and ran a hand into the thick, chestnut strands.

When they came up for air at an impatient whinny, they let their foreheads touch. The horses could wait a few more minutes while she breathed in the scent and very being of her lover. The day she'd met Chance had changed her life. She'd lost her way over thirty years ago and managed to find the road back home a few months ago, back into Chance's arms. Standing in a renovated barn with the smell of Timothy hay and alfalfa all around her, she was reminded of how things had changed for her.

"What's that smile about?" Chance nipped gently at her earlobe.

"I was thinking about how blessed I am that you love me."

"It's me that's blessed. I'll show you how much if we finish up the chores here. Sorry I didn't get home in time for a ride."

Jax raised an eyebrow and moved in to kiss her again. She caught Chance's lower lip and nipped before soothing it again with her kiss. "I'll think of some way for you to make it up to me. Kelly over there will take a little more convincing." She felt Chance shiver in her arms and delighted in the power she had to arouse her fiancée.

"You are dangerous. I'll look forward to my penance later." Chance pulled back and walked over to her horse, who nodded fervently.

Watching the connection Chance had with Kelly warmed Jax. "I swear she understands exactly what you say."

Jax watched as Chance grabbed two flakes of hay from the bale and put it in the corner feeder, just inside the stall. Jax grabbed the grain bucket and handed it to her as she went to feed Mac one stall over. Through the open bar's half wall, she watched the muscles of Chance's arms and shoulders bunch and roll. She was so turned on; she considered throwing Chance down and attacking her in one of the empty stalls.

Chance reached up and patted Kelly's neck. "She does. We worked a great deal on communication when I trained her as a search and rescue mount."

Jax knew horses learned in a variety of ways and reacted to the stimulus they were exposed to. Operational conditioning was achieved through trial and error, with positive and negative reinforcement. She also knew that desensitization was important for horses used in law enforcement in order to allow them to work in highly unpredictable situations. Chance was a natural with horses and animals. Jax was sure that was one of the reasons they made a compatible couple. They shared that love and sensitivity. She watched Chance move around the stall, grooming and caring for her equine partner. The deep rumbles of contentment Kelly emitted proved Chance was still in her good graces, despite the absence of their evening ride. Jax was brought out of her musings by the rich voice that always brought her to attention.

"I really missed going on our ride tonight. Promise. I'll be home in time tomorrow. I spent longer with Kendra than I'd expected."

Jax stepped out into the center aisle, closed the stall door, and made her way to Chance. She wrapped an arm around her waist as they headed for the house. "How is she?"

"In love."

"Do tell."

"Too much for this short walk. I will tell you something funny. The girlfriend is a veterinary student from California."

Jax's laugh cackled out into the night. "Following in her big sister's footsteps awfully close, don't you think?"

"That's what I thought. She hadn't even told Brandi about you, for which she got a pretty good punch to the arm."

"Kendra lacks your confidence. It'll come. I have no doubt about it. So, Brandi, huh?"

They walked to the house and stepped up onto the porch. "Let's eat, and we'll settle into the swing with a cup of coffee. I'll tell you all about it."

"Deal."

Jax opened the insulated bag Chance kept in her cruiser for bringing takeout home. The meal would still need a bit of reheating. She plated the tamales and put them in the oven to heat. The microwave tended to dry things out, and she could be patient a little while longer. Chance handed her a bottle of beer, which Jax accepted gratefully.

"I saw Penny today. She's glowing, and Taylor is like a mother hen."

"I know. Both of them are so excited. I helped her move some furniture the other day. They have the nursery set up. Offering them the house was one of the best ideas I've ever had."

Jax threaded an arm around Chance's waist and kissed her. The taste of hops lingered on her tongue. "No regrets about moving into this place with me?"

"Not after the contractors got it in gear. Once you gave Arlen the go-ahead to hire as many workers as he needed to get it done, it was amazing how fast this place was ready. I know Taylor and Penny were grateful they didn't have to sign a lease extension for their old place. The upstairs still needs to be finished, and I know the constant mess hasn't been fun for either of us. The upside has been being with you every day." Chance stroked down Jax's back, drawing a delicious shiver.

"I'm pretty fond of waking up beside you, too. Like I said, I was fortunate enough to have the funds to make it happen. I wanted Penny settled with one less thing to worry about while she's concentrating on making a little person."

"I know it's eased Taylor's mind. She didn't want to be moving in winter." Chanced kissed her again. "On to other topics. How was work?"

"Uncle Marty came in to make plans with Lindsey for the free checkup clinic at Leaf Peepers, and I had a pretty full day of appointments. One barn call over at the Butler farm. Their sheep herd was due for a good checkup. All was well, and I ended the day with an adoptive family bringing in a new kitten from the shelter for her shots. The adorable little girl was so afraid she'd hurt the calico."

"And if I know you, you made her an assistant, so she felt involved in the care. I've watched you work. You are pretty outstanding when it comes to calming those fears."

Jax hugged Chance before releasing her to put out silverware on the table. "It's scary for kids. They don't like getting shots and seeing the apprehension on their faces over their pets breaks me. Letting them help with the weighing and simple things helps put them at ease." She could finally smell the tamales. She reached for her hot pads and pulled the two steaming plates from the oven. "Can you grab the chips and salsa?"

"On it." Chance brought the oily brown paper bag to the table, along with the salsa Jax loved. Chance tore open the bag, revealing the chips.

With everything on the table, the two sat down to dinner. Jax lost herself for a moment in the domesticity she'd found with Chance. Here in her newly renovated kitchen, she and her fiancée were about to enjoy a meal, a simple pleasure she'd gone years without. *Let the past stay in the past, Jax. Enjoy the present.* Her first bite of the spicy tamale brought her back to the here and now. "My God, this is so good. How was Anita?"

"She said to tell you hello. Poor thing has been relegated to sitting behind the checkout register. Pasqual was busy in the kitchen. His mother has taken over a great deal of the hostess duties. Another month and Pasqual said he would make Anita stay home. I told him to let me know how that goes." Chance shook her head. "Anita never has been one to be told anything. I won't be surprised if she gives birth and is back in the restaurant ten minutes later with the baby strapped to her."

"I won't be either. This salsa is to die for. I need to make some to have on hand. I originally thought about having you grill burgers until this idea popped in my head. Now, tell me what you found out over at the sheriff's office."

Chance tipped back her beer then rose for another, pointing to Jax's bottle.

"Yes, please."

"Will said they're seeing an increase in the heroin calls with the influx of transient workers. His pipeline seems to be coming from the north. Not likely the same suppliers. We're all in the same boat, trying to find the head of the snake."

"Any word on what's going on with the guys who kidnapped Uncle Marty?"

"With the kidnappers being from Baltimore and the drugs found in that cabin, the feds have taken over the investigation and prosecution. When they kidnapped Martin, those guys put themselves in a different level of felonies. I talked with the feds. They wanted to take the lead, and I can't say I'm unhappy about that. Larry would be in way over his head prosecuting this. He'd likely plead the thing down to the equivalent of jaywalking. I wasn't going to let that happen." She put another beer down on the table.

Jax put a hand on Chance's forearm. "I will always be grateful for you that night. I don't know what I'd have done without you."

Chance bent down and kissed her softly. "I don't know what I'd have done if they'd taken you instead of Marty."

Jax stood and stepped away from the table, gathering Chance in her arms. "It didn't go down that way. You can't spend time dwelling on what didn't happen. We're together, and I feel so completely safe with you, my love. I could spend hours and hours thinking about what could have happened to you and Zeus. I won't, because I know it has no purpose. I live for today, for the here and now. What is, not what was." She drew Chance closer. "I know that you are damn good at what you do, and I trust you to come home to me. That's where my mind and heart live. In you." She pulled back and kissed Chance again. "Now, let's eat before this gets cold again. We've got a lifetime to work through all our concerns."

Chance nodded and opened their beers. "I'm starving. Do you have any idea what it's like to drive an hour smelling this?"

Jax dug into her meal and smiled at the simple pleasure of dinner with the woman she was going to marry. If she had anything to do with it, they'd be doing this same thing when they were eighty. Jax was exactly where she wanted to be, and for the first time in many years, she was completely herself and intent on living her own dreams.

Chapter Three

CHANCE PUSHED THE SWING lazily with her foot. Jax sat curled into her side, her feet drawn up beside her. The fall breeze smelled of damp earth. The leaves had yet to change. Chance always chuckled that the Leaf Peepers festival was held when the leaves were still green. Two other counties held large festivals later in the season, leaving Tucker with little choice. The other festivals pulled in large crowds that would draw participants away. Jax broke through her musings.

"Think we'll have color this year?"

Chance looked out at the mountains. "I never know. Some say if we have a dry summer, we'll have color. Others say the exact opposite, that wet summers make them brighter. I tend to believe that no one knows until they turn. For you, I'll hope for rainbows of crimson, amber, and vibrant orange."

"If wishes were horses, then beggars would ride."

"I haven't heard that in ages. I have much more important wishes that I plan to make come true."

Jax tilted her head up and met Chance's gaze. "Like what?"

"Marrying you. We haven't talked about the wedding in a while."

"I'd do it tomorrow if you wanted."

Chance kissed her softly. "As would I, but I'm only doing this once. That means we're doing it right. The moms-squared would kill us if we did it any other way." She paused, and a thought passed through her head.

Jax reached up and rubbed between Chance's eyes. "Hey, what's going on up here?"

"Have you said anything to your parents? Hell, this whole damn county knows. Even if you haven't told them, your mother's spies probably have."

Jax took a deep breath. "I called Daddy and the twins. They're all very happy for me."

"And your mom?"

"I have no idea and have no intention of trying to figure out if she cares or not. The last time we attempted a conversation, she brought up that she'd been talking to my ex. I've discovered that life is simpler if we stay in different states and talk as little as possible."

Chance tipped Jax's chin up so she could look into her eyes. It killed her that this divide existed between the woman she loved and the woman she'd only met once. "I'm sorry, honey. You have two moms a few miles away who love you like mothers should. Remember that."

Jax wiped at a tear. "For those two women, I am eternally grateful. Now, tell me about Kendra's new love."

Chance shifted Jax until she was lying across her chest, nestled in under her chin. "Brandi Antolini. A real spitfire and seems crazy about Kendra, who by the way is all thumbs around her. She's a sophomore planning on being a vet."

"I wonder if her mom is Beth Antolini? She's a vet from around the bay area. I met her at a few continuing-ed conferences. If so, Brandi comes from very good stock. I wonder why she didn't stay in California for school? UC Davis has one of the best veterinary schools in the country."

"Well, you can ask her next weekend. She's coming home with Kendra for Leaf Peepers. She's looking forward to meeting you."

Jax sat up with a hand on her chest. "Kendra is bringing home a girl?"

"I know. Momma D will tease her mercilessly. Kendra is all worried about where they'll stay and if they can sleep in the same room. I know she'd rather stay here, but our guest room isn't really habitable. That means she'll have to stay with the moms."

"You think Maggie is going to let them stay together? I know they're adults, but letting her kid bring her girlfriend home and sleep in the same bed might put Maggie over the edge."

Chance put her head back against the swing and shut her eyes, taking in the sounds of the evening. In the distance, she could hear one of the horses pawing at the stall gate and the rustle of tall grass. Zeus was softly snoring at her feet. "I told Kendra it was hers to work out. She knows what the situation is here. Brandi said she's okay that they might not be allowed to. It's pretty obvious she's crazy about Kendra. I've never seen Bullseye so nervous. It was almost comical."

"Don't tease her too much. She worships the ground you walk on. She needs your approval more than anyone's."

"Wow, look at that sky." Chance pointed, as Jax turned in her arms. It looked as if someone had painted the horizon with a broad brush of tangerines and sharp yellows.

"One of my favorite things about fall, the incredible sunsets." Jax yawned.

"I think it's time we put you to bed before you turn into a pumpkin. You planning on running with us in the morning?"

"Absolutely, next to making love, it's the best way to start the day."

Chance rose with Jax in her arms. "I think we might be able to arrange both of those." Chance kissed her. "I love you, Jax. I can't wait until you're my wife."

***

The next morning, Chance strode into her office with a takeout cup of peppermint tea. She placed it in front of Penny, who sat looking at her computer screen intently. "Morning little momma. How are you two?"

"Cranky. I think giving up caffeine is going to be the death of me. If not me, then Taylor. Thank you for the tea. It's very sweet of you. Molly's shop is out of my way or I'd be in that place every morning. Her peppermint tea seems to be the only thing that keeps me from tossing my cookies. This kid has a serious issue with me keeping anything down."

"Which is why I brought you another bag of her special blend. I plan to keep you well supplied."

Penny rose and hugged Chance. "You're the best."

Taylor stepped from the back offices. "I turn my back for one minute, and you're trying to steal my wife and child. What am I to do with you, Sheriff?" Taylor quirked a grin and handed Penny a stapled set of papers.

Chance released Penny but kept an arm around her waist. "Hey, I'm planning on being an awesome godmother. Your family is my family, but I'm leaving all the sleepless nights *and* three a.m. feedings to the real moms. I've got my own set of wedding vows I'll soon be abiding by."

Penny went back to her desk. "Just when might that round of I dos be taking place?" She sipped her tea. "That's it, Taylor, I'm leaving you." Laughter filled the office until the unmistakable smell of sweat and polyester entered the room.

Chance turned and narrowed her eyes at her deputy assigned to courtroom security. "What can I do for you, Brad?"

The overweight man grabbed for his gun belt and hitched it higher on his hips. "I need to talk to you about my cruiser. It's time to replace it."

"Brad, you drive that vehicle a total of twelve miles, five days a week. It was purchased two years ago and still has under thirty thousand miles. It receives regular maintenance and all the reports show the vehicle is roadworthy. Now, if you need tires or an oil change, I suggest you make an appointment with Tommy to have it seen. I have no service requests for repairs on my desk, so just what is it that makes you believe it needs to be replaced?" She watched as his face turned red.

"I'd like to discuss it in your office, Sheriff."

Chance looked at her watch. "You're due in the judge's courtroom in twenty minutes. I suggest you come back and see me at the end of the day before you go home. I'm aware that the judge has an appointment this afternoon at one, so I know you will be adjourning long before the end of your shift."

Brad glared at her. "Are you refusing to see me, Sheriff?"

Chance took two steps forward, Zeus at her side. "Deputy Waters, I've just advised you that I'll see you when the court adjourns for the day. You'll still be on the clock when Judge Landry leaves. With two other witnesses in the room, I've set a time for you to talk about your concerns. Not that I have to justify anything to you, but I have a prearranged meeting at the barracks, with Sergeant Harley Kincaid. It'll take me twenty minutes to drive to that meeting. Unlike you, I like to be punctual so as not to hold up others. I suggest you find your way across the street and to the screening device. Precisely at nine, you are to walk into the courtroom and announce the judge as your job description requires. Do I make myself clear?"

She watched Brad's hand bunch into a fist. She felt Zeus surge forward two steps, before she spoke with power and dominance. "Zeus, *zit*." The dog sat, barely in front of her, ears still in the alert position. If Brad so much as took one step toward her, she could only pray his obedience to her was stronger than his need to protect her. "Deputy Waters, don't make me repeat myself. I will be in my office at two. Knock before you enter to avoid a repeat of what happened the last time you barged into my office. Dismissed."

Taylor spoke up. "Brad, if you don't make your way out that door, I will personally write you up for insubordination. That was a direct order from a superior officer and your boss. I suggest you follow it."

Brad's jaw twitched once as he turned his considerable girth and made his way back out the door.

"Worthless piece of shit. I wish with everything I am that we could fire his ass. He knows where that line is." Chance used her finger to draw an imaginary boundary. "He puts the toes of his uniform boots right up to the edge of it. Biggest mistake I ever made when I became Sheriff."

Taylor clapped her on the shoulder. "Lessons learned, my friend."

Chance shut her eyes. "Hell of a way to start the day." She took a deep breath and looked at Penny. "What's on my agenda today, boss?"

Penny looked at her list. "After you meet with Harley, you have a regional sheriff's meeting over in Elkins at ten. After that, there is a meeting with the federal prosecutor, Taya Chapel. She has some questions about the kidnapping case. Unfortunately, I need to let Dee know you won't be at the Leaf Peepers meeting so you can meet with Brad. I also have an edict from Jax that you make it home in time for a ride."

Chance let out a laugh that filled Penny's office. "Yeah, I missed last night, trying to get some information from Will over in Clarksburg. Kelly was none too happy she didn't get to go. It's how we wind down our day. I need to get over to see the other girls too. I haven't made it there this week at all."

Taylor waved her arm. "They're good. I'm there every day. I need to run over to the magistrate's office. I'll see you later. I'll bring lunch back." She kissed Penny and strode out the door.

The clock on the wall chimed eight thirty. Chance wanted to stop by the clinic before she headed to Elkins. "Is there anything on my desk that I need to attend to immediately?"

"There are a few concealed-weapon background checks you could sign for me and a purchase order for the rest of Daniel's uniforms. A few other things of minor importance. How's he doing at the academy?"

Chance couldn't help the smile that grew. "He's doing great. Top of his class so far. I know a few of his instructors, and they are very pleased with him. They tell me he's going to make a really good officer. Not like I didn't already know that, but it's nice to hear."

"How are his mothers doing with his choice?"

"A little worried, considering what I went through earlier this year. They also know he's never wanted to do anything else. I promised them I would do everything I could to keep him safe. Which reminds me, I need to start making calls about the K9 training he'll need after he gets out of the academy."

"One more thing on your list. Go sign those things and get to your meeting with Harley." Penny pointed her finger at Chance. "Tell Jax hi for me and remind her we have a date to start wedding planning."

Chance saluted. "Yes, ma'am." She strode back to her office and signed the papers she needed to. The next few moments were spent catching up on the morning intelligence reports before she brought the paperwork back out front to Penny. "Okay, we're out of here. Behave yourself."

Penny crossed her arms and furrowed her brow. "You and Taylor are cut from the same cloth. I'm pregnant, not an invalid." She pointed to the door. "Go."

"Come on Zeus, I believe we have been dismissed."

Outside, the sky was a pale blue, and a few discarded leaves rustled in the street. Most were still on the trees and green. It would be October before the inevitable turn would begin. She loaded Zeus into her Suburban and turned to go to the clinic. The morning run with Jax had been enjoyable, as had the cup of coffee with their meal. Breakfast had been quick, after they'd made love in the shower. She could still feel Jax's lips on her skin. Making love with Jax was a near addiction, and Chance vowed to make her feel treasured every day of her life.

Her radio crackled. "Comm Center to SD-1."

She picked up her mic. "SD-1. Go ahead."

"State Police Unit 207 is requesting backup on a domestic call on Route 72."

Chance flipped on her lights and made a sharp U-turn in the road. "SD-1 responding. Size up?"

"Man barricaded in his house with a gun, holding his wife and one of his children hostage. An older child escaped and ran to the neighbors to make the call."

Chance wanted to make sure Taylor had copied the radio traffic. "SD-1 to SD-2."

Taylor came up on the radio. "SD-2 is responding."

"SD-1 to 207."

Harley answered the radio. "Let's move to encrypted, Chance. I'm near St. George."

Chance flipped her radio. "I'm passing Holly Meadows now. Not sure of Taylor's location. Five to seven-minute ETA."

"It's Chuck Wilson. He's got his wife Mary and a six-month-old infant barricaded in the back bedroom of the house. The seven-year-old ran next door. The kid that made the call was at home because he was sick. All he could say was his dad had a gun and wouldn't let his mom go. No clue what kind yet. When she signed the domestic against him last month, we took an arsenal out of there. She's filed for divorce."

Chance thought about her run-ins with Chuck. He was likely high or drunk. "He's probably on something if his priors hold true. Any other troopers coming?"

"From off the mountain. I've also got one coming from the Preston County end, but it will be a while for that one."

"Break. SD-2, what's your location?"

Taylor's voice came over the radio, blended with the sound of the siren. "On Route 72, about five behind you."

Chance put down her mic and concentrated on the road. In less than three minutes, she pulled near Harley's cruiser. Once her vehicle was in position, she released Zeus and came to Harley's side.

"I'm hoping this doesn't go south any more than it already has. Chuck threatened to kill her the last time. No shots fired as of yet. As soon as I see Taylor's cruiser, I'm making a call to the house."

"Okay, Zeus and I will make our way around the backside. Taylor has Midas with her. How close is your other trooper?"

"He was coming down Sugarlands a few minutes ago."

"Keep your head down. There's Taylor." Chance crouched and ran back to her chief deputy. Midas jumped out to his partner's side. "Make your way around to the back toward that kitchen door. I'm betting he's in that master bedroom. I'll be on the other side. I've got reinforcements coming. He's got the baby and Mary in with him. I'm assuming little Charlie is still with the neighbor."

A shot broke through a window, followed by an angry voice. "Clear the fuck out of here, or I'll kill them both."

Chance and Taylor rolled to the right side of the house and took cover behind the disabled vehicles dotting the overgrown yard.

Harley took the lead in negotiations. "Chuck, you need to let them go before this gets out of hand."

"It got out of hand the minute she threw me out. This is my house. She's my wife, and these are my kids. I'm in charge here, not this bitch."

Chance could see movement in one corner of the room through a window on the opposite side. She made her way to below the window and peered in. Mary sat on the bed, holding the baby, as Chuck paced the room near the window. He had a pistol in his hand. She could hear him screaming at Mary.

Harley yelled. "Chuck, you have to let them go. No matter what's happened, we can work it out. If you harm them, it will only get worse."

"I'm not going back to jail. I'll kill us all before that happens."

Taylor moved closer to the side of the house, within Chance's sight. Chance needed to figure out a way to get Chuck separated from Mary. She didn't see a way to send Zeus or Midas in safely, unless she could get them into the attached bathroom. The window was partially opened. She stood and tried to raise it. The sash stuck at first, then finally moved up. Harley still had him engaged. Chance looked around the yard and found a milk crate that would allow her to climb in the window without difficulty. She was grateful this was an old farmhouse with large windows and not the smaller windows found in most modern construction. Zeus was at her side. She bent down to pick him up and help him through the window. She whispered, *"Zit."* In the background, she could hear Harley continuing to negotiate and the sound of another siren approaching. She followed Zeus through the window.

"Get off my land! I'll kill the first person who comes through my door."

Harley's voice remained calm and measured. "Chuck, you've got to put down the gun and come out. Don't harm Mary or the baby. Doing that won't serve any purpose and will land you in jail for the rest of your life."

"Not if I'm dead too."

"What about Charlie? Who's going to take care of him if you and Mary are gone? How does he live with the fact that his father killed his mother and baby sister? Don't ruin his life, Chuck."

Chance pushed the door open an inch. She could see Chuck covering his ears, gun in hand. She leveled her gun at him. She whispered to Zeus again, *"Bewaken."* Chuck moved to the end of the room, opposite of where Mary cradled the crying baby. When his back was turned, she stepped out and put herself between Chuck and his hostages. "Drop the gun! Drop the gun, or I release the dog!"

Chuck spun and pointed his gun at her.

"Stellen!" Chance bellowed, and Zeus lunged forward, catching the man by the arm that held the weapon. Chuck had no time to react. "Mary, roll off the bed. Get down." Zeus growled and snarled as Chance shouted commands. Taylor and Midas broke through the bedroom door, with Harley right behind her. Midas engaged and had Chuck by the ankle with a simple command from Taylor. He was screaming in pain as the dogs sank their teeth into him.

"Drop the gun! Drop the gun!" Chance screamed at Chuck, with her gun pointed at him. She maintained the physical barrier between him and his wife, who cowered on the floor on the other side of the bed. Chance heard the gun clatter to the hardwood as Chuck screamed for them to call off the dogs.

"Zeus, *houden*." She called for Zeus to stop the attack and hold the suspect. Taylor's command followed suit.

"Roll over. Hands behind your head," Taylor shouted at Chuck, who tried to comply as she cuffed him.

Chance turned to Mary, who held the baby tight to her chest. "Mary, are you and the baby all right?" A bright red handprint on Mary's face and finger-sized bruises around her neck told Chance she was anything but. "I'm going to call for an ambulance to check on you and the baby. Let's get you out to the living room." Chance helped her up, while Chuck screamed obscenities at her.

"You fucking bitch, this is all your fault. I'm the master of this house, and you do what I say. You hear me? You hear me? You belong to me."

Chance pointed to the door. "Get him the hell out of here, Taylor." She stood between Mary and her officer, who was pulling Chuck to his feet and pushing him out the door.

"We've got him, Sheriff." Harley held Chuck's arm, as she led him through the house and out the front door.

"Come on, Mary. Let's check you out. Little Charlie's safe. Where are you hurt?" Chance tried to completely block Mary's view of the man who'd abused her.

Mary's sobs prevented her from saying anything coherent. She whispered a weak thank you. Once Chance had her and the baby settled on the couch, she went to the drab kitchen and found a glass in the drainer. She filled it with water and carried it back to Mary. "Take a sip of this." Chance found a tissue box and put it near Mary as well.

Mary held her hand to her mouth and sobbed as the baby cried. "She's hungry. I need to feed her and change her diaper."

"If you change her, I'll fix her bottle. Tell me where everything is."

"There's one made up in the refrigerator. It needs to be heated." Mary stood and grabbed the diaper bag at the end of the couch.

Chance headed to the kitchen and heated the formula. She brought the bottle back in the room with her when it was warm enough. "Can I feed her? Give you a chance to settle down."

Mary handed Chance the baby. "Carissa has a hard time eating unless you bounce or sway her."

Chance noticed the rasp to Mary's voice. "I can do that." Chance put the bottle to the baby's lips and smiled as the baby greedily took the nipple.

Mary smoothed her dress with her hands. Tears continued to roll down her face.

"The ambulance will be here soon to check you both out." Chance swayed with the baby in her arms. "Mary, I hate to have to ask you this. Did Chuck sexually assault you?"

Mary held her hand to her mouth and stifled a cry as she nodded that he had.

"Whatever you do, don't take a shower or bath. It's important that we preserve evidence. I want him to go away for good this time. Mary, you and your children need to be free of him and protected. You'll have to testify and tell the court what happened. Can you do that?"

Mary looked Chance directly in the eye, tear tracks streaking her face. "I'll scream it from the courthouse steps if I have to. That man will never have the chance to hurt my children ever again. I made the mistake of marrying him and forgiving him every time he hit me. I believed him when he said it was my fault that dinner wasn't on the table, hot and ready for him, no matter when he decided to stagger in here. I'm done, Sheriff. My children didn't choose this life, and I won't shackle them to it for a single day longer. I watched him put that gun to Carissa's head then threaten to kill her if I didn't do what he said. He told Charlie he'd kill the baby if he didn't behave. Where Charlie got the courage to run, I'll never know. What I do know is it's time for me to show that same courage." Mary turned and went into the bathroom.

Taylor came back inside. "My other troopers are here, and Chuck is secured in one of the cruisers. Harley went to get Charlie." She pointed her chin in the direction Mary had disappeared. "How's she doing?"

"A determined mess. When EMS gets here, let them know we have a sexual assault victim. Tell them to advise the ER to have a rape crisis advocate on hand."

Taylor shut her eyes. Chance understood her frustration. The court system had let Chuck off numerous times for a variety of infractions. Mary had rescinded several orders of protection, always letting Chuck come back home. He'd never gone this far, and they could only hope that Mary would follow through this time and go through with the prosecution. Chance hoped, eventually, the family could completely get Chuck out of their lives. Mary came back into the room. Chance moved the baby to her shoulder. After a few gentle pats, she felt Carissa burp.

Taylor grabbed a cloth diaper and wiped the baby's mouth. "She spit up a bit on your shirt."

"Par for the course. No worries." Chance heard the siren of an ambulance. Charlie ran through the door crying and into his mother's arms. Mary dropped to her knees and held her son tightly.

"I'm okay, Charlie. It's going to be okay."

"Mary, the ambulance will take the three of you to the hospital to be checked over." She looked at the bruise forming on Charlie's face. The anger began to bubble up. *No child should have to go through this. Not one.* She handed Mary the baby. "Let's find Carissa's car seat. Charlie, do you have your booster around here?"

Charlie wiped at his tears and nodded. She held out her hand and he led her through the house. She could feel how badly he was shaking. She stopped and knelt beside him. Tears streamed down his face. "You're safe now. Your mom is okay, and so is your baby sister. I won't let anything happen to you."

Charlie wiped his face. "You taking my daddy to jail?"

"Yes, Charlie, I am. He hurt you guys. That's wrong."

"Good. He's mean, and he hurts Momma."

Chance gathered the small boy into her arms and wiped his tears. "He hurts you too, doesn't he?" She watched, as the little boy nodded. "We're not going to let that happen ever again, okay? You were very brave today. You saved your family. That makes you a hero. I'm proud of you."

Charlie nodded again and grabbed his booster seat as the medics entered the house. Chance brought him back to his mother and made her way to Harley. The entire incident would generate tons of paperwork and take hours to wrap up. She wouldn't make the regional meeting but felt she could make the meeting with the federal prosecutor. That was extremely important to her. Putting away the men who'd kidnapped Martin held a very high priority in her life. She would do everything she could to make sure they went away for what they'd done. The thought that it could've been Jax still rattled her.

Taylor met her in the yard. "Penny called the regional meeting organizers and told them you wouldn't make it. She also called Taya Chapel and let her know what was going on. Your meeting has been moved to three. She said if you needed to cancel, she'd understand and could reschedule it if necessary. My half unit also called to tell Brad that your meeting with him is rescheduled for tomorrow at two."

"I'll bet he had a few things to say about that. I'd be lost without your wife."

Taylor clapped her on the back. "That makes two of us. Let's see if we can get this wrapped up. Zeus and Midas are in my vehicle. They did really well, given the limited space. I know I've said it more than once, our K9s certainly make our job easier and safer. I want to make sure they both get a good checkup."

"I'll call Jax and see if she can see them." Chance looked at her watch and pulled out her phone. "She should be in the office."

"Three Rivers Animal Hospital," a female answered.

"Hey Lindsey, this is Chance. Is Jax busy?"

"Oh hey, Sheriff. No, she's finishing up a chart. Hang on."

The local radio station filled the silence until the line was picked back up again.

"Hey gorgeous, how's your day?" Jax asked.

"Rather busy for a Thursday. Do you have time to check Zeus and Midas over? Neither appears hurt, but they had to engage a suspect."

"Of course, I'll see them. Are you all right?"

"I'm fine. Domestic violence call. The victims are headed to the hospital to be evaluated, so is the suspect. The boys got a hold of him. Too much paperwork to even think about. I'd feel better if the dogs were looked at. Midas got tossed around."

The urgency in Jax's voice went up. "You didn't get hit, did you? I know you, Chance. You'll think because it hit your vest, you're fine. Did you get shot?"

"No, he never fired at me. Zeus and Midas made sure of that. If you can see the dogs, Taylor will bring them by. I'm still on the scene, and I'll need to make out a report. I'm supposed to head to Elkins to meet with the federal prosecutor. I'm likely to be home later than I'd like. Keep your fingers crossed I'll make it in time to go for a ride. If I don't, will you take Kelly out with you? She'll go nuts if she doesn't get to go."

Jax chuckled. "I can do that. Try to make it home. Remember, I'm pretty fond of her rider. Stop by the office if you get a minute. I love you."

"I'll try. Love you too."

They ended the call and Chance found Taylor. "Take the boys over to Jax. She'll see them. I'm going to follow up at the hospital. I can do my paperwork there, and it will put me that much closer to my meeting with Taya Chapel."

"You got it. Good job today. I'll tell Harley where you're headed and take the dogs to the clinic."

"Thanks, catch you later." Chance strode over to her Suburban and climbed in. She grabbed her mic. "SD-1 to Comm Center."

"SD-1, go ahead."

"This unit will be clearing the scene en route to Davis Memorial."

"Copy, SD-1."

Chance drove away from the two-story farmhouse. It was a call like this that took her father from her. She'd pushed herself to back Harley up, determined to bring the incident to a successful outcome. She looked at the dash clock that read eleven thirty, astonished that somehow two hours had slipped by as Chuck held his family hostage. *Lessons learned the hard way. Let's hope they aren't repeated.*

Chapter Four

JAX STARED AT THE RECEIVER as she placed it back in the cradle. She took comfort in the knowledge that Chance was an exceptional officer, well trained to face those who wanted to hurt her. Jax was proud to be the type of partner who could accept the danger Chance faced, without burdening her with unnecessary fear. Jax wanted her always to know she could handle whatever happened, as long as Chance told her about it. A voice in the doorway brought her out of her thoughts.

"Sheriff Fitzsimmons okay?" Lindsey walked in and offered a steaming mug to Jax.

Jax took a deep breath and released the tension. "She said she is. Taylor's bringing in two of the K9s to be looked over. Nothing seems wrong; she wants to make sure. Call and see if you can cancel my one o'clock, so I'll have time to see them without being rushed."

Lindsey nodded. "That's no problem. It's just the animal shelter bringing a few new intakes for a checkup. We can do that tomorrow. I'll call them." Lindsey started to walk away and turned back. "It's not always easy, is it?"

Jax smiled. She knew Lindsey was in the same boat she was rowing, now that Meg was out of the academy and on active duty in Elkins. This was the life they'd chosen because of the women they loved. "Loving her is, worrying about her, not so much. She says she's fine. That's all that matters."

Lindsey squeezed her hand. "We'll lean on each other, okay?"

Jax squeezed back. "Yes, we will. How's Meg doing?"

Lindsey's smile grew wide. "She's patrolling by herself and happy to finally be putting her academy training to use. I wish she had a K9 with her all the time, like Chance's officers. I know she loves being a trooper and wants to make a difference in the community. It's important to her that her mom is proud."

"Chance told me the same thing. Okay, let's get ready to see the boys."

Lindsey turned on her heel. "I'll make that call and get Room 3 ready. It should give you enough space to see them both."

Jax looked at her hand and the diamond Chance had placed there.

Soon, her dreams would become a reality, and she'd marry the woman she'd always loved. Her phone rang. The number displayed was her dad's. "Hey, you."

"Hey, Jibber Jack. How are you?"

"I'm fine, Daddy. How about you?"

"The same. And Chance?"

"She's good too, Daddy. It's nice coming home to someone who looks forward to spending time with me. It's something I haven't known in a very long time."

"Have you two set a date yet?"

Jax rolled her ring around with her thumb. "No, we've been throwing dates around. We just haven't settled on one yet. I promise to let you know. I'd love for you to come."

"You give me a date, and I'll be there. I'll drag your mother there kicking and screaming if I have to."

"I love you, Daddy, but if it requires you to drag her, I'd rather you not bother."

"Jax, your mother is a complicated creature who's set in her ways. You know her. She keeps her armor up. If Jacqueline isn't in charge and calling the shots, everything feels out of control."

"I've heard all this before, and I'm not disputing the facts. She can be in charge of whatever she wants, except me. I took control of my life the day I left for California, and I have no intention of changing that. I'm sorry, Dad, I've got to go. Chief Deputy Lewis just pulled into the back lot. She's got two of the K9 units for me to check. I'll call you soon. I love you."

"Love you too, kiddo."

They disconnected as Taylor walked in with Midas and Zeus. Both dogs greeted her with exuberant tails. Jax knelt and rubbed all over both of them. "Hey, boys, how are you? Such good boys. Let's get you back in the room. Everything okay, Taylor? Chance told me a little about the incident. Everyone come away unharmed?"

Taylor walked down the hall and into the room with Jax. "Our suspect has a few bite marks on him, so I'll need the shot records for the hospital. The guy terrorized his family. Unfortunately, his wife took the brunt. I'll never understand it. If anyone ever laid a hand on Penny or our baby, I'd—" She stopped. "Well, let's just say that person better hope someone else gets to them first. I'll leave it at that."

Jax ran her hands over Zeus, checking for any unseen wounds or any discomfort Zeus might show. She felt down each leg and over each paw. Zeus showed no sign of injury and licked her cheek.

"Love you too, boy. Let me listen to your heart." Jax pulled her stethoscope from her lab coat pocket, settled the earpieces in place, and put the bell on Zeus' chest. The rhythmic thump she heard put her mind at ease. His lungs sounded clear. "Let's check those teeth." She lifted his gums and checked the prominent canines for stability. Everything seems to be in order."

"Midas took a good hit up against the wall when they took the suspect down. He's favoring that right front leg." Taylor pointed to where Midas was holding up his paw.

"Let's take a look." Jax slowly palpated all along the leg. When she reached the elbow, Midas whimpered and withdrew. He showed no indication he would bite, but she used caution. "Hey, Lindsey?"

"Right here." Lindsey appeared at her side.

"Let's get an X-ray and rule out any fracture. It's probably a bruise. That won't show on the films." Jax turned to Taylor. "We'll check everything and follow a course of treatment for whatever we find."

Taylor nodded. "I trust your judgment. I know Chance does too."

"That means a great deal to me. Okay, let's get him back there. I'm going to put him on a rolling cot to keep him from injuring himself further. Can you pick him up for me? If you keep Zeus busy, we'll go take a look. I'll let you know as soon as I see anything."

Jax let Taylor pick Midas up and place him on the soft surface before she fastened a Velcro strap across his middle.

Taylor stroked her dog's head. "Okay, we'll be out front."

Once in X-ray, she and Lindsey manipulated the limb to get several shots of the affected area. Midas was tolerant, and while Lindsey went to develop the films, Jax wheeled him back to the treatment room. She waved Taylor back and heard the bell over the door ring. Jax stiffened.

The hair on the back of her neck pricked, as Leland Kurst came through the door. He eyed her from head to toe, then settled on her chest. She'd never been so glad for her lab coat and to have Taylor with her. Kurst masked his gaze when he saw Taylor.

"I'll be with you in a minute. I have a patient." Jax felt him watching her as she continued past him with Midas to the back room, Taylor and Zeus a step behind.

"That guy gives me the creeps like no one I've ever known. Once I get back here, please go check on Lindsey. Chance would shit if she knew he'd come in when she wasn't here."

Taylor adjusted her gun belt. "You aren't here alone. Zeus, stay with Jax."

Jax could hear Leland trying to make conversation with Lindsey, and then she heard the clear order from Taylor telling Leland to let Lindsey pass.

"I'm not going to tell you again, Leland. Let her pass. Go ahead back to Jax, Lindsey. I'll handle this." Taylor's tone was louder and more authoritative than usual.

Jax stepped close as Lindsey entered. "Are you okay?" Lindsey was shaking as Jax closed the door and pulled her into her arms. "What did he say to you?"

Lindsey dropped her head to Jax's shoulder and wiped furiously at the tears that streamed down her face. "The same crap he used to say in high school. He called Megan a dyke and offered to show me what a real man could do for me."

Jax bristled. No one would threaten her staff. She had to keep her head. "You stay in here with Midas and Zeus. Do not open that door for anyone until I come back."

Lindsey grabbed her arm. "Don't go. He takes a threat as a challenge. It will make things worse."

"Well, he's not going to threaten anyone in my place of business, and he certainly will not talk like that to people I care about. Stay here." Jax walked out and shut the door behind her. Taylor stood almost toe to toe with Leland, her hand resting on her hip near her gun.

Jax put her hands on her hips. "I want him out of my business. Don't ever come back, and if you ever say anything to Lindsey again, we'll slap you with a restraining order. Frankly, I don't need your business, nor do I want it. Get out." Jax pointed to the door.

Taylor took another step toward him. "What did you say to her, Leland?"

He held his hands in the air. "Nothing illegal about talking to a pretty girl, Deputy Lewis. If so, most of the men in America would be in jail."

"Threatening to rape her is more than just talking to her. Now, I want you out of here. Don't come back, ever." Jax walked to the door and opened it. "If you don't leave, I'll have you removed."

"I think you should do as the doc asked, Leland. I can, and will, remove you if you are unable to comply."

Leland glared at Jax. "You dykes are all alike. You need someone to put you in your place."

Taylor grabbed Leland's finger and twisted his arm behind his back as she frog-marched him to the door. "If I hear of you being within twenty feet of Dr. St. Claire or Lindsey, I'll be closely examining your vehicles for violations every time I see you. Last warning, Leland. Take my advice and mind your manners." They disappeared through the door, and Jax drew in a pained breath with a hand on her chest. She hadn't realized how badly she'd been shaking until she saw her hands. He'd threatened them. A court of law might not see it that way, but a threat was implied.

Minutes later, Taylor reappeared at her side. "You okay, Jax?"

"Yeah, just shaken up. Lindsey's worse. Chance will shit a brick."

"You've got to tell her. Don't keep things from her to protect her. She needs to take care of you, and it would hurt her more to know you withheld the incident, even if you think it's in her best interest. What she needs most is your honesty and belief in her. Let's go check on Lindsey."

Jax leaned in and let Taylor wrap an arm around her as they walked back to the treatment room. "It's us, Lindsey, open the door."

Lindsey let them in. "Is he gone?"

Taylor nodded. "What time does Meg get off? I want someone with you, especially when it gets dark. No arguments. Leland Kurst is no one to mess with, and he's been taking an interest in you for years."

"Meg gets off at four, which puts her in town just before five. I don't want her to lose it and go after him. In high school, he terrified me, because he wouldn't take no for an answer. He stalked me all over the county. Mom and Dad wanted to pull me out of school, but I begged them to let me stay. They went to the school, and the principal suspended him. I was so grateful when he left town and stopped terrorizing us." Lindsey broke down in tears again.

Jax held her in her arms. "Let's get Midas taken care of, then we'll call Chance and Megan. I know they'll want us to be careful. Come on." She squeezed her. "I'm betting Midas would like to go home. I say we cancel the rest of our appointments, go to my house, and fix dinner for them. Meg can pick you up there."

Lindsey wiped her eyes. "I'd like that."

"And I'll follow both of you there with the boys. That way, we can wait together for them to get home. I'll have Carl take Penny home. No arguments."

Jax nodded. "Okay, let's look at these films."

***

Chance walked out of the emergency room and stepped off to the side of the entrance to wait on Harley. The phone call she'd received from Jax put her nerves on edge. Harley needed to be aware of Leland's latest threat and be assured that Lindsey was safe. *He's not getting within two feet of either of them, ever again.* She started a loop around the perimeter. The phone call wasn't the only reason she was pacing in the emergency room's ambulance bay. The incidents at the Wilson's had unearthed painful memories of her father's death.

"Aunt Maggie, someone's at the door!" Chance looked up to see a uniformed figure through the glass.

"Who in the world would be calling at this time of night?" Maggie tightened the belt on her robe and turned the knob.

Chance watched, as her dad's boss, Sheriff Owen Knight, took off his hat and ran his hand through his hair.

"Maggie, I need to talk to you." He looked at Chance. "In private."

"Owen—"

"Please, Maggie." Owen put a hand under Maggie's elbow as Dee came into the room. "Dee, can you come with us? Chance, stay here."

Chance was thirteen years old and knew something was terribly wrong. "Sheriff, where's my dad?"

He turned to her. "Chance, let me talk to them first, then I'll sit down with you."

Chance balled both of her fists. "No, if this is about my dad, tell me now!"

Dee stepped beside Maggie and wrapped Chance in her arms, as she led her into the living room. "Owen, we're a family. Whatever you need to say, we'll hear it together."

The sheriff followed them into the living room. Dee settled Maggie on the couch with Chance between them and turned off the television. Maggie pulled her close, and all eyes turned to a visibly shaken Owen.

"Chance, your dad has always been one of the finest officers I've ever known, the bravest as well. He took an oath to protect and serve. Tonight, he stood between an innocent and someone who wanted to do harm. I don't even know how to tell you how sorry I am."

Maggie's hand flew to her mouth but didn't stop the cry that left her body. Dee wrapped her arms around them both, as Chance sat in stunned silence. Her father was gone, and her whole life would never be the same. In the blink of an eye, everything had changed.

Harley cleared her throat. "I'd offer a penny for your thoughts, but that look tells me whatever is on your mind might cost me a Benjamin or more. I'm saving for a wedding, so you'll have to give me a discount."

Chance took a deep breath and chased off the ghosts of the past. She needed to deal with the monsters of the present. All the details needed to be taken care of so that Mary Wilson and her children never had to fear Chuck again.

Harley stepped close and filled her in on the current situation. "Chuck has a dozen stitches and is on his way to the regional jail. Mary's mother is on her way from Clarksburg to pick up her and the kids. They'll stay there a while to recuperate. She has a bruised larynx, and the sexual assault happened before we even got the call. No matter how fast we got there, we couldn't have prevented that horror for her."

"At least we're going to be able to give her the security she needs to know he's going away for a long time." Chance looked at her watch; she was supposed to meet with the prosecutor in twenty minutes. "You have my report, and I'll make you a certified copy of the body-camera footage when I get back to the station. I need to tell you about something that happened at the animal hospital today."

Harley's posture sharpened and she stepped closer to Chance. "Is everyone okay?"

"Both are a little shaken, but I can assure you they're safe. Leland Kurst came into the office and made some lewd comments to Lindsey. Jax told him to leave, and Taylor escorted him off the property. After that, they closed the office and went to our place. They made a call to Meg, and she'll pick Lindsey up at our house when she finishes her shift. Taylor's going to stay with them until I get home. I can promise you she won't be alone."

"That bastard harassed both of them in school. It was so bad, Lindsey's parents tried to make her switch schools. I give the girl credit. She refused to leave Meg there by herself. We were all grateful when he moved away." Harley repeatedly clenched her hands into fists.

"Apparently, he's making a habit of showing up at the animal hospital. I ran into him there one time, right before someone kidnapped Doc. He's got some fixation with one or both of them, and I'm afraid these run-ins are going to continue. You and I both know he hasn't done enough to warrant a restraining order. Even with one in place, he has to break it before we can do a damn thing." Chance's phone vibrated. She pulled it from her pocket and read the text from the prosecutor's office.

Prosecutor is in chambers with the judge. Need to reschedule.

Chance typed out a quick reply and put a hand on Harley's shoulder. "My day just freed up. I'm going to head home and stay with them until Meg gets there. The girls are cooking dinner, stop by if you can. Don't worry, Harley. As far as I'm concerned, the surveillance on Leland Kurst moved to another level after his stunt today. He steps out of line, and he'll find himself a guest of the Huttonsville Hilton. I'm going to suggest Jax put in a monitored camera system and that both of them wear panic alarms. After what happened to Doc, she'll want to make sure to protect Lindsey. I'll certainly feel much better about them being there by themselves."

"I'm sure that would help ease Megan's mind. We might want to give both of them a few lessons in self-defense. We can't be with them twenty-four hours a day, and there are a lot of Leland Kursts out there. They need to be prepared."

"Good idea. I taught Kendra several moves to protect herself when she went off to college. Sarah Riker is a Krav Maga instructor. She took a weekend course at a conference several years ago and continued her education after. I'm sure several others would be interested in having a class."

Harley held out her hand for Chance to shake. "Thanks for your help today. I felt a lot more confident of the outcome knowing you had my back."

Chance shook the proffered hand. "Any time, my friend, any time."

Chapter Five

CHANCE OPENED THE DOOR to Trooper Megan Kincaid. The panic on Meg's face nearly broke her. Immediately, Megan stepped forward and gathered Lindsey in her arms.

"I'm here, baby. I'm right here."

Lindsey's sobs were muffled, as she cried into Megan's chest. "He's back, Meg. He's back."

"She's okay, Meg, and we're going to make sure she and Jax stay that way." Chance raised an arm and tucked Jax under it as she approached.

Jax chimed in with a few more reassurances of her own. "I promise you we're going to make the animal hospital safer and more secure. We've already talked about simple steps we can take every day. Let's have dinner, and we'll tell you what we're thinking."

Chance saw the fire in Megan's eyes and realized she needed to acknowledge the anger. "Trust me, Meg. I'm pissed and ready to grind Leland under my boot heel like a discarded cigarette. We're officers of the law, and we can't become what we stand as a shield against. It's not fair, and it's not easy, but it is the law. The good thing is, it's on our side and he's on notice. Take a deep breath and be the strength Lindsey needs, not another reason for her to worry. I've got your back on this. Rest assured, Lindsey's safety is as important to me as Jax's." She watched the flames die down to smoldering coals.

Megan nodded as if she understood. "You've always been a straight shooter with me, Sheriff. If you say this is the right way to go about it"—she looked to Lindsey—"then I trust you with the one thing most precious to me."

Chance tilted her head in the direction of the kitchen. "There's a table full of meatloaf and mashed potatoes waiting on us right through that door. I say we tackle that first, then sit down over coffee and lay out a plan." Megan met her eyes, revealing much more than Chance was sure she intended. Alongside the anger, fear and a sliver of helplessness wavered in the gray fathoms. It would take time for the reassurance to get a foothold.

Megan shook off the stress and found a small smile to offer. "It smells good, and I'm starving."

***

Platters were passed from hand to hand until the dinner plates were full and the clatter of forks against the ceramic blended in with the conversation. Jax took in the interaction between the two officers at her table.

"Mom said you guys had a pretty hairy incident today out near the county line." Megan lifted a forkful of potatoes to her mouth.

"It was for a while. It was Chuck Wilson. I'm sure you've heard of him. Domestic assault and a list of other atrocities he'll go away for. I've never understood how someone can hurt their family that way. Little Charlie was the hero when he got away and found help. The things he's seen will take time for him to get over." Chance sipped her beer.

"I met Mary last month when I went out to check on some of their goats. She looked like she's lived a rough life." Jax spooned some applesauce onto her plate.

Megan shook her head. "Domestic violence calls are way up. We've been running ragged in Elkins trying to serve protection petitions. I did three yesterday. Can you pass me a roll, babe?"

Lindsey handed the basket to Megan. "I'm grateful I didn't grow up in a house like that. My dad respected my mom. I never heard them have a harsh word for each other."

Once everyone had their fill, they moved to the living room. Lindsey handed Megan a piece of pie and a cup of coffee before settling on the couch beside her. Chance piled up a few small pieces of kindling in the fireplace and lit them with a long wooden match, and then added a few substantial logs.

Jax patted the front of her chair and splayed her feet for Chance to sit between. She put her hands on Chance's shoulders and began to rub. "Good Lord, your neck is tight. You carry all your tension right here." Her thumbs pushed deep into the knotted muscles.

Chance leaned her head forward to allow Jax better access. "I'm sure I'm still a little keyed up from earlier. Let's talk about what we are going to do about Leland. Megan, I want you to listen to what I have planned to protect Jax and Lindsey at the animal hospital. If you can think of anything else, I'm all ears."

Megan nodded. "I'm listening."

"Tomorrow morning, I'll make a call to Billings Security and have them install a camera system with a monitored alarm. Both of them will wear panic pendants, and a silent alarm button will be installed in each room as well as at the reception desk. I talked to Sarah Riker earlier. She's agreed to teach a self-defense class when everyone can find the time. Both Jax and Lindsey along with Maggie, Dee, and a few others will have an excellent instructor. Those are the first things we're going to do. Unfortunately, he hasn't done enough for Jax to get a restraining order, but given Lindsey's history with Leland, I think we can convince a magistrate to issue one on Lindsey's behalf. The good thing is it will include her place of employment, which will offer some protection for Jax."

Lindsey had curled her feet under her and leaned into Megan. "That paper won't stop him. I'll get it but getting him to abide by it will be a miracle. We went down this road before. The only thing that stopped him the last time was when he left town after he wrecked that truck he stole."

"We heard later that his dad paid the guy off. After that, they hustled him off to Maryland with another family somewhere over in Baltimore. Up until recently, I hadn't seen him since that last day he got kicked out of school. After Lindsey went to work for Jax, it seemed like he was everywhere we went. Two weeks ago, we went to a movie and passed him on the way out of the theater. His obsession with Lindsey is starting all over again. It's like we're back in high school."

"I understand, Megan. That's why we've got to get a handle on this now. The longer we let it go, the more brazen he'll get. If I have to work out of the clinic as their armed security, I will. I've already made plans to do just that over the next week or so, until the alarm systems are up and running. I ran some background information on him a few months ago. He was under surveillance by several drug task forces over in the Baltimore area. They had a suspicion he was running drugs for the Murdaland Mafia Piru. Low-level stuff they don't want those closest to them getting caught with. He was expendable, you could say. I made some calls to the task force over there, and they told me they aren't sure why he came back over here. Personally, I think he's tied in with the guy who tried to shoot me. Our task force is looking into the connection to see if the gang from Baltimore is trying to funnel product into the tourist industry here. Taylor's digging a little deeper with them to pinpoint the connection."

"Jesus." Megan sat forward and ran her hand through her sandy-brown hair. "This isn't good."

"Megan, look at me." Chance waited for her to comply, and then dropped her voice. "We're not going to let him get to either of them, nor mule a drug train here under our noses. We'll work on the security system and the restraining order. If I have to dog him day and night to find the chink in his armor, I will. Make no mistake, he's a problem right now, and we're going to take care of that, one way or another. We have resources and a plan of action. We will fix this, I promise you. He's not getting to either of them."

Jax spoke up. "Megan, I want you to know I won't spare any expense to make sure we can go to work and be safe. Lindsey isn't just my employee...she's my friend. I'm not going to let anything happen to her."

Lindsey wiped away a tear. "I consider you the same. We'll keep each other safe."

***

They all sat watching the fire until Chance noticed Lindsey was starting to fade. "I think you'd better take your best half home before she turns into a pumpkin. It's been a stressful day. Tomorrow, we start fixing the issue."

Megan rose off the couch and pulled Lindsey up. They walked to the door where Jax hugged them both before they headed out. "Be careful you two. Lindsey, text me that you made it home. Do you feel like coming to work tomorrow?"

Lindsey straightened, and Chance watched the slight woman find her strength. "I'll be there. I won't let him control what I do, and he's not going to intimidate me into hiding ever again."

"Then I'll see you at nine." Jax waved at them. Lindsey climbed into her car, followed down the driveway by a blue and gold cruiser.

Chance wrapped Jax in her arms from behind. "Okay, let's go sit in front of the fire and talk." She led Jax to the couch and cradled her while the emotions bubbled over. The tears rushed forth in hot waves as she sobbed.

"I was so angry. I could have slapped that smug look right off Leland's face. It was bad enough the way he eyed me, but what he said to Lindsey? That was beyond crude, and it shook her badly. I don't care what it costs, Chance. I don't want that to ever happen again."

"I'll take care of it. I called Penny while you and Lindsey were talking. She'll forward all my office calls to my cellphone. I have to meet with Brad tomorrow and handle a few things out of the office. After that, I'll be working out of the animal hospital until we get things under control. I know you don't want to be under armed guard. All I ask is, for a little while, you let me take care of this, and you."

"I'm not arguing. I wouldn't complain if I spent every minute of every day with you. I know that's not practical. You have work to do, and so do I. We'll get the security system up and running. If need be, I'll hire a bodyguard who can act as an assistant. Leland Kurst isn't getting anywhere near either of us ever again." Jax settled with her feet tucked beneath her.

"Now that we have that out of the way, I'll tell you about Midas. When I checked him, I didn't see any major injuries. I think it's more of a bruise in the shoulder area making him limp. A few days' rest and I'll recheck him."

Chance patted Zeus' head where he rested it on her thigh. "They brought him down quickly. The second he raised that gun, Zeus was already in motion as I gave him the command. Midas was right behind him."

"I'm so glad you're okay. Thank you, Zeus." Jax turned and kissed him between his ears. She looked at Chance and started again. "Now, tell me what has you on edge besides Leland Kurst."

Chance let her head fall back on the couch. The only way the lines of communication would remain open was if they talked about their dreams and their nightmares. "The call at the Wilson's brought up some painful memories. It was a similar situation that took my father all those years ago. He put himself between an abusive husband and his terrified wife, just like I did today. The difference was I wasn't alone. I had Taylor, Zeus, and Midas. Harley was outside, and Chuck Wilson didn't get a shot off. My father had no one when he put himself in the line of fire to protect an unarmed woman, a woman just like Mary Wilson."

"I'm so sorry, honey. I wish things had been different for your father. I'm eternally grateful today's incident didn't turn out the same way." She tapped Chance's chin. "I'm looking forward to many years as your wife. Your father didn't die in vain. His sacrifice made you a more conscientious officer. It also drove you to find a solution to the backup issue when you became Sheriff. I've spent half my life missing something that made me feel whole. That something was you."

Chance pulled Jax close and held her so tightly she was afraid she might hurt her. Jax clung to her just as tightly, and both let the stress of the day melt into the embrace.

***

Chance sat behind her desk; the phone held to her ear. She looked at her watch. Agent Andy Treeland had pulled a case file from the DEA's active investigations. Chance was trying a different avenue for information than she'd gathered through the other task forces.

"Leland Kurst, yeah, we have a file on him. Always seemed to avoid trouble when it was going down. We could never pin anything directly to him. That doesn't mean there's a single one of us that doubts his involvement."

Chance rubbed her eyes. "Any chance he's connected with the names I gave you from the kidnapping or shots-fired incidents we had earlier this year?"

"There is a very thin line connecting him with Dennis Cooley. They both worked at a small tobacco store chain in a rough Baltimore neighborhood. That store is owned by the wife of one of the higher-ups in Murdaland. We're pretty sure they're selling more than cigarettes and beer in those places. You know how it is, long drawn out months, sometimes years, of surveillance. It's one of those cases we have to have locked down tight before we go busting in with a warrant. Sorry, I don't have a lot for you, but I'll keep digging, Sheriff."

"Don't worry, Agent Treeland. Every little piece of information helps. I need to cut this pipeline before it floods my jurisdiction. I've got plenty of drugs that originate here in my county. Thanks again. I'll let you know if I dig up any connection. Let me know if you need anything." She disconnected the call and lowered the phone back into its cradle before picking it back up and calling Jax.

"Well, this is a nice surprise," Jax said when she answered.

Chance leaned back in her chair. "I like surprising you. Sometimes, I need to hear your voice."

"You can call anytime, you know that, right?"

"I do, but I know you're busy."

"I love you, so I'm never too busy for you. I want to try and get out of here early tonight. Isn't Kendra stopping by our place for dinner with your parents?"

"I love you too. Poor Kendra, I'll bet she has hives by now, worrying about next weekend. I'll stop by the store and grab some steaks. Wonder if Mags will let Dee have one or if I should pick up some chicken instead."

"Let's make Maggie happy. Get chicken, and we'll make grilled chicken salads."

"Your wish is my command. Okay, back to work for both of us. And Jax?"

"What, honey?"

"You make everything in my life better. Love you."

***

Chance waited for Deputy Brad Waters to make his appearance. She'd pulled all the maintenance records on his cruiser. She'd even gone and checked the vehicle while he was performing his court duties. As the sheriff, she had keys to every cruiser. The test drive she'd taken it on revealed no issues. The lights and siren worked, as did the radio, air conditioning, and heat. She knew this was just one more way of Brad trying to establish his seniority. She looked up at the knock on the door. "Come in." She looked back at her papers, purposefully ignoring Brad for a few minutes while she organized her notes. "What can I do for you, Deputy Waters?"

Brad sat in the chair across from her desk. "It's time to replace my cruiser. Give me a new one and give Daniel one of the older cruisers. I've earned it."

She checked a box beside her notes. She'd put a list together of the things she was sure Brad would bring up, and Daniel was one of them. "Deputy Waters, your current cruiser has twenty-seven thousand miles on it. Its last service at the garage was three weeks ago for inspection and regular maintenance. I'm not—"

Brad interrupted. "I don't give a crap what the mechanic says. I'm owed a new cruiser, and if I have to file a grievance to get it, I will."

Chance checked another box. "On what grounds?" She stared at him with true disgust.

"Differential treatment." Brad sat back and crossed his arms over his chest, grinning.

"Deputy Waters, your cruiser has lower mileage than all of the fleet except my new vehicle. A cruiser is provided to you as part of your job. You have a uniform allotment and are afforded training opportunities based on your job duties here. You have all the same holidays, all the same insurances, you get the same pay raise, and you never have to do shift work. I see no place where you are being treated differently than any of the rest of the department. I took the liberty of test driving your vehicle and found it to be in excellent shape, except for the driver's seat. I've made an appointment to address the broken welds with Tommy. You need to have it to him this evening. One of the deputies will pick you up at the shop and transport you home. Your request for a new vehicle is denied. If there is nothing else, sign for your written answer to your request." She slid a piece of paper across the desk and pulled a pen from the cup at the corner.

"I'm not signing shit. My attorney —"

Chance cut him off and called for Taylor, who was walking by. "Can you stop in for a minute?"

"How can I help you, Sheriff?" Taylor's eyes tracked to Brad, who sat red faced.

"I need you as a witness, since Deputy Waters refuses to sign." Chance read off the statement then looked to Brad again. "Do you want to sign now, or do you want me to have Chief Deputy Lewis sign that you received this notification but refused to acknowledge it with your signature? It's up to you."

"It's my right to report equipment I feel is inadequate and unsafe." Brad bristled.

"As I mentioned, it was inspected three weeks ago, and I personally ran it through its paces not thirty minutes ago. I found no deficiencies except for the broken seat. Taylor, can you sign here please?"

"Wait a fucking minute, are you even listening to me? Fucking females. Things always have to be your way. Having women in law enforcement is a joke. Should have stayed at home where a woman should be. Oh, that's right, you're some big dyke who never understood what a woman should be. You probably slept with half the women in this county to get their vote. No way you beat me fair and square."

Chance came around her desk so fast, Brad nearly toppled backward in his chair. Taylor grabbed her arm. "You are now guilty of insubordination and sexual harassment, have your attorney look that up. You're suspended. Leave your badge and gun with Taylor and get the hell out of my office. I'll notify you of your civil service hearing. I advise you to bring your attorney. This also means you'll not have access to your cruiser. I suggest you call someone to pick you up, because no one in this department will drive you anywhere. Dismissed!"

"You can't fucking suspend me. I haven't done anything wrong. Fucking bullshit. You don't know who you're fucking with."

Chance walked to her filing cabinet and pulled out the county personnel policy, as well as the sheriff's department policies. "You really should read the personnel manual you've been working under all these years. I can suspend you and will take steps to fire you under the following provisions listed under the Disciplinary Action section of the policy." Chance began to read. "Suspension, Dismissal, or Termination of Employment. The following actions are among those that may result in suspension, dismissal, or termination from employment with the county. The infractions listed below are illustrative, but are not all-inclusive, of the type of conduct warranting discharge. Section one. Insubordination. Insubordination includes the act of either carrying out an action in a manner contradictory to the spirit of an order or failing to carry out an order as presented by the employee's department head or the city manager. In case you don't understand who that is"—Chance pointed to her chest—"that would be me. Section Two. Sexual Harassment. Consistent with the sexual harassment section of this booklet. I'll let you look that part up for yourself on the copy you signed for last year when we updated it. That's just the first two violations you are guilty of in the last ten minutes. You are hereby relieved of duty. Taylor, adjust the schedule to reflect his suspension. Advise the rest of the staff we are looking for officers on shift work to work overtime until further notice. I'll need you to type up what you witnessed today. Have Penny pull a set of suspension papers along with a comprehensive list of all equipment assigned to him." Chance pointed to Brad.

Brad made his way out of the chair with his hands held up. "Now, Chance, be reasonable."

Chance whirled on him. "I've been reasonable for the last two years. I gave you a job when you lost the election. You've done nothing but stomp on my generosity. I'm done. You have a right to an appeal, so I suggest you get that lawyer on a retainer. You'll never work for this department again if I have any say in it. Your attitude is toxic, and I'm no longer letting it poison the rest of the good work we do here. I'm done talking. Taylor, get him out of here before I show him the door myself!"

Brad shook his finger at her. "You'll live to regret this, you bitch. Nobody treats me like this. I'll be back, and you won't be able to stand behind that badge and gun. We'll see who has balls around here."

Chance took two steps toward him. "Are you threatening me? Forget the suspension, you're fired!"

"Let's go, Brad. This meeting is over, and you need to clean any personal items out of that cruiser and your locker. I suggest you get to it. As a matter of fact, I'll call Carl and have him accompany you while you clear out. If it was issued to you by this department, leave it behind."

Taylor escorted a cussing Brad out the door. Chance gripped either side of the door frame. Releasing the internal volcano would have to wait. She needed to document the entire personnel incident and begin formal termination notifications. She needed to cancel his department-issued credit card and notify the state. There was little doubt Brad would sue to try and get his job back. That was the least of her worries. Inside the tall cabinet was a file on Brad as thick as the penal code. In all her years in management, from being a crew boss of smokejumpers to being a Fish and Wildlife officer, she'd never had to fire anyone. She wasn't looking forward to this process in any way. It had to be done. If she let Brad get away with talking to her like that, it would undermine her authority with every member of her department. This was a justified termination after the threat, and she needed to lay out the framework that would seal his fate. Minutes later, Taylor came into her office.

"It had to be done, Chance. I have no idea how you didn't feed him his teeth."

"With great self-restraint and all the will power I could muster. Let's get our thoughts down while they're fresh. I'm not overlooking this time. His termination has to be ironclad. He'll never work as a deputy in this county again."

"Agreed. I'll get on it. Carl is out there with him in the locker room. I told him to accompany Brad to the cruiser then call me. I'll go take his keys."

"Good thinking. Somedays, this job sucks. This is one of them."

"You did the right thing, Chance. We'll be a better department, now that we aren't dragging that anchor. I'll start working on covering the courts, too."

"I wouldn't know what to do without you, Taylor."

For the next hour, Chance documented the incident until she heard a ruckus. Loud voices followed by a crash brought Chance and Zeus out of her office into the lobby. She found Brad Waters being restrained by Carl, with Penny on the floor. Carl's dog, Petra, stood in front of Brad nearly in attack mode.

Chance dropped like a stone to her knees beside Penny. "What the hell is going on here? Penny, are you all right?"

Penny lay on the floor, holding her abdomen. "I think so."

Chance hit the phone intercom. "Taylor, I need you in the reception area now." She leaned down to Penny and looked up at her deputy. "Carl, you hold onto him until I tell you differently." She could hear

Taylor's pounding footfalls coming down the hall. When she got to the front, Chance watched her go ghostly white at the scene. Midas immediately went on alert, seeing Zeus and Petra in a protective stance. All three dogs bared their teeth in Brad's direction.

Taylor dropped to her wife's side. "Penny! Are you okay, honey? What the fuck happened?" Taylor looked up to Brad, who was being forcibly restrained by Carl. "What did you fucking do?" Taylor attempted to stand up until Chance put a hand on her.

"Stay with Penny." Chance stood and left Penny to Taylor's care. She took three long strides toward a visibly nervous Brad. "What happened here? You'd better start explaining, or I'll have you sitting in Huttonsville so fast, you'll think we time warped. What did you do?"

"I didn't do anything. It was an accident. She got in my way. All I was trying to do was come back to your office. She blocked my path. When she wouldn't move, I pushed past her. It wasn't a hard push. She's just being a good actress."

Chance turned just in time to catch Taylor by the shoulders of her vest.

Taylor's face was blood red, and spittle came out with each word. "You son of a bitch. You better pray my wife and baby aren't hurt. If they are, even God can't save you from what will happen to you."

"Go back to Penny and let me handle this. I promise you, I'll take care of it. Penny and the baby need you. Check and see if she needs an ambulance." Chance released Taylor and directed her back to Penny.

Chance whirled on her former deputy. "Brad Waters, did you make physical contact with my office administrator?"

"I was trying to get to your office. I didn't push her that hard."

Chance stared him directly in the eyes. "Brad Waters, you're under arrest for assault and battery, as well as intimidating an employee of the sheriff's department. Read him his rights, Carl, and take him to the magistrate's office. I'll be there shortly with the criminal complaint. Cuff him."

Carl pulled the handcuffs off Brad's belt and locked his own with them to form a larger set of restraints. He pulled one of Brad's arms behind his back.

"Get your fucking hands off me." Brad wailed at Carl who stood nearly a foot taller. Petra put her ears back and stepped forward.

Carl followed department procedure to the letter of the law. "Brad Waters, you have the right to remain silent. Anything you say can and will be used against you in a court of law. You have the right to an attorney. If you cannot afford an attorney, one will be provided for you. Do you understand the rights I have just read to you? With these rights in mind, do you wish to speak to me? Settle down and stop fighting me, or Petra will hold you in place. Do you understand?"

"Every one of you will pay for this. Mark my words." Brad continued to thrash.

Carl leaned in close to the man he restrained. "Brad, I'm only going to tell you once. If you resist, I will have no choice but to tell Petra to subdue. If that were my wife on the floor, you'd be in a coma by now. Come peacefully, or I'll make this public spectacle a great deal more embarrassing than this is likely to be."

Brad glared at Chance. "Dyke lovers, every one of you. Fucking dyke lovers. This whole place is a joke."

Chance pointed to the door. "Get him the hell out of here, Carl, now!"

Carl turned Brad around and pushed him through the door and onto the sidewalk. When he was out of view, Chance came back to Penny's side. "Penny, I want you to go get checked out, even if it's just at the clinic. I'd prefer you go to Garrett, but I know you're going to fight us. So, as your boss, don't make me order you to go, please?"

Taylor cradled Penny's head in her lap. "Please, honey. Do it for our baby if you won't do it for me. I won't be able to stand worrying."

Penny reached up and cradled Taylor's cheek. "For you, I'll go. Cancel that ambulance or no deal. We'll go over to the clinic. If they find something, I'll go to Garrett. We're okay— nothing more than a little shaken up."

Chance looked at Taylor and put her hand on her friend's back. "I'll take care of everything with Brad. You go with her and call me if you need anything."

They both helped Penny get up. Chance held onto her as Taylor grabbed her purse and jacket. They walked her out to Taylor's cruiser and put her inside. Taylor turned to face Chance. "Whatever you can do, do it. She's got bruises on her upper arms. He did more than push her. Rest assured, Penny will press charges. Nail his ass, Chance. I'll call you as soon as I know anything. If she's okay, I'll bring her by the magistrate's office as soon as possible."

"Okay, I'm going to call Jax and see if she is close to finishing. I know Penny would appreciate her being there with you." Chance leaned in and pulled Taylor close. "They're going to be okay. Hold it together for Penny. I'll make sure he never wears a badge again."

Taylor nodded then got in the cruiser. As they drove away, Chance called Jax and filled her in. Jax was pissed and said she'd be right down to the health clinic. Back in her office, Chance gathered the paperwork she'd need and made a copy of the lobby video surveillance. Few people knew about it, and Chance rarely had reason to view the footage. Brad Waters was done. If the video showed it, he'd lose more than just his job.

Twenty minutes later, she walked into the magistrate's office where Brad Waters sat fuming. He might be pissed, but Chance could see how nervous he was. He had a tell; his leg bounced like there was a spring in his foot. She didn't acknowledge him, as she made her way to the clerk with the paperwork and a CD copy of the confrontation in the office. Brad was saying something derogatory, though Chance didn't bother to answer.

A slight woman with gray at her temples met Chance at the desk. "Sheriff, what can I do for you?"

"I need to see the magistrate on duty. Is he in?"

"I heard him come in the back door a few minutes ago. Go on back to his office. I'll let him know you're here."

"Thank you, Nancy." Chance made her way back to the door marked *Dean Halsey*. She was grateful not to have to deal with Lonny Reap, brother of the prosecutor. Even in his seventies, Dean wasn't afraid to take on the tough cases. She knocked on the open door.

"Come on in, Sheriff."

Chance greeted him, and then took a seat in the chair opposite his desk. She put a packet of papers in front of him. "I wish I were coming with something that wouldn't stir up a hornet's nest. I'm charging Brad Waters with assault and battery, and intimidation of a Tucker County Sheriff's Department employee."

Dean's eyes got wide as he read through the notes. "What the hell, Chance? I've known Brad for twenty years. There was no doubt he was bitter about losing the election, but this?"

"I fired him this morning for insubordination and a few other things. He came storming back into the office. When my secretary tried to stop him, he grabbed her by both arms and threw her down." She held up the CD.

"Holy Shit. You have that all on video?"

"The assault and battery, yes. The things that happened in my office were witnessed by my chief deputy and are also on the CD. Penny Lewis is pregnant and on her way to the clinic to be evaluated."

"Let's check out the footage." He held his hand out and put the CD in the laptop. After watching the incident, he grabbed the paperwork. "I assume he'll post bail?"

"I don't have a clue, and I don't care. Brad's no longer a member of my department. He broke the law. No professional courtesy, Dean. I'm sorry, but he put his hands on a pregnant woman. There are bruises on her arms. God help him if something happens to Penny's baby."

Dean stood up and led Chance from his office. "Let's go arraign him."

Chance's cellphone rang with Taylor's number on the display. She didn't even bother with a greeting. "How is she?"

"She's spotting. We're on our way to Garrett. Her obgyn is going to meet us there. All her vitals are strong, and the ultrasound doesn't show anything wrong. It's more of a precaution. I swear, Chance if something happens, I—"

"They're going to be all right, Taylor. You have to believe that. I'm about to hand Brad his ass. I'll make my way to the hospital after I finish with this."

Chance stood at the counter signing papers, with Brad bellowing in the background. Petra and Zeus stood at attention, staring directly at Brad with an occasional, deep rumble growl.

Brad was led to the counter where Carl uncuffed his right hand to allow him to sign paperwork. His left wrist was handcuffed to a pipe affixed to the surface, designed to hold prisoners in place. It took an hour for him to be charged and entered into the system. Once everything was official, Carl moved him into a holding area where he could make a call.

Brad pointed a stubby finger at Chance. "This isn't over. I'll see you in court, and I'll hand your ass to you. You won't get away with this. I'll sue you until you don't have a dime to your name."

Chance walked over to the holding cell and stood with her hands on the bars. "You'd better hope Penny and that baby are all right, or you won't see the outside of a jail cell for years. I promise you that. You've got one call; I'd make it a good one. If you don't post bail, you'll be spending the night at Huttonsville."

Brad surged forward. "You can't do that! I'll be in danger as a police officer in there."

Chance narrowed her eyes. "Former police officer."

"Fuck you."

"Not if you were the last human being on earth, and I was

desperate for the human race to continue." She stepped even closer to the bars of the cell. "You say what you want about me. Think what you want about me. The minute you put your hands on Penny, you went over the line."

Brad sneered. "It's my word against hers. Who do you think they're going to believe? You're expecting them to believe the word of a glorified secretary over a twenty-plus year law enforcement officer? Not likely."

"I think they're going to believe the video evidence." Chance let a thin smile cross her lips, as she watched Brad's jaw drop. "Oh, did I forget to mention the reception area has two cameras that record everything? Must have slipped my mind. You apparently missed that little sign on the door. It's all in the details, Brad. I'm pretty sure it's you who's going to get your ass handed to them. Count on it."

Chance turned and strode out of the magistrate center and holding area. She pulled out her phone. The minute she heard Jax speak, her mind settled. "How is she?"

"She's stable. They have her on a fetal monitor and the heartbeat is strong. The doctor thinks she'll be fine but has her on bed rest for a week. What in the hell did Brad think he was doing?"

Chance rubbed her eyes as she and Zeus got into the Suburban. "Brad's been arrested and arraigned. After that, I couldn't give two shits about what happens to him. He's in a hell of his own making, and it's not up to me to dig him out. Are they keeping Penny tonight?"

"Yes, they want to monitor her and the baby overnight. I already called Kendra and Maggie to tell them dinner was off. Are you coming over?"

Chance buckled her seatbelt. "Thanks for that. I completely forgot about them. I'm on my way. Unless I miss my guess, Taylor is going to stay with her. I'll be there in about an hour, and I'll bring Midas home to stay with us for the night. I need to ask Randy to take care of the horses. Thanks for being with them, Jax. I'm sure Taylor and Penny appreciate it."

"I can't do much beyond offering a hand to hold, or another set of ears to hear what the doctor is saying. I wouldn't be anywhere else. Drive carefully, babe. I'll see you in a bit."

"You're doing more than you'll ever know. I love you." Chance disconnected the call and got on the road.

Chapter Six

A FEW MINUTES PAST four in the afternoon, Jax paced the waiting area in the emergency room. She was waiting for Taylor to come and get her, or for Chance to arrive. The phone call from Chance explaining what had happened to Penny incensed her. *How could he have thought that was okay?* On her next turn, she came face to face with someone she recognized.

Dr. Faith Riker approached. "Jax, what are you doing here? Is Chance okay?"

Jax braced herself and looked directly at Chance's ex, who was determined to get her former lover back. "Faith. Chance is fine. Penny and Taylor are back in the exam room meeting with their obgyn."

Faith crossed her arms. "Is Penny okay?"

"She and the baby seem to be. I don't have much information."

"And you probably wouldn't reveal it to me anyway."

Jax bit the side of her cheek to slow her response. "Probably not. That's Penny and Taylor's personal information. I'm here as moral support."

"And standing in for Chance, unless I miss my guess. Sooner or later, you'll figure out you're nothing more than a part of Chance's routine. One more obligation, like her job or volunteer work." Faith crossed her arms over her chest in a defiant stance.

"Faith, I'm not here to get into a pissing match with you." Jax held up her hand and pointed to the ring. "Nothing you say to me will ever change my mind about spending my life with her exactly as she is. Over thirty years ago, I walked away, looking for something I didn't realize I'd already found. I was a fool, and I've spent my time in hell paying for it. I won't make that mistake again. Your former relationship with Chance has no bearing on our current one. Your mistakes aren't mine, and mine aren't yours."

"All that might be true, but Chance is still who she's always been. A woman haunted by losing her father and always seeking the next natural high. Settling down might be fun for a while, but she'll get bored and start looking for that next rush. When that happens, I'll be right on

57

your heels. I'm not done with Chance."

Jax shook her head. She had to give it to Faith for her persistence. "Did I miss something? I thought you were already married to Theresa. That probably puts a real crimp in your plan to get Chance back, doesn't it? Did your wife ever mean anything to you, or did you just use her to get back at Chance? How can you be so cruel to someone you professed to love so much you married her? Do you even care how badly you're hurting someone who doesn't deserve any of this? What you're doing to Theresa is beyond cruel and completely demoralizing."

Faith interrupted her. "My relationship with Theresa is none of your business."

"You're absolutely right, and neither is my commitment with Chance any concern of yours. I feel sorry for you. You're burning your life down around you and pouring gasoline on by the gallon."

Faith looked like a warrior ready for battle. "I love Chance, and I'm not giving up. We will be together." She spun around at the sound of a choking sob.

"Nice to know I don't factor into that decision at all." Theresa stood behind Faith with a bouquet in her hand, tears streaming down her face. "At least I know where I stand. I'm done fighting for something that obviously doesn't mean a damn to you. I don't have a clue who you are anymore, certainly not the woman I married."

Faith reached out to grab her wife. "Theresa, wait!"

Theresa shook off her hand. "Nothing to wait for. You made yourself perfectly clear. You have no intention of spending your life with me. God, what a fool I've been." Theresa looked at the roses in her hand then jammed them into the trash receptacle as she walked out the door, right past Chance.

Faith tried again. "Theresa!" Theresa never turned around.

Chance approached Jax and took her hand. "Faith, what was that?"

Faith said nothing. She looked at Jax before she turned and walked through the doors to the treatment area, leaving the two stunned women behind.

Jax leaned into Chance's chest and put her arms around her fiancée. "My heart is breaking for Theresa. I've been in her shoes. Nothing hurts worse than to know the person you gave your heart to doesn't feel the same."

"I'm sorry she's dragging you into this mess."

Jax pulled back and looked into Chance's eyes. "Honey, we're in this together, no matter what happens or who tries to step in our way.

None of this is your fault. I feel so sorry for Theresa. She walked in on Faith professing her determination to get you back. I'm starting to really worry about her obsession with you."

Chance pulled her close. "I think you're in a unique position to talk to Theresa. You've been in her shoes."

"I'm not the only one. You've had someone cheat on you. I'm sure you have some wisdom you could share with her." Jax caressed Chance's jaw.

"Talking to me is like pouring salt in a wound. Nothing I say will make this any better. Theresa's lost in this storm. She needs someone who can show her she will come out on the other side of the pain. You're in a better position to do that. Why don't you go see if she's still outside?"

Jax nodded and kissed Chance. "You know, you're a big teddy bear inside. Don't worry, I won't reveal your secret."

"Whew, I was worried there for a minute. I love you."

"Love you too. Go check on Taylor and Penny. I'm sure they could use your support." Jax left her arms and followed the path Theresa had taken. She wasn't sure about Chance's assessment that she could help, but Chance had asked her to try. The palpable memories of how painful it had been to learn of Lacey's betrayal brought bile up in her throat. When she'd cleared the doors to the hospital, she saw Theresa sitting under a tree on a stone bench.

"Can I join you?" Jax pointed to the space beside Theresa.

"Free country. Be my guest. I'll warn you, I'm not very good company right now." Theresa ran her hand through her hair and leaned forward, resting her elbows on her knees.

Jax folded her hands in her lap. "I can't imagine you would be, after what you witnessed. I'm sorry if I've personally caused you any pain. I can empathize with what you might be feeling, and I know it's awful."

"Ever witness your wife professing her undying love for someone else?"

"Not in those words, no. I had to hear from our colleagues about her exploits. Someone even provided me with pictures. The straw that broke the camel's back was when I found her fucking one of our vet techs in her office. She thought I'd left for the night. My experience might not be exactly like yours, but I can certainly understand what you're going through. You love her. That's obvious."

Theresa rubbed her face. "I do, or I should say I did. When I said for better or worse, I didn't think worse meant her loving someone more than me. I don't think I can do this any longer. I've tried, and it's killing me. I won't play second fiddle to anyone. Before you say it, I don't blame Chance for any of this. No one owns this failure except Faith. I've been putting off serving her with divorce papers in the hope she'd come to her senses, hoping just maybe, we could get past this. After what I just heard, I have zero confidence she ever will. I can't start to get over this and heal until I've cut out the infection. If I was being honest with myself, I should have known she wouldn't be faithful. Hell, she left Chance for me."

Jax placed a gentle hand on Theresa's shoulder. "Only you know what you need to do to be whole. Faith has no place in our lives. Chance changed doctors and doesn't even call Faith for assistance on scenes. I can tell you that she's close to putting a restraining order on her. Her relationship with Sarah is the only thing that keeps her from doing that."

"Sarah's pissed at her and with good reason. Faith's always been hard on her, and she practically ignores Kristi." Theresa stopped talking and shook her head. "I have no idea why I'm telling you any of this. It's not your problem."

"No, it isn't. That doesn't mean we don't care. Chance never meant to cause you any pain or put a rift between you and Faith. Please know that we will be here for you if you need us. All you have to do is reach out."

Theresa stood and held out her hand to Jax. "I have a lot to think about and an appointment with my attorney to make. It's time to protect myself. Thanks, Jax. The fact that Faith never bothered to come out and check on me says all I need to know. Take care."

There was a cool breeze, and it felt good against Jax's heated skin. She watched Theresa climb into her truck and leave the parking area. Falling out of love was painful. It took time to work through all the complicated feelings and untangle all the threads of physical and emotional connection. She didn't envy Theresa the days to come.

"Hey, you."

The smooth voice she knew well brought a smile to her face. "Hey."

"How is she?" Chance joined her on the bench and wrapped an arm around her shoulders.

"Broken and resigned. I feel so bad for her. Her whole world is upside down. You invest your heart and soul into the person you think you'll spend the rest of your life with. Unfortunately, you wake up one day to find the other half of the equation doesn't feel the same. It's soul wrenching."

"That's why I wanted you to talk to her. When I walked in on my ex, we were only dating. We weren't married or even engaged. It hurt. I can admit that. I also know she wasn't my one true love."

Jax scooted closer. "I certainly hope I qualify for that position."

Chance kissed her. "You definitely have the job. I only caught the tail end of what happened. What brought all this on?"

"First tell me how Penny is."

"She and the baby are fine. She's resting, and everything seems under control, other than Taylor's anger. Brad Waters would do well to keep a full ten miles between them, which won't be hard since he's currently jailed. I can't say that I blame her. It took everything I had not to deck him right there in the lobby. I regret trying to be a decent human being by keeping him employed. My bad decision could have cost Taylor her child. For that, I'll never forgive myself."

"Chance Fitzsimmons, you look at me. None of this is your fault, not Brad and not Faith. You can't take ownership of what isn't yours. We all have faults and make mistakes. None of this bullshit is on you."

Jax watched as Chance closed her eyes and lifted her face to the sky.

"I wish I could believe that. I'll be buying Penny a big bag of peppermint tea from Molly's shop for the rest of my life."

"Penny might just divorce Taylor for that tea, and I'll have to fight two women for you."

"Not a chance in hell. Penny loves Taylor like I love you. Nothing's ever going to change that. How about we check on the patient one more time, then take the dogs home? I need a beer and some time on the swing with you in my arms."

"Sheriff, that's the best offer I've had all day. Lead the way."

***

Jax stood at the breakfast counter, buttering a bagel. A plate of bacon and eggs waited on the counter for Chance. Jax couldn't stop thinking about Theresa and what faced her. The pain of ending a committed relationship went far beyond what anyone could see on the outside, and the scars ran deep beneath the surface. She was grateful she had Chance's love to replace the horrible memories and pain. She hoped Theresa would eventually find the same.

"Morning, love." Chance snuck up behind her with a kiss to her cheek on the way to let the dogs out into the yard.

Jax smiled at the mere sight of Chance. Lean and strong muscles rippled under her uniform. She was blessed, and she knew it. "I hope you have something more substantial planned for me than just a peck?"

Chance's grin added more light to the sunny kitchen. "Of course I do. I just didn't want to have to compete for your attention with those two." She pointed her thumb to the two dogs roughhousing outside the door. "I took care of the horses after our run, so you don't have to worry about them this morning. What's on your agenda today?" Chance wrapped her arms around Jax's waist and kissed her soundly.

"Well, after that kiss, I'd like to say we are headed back to bed, but Lindsey and I have a full day of barn calls. The Timms want a check up on their goat herd, and Cliff Minor has a batch of new calves he wants vaccinated and a horse with a bad tooth. It'll be a busy day out of the office. How about you?"

"If Penny is up to it after she gets home, I'm going to stop by the house with paperwork to finalize the charges against Brad. Taylor wants her to rest. I'll have that mess to clear up. Brad's dismissal, plus the fact I'm already down one patrol deputy, is going to create a scheduling nightmare. Daniel is still at the academy and won't begin his K9 training until after that's complete. I know you aren't going to like this, but I'm going to have to take on some shift work. I don't want Penny home alone at night. She'll likely return to work in the next few days, and I'm going to have Taylor handle the court duty and office work. That way, she can keep an eye on Penny. I'll likely take the afternoon patrol and divide up the other shift with Carl and Randy. Until the whole termination hearing is settled, things are going to be up in the air. I might be able to hire someone temporarily, until I can get Daniel on shift. I'll need to check with civil service and our attorney to see if I can fill the vacancies immediately off our current list. As badly as I wanted to get rid of Brad, this wasn't what I had in mind."

Jax ran a hand across Chance's back. "Sit down and eat. It sounds like your day is going to be as crazy as mine. Try to make sure you get some lunch."

"I need to go see Mags and Dee today, so lunch is under control."

"With the schedule being so messed up, how are you going to handle Leaf Peepers?"

Chance shook her head. "Don't remind me. I need to meet up with Harley and see if she can pull some strings to get an extra trooper assigned. Daniel will be home for the weekend, so I can put him in the car with me for some ride-along time. He can't do much else until he finishes the academy in another month."

"When Brad's firing becomes finalized, you're going to have another problem on your hands, you know?" Jax bit into her bagel.

"What's that?"

"Your Mini-Me." Jax laughed.

"I know. The list is still good for another fifteen months. Unless I don't have a viable candidate, I have to hire off that list. There are three other names on it, two of which have already been through the academy. Kendra won't like it, I know. She will understand. I have at least another year before I have to worry too much. The moms will kill her if she drops out of college."

Jax reached up and wiped some mustard off Chance's lip. "Safe for now then."

"She'll still gripe, trust me."

Jax wiped her hands. "I've got to get going. I'm picking Lindsey up at her place. I'll call you later." She bent down and brought her lips to Chance's. "Be careful. I love you."

Chance cupped the back of her neck. "Right back atcha, Doc. Call me later."

Jax let the two dogs back in on her way out. "Will do."

Chapter Seven

IT WAS MIDMORNING WHEN Chance pulled up to Taylor's residence. She let Midas and Zeus out of the Suburban. Taylor had texted her that they were home and she could stop by when she got the opportunity. The front door opened, and Taylor greeted Midas with a vigorous scratch along his sides, then greeted Zeus as well.

"Thanks for bringing him by. Penny's settled in on the couch. She's really grouchy, because I wouldn't let her go to work today."

"Well, her boss is here now. Don't worry, I'm ordering her off for the rest of the week and more if she needs it."

Taylor sighed and ran her hands through her hair. "I appreciate that. I love that woman, but she's stubborn as a mule. The doctor said she and the baby are fine. She wants Penny to take it easy for the next few days, and I'm determined that she will do as the doctor ordered if it kills me."

"Let's keep it from going that far. I brought peppermint tea, that should help soothe the savage beast."

Chance followed Taylor through her former home. It occurred to her that it truly had become that, a home. When she'd lived there, it was a house. Now, Taylor and Penny were starting their family, expecting a little one to grow up under the roof she'd built. That fact made Chance happy, and she was glad she'd offered the place to her friends.

Penny sat with her feet up and a blanket across her lap in the living room. "I see she brought reinforcements." She kissed the top of Midas' head as he sat at her side. "Okay, out with it. I'm sure you're here to issue some directive. Let's have it so I can argue my point."

Chance smiled and shook her head. "You are a stubborn cuss. There will be no argument, because I'm your boss, at least in name. The office will be fine for a few days. I can handle it. Anything in dire need of attention, I can send to your laptop, which I brought with me. Take it easy and let things settle down. If not for your nerves, for Taylor's. Tomorrow is Friday, and you'd be off the weekend anyway. Taylor and I are going to work on the schedule. Carl's handling court today for overtime. I'm going to handle the afternoon shift, and Randy has the midnight turn. Taylor will handle court tomorrow. I promise we have it all worked out. We'll make do, and you will rest. That's an order from your boss. I brought you a peppermint tea and a bag of doughnut holes as a peace offering. I have some paperwork with me from the magistrate's office for you to fill out to get the ball rolling on the more severe of the charges against Brad."

"With pleasure. I hate that this is how his career is coming to an end." Penny picked up the pen and began filling in the boxes Chance had made marks beside.

Taylor handed Chance a cup of coffee. "The jackass should have retired when he lost the election, not come begging to you for a job."

"True, but I take responsibility for giving him the job. Penny, document everything that happened in as much detail as you can. He made bail late last night and didn't have to go to Huttonsville. Carl said he cussed me the whole time. Our case is ironclad with the video evidence. I know he'll sue, and we'll go through the process. He won't be back. You can rest assured of that."

"It won't bother me not seeing his face every day. I can tell you that. Here you go. Do I need to come to the magistrate's office, or will this do?"

Chance folded the papers and put them in her shirt pocket. "This will be fine. I know what will happen. I'm going to try and recommend a special prosecutor on this to avoid any conflict of interest. When this goes to trial, Larry would likely try to plead this down to a misdemeanor. I want more than a little slap on the wrist. The big fight will be when he goes after us for wrongful termination. I'm ready for that one too. Now, I want you to rest and not worry about anything. Do not pick up that laptop unless I call with something I can't fix. Watch TV or read, but please take it easy. Taylor and I are going to the kitchen to work on this schedule."

"I'm doing this under protest, just so you know."

"Noted. Taylor, let's get cracking."

***

Around one o'clock, they had the next two weeks on a schedule. Each officer was working at least sixteen hours overtime, with Chance filling in as well. She was going to call over to Randolph and Preston counties to see if some of their deputies could provide relief on their off days. She'd made calls to several of the regulatory agencies and determined what she'd need to do in order to have them work outside of their normal jurisdictions. She had a temporary solution until Daniel could get out of the academy. His K9 training would have to wait. She would shift him into court duty until they could get another officer hired. Circumstances being what they were, she could put in for hardship rule and hire out of order with a candidate who was already a certified officer.

"A temporary relief officer won't have a K9 backup." Taylor pointed out the deviation from their norms.

"Not true, one of them owns his own K9. We'll overlap as much as possible, and we'll coordinate with Harley to ensure county coverage no matter who we choose. I'll back up officers as needed. I'll do split shifts for a while to ensure we have backup for our people." Chance highlighted her days on the schedule.

Taylor shook her head. "You're going to get fatigued trying to keep up."

"I'll rest as I have to. The good part about being the boss is I can set my schedule. Jax will be fine with it as long as we see each other once a day. Kelly is the one who's going to be miffed. Jax will have to alternate the horses for rides, and I'll get Dee to help. Honestly Taylor, we'll make it work until we get back up to full staff. Right now, it's the best we can do."

"I won't argue except to say I'll take call as well. You can't do that all by yourself. You go out at dark, so do I, or no deal."

"Taylor, I know you're my chief deputy, and I respect your opinion. Penny needs you at home for a while. She won't tell any of us, but I know this has shaken her up. She needs to feel secure, and that means you being home. I'm going to head over to see Mags. I'll call you later." Chance got up and grabbed a copy of the schedule to post.

"Chance, I know I've said it before, but it's a pleasure working for someone like you."

Chance and Zeus headed for the door. "That works both ways, my friend. Go spend some time with your wife."

***

Fifteen minutes later, Chance stopped in at the real-estate office. Maggie came out from behind her desk with a hug. She led Chance to the break room and put a sandwich in front of her. "Rumor has it, your department is a deputy short. Want to talk about it?"

Chance sighed as Dee joined them. "Not really. I'm dealing with things but need a little help. I'm going to be working some odd shifts and need a little help with the horses. Think you guys would be up for some evening rides with Jax for a while?"

Dee held up her hand. "I'm game. I have a few things on my schedule with ball practices. Otherwise, I'm good for it."

"Thanks, Momma D. Jax has a full schedule making it nearly impossible to exercise all three horses without me."

"I understand that, too. I'm down an assistant coach for the girls." Dee looked at Chance with understanding eyes. "Before you say anything, Theresa knows this isn't your fault. She's taking some time off. She's asked the school for a leave of absence. Fortunately, we're in the off-season, so it's only practice that's currently affected. She told me what happened with Faith at the hospital."

Maggie sat back in her chair and motioned for Chance to eat. "Faith called me that night. She's a mess. To be honest, I don't know what to do for her at all. She's headed down a road that'll only lead her to more heartbreak. I haven't been able to get through to her."

Chance shook her head as she chewed and swallowed. "I can tell you this, nothing she does will change the fact I intend to marry Jax. I need to call Sarah, but it's been nuts today, trying to deal with the schedule and Brad's arrest. Faith stopped in my office not too long ago and I nearly had to throw her out. She was hardheaded when we were together, now she's pure obstinance. Sarah's on my side, and I hate that it's going to cause an even bigger rift between them. Faith doesn't want to take no for an answer. It burns my ass that she acts like I have no choice in this."

Dee squeezed Chance's neck. "Think Sarah can talk any sense into her?"

"Doubtful. Faith takes nothing Sarah says to heart. If it wasn't for Daniel, I doubt they would have much at all to talk about. It's the one link they have since their parents passed."

Maggie took a drink of her coffee, then set the mug down. "This isn't your fault, Chance. Faith let you go a long time ago. Apparently, she thought you'd wait around. She's seen you with others over the years, after you separated. The one that's getting the worst of this is Theresa. She certainly doesn't deserve this."

Chance finished the sandwich and drank the last of the glass of water she'd been given. She rose out of the chair and put her hat on. "I've got to get back at it. Tell Kendra I'll try to catch her before she goes back to school. Maybe dinner tomorrow? I know she'll be home for Leaf Peepers. Have you guys come to an agreement about the sleeping arrangements?"

Dee held up a hand. "Oh, don't go there. The discussions are ongoing. That one over there has taken the protective, mother bear position." Dee laughed, then covered it with a cough before reaching down and scratching Zeus' side.

Maggie crossed her arms. "I can't help being protective. I have a right to be. I've never met this girl. I've got more than one bedroom available. My mind is made up that they'll stay in separate rooms."

"Yeah and sneak in to visit after you've gone to sleep." Chance couldn't hold her laughter, knowing how many times over the years she'd done the same.

Maggie pointed at Chance. "I know what you're thinking, Chance Raylynn. I know what you did years ago, and it might happen next weekend too. I don't have to give my approval."

Chance stood and stretched as Zeus made his way to the door. "I get it, Mom. Don't get your dander up. I have no doubt you're going to like Brandi. You have nothing to worry about, but I'll let you judge for yourself. I need to head out. I got a text from Sarah. She's working today and asked me to stop by. Maybe we can come up with something together."

Maggie came around the table and hugged her. "Be careful out there. I know you're running short. The bad guys know what's going on too. Don't take any chances. You have people depending on you."

"You got it. I'll call you later. Thanks, you two, I wouldn't know what to do without you. Thanks for the sandwich. Let's go, Zeus."

"That's what parents do, no matter how old their kids are. Go, we've got you covered with the horses and anything else Jax needs. Call if you think of something else." Maggie kissed her cheek.

Chance tipped her hat and headed out the door. She'd barely made it inside her cruiser when she received a radio call.

"Comm Center to SD-1."

"This is SD-1. Go ahead with your traffic."

"State Police Unit 206 requests you meet him at Valley View Road in Timberline. Missing juveniles."

She pointed the Suburban in the direction of Timberline. She was ten minutes out from where Quade wanted to meet her. "Do you have any more information?"

"Two twelve-year-old males, last seen near the Valley View trail over two hours ago. Parents have been looking and calling for them since discovering they were missing. One is in a blue hoodie and jeans. The other has a black jacket and jeans. Neither is from the area. One is diabetic. It's unknown whether they took any provisions."

"SD-1 received. Go ahead and notify Canaan Valley Fire Department and the Saddleback rescue unit. With a two-hour head start, we need to locate those kids ASAP. Break. SD-1 to 206."

"This is 206. Go ahead."

"How close did the boys enter the woods in relation to the trail parking area?"

"Chance, from what I can tell, they went in about a quarter-mile from the rental house. The parents haven't seen or heard anything from them."

"Does either boy have a cellphone?"

"Negative. I thought of that too. No luck there. I'm going to drive Valley View with my siren on and see if I can give them a target to head for. I heard you called the horses in. Hopefully, we can get them in here quickly."

"Received. I'm on my way, 206." Chance's cellphone rang and she answered without looking at the caller ID. "Sheriff Fitzsimmons."

"Chance, it's Taylor. I'm headed to your place to load the horses. Jax is on her way to meet me. We'll load up your two, then I'll get Sabrina. I'll make contact with Matt Carson. Anything else you want?"

"Yes, contact Pete Doran out at the Rubenstein Center. See if he and his search dog can head our way. Let's set up a command post at the trail parking area."

"You got it. See you there." Taylor hung up.

Chance grabbed her radio. "SD-1 to Company 30."

"This is Company 30. Go ahead, Sheriff."

"Ike, can you run the scene? As soon as my horse gets here, I'm going to head out on the trail."

"I'll take command. We're leaving the station in five."

Ten minutes later, Chance pulled near Quade's cruiser and stepped out beside a frantic couple. "I'm Sheriff Fitzsimmons. What can you tell me about the boys?"

A man who looked in his late thirties stepped forward. "We rented a cabin on Valley View. The boys were playing in the back yard, and I went inside to take a phone call. When I came back out, the boys were gone. I tried to find them myself, then came back and got my wife. We've been calling for them nonstop until I made the call to 9-1-1."

"What are the boys' names?" Chance pulled her notebook out.

"They're twins, Laken and Brayden. Laken is diabetic and takes insulin shots twice a day. He ate lunch, and we normally would have checked his blood sugar by now. We do that about every three hours. We're well past that."

"Okay, what's your name?" Chance made notes.

"I'm Joseph Clarkson, and this is my wife, Eve. We're vacationing from Columbus, Ohio."

"Please, Sheriff, we need to find them. Laken could easily slip into a diabetic coma. He didn't take his kit with him." Eve trembled as she wrapped her arms around herself.

Chance stepped up beside Joseph. "We're going to do everything we can to find them. Would the boys stay together?"

Joseph pulled his wife close. "Without a doubt. When you find one, you'll find the other stuck right to him. They're inseparable. Laken is actually the more adventurous of the two. Brayden will follow his brother to the gates of hell and back, but he won't lead him there."

Chance asked several more questions about the boys' heights and weights. "Okay. Do you have anything of the boys with you? I'm hoping one of the dogs might be able to get a scent trail."

"No, we took off walking, trying to find them." Joseph shook his head, still holding his wife close.

"Then here's what I need you to do. Go back to the house and get Laken's insulin and something the boys have worn recently. Our medics will have medication with them, but you've been dealing with his condition his whole life. Once we find him, we can make sure he quickly gets the attention he'll need. We're going to set up a command post here in the parking lot. When you get back, stay here. This is where we'll bring them when we find them."

Joseph tried to protest. "I want to go out and search with you."

Chance put a hand on his shoulder. "I know that's what you want to do. The problem is, you aren't a trained searcher. I'm going to be on horseback. The safest and most helpful place for you is to be in the command post if we have questions. I know it's hard, I do. We've handled hundreds of these searches. You have to trust us." Chance turned at the sound of a siren, as the rescue truck showed up along with a Sheriff's Department truck pulling a horse trailer.

She coordinated with Quade and Ike, as Taylor unloaded Kelly and Sabrina. Chance joined them and put an arm around Jax who stood holding Mac's reins. "Thanks for coming. Hopefully, we can find the kids before it gets dark. We only have a couple of hours before dusk sets in. We've got to get moving. I'm going to take Jax and head north. We'll work off tactical channel two. Ike are you okay with all that?"

Joseph ran up to them with the boy's pajamas. "Here, they wore these last night."

"Excellent." Chance looked up to see Pete walking into the scene with Booney, a loveable bloodhound. "Just in time, Pete. Were you already close?"

The man with salt and pepper hair stood beside a tall Appaloosa and held a very long leash. "We were doing some training over at the ski lodge."

Chance filled him in on the call and handed him the garments. Pete bent and let Booney smell the pajamas.

Taylor stepped into the stirrup and threw her leg over Sabrina. "I'll head opposite of whichever way you guys go, Chance, just to cover all the bases. Get moving."

Jax handed Chance Kelly's reins. "I'm right behind you."

Booney put his nose to the ground at the track command, and he and Pete took off north, with Chance and Jax following along the Valley View trail, one horse directly behind the other.

Ten minutes later, Taylor came up on the radio. "Anything?"

Chance keyed her mic. "They were out here a long time before the parents discovered they were missing. No telling how far they got."

Small huckleberry bushes dotted the grassy areas and the horses were forced to navigate around thick laurel patches that snaked out into their path all along the trail. Eventually, they made it to the ridge and the rocky vistas of Dolly Sods.

Booney smelled the ground all around and looked up at Pete. "It's okay, boy. We'll find them."

Chance stopped and cupped her hands around her mouth to yell. "Brayden! Laken!" She stopped to listen for any noise that might indicate the boys. She tried again with no result. "Two boys that age could get pretty far. I'm hoping they didn't make it to the cliffs."

Pete rubbed his neck. "Boys tend to push each other when it comes to outdoing the other. Laken is the one that's diabetic, right?"

Chance nodded. "Yeah. His mom said he doesn't have anything with him. He'll be burning a lot of energy in this kind of terrain. I threw an orange juice and some glucose tablets in my pack." She turned to Jax. "I assume you have your jump kit?"

Jax patted her saddlebag. "I do, but we don't carry insulin. That's the worst-case scenario. I have a glucometer, so we'll be able to check his blood sugar right away. Then we can get him to his mom with the insulin if that's the issue. Come on, let's keep going."

They traveled farther up the trail, stopping to call for the boys frequently. Chance looked at her watch, concerned about the late hour. If they didn't find the boys soon, there was a possibility they'd be spending the night out in the elements. Without provisions, Laken could lapse into a life-threatening coma. Chance stopped when she saw Kelly twitch her ears and nicker. "What is it, girl?" Chance twisted in her saddle. "Laken! Brayden! Can you hear us?" Booney cut off the trail and down toward the rocks and the cliff faces. "I don't like where this is leading." Zeus pranced beside them.

Jax looked concerned. "You don't think the boys would try to climb down the face, do you?"

Chance shrugged. "With boys, it's hard to say. I wouldn't put it past them."

Pete shifted in his saddle. "I hope we find them before they get into too much trouble."

Booney took off in the direction of the cliffs, and Chance nudged Kelly to follow until they reached a point where the horses were no longer able to travel. Pete, Chance, and Jax dismounted and secured the horses and grabbed equipment that might be needed. They yelled the boys' names again before stopping to listen intently. Booney howled in front of them as Zeus raised his nose in the air.

Jax adjusted her pack. "Let's hope the way he's carrying on means they're close."

Pete took off at a run, with Booney's long leash in his hand, Chance and Jax close behind. They followed the distinctive bay until they found him standing on top of a large granite stone looking down. Chance leaned over and saw the boys huddled together on a rocky outcropping. "Brayden? Laken?" She watched one of them look up and raise his arms. "You two sit tight. We're coming down to you." She turned to Jax. I'm going to start working on a way down to them. Get on the radio and let command know our location." She handed Jax a GPS unit.

"Chance, it should be me that goes over the hill. I can start an IV. You and Pete need to set up the haul and direct operations from up here." Jax began tying a simple harness out of a piece of webbing.

"I don't like it, but you can render more medical assistance than I can." Chance went to look for an anchor while Jax called in their coordinates.

Chance ran back and checked Jax's seat harness knots and attachment points. "Okay, let's get you over the side. That webbing is going to hurt if you have to hang very long. Luckily, they're only about thirty feet down. You ready to rappel?"

"Let's go. We're burning daylight, and we don't know what condition Laken is in." Jax connected to the rope and Chance checked every knot and connection again.

"Your riding helmet will help protect you in case anything falls from the top. I'm going to warn the boys to cover their heads. Be careful. I love you."

"I love you, too. Now let's get me down to the boys."

"Your wish is my command." Chance leaned over the edge and yelled to the boys. "I'm sending someone down. Cover your head with your hands, and don't look up." She turned back to Jax. "Okay, baby, over the side with you."

***

Jax stepped back and leaned into the makeshift harness and walked her feet down the steep wall. She could see where the boys had disturbed the ground on the side as she made her way down to them. Jax called out her distance to keep Chance apprised. "Twenty feet. Fifteen feet, five feet. I'm with them. Off rope." Jax unclipped and knelt by the boys. Brayden was talking a mile a minute, but Laken was still. She grabbed his wrist. His pulse was thready and his breathing faint. "Brayden, has Laken eaten anything recently?"

"No, we didn't plan to be out this long. He needs to eat." The small boy shuffled closer to his brother.

"I'm going to check his sugar, then I'll get something to help him, okay?" Jax wanted to reassure Brayden that she was going to try and make Laken better.

"Laken wanted to keep going, but I couldn't tell where we were. He saw this place from up there, and I couldn't stop him."

"We won't worry about all that right now. I'm going to check Laken's sugar and see if we can bring him around. Are you hurt anywhere?" Jax looked him over and could see mud on the sleeve of his sweatshirt.

"I slid down part of the way. I think I cut my elbow, but I'm okay. Help Laken."

"I'm going to do just that, buddy. How about you hold his hand while I stick his finger? You've seen him do this, right?"

The boy nodded as Jax lanced his brother's finger and let a drop of blood soak into the test strip. She pushed the strip into the small, handheld monitor. She waited for a few minutes for the digital reading to appear. *Dammit, thirty is way too low.*

Brayden's eyes grew wide. "That's really low. He needs sugar."

"Yes, he does, and I can do that. I'll need your help, but I need to let my partner up top know what's happening, okay?" She watched the boy nod. "Okay, you tear open this plastic bag." She handed him the bag of dextrose, while she called for Chance using her Saddleback unit number. "SB-17 to SD-1."

"Go ahead, Jax."

Jax could hear both Zeus and Booney barking and howling in the background. "Both boys appear mostly uninjured. Laken's sugar is thirty. I'm going to start a line and follow the diabetic protocol. There's no way to climb back up out of here, so we'll have to use a stretcher for Laken. I'm guessing I can put a harness on Brayden and clip him to me, then have you haul us."

"Okay. The rescue group is on their way to us with equipment. I've got an ambulance standing by at the trail parking area. Do you need anything else down there?"

"A couple of real harnesses and the basket should do it. I'm going to get this line started."

"Copy."

Jax opened the tubing and pushed the bulb into the connector. She rolled the small wheel to allow fluid to come out of the tube. "Laken, can you hear me? I'm going to start an IV on you. You're going to feel a stick."

Jax pulled a needle from the plastic packaging and put a tourniquet around Laken's arm. The boy still wasn't responding to her voice but winced when she slid the catheter into his arm. She immediately saw the telltale signs of blood flashback. She connected the tubing and let the fluid run wide open to get the solution into his system as soon as possible. She could hear the radio traffic of the crews coordinating to bring in the necessary equipment.

"You guys didn't fall or anything, did you?" She looked over Brayden and ran her hands over Laken's extremities to determine if he had any injuries.

Blond hair fell into Brayden's eyes and he pushed it to the side. "No, we slid down here and tried to climb back up. Laken started saying he was tired, so we sat down. I thought about trying to get back out to find help. I didn't want to leave him. I was afraid he'd roll around and fall off."

"You did the right thing staying with him. He'll feel better in a little while, and we'll get you both back to your mom and dad soon."

"We're going to be in big trouble, aren't we?"

Jax smiled at him. "I think we'll worry about that later. Your mom and dad are very worried about you. I think they'll be glad to know you're okay." She wrapped a blood pressure cuff around Laken's arm and assessed his vitals. Everything was looking good. Half the bag of fluid ran into his arm before the boy began to flutter his eyelids and look around. Jax could see his confusion and spoke in quiet tones to assure him he was all right.

"Laken, you're awake!" Brayden squeezed his brother's hand.

The boy rubbed his eyes. "Where am I?"

"Hi, I'm Jax. Unfortunately, you're over a hill in Dolly Sods. My friends are on their way with some equipment to help us get back up. You let your sugar get really low, and you passed out. Your brother's been doing a great job of watching over you. I started an IV, and I've given you some medicine to help bring your sugar back up. How are you feeling now?"

Laken rolled his head and rubbed his eyes. "Tired, really tired, and a little sick to my stomach."

"That's to be expected. You'll start to feel better after all this runs in. Are you hurt anywhere?"

"I don't think so."

The radio drew her attention with a direct request for a situational update. "SD-1 to SB-17, how are things down there?"

Jax filled Chance in on Laken's progress and was given a twenty-minute ETA for the rest of the rescue party. She turned her attention back to the boys.

"Let's check your sugar again. Brayden, can you get me the box of test strips?" Jax wanted to keep both boys engaged and not thinking about being in trouble or moving around. After repeating the glucometer test, Laken's sugar was up to eighty. Still lower than she'd like, but closer to stable. "Let's get another bag of fluid ready to go while we wait for my friends to come and help us out of here." She watched the sun start to drop below the horizon. She was sure the crew would be bringing lights with them to illuminate the scene. She flexed a glow stick, releasing the chemicals to give her some light. She heard

Zeus bark excitedly. "I'm betting that's our ride out of here. You guys sit tight for a minute, okay?"

Both boys nodded as Jax got to her feet and dusted her hands off on her pants.

"SD-1 to SB-17."

Jax clicked her radio. "Go ahead, Chance."

"Want some company down there?"

"Always. If you stay to the left of where I went over, you'll come down right beside me."

Within minutes, Chance stood on the ledge with her and unclipped the basket Laken would ride in up to the top.

Chance introduced herself. "Hey guys, my name is Sheriff Chance, and we're going to get you out of here now. Okay with you?"

A tear slipped out of Brayden's eye. "Please, I want to go home."

"That's what we're going to do. Come over here, so I can put this harness on you. Jax, here's yours."

Jax was grateful. She'd barely felt her legs when she'd used the webbing harness to come down to the boys. One-inch webbing wasn't comfortable and cut off circulation quickly. She slipped into the harness and helped Brayden do the same, then helped package Laken in the basket for transport.

"I'm going to take Laken up and let you bring Brayden, okay?" Chance relayed more of the plan on how they would be hoisted.

"We're good with that, right Brayden?" Jax put a hand on his shoulder.

"Yup, I'll do whatever you tell me to." Brayden wiped his face and let Jax check the fastening points on his harness.

They watched Chance keep her body between the rock face and the rescue basket on their ascent. Once the basket had cleared the top of the rocks, the ropes were dropped back down.

"Okay, buddy. Our turn to get out of here. You ready?"

Brayden nodded enthusiastically. "Like, yesterday."

Jax laughed and spoke into her radio. "On rope." She felt all the slack leave, and the rope took their weight. "You relax and enjoy the ride. Put your hands right here." She placed Brayden's hands on the rope above the connection and put her feet on the rocks to keep them off the face. Slowly, they made their way up until they reached the top, where several sets of hands helped them up and over the edge. She high-fived Brayden. "Good job, buddy. You did great!"

The boy put his arms around Jax and squeezed. "Thank you, Jax.

You're awesome."

Jax went to one knee and held Brayden's hands. "So are you. You did a great job taking care of your brother."

Chance was waiting as the two walked over to where the horses and Zeus waited. Chance wrapped an arm around Jax and shook Brayden's hand. "I'm proud of you. You kept a cool head. I know your mom and dad are going to be proud of you as well."

Brayden shoved his hands in his pockets. "Maybe after they get done grounding us for a million years."

Jax bent down and took his hands. "I'll put in a good word for you."

Brayden encircled her for another hug. "Thanks for everything."

Jax soaked it in. She was riding a rescue high and enjoyed every second of working for a positive outcome. She looked up at Chance. "You're very welcome."

***

Hours later, Chance and Jax stood in the barn to brush Kelly and Mac out. It had been an intense rescue. They were both exhausted as they finished the care of the horses and shut up the barn. Chance wrapped an arm around Jax. "You did great out there today. Damn proud of you."

"I'm just glad the boys were okay. I talked to Eve a few minutes ago and she told me they were passed out in bed. The hospital released Laken with orders to rest. That whole thing could have turned out so much worse."

"Luckily for us, it didn't. You got that line started and got Laken's sugar up while reassuring Brayden. That was exceptional."

Jax sighed. "I saw Kendra out on the scene. She helped transport Brayden out on one of the Saddleback unit's other horses."

"I saw her too. I told her we'd have dinner tomorrow." Chance looked at her watch. "Well actually, today. I think we need a shower."

Jax held open the door to the house and let Zeus go in front of them. "That sounds like the best idea you've had all day. You and me, naked, with hot water all around us."

"Lead the way."

Jax pulled off her scrub top and dropped it on the floor, along with the tank top that had come off with it. Chance watched Jax slip out of her boots and leave them behind as she walked. The sight of Jax's naked back suddenly erased the tension of the day. The jeans went next, until all Jax was wearing were the lacey bikini bottoms she favored. Chance increased her pace, picking up the discarded clothing and throwing it into the laundry room. When she looked up, the last bit of fabric left on Jax's body was dangling from her index finger. *She's trying to kill me.* As they drifted to the ground, Chance quickly shucked out of her own clothes and made great strides toward the bathroom. The sight of Jax's naked body stepping into the large, walk-in shower made her center clench.

Chance was grateful for the instant hot water heater she'd insisted on when they remodeled the bathroom. If there was one thing she loved, it was touching Jax under the steaming pulsations of the shower heads they had installed. "God, you're beautiful."

Jax turned in her arms and put her head back. Chance smoothed back her dark hair and let the hot water soak it through. With a need so great she could barely contain herself; she pulled their bodies close and let her lips linger on the soft flesh between Jax's neck and shoulder. She nipped, and then licked the spot, enjoying the groan of pleasure that escaped Jax's mouth.

"Chance, I love you so much. Please touch me."

Not one to ever deny the woman she loved anything, she bent her head and captured Jax's nipple in her mouth. She sucked and licked until the flesh became puckered and hard. Her right hand roamed down Jax's sleek body, the water aiding the sensuous glide. Her left arm held Jax tightly to her while her lips traversed the landscape of skin over and around each breast. Jax's hands had migrated to her hair and were holding her head tightly to the nipple she'd just drawn between her lips.

"So beautiful."

"Chance, I love everything you're doing to me, but if you don't touch me soon, I'm going to explode on my own."

Chance raised her eyes to Jax's. "We can't have that happen, now can we?" She backed Jax over to the tiled bench seat built into the shower and lowered her to it.

Curiosity danced in her eyes. "What are you doing?"

"This." Chance used her hands to draw Jax to the edge of the seat, then dropped down to her knees on the tile floor. Water cascaded all around them. She pushed Jax's knees apart, then lowered her head to Jax's center. Though diluted by the water, Chance could smell Jax's arousal and moaned at the very thought of tasting her. She pointed her tongue and used it to part Jax's silken folds. Chance nearly gasped at the delectable flavor of her lover's desire. Her lips enveloped Jax's center.

Chance sucked. She licked and flicked across every tender surface, drawing moans of pleasure from her lover.

"Oh my God, Chance. Yes."

Chance's knees were uncomfortable, but it paled in comparison to the pleasure of making love to the woman who would be her wife. Her tongue explored every inch of the swollen flesh. She felt Jax dig her nails into her scalp. She buried her tongue deep inside Jax, stiffening it for greater penetration. Moving in and out, she listened to the whimpers of the woman before her and drew her head away only to join her lips with Jax's in a passionate kiss. The desire to be inside Jax was overwhelming, and she moved her right hand between their bodies.

"Please baby, go inside. I need to feel you."

Chance wanted to fulfill Jax's every desire and she entered her with two fingers, watching as her head fell back in pleasure. She moved in and out of the heat as the water poured over Jax's thighs. With each and every thrust, Jax met her with urgency. When their eyes locked, Chance brought their faces close together and growled out her demand. "Come for me, baby. Let go."

Jax's eyes started to flutter, and Chance increased her speed, dropping her mouth once again to the erect nipple. When she nipped at it, she felt Jax clench around her fingers and pull her in even deeper. A deep tremble started in her lover. The spasms around her fingers increased, until she felt the hot rush of Jax's climax coat her hand. She moved her body to prevent the spray from erasing her prize. She bent her head down and lapped at Jax, as she continued to push into her lover's body. A second, more intense spasm clenched her fingers so tightly she couldn't have withdrawn them if her life depended on it.

With a final gasp, Jax came again. "Chance!"

Chance gentled her licks and strokes, drawing out every aftershock from the two intense climaxes. Her love for this woman grew every second, and she vowed to bring a lifetime of pleasure and safety to Jax. When she stopped her motions, she withdrew gently and pulled Jax to the floor of the shower with her, cradling her in her arms. "I love you, Jax. More than you'll ever know."

Chapter Eight

THE NEXT MORNING, CHANCE decided Glenny had earned a ride since she'd missed out on the rescue adventure. Chance called Kendra and invited her to join their run and to go for a horseback ride after breakfast. She needed to pull an afternoon shift on patrol to cover a hole in the schedule. The ride would do everyone a world of good.

The horses traveled through the woods on the farm property that bordered the Monongahela National Forest. "Mom says she's enforcing the separate bedroom rule on you when you come next weekend for Leaf Peepers." Chance shifted in her saddle.

Kendra rolled her eyes. "Mom's house, Mom's rules. We're practically living together on campus. I'm either in her dorm or she's in mine, every night. I don't get what the big deal is."

Jax pushed a branch out of her way. "It's not that she doesn't trust you. She needs to get to know Brandi and get used to the fact her baby isn't a baby anymore."

Chance leaned over in the saddle to pinch Kendra's cheek. "You'll always be the baby."

Kendra shoved her. "Cut that out."

"Let's hit part of the Loop Trail." Chance pointed to the trailhead. "I need to talk to you about the job opening at the Sheriff's Department. You aren't going to like this, but I can't avoid it. I know you want the position and the truth of the matter is I want you there. We can't do it this time, and I don't know when the next position will open up. When I fired Brad, it put us in a bad position with Daniel still in training. I have to have someone I can put on the road right now."

Kendra groaned. "This just sucks."

"I know it does, and I wish I could avoid it. I'd been hoping he'd max out in two years. You'd be finished with college and able to test. That's not the way this is going to play out. I have an opening I have to fill now with someone already through the academy until I can get Daniel ready to go. I have two viable candidates I'm interviewing this week."

Kendra played with Mac's mane. "I know you have to do what's best. It doesn't mean I have to like it."

"Doing what's right isn't always easy." Jax offered her perspective. "The people of this county elected Chance to provide them with protection. She has an obligation to make that happen in the most efficient method possible."

"It still sucks."

Jax chuckled. "It certainly does."

Kendra blew out a long breath. "Who are you considering?"

"Khodi Lahman is currently an officer with the Bridgeport Police Department. His parents have a house down in Dry Fork. Then there's Steve Parsons. He's currently a deputy over in Barbour County and has family over here. Both are good officers. The benefit with Khodi is that he's already a K9 officer and owns his own dog. He'd be able to start patrol right away." Chance stopped and let the horses rest and grab a drink in the small stream.

"Is it unusual for an officer to personally own a K9?" Jax questioned.

"Usually the dogs are owned by the department. His department wouldn't pay for the dog but agreed to pay for the training. He's been working there for nine years and wants a change. According to the chief, he's an excellent officer. His K9 is exceptional and trained in narcotics detection as well as apprehension. Between us, he's my top candidate if his next interview goes well. I can't imagine being able to get anyone on by Leaf Peepers, but I hope to have someone on by next month. I may have to delay Daniel's K9 training and have him work the court detail until I can bring on another patrol officer."

"Oh, he's going to be bummed. He was looking forward to that." Kendra shook her head.

"Can't be avoided. Brad put us in an impossible position and has the department spread thin. Until I get the department up to full speed, we'll have to cover the shifts as best we can. I promise, Kendra, you will have an opportunity to be a deputy. I've got a lot of years left."

Chance could tell Kendra was disappointed. She also knew her sister well enough to know she would understand that the needs of the public outweighed her personal needs. That altruism would make her an excellent officer.

They finished up their ride, and Chance got ready for work. She slid Zeus' vest on and fastened it on the excited dog. Jax met her at the door and smoothed down all the Velcro on her vest.

"Be careful out there tonight. Stop in for dinner if you can?" Jax kissed her.

"You bet. I'll call when I'm on my way. Let's do simple. We have that chicken we planned for salads, how about putting that together? That way there won't be any cook time in case I have to go."

"You got it, Sheriff. I'll even make that honey mustard dressing you like."

"Excellent. Call if you need anything."

"Will do. Zeus, keep her in line, okay?"

A quick bark let everyone know he was ready. "Okay, okay, we're going. See you later." Chance gave her a long, lingering kiss, full of promise, before she put on her hat and stepped out the door.

Chapter Nine

THE FOLLOWING WEEK CHANCE sat at her desk, looking over the mounds of paperwork heaped on top of it. Zeus whined softly. "I know boy; we've got more office work to do before we can go out." She looked over the applications again. Nearly a week had now passed since she'd fired and arrested Brad, and she needed to get someone hired. Leaf Peepers started the next morning and would run through the weekend. The previous day's interview with Steve Parsons had gone well. She still had concerns about what training he would need in comparison to Khodi. The Bridgeport officer was due for his interview in fifteen minutes.

Taylor strode in and collapsed in the seat by her desk, a manila folder in her hand. "Ready for this?"

"I am. I'm hoping Khodi will be a good fit. It would solve several problems." They heard the buzzer on the front door. Zeus picked up his head and looked in the direction and growled. Chance followed Taylor out to see a man wearing an ill-fitting suit, who stood there with paperwork in his hand.

"How can we help you, Mr. Dexter?" Taylor asked.

The man hitched up his pants, then ran a meaty hand across his sweaty brow. "I'm here to deliver some paperwork to the sheriff."

Chance moved in front of Taylor. "What kind of paperwork?"

The man held up a thick envelope. "I'm representing Deputy Brad Waters in his civil lawsuit against you and this department, Sheriff. My client was wrongfully arrested and terminated. You've been served. I've filed all the paperwork with the courts, and we'll be moving forward with our lawsuit unless you'd like to drop all charges and reinstate my client."

Chance rose to her full height and stepped a few inches from the man who was barely above five feet tall. "Mr. Dexter, Brad Waters will never work for this department again as long as I'm Sheriff. I hope you're a defense attorney as well, because a special prosecutor has been assigned to handle the criminal charges in this case to avoid any conflict of interest. You can take up his termination with the civil service board." She walked back to her office and picked up a stack of paperwork as thick as a dictionary. "This is his personnel file. I can assure you I have all I need to back up his termination. The second he put his hands on my assistant, he sealed his fate. Good day, sir."

"You can be as high handed as you want, Sheriff. We'll go to court, count on it. Might be you looking for a new job by the time all this is over." He threw the packet on the counter in the reception area.

Taylor stepped forward, Midas at attention by her side. "I think it's time to go, Mr. Dexter."

The attorney glared at her and moved a toothpick in his mouth to the other side. "Don't think you're in the clear. As Chief Deputy, a lot of this falls in your lap too."

Chance moved across the room, Zeus on her heels. "Good day, Mr. Dexter."

Dexter backed up so fast, his shoulder hit the door frame. "You get that mutt under control, Sheriff, or it won't just be Brad suing your ass."

"If you have no more business here, see yourself out before you have to be escorted out. Last chance, Mr. Dexter." Chance crossed her arms over her chest and took another step forward.

He adjusted the skewed necktie and glared at her. "I'll see you in court." With those parting words, he turned and went through the lobby door and out to the street.

Taylor picked up the packet, and Chance followed her back to her office. Chance counted to ten while Taylor perused the contents.

"It's all bullshit, Chance. Typical of what you'd expect. He's claiming you've discriminated against him because he's a heterosexual and doesn't applaud your life. Reverse discrimination, in that you've appointed me because I'm a lesbian like you. What a jackass. Shit, we didn't need this. This incident is going to start a public relations war, and he'll be able to say whatever he wants while we have to stay quiet because of personnel policy."

Chance put a hand on Taylor's shoulder. "Take a breath. We have video evidence of what he did to Penny and more verbal warnings and written reprimands than the rest of the department combined. He doesn't have a leg to stand on. This is a desperate attempt by a desperate man. We've got the truth on our side. He has nothing. I'm not worried in the slightest. Khodi will be here in a few minutes. I'd like you to sit in on this interview. If it goes well, I want to offer him the position. Hiring him puts a K9 unit on the street immediately."

"Sounds good."

The door chimed again, and Chance stepped back out into the

lobby. A man in his early thirties stepped forward with his hand extended.

"Sheriff Fitzsimmons, Chief Deputy Lewis, good to see you again." Khodi Lahman shook hands with both women.

"Nice to see you again, Khodi." Taylor greeted the guest.

Chance waved them into her office. "Let's go have a seat. Good trip over?"

"Made the trip a thousand times. I could drive it in my sleep." Khodi had a seat in the chair indicated.

Chance appraised the way Khodi carried himself as he interacted with Taylor. Khodi was a few inches shorter than Chance and healthy according to the physical she held in her hands. A physical ability test had been given to each candidate, and Khodi had smoked his. The man sat before her in crisply ironed pants and a smartly tailored jacket paired with a pale-blue shirt. The leather boots he wore were polished to a high shine.

Khodi's hair was neatly trimmed, and he sat straight in his chair, his sharp eyes taking in everything around the room. Chance noticed he'd adjusted the seat to keep from having his back completely to the door.

Cautious and alert. "So, let's talk about the job. Why do you want to leave Bridgeport? Are you unhappy over there?" Chance shifted papers in the file she had.

Khodi sat up straighter. "No, I'm not necessarily unhappy over there, Sheriff. The reality is, I want to come back home. Mom has multiple sclerosis, and Dad isn't in the best of health either. They could use some help, and to be honest, I miss being home. Not planning to move in with them but being close by would make things easier. I'm tired of being in the city, away from the mountain."

Chance smiled. She understood. That same feeling had brought her home after her time as a smokejumper.

Khodi shrugged. "I like to ski and ride dirt bikes. I spent my high school years running and hiking up in the Sods and fly-fishing the Blackwater River and Red Creek. These are still the things I do in my downtime. The problem is, living over there, I have to drive back over here to enjoy them."

Taylor had a few questions of her own, and Chance let her lead for a while. Taylor took notes on a legal pad she balanced on her thigh. "How are you around horses?"

"Mom and Dad used to raise quarter horses. I grew up taking care of them and riding them on the farm. My farrier skills are probably a little rusty, but it wouldn't take much to get back into practice."

Chance listened, as Taylor questioned him about his marksmanship skills. She was pleased both with what she could see on paper and in watching Khodi. There were several commendations listed in the file for him and his K9 partner, Echo. When Taylor wound down her line of questioning, Chance picked it back up.

"Tell me about Echo." Chance watched as the smile grew on Khodi's face.

"He's a black German shepherd from the Netherlands and a beast. He's trained in patrol and narcotics detection. We've kept up with every certification, and you should have his health record in your file."

Chance reached down and ran a hand across Zeus' head. She knew what a close bond the handler and their K9 had. She appreciated the pride she saw in Khodi when he spoke about his dog. "How is he around horses? We have a stable of several that we use frequently."

"No problems being around them. Mom and Dad still have a few, and he's learned how to travel beside them. Sheriff, I know I'm not your only candidate, but I'm a good officer and ready to work. I can start whenever you need me. My current chief knows I'm trying for this position, and he's told me I can leave immediately if you hire me. I'm on vacation for the next two weeks. I can use that as my two weeks' notice, so it wouldn't leave them short-handed. I'm a quick learner. Give me a copy of this department's policies and procedures, and I'll learn them in a few days. I can qualify with my weapon today, if you'd like me to. I want the job. I can promise you won't regret hiring me."

He leaned forward and settled his elbows on his knees as he steepled his fingers. "I need to come home. I'll fully understand if you choose someone else because they are better qualified. I'll walk out of here and say thank you for considering me." He sat back up. "If you chose to bring me on, I'll work harder than anyone you've ever hired in my position. I was born and raised here. I know the people and the county inside and out. I've got applications in with several other agencies. Even if you don't hire me, I'm coming back to this area, even if I have to travel to work. For that matter, I could stay where I am and commute until I find a job. It's that important."

Khodi paused. "I want to work for you because I've respected and looked up to you my whole life, well before you ever pinned that badge on. You need a K9 officer; that's a fact. I'm honestly not trying to brag, but I'm a damn good one with references to back me up. I hope you'll consider that I want to give back to the people and the county that shaped me."

Chance looked at Taylor and saw the barely perceptible smile that formed on her lips. She could read Taylor's thoughts and knew she was in agreement. She stood and stretched out her hand to the officer before her. "Welcome to Tucker County Sheriff's Department, Deputy Lahman. I look forward to working with you and Echo." Khodi's broad smile swallowed his face, as he rose and firmly shook her hand.

"You'll never want for cookies or brownies ever again. My mom said to throw that in if it would get me the job. Hell, she sent a full tin to push you over the edge."

Chance looked to the left and right of her, watching as Khodi's brow scrunched.

"And?" Chance held out her hands, palms up.

Khodi shook his head, and Taylor started to laugh. "And what?"

"And you ate them on the way here? You gave them to Echo?"

Khodi blushed and chuckled. "Oh, the cookies. No, I didn't eat them. I didn't want to be seen as bribing the sheriff. They're in the truck."

Chance came around the desk. "Okay, then you go get the cookies, and we'll get some paperwork together for you to sign. I will be calling over to talk with your chief. I want to do this right and leave no bad feelings behind. I trust what you've said, but it's my reputation on the line as well."

"Want his cell number? I told him I wouldn't be surprised if you wanted to call, and he said to give you that one and his home number."

Chance pulled out her cellphone. "Let's see if it's the same one I got a few years ago at a regional meeting."

They compared numbers while Taylor slipped off to get the new-hire paperwork. An hour later, the cookie tin was empty, and Taylor was ready to take Khodi to the range to qualify on the weapon he would be issued.

"Khodi, you tell your mom these were great. Now, are you staying for Leaf Peepers?"

"Haven't missed one yet. I'm on the team for the Mountaintop Library. I always come home to support the place my mom helped establish."

Chance nodded. "Excellent, my mom adores yours. Do you have any plans after you do the Run For It? Could you do a ride-along with me as an orientation shift? I know you don't have a uniform yet. A set of black tactical pants and a long-sleeved, black T-shirt will work for now."

Khodi's face lit up. "That would be great. I've got a vest and some basic equipment of my own until you can issue me gear from the department."

"I'll let you work all that out with the chief deputy. She'll issue you your badge and service weapon. If you're up to it after the run, grab a shower and join me at the Davis Fire Hall. That's where I'll be for the remainder of the evening unless we get a call."

Khodi reached out and shook Chance's hand. "I'll be there."

"Welcome aboard, Khodi. I look forward to having you as a member of the Tucker County Sheriff's Office. I have one in the academy that will finish in a few months. With your addition, this brings us back up to full staff, minus one K9 until Daniel goes through his training. We're going to hit the ground running. Your former chief said he expects a call from you and the promise of your mom's cookies at Christmas."

Khodi crisply saluted Chance. "Roger that, Sheriff. Thanks for the job."

"Don't thank me yet. Once you've dealt with the Malone sisters for the fifteenth time in a month and stood at Wild Maggie at three degrees below zero for a stuck tractor-trailer, for the third time in one night, we'll see how thankful you are."

"She's right, you might not agree in a few months." Taylor laughed and pointed to the door. "Let's head to the range."

"I'm going to go home for a while and come back out around eleven. I assume you can hold down the fort? I think Harley has someone out as well." Chance put her hat on and gathered her things.

Khodi stopped and turned around. "Is Sergeant Harley Kincaid working tonight?"

"Not sure. Let me check the schedule." Chance walked back over to her desk and pulled up the West Virginia State Police Parsons Detachment Schedule. "She's on now but will be done at midnight. You know Harley?"

"I do. One of the finest officers I've ever met. I'll see you Saturday, Sheriff." Khodi waved as he walked out the door and headed to his vehicle.

Taylor lifted an eyebrow and tilted her head in Chance's direction. "Seems he's a fan."

"Indeed. Anyway, tell Penny hi for me when you get home. I'll check in on the horses on my way to Mom's house. Poor Kendra is bringing her girlfriend, Brandi, home for the first time. She's as nervous as a long-tailed cat in a room full of rocking chairs. We're going over as a buffer between Mags and Kendra. I swear, sometimes those two are like a match and gasoline."

"Kendra's an incredible young woman who's not a kid anymore, and your own personal Mini-Me. How disappointed was she about the job?"

"Took the news as I expected. She understands. Kendra wants the job so bad she can taste it. She also knows I need someone on the street right now. Charley would be next up for retirement, and he's not planning to go anywhere for at least five more years. I think we need to talk with him about the court security position after Daniel gets his K9. His wife and grandkids would probably like to see him more on weekends and holidays. Not to mention no more night shifts. It's worth the discussion. I can't do any of that until I have a full complement of deputies and K9s ready for the road. Until then, we'll make do, and Kendra will stay in school."

Taylor grabbed her coat off the hook. "I've got a few hours of patrol left before Ray comes out. If you're planning to come back out this evening, try and get some rest before you do. Leaf Peepers will kick off tomorrow morning. I've got everyone out for this one in twelve-hour shifts, including Daniel—who will ride with Randy. With the good weather, the tourists come out of the woodwork."

"It will be good for the festival and unfortunately, just as good for all our less-than-stellar citizens. Lots of visitors coming in with a lot of money to burn. Tell everyone to keep their eyes open."

"Will do, Sheriff. Get out of here. I'll go to the range with Khodi and let you know how he does."

Chance waved and loaded Zeus into her vehicle as she placed a call to Jax.

"Hey, stranger. How's your day?"

"Better now."

Jax's voice was like sunshine. She and Jax exchanged plans, and she hung up. On the way past the convenience store, she spotted Leland Kurst's truck parked off to the side, with another car parked nearby. She pulled into the lot and rolled slowly by. Leland and another man stood talking. She let her dashcam catch the license plate for later reference. She glanced down at the plate reader that pulled up a registration out of Baltimore. Zeus barked in the back seat, and Leland turned away from Chance's view. *Nope, nothing going on here. Sure there isn't.*

Several messages pinged and she pulled out her cellphone. One from Maggie, *Call when you can.* One from Dee, *Kendra's going to jump out of her skin.* And finally, one from Kendra. *Get your ass here now! Please? Not kidding, get here soon!*

Chance couldn't help laughing at Kendra's desperation. She called Jax.

"Forget something?" Jax asked.

"Nothing other than how intimidating it is to bring a girl home to the moms-squared for the first time. Kendra's freaking out. How long before you can get to their place?"

"I'm on the way now. Still about ten minutes out. I need to fill up the Tundra."

"I'll send Kendra a message to relax, help is on the way. I love you. Drive carefully."

"Love you too...see you soon."

Chance pulled into the small gas station where they got their fuel. When she stepped out, Faith pulled in beside her on the other side of the pump. *Perfect.*

Faith slid the fuel handle into her fill point and turned to Chance. "You can't keep avoiding me."

"I can, and I will."

Faith tried another tactic. "I saw Kendra pull into town earlier. How's she doing in her classes?"

Chance squinted and tilted her head. "Faith, you couldn't give a rat's ass about Kendra's classes. You're trying to prolong this conversation, and I'm not doing it. Kendra's fine."

Faith took a deep breath. "Daniel's graduation is coming up next month. I'm going to be there. I'd rather us not be biting each other's heads off. We have to find a way to be civil, for his sake."

Chance seated her hat on her head tighter and adjusted her vest. "I've never had a problem being civil. Perhaps you need to look up the definition." She closed her eyes and held up her hands. "Let's stop right now." Chance pulled the gas handle out and replaced it on the pump. She waited for her receipt, then turned to Faith. "We're done here. Daniel is my employee. More than that, he's my godson. Don't push me, Faith. It's his big day. If you do anything to ruin it for him, my forgiveness will be the least of your worries."

Chapter Ten

JAX SAT QUIETLY, OBSERVING Brandi as she completely entranced Maggie and Dee. The young woman was entertaining the moms with tales of her life in California, where she'd followed her veterinarian mother around her office, begging to be taken on stable calls. Kendra was grinning from ear to ear. The only sign of her nerves was the endless tapping of her thumb on her tea glass.

Brandi played with the short fringe hair at her neckline. "I've come to believe some client of Mom's patterned that cartoon, Doc McStuffins, after me. I patched up my dog and the office cat all the time. I'll bet I ran Mom's bandage bill through the roof. Poor Tink and Rocky spent a lot of time with one appendage or another wrapped in gauze, while I traipsed around in a little lab coat."

Jax laughed. "I remember those days. Uncle Marty took me all over the place when I came to stay with him. Learning at his knee solidified my decision to become a vet. He's also the reason I came back here to take over his practice."

Kendra snorted. "Yeah, right. Wouldn't have anything at all to do with a certain law enforcement officer. Nope, it's all about the animals."

Jax couldn't help but blush, as she heard a vehicle door close. "Well, I'll admit there were other deciding factors."

Maggie opened the door and let Chance and Zeus enter. Chance waved to the group. "Brandi, nice to see you again. I see they don't have you sitting in a hard chair under a bare lightbulb."

"That's next." Dee quipped.

Jax kissed Chance. "Somehow I think you're way past that. I was right; I do know her mother." Jax pointed to Brandi. "This one is a chip off the old block. Smart and commanding, much like Beth."

"Mom would say demanding smartass, but thanks for softening the blow. Good to see you again, Sheriff."

"Brandi, call me Chance. We're not big on formality and titles around here. I'm starving. What are we eating?"

Maggie called from the kitchen, as Jax caught Dee making a face. "Beer-can chicken, green beans, roasted red potatoes, and a salad. Kendra, can you and Brandi set the table, please?"

Dee shuddered. "I'm going to start clucking any day now. Every night, chicken, fish, or turkey. Beef, my kingdom for a burger!" Dee held her fist into the air.

"Keep it up, smartass, and you'll be testing out how comfortable that couch is beyond a cat nap." Maggie walked to the dining room and put the side dishes out. "Chance, will you get the chicken out of the oven?"

"Sure thing, Mom. By the way, I love your beer-can chicken." Chance squeezed Dee's shoulder.

"Traitor!" Dee flinched when Maggie came by and flicked her ear.

"I'll traitor you. Bring the pitcher of tea to the table. Good Lord, trying to keep you alive is going to send me to an early grave." Maggie kissed Dee sweetly.

Jax hoped she was watching a living example of what she and Chance would be like after decades together. Jax knew the story, how they'd met in high school and never looked back. They'd started a life together when it wasn't easy or safe. Somehow, they'd raised two daughters and cared for more than one foster child over the years. She envied Chance and Kendra. They weren't Maggie or Dee's natural born children, yet they'd grown up in a home that accepted them exactly as they were. She, on the other hand, had been born to a woman who seemed to despise her for all the choices she'd made. How grateful she was to be part of this family.

Dinner was two hours of stories and laughter. Kendra blushed bright red with every embarrassing or brag-worthy story the family told. Chance expounded on how her sister had become known as Bullseye for both her archery and basketball skills. Several discussions centered around the Christmas wedding they were planning. When they were talked out, dessert was devoured. The house rule was that clean up fell to hands that hadn't prepared the meal. Jax stood at the sink washing pans, while Chance dried. "So, how did the interview go?"

"Khodi will start working for us right away. He's burning vacation time from his other department, which will make for an easy transition. We're going to have him do some ride-alongs during the festival. By the way, what are your plans?" Chance dried a plate and put it in a cabinet.

"Uncle Marty and Lindsey are going to help with the free clinic over in the Shop 'n Save parking lot. We've rented a tent and plan to do basic checkups and free shots. Maybe I'll ask Brandi if she wants to help since she'll be here with Kendra." Jax scrubbed at a stubborn bit of burnt-on food in the chicken pan.

"That young lady is going to fit in here really well. She's got Maggie and Dee eating out of her hand. The only girl I ever brought home who made them act like that was you."

"I'll take that as a compliment. Otherwise, how was your day?"

"Good, other than running into Faith when I got fuel." Chance put down the red-and-white checkered dish towel and turned to Jax. "She's planning on coming to Daniel's graduation."

"Ah."

Chance put another dish away. "Yeah. Anyway, we'll see if she keeps her word about not causing a scene. On another front, I want to schedule an appointment with you to do an exam on Echo, Khodi's dog. The health records are all in order. I'd like him to have a baseline with you."

"That's a good idea. How about we see if Khodi's free on Monday?" Jax let the water out of the sink and rinsed the dishrag before wringing it out and laying it over the center divider to dry.

"I'll check with him tomorrow. So, how can I help you set up for the clinic?" Chance put the drying rag over the handle of the stove and leaned on the counter.

"If you can set up the tent and tables, that would be great. Lindsey and Meg are going to be there to help so that Uncle Marty doesn't have to do much. With Brandi there, we'll be able to get people in and out quickly."

Jax walked over and wrapped her arms around Chance's neck. Their lips met with slow, luxurious heat. She'd been on simmer from the moment Chance walked in the house. The mere sight of her had Jax's center in a constant clench. What she felt for Chance was a tangible thing she needed to put her hands on.

"Ew, mushiness." Kendra walked by them with two empty glasses that she filled from the tea pitcher in the refrigerator.

Jax snuggled into Chance's side and grinned. "Oh, and that wasn't mushiness I saw a few minutes ago with you and Brandi sitting on the front porch swing?"

Kendra turned quickly on her heel. "As you were."

One more private kiss, and they walked out to join everyone on the patio to watch the sunset.

Chapter Eleven

SATURDAY MORNING, CHANCE AND Jax took their early morning run out at the Canaan Valley State Park. She called into Tucker Comm to let dispatch know they were clear of T3. With Zeus tucked in the back, they drove home. The rental houses along the way were packed with out-of-state vehicles from as far away as Florida.

"How many runners are they expecting today?" Jax drank deeply from her water bottle.

"According to Dee, they've had over five hundred preregister. They'll have more sign up this morning. It seems like it gets bigger every year." Chance drove along the Appalachian Highway thinking about the logistics of the 2K walk/5K run for charity. The event helped fund many grant projects throughout the county. "I predict this weather will bring out a record crowd. I never worry about the runners causing problems. It's the others that come to prey on the tourists attending the festival. Last year, we confiscated everything from methamphetamines to heroin. Every year it gets worse."

"This will be Uncle Marty's first big outing since the incident earlier this summer. I've told him he could go home any time if he's feeling overwhelmed. I don't want him to get too tired out."

"That guy is tough. If you think he's going to let you outlast him, you're crazy." Chance threaded her fingers through Jax's. "He'll be fine. Let him do whatever he wants to, or he'll get pissed that you're babying him."

Jax sighed deeply. "I know you're right. I can't help worrying about him."

"Have you talked to your parents lately?"

"With Dad a few times. I send Mom's calls to voice mail and screen them. She hasn't said anything I've felt required a return call. Blah, blah, blah, bad choices, blah, blah, blah. Someday she'll give up calling. As far as I'm concerned, that day can't come too soon."

Chance wished she had a way to bridge the divide. Every time she tried; she disliked the woman even more for the way she belittled Jax. The woman beside her was intelligent, beautiful, and had a heart bigger than the Blackwater Canyon. "When we get home, you shower. I'll throw together breakfast sandwiches for us, then I'll shower while you gather your things."

"I say we shower together to conserve water."

"Our showers are twice as long that way and will take three times as long when I decide to devour you. We have to be out the door in less than two hours to get that clinic set up for you."

"Must you be so practical?"

Chance pulled into their driveway and shut the vehicle off. "I promise, later tonight, I'll be as impractical as you'd like."

"Deal."

***

Two hours later, Chance set up the last table inside the tent and looked around for the equipment box to move into place. Lindsey set up instruments, while explaining to Brandi how to fill out the intake forms and where the rabies tags were. Kendra carried in the last cooler of medications and placed them in a secure area.

Marty Hendricks yawned as he filled a green cup with coffee from an ancient thermos.

"You going to make it Marty?" Chance teased him. "You slip up and grab decaf this morning?"

"Wouldn't drink that garbage. What's the damn point?" Marty grumbled. "You working the run from this side of town or the other?"

"I'm handling this side near you guys. Taylor will have the other. I'm supposed to meet the race administrators at the fire hall in about ten minutes. The race starts at eleven."

"Well, try to keep it to a low roar today. We'll hold down the fort here," Marty said, as he took another drink.

"Will do. Need to find Jax for a minute. See you later." Chance walked to the other end of the tent and put a hip on one corner of the table Jax was setting up.

"Hiring out as a paperweight, Sheriff?"

"Are you saying I'm getting fat?" Chance grinned and raised an eyebrow.

"Smartass. You headed out?"

"Yeah, need to get command established and put officers in place at the different intersections for when we shut everything down. I'll call you later to check in. Will you be able to get something to eat?"

Jax waved to a cooler sitting beside her black bag. "Gifts from

Maggie that Kendra and Brandi brought with them. We're good here."
She reached into the cooler and produced a small thermal bag. "She
didn't forget you either. Be careful, I love you." She leaned up and
kissed Chance.

"I love you too. Okay, I've got to roll. If you need anything, call me.
Let's go, Zeus."

***

Once at the fire hall, the wall of noise emanating from the race
officials, craft booths, and auxiliary personnel was deafening. Chance
found a quiet spot to call Taylor to determine her location. The roads
would remain open until thirty minutes before race time. Anyone who
needed to get to the other side of town, this was the time to do so.

"Taylor, are you at the bridge?"

"We're in position. Carl and Randy are up near Fifth and
Blackwater. Harley has troopers at Fairfax and Kent. Quade and a few of
his crew are taking some of the side streets. I think we're covered."

"How's Penny doing?"

"Cranky. She wanted to walk this with Becky and Kristi. She even
called her doctor after I overruled her. He wants her to rest. I have her
set up on the couch with snacks and whatever else she'll need for the
next few hours. Her partners in crime are going over to visit after they
do the 2K walk."

"She still cleared to come to work on Monday?"

"And chomping at the bit. I've got a few of our horses tethered in
behind Shop 'n Save, near Jax, so we can get to them if we need them
later."

Chance adjusted her hat and rubbed Zeus' ears. "Good thinking.
I'm going to stick to the Suburban for now, with Khodi joining me after
the run." She laughed. "He's anxious and can't wait to change into a
uniform."

"Daniel's the same. I think they're both going to fit in just fine.
Okay, I'm in position. Are we using a tactical channel?"

"Yes, switch to encrypted Tac-1 for today. See you after the race."

Chance drove out to the main road, where she and Zeus marked up
with Tucker Comm that they were in position. She looked at her watch.
In another twenty minutes, she'd shut down the roads until the majority
of the participants had crossed the finish line. The walkers took the
longest and often included children in strollers or participating with

parents. The large event drew a significant crowd to the small, tourism-supported town. From her vantage point at the main road, she watched several individuals she had on her radar drive into town. Leland Kurst was among them, in the same vehicle she'd seen him with at the convenience store. They pulled into a parking area near the festival.

A cruiser pulled up alongside her with Sergeant Harley Kincaid at the wheel. "Sheriff, I see you claimed prime real estate for the race."

"Being the boss has its perks. I figured Meg would be working this. I know you called in some troopers from surrounding counties. I left her and Lindsey with Jax earlier."

"I thought about it, even talked to her to see if she wanted the overtime. Lindsey wanted her help at the clinic. They have wedding plans to work on if they get slow. The big day is less than a month away." Harley adjusted her rearview mirror.

"Jax said Lindsey is as excited as a five-year-old in a Build-A-Bear."

"Meg's right behind her. They've been in love for a long time. You guys are coming to the wedding, right?"

Chance nodded. "It's in the meadow at her parent's farm, right? Then the reception at the big barn?"

"Yup. They wanted simple. Lindsey's dad offered a big wedding or a piece of property on the farm and help with building their house. Always the practical ones, they chose a small wedding and reception."

"They don't seem like the big wedding type to me anyway. Heads up, I saw Leland pull into the lot over there." Chance pointed off to her left.

Harley turned her head where Chance indicated. "Damn him. Let me know if he moves. Okay, headed to my spot. Tac-1, right?"

"That's it. See you at the firehouse after the race." Chance waved Harley off. She watched the traffic and wished she'd been able to convince the commissioners to let her install the license plate reader at the major intersection. With this many visitors in town, she knew drug dealers were selling out of vehicles and in dark corners. Illegal drugs were a growing problem that she currently had no solution for. She watched another one of the Kurst vehicles pull into the Sawmill restaurant. Ronny and Danny Kurst got out and looked around before locking the beat-up Ford truck and going inside.

"What are you guys up to?" Chance mumbled to herself. That many Kursts in town spelled trouble. No one in that family had a charitable bone in their body. She texted Jax to warn her and Lindsey.

Heads up, Leland Kurst is in town. I don't have eyes on him so keep your wits about you.

She didn't have time to run over to the clinic. It was time to shut the road down. Chance pulled her Suburban across the main road and put on all her emergency lights, before she and Zeus stepped out of the vehicle. She pulled her Stetson on and took up her post. The chatter on the radio let her know that everyone was in position. She could see the fire hall and all the participants milling around in the roadway warming up. She spotted Khodi with his K9, Echo. Khodi was standing in among others, all wearing T-shirts with Mountaintop Library written across the back.

"SD-2 to SD-1."

Chance clicked her radio mic. "This is SD-1. Go ahead."

"Heads up, camera crew headed your way."

Chance turned to her left in time to see Mya Knotts headed directly for her. She was grateful for Taylor's advance warning. She rested her hands on her gun belt and looked back at the crowd.

"Chance, I'm still waiting to talk to the source about your heroic rescue of those lost boys. I've made several requests for a sit-down interview with you, and I'm starting to get the feeling you're avoiding me."

Chance chuckled. "Ya think?"

"I have a job to do, Chance, just like you. There used to be a time when you didn't mind a little one on one with me." Mya flipped her hair and adjusted her camera bag on her shoulder. She sat the tripod beside her.

"You do realize you're flirting with an engaged woman who has no interest in *one on one* time with you? If it's not about business, we have nothing to talk about. I have a standing rule that I don't talk about myself."

"Fine. I just thought you'd like to know that I'm investigating the arrest of Deputy Brad Waters. If you don't want to refute what his lawyer is saying, then I'll come to my own conclusions. I've seen the arrest record. People are asking, and you might have kept it quiet, but it won't stay that way." Mya picked up her equipment. "Makes me think there's something more to it. Rest assured, I'll get my story, one way or the other." She turned her back on Chance and continued away from her to the starting line.

I'm surprised it's stayed under wraps this long. Chance took a deep breath, then pulled her cell phone out to call Taylor. She didn't want any of this going across the airways, encrypted or not. Taylor answered her phone.

"I assume hurricane Mya blew through?"

"She did. Thanks for the warning, by the way. She knows about Brad's arrest. We need to formulate what we're going to say. Talk to Penny; I don't want Mya blindsiding her by shoving a mic in her face on the way to a doctor's appointment. That's it for now. Nothing more we can do until the festival is done. It looks like they are getting ready to start the race. We'll talk later."

"You got it, Chance."

Down at the starting line, the runners were lined up. A man dressed in an Uncle Sam suit, complete with a red-and-white striped top hat, held up an air-horn can. At the sound of a loud blast, a sea of people ran away from the fire hall and up William Ave. Many of the serious runners touched their watches to start their lap time. There were teams dressed in colorful T-shirts, while others donned outrageous outfits befitting their team names. The Doggy Sodds team wore cat and dog ears on their heads. Chance saw the tails sewn on the bottom of their shirts as they ran past another group. Team Tiny Dancers wore tutus over their running clothes and carried a banner with them. This group moved a little slower, with all their young participants in tow. The Hospice Angels were wearing scrubs with angel wings protruding from the back and halos on their heads, while another mob was dressed from head to toe in bright pink for the team supporting breast cancer awareness. Every team was vying for donation money for their cause. Before Chance had become Sheriff, she'd run the event many times as part of the search and rescue team.

"SD-3, all units, runners are passing Fifth and Blackwater."

Chance acknowledged Carl's transmission and waited for one from the trooper at the next intersection. Once the mob was clear of William Ave and onto the back streets of the course, the westbound lane would be opened to relieve the traffic tie-up. This change would require more vigilance from officers to keep the participants safe. Several more reports came in with positions of the runners, including Randy, her final deputy on duty today and the man Daniel was riding with. Chance checked her watch. The fastest 5K times would normally be under seventeen minutes, the longest, over an hour. Fourteen minutes from the time the starting blast sounded, Taylor called in that the first of the runners were approaching the intersection of Second and William. Within seconds, they would make the final turn toward the finish line.

A call for an ambulance was dispatched to a local address. The comm center gave a size up of a twenty-eight-year-old male, not breathing as the result of a possible overdose. A call like that would require an officer to go and make a report. Chance was the closest to the incident, though her position on the roadblock prevented her from leaving.

Another officer answered the call. "SD-3 to Comm Center." Carl told dispatch he would respond. Chance was increasingly worried this type of call was becoming the new normal in her jurisdiction.

Check-ins from other law enforcement officers reported the progression of the walkers and slower runners. Nearly forty minutes had passed since the start of the race. Chance had seen Khodi and Echo finish in with some of the top runners. She called Jax. "How's the clinic going?"

"Steady. We've probably seen twenty dogs and that many cats, at least. Uncle Marty's line is a little slower in production. He's enjoying the interaction with people he's known for years." Jax laughed.

"Any problems?"

"No, I stopped for a moment to shove my sandwich in my face. Brandi is going to make an excellent vet. Lindsey's decided she wants to take me up on the offer of the scholarship, after they get married and settled into the house they're building. We'll go ahead and start the paperwork for her, then decide on when she'll start. How's the race going?"

"The first runners crossed the finish line a few minutes ago. Times were about what you'd expect. I'll wait for the walkers. Hopefully, I can come and see you in another hour or so."

"Be safe out there, Sheriff. I love you."

"Love you too, and you do the same. Megan still with you?"

"She's never left Lindsey's side and been a big help today."

"Were you able to alert Megan about Leland without worrying Lindsey? I have an eye on the truck and will let you know if it comes your way. Remember to keep your eyes peeled in case they approach on foot."

"I think Harley called her a while ago. I saw her stiffen and look around while they were talking. I'll be careful. See you in a bit."

Chance disconnected and glanced over to where Leland's truck sat. Her gut told her he and his brothers weren't there to take in the festival. The runners had cooled down by slowly jogging up and down the street, while the walkers crossed the finish line. A delicious scent tickled Chance's attention.

Dozens of chickens were roasting over a large, charcoal pit erected from cement blocks and covered with a metal grate. The chickens were skewered on long, metal rods the length of the pit. Men and women from the Rotary Club wore heavy welding gloves and slowly turned the rods, while juices from the chickens dripped onto the hot coals. In twenty minutes, there would be a long line that snaked back through the vendors booths. Supporters would leave with Styrofoam boxes filled with chicken, a roll, and baked beans. Rows of picnic tables were set up under a pavilion, where diners could sit and enjoy their meal while listening to live music coming from the stage.

Walkers continued to come across the finish line as Chance's radio came to life with another dispatch for EMS. Another possible overdose, this time for a thirty-two-year-old female, followed immediately by another call for a nineteen-year-old male in a different location. All these calls were within a ten-block area. *Something's not right.* Chance turned to see Leland Kurst and the other individual he'd parked beside climb into their vehicles and leave. Across the street, she watched Leland's brothers leave the restaurant and drive away. An idea hit her prompting her to speed-dial Harley's number. When she picked up, Chance started right in.

"Harley, are you hearing those overdose calls?"

"I am. I sent one of my troopers to the first one. Randy marked up on the last one. We've got a problem."

"I agree, and I think the Kurst brothers have a hand in it. All three of them and the company they brought with them are currently headed back toward Thomas. I wonder if they sold everything or if they're still carrying. Do you have anyone you can shake loose to tail them, see if they can pull them over on a moving violation?"

"My closest unoccupied trooper is down in Parsons. I'll have him watch for the vehicles. Something tells me this overdose run isn't over."

"That's my fear as well. I'm going to call Sarah and put her on alert and talk with Taylor."

"Call me back if something else goes down I can't see. I'm going to text Meg as well."

They hung up, and Chance thumbed her keypad.

"This is Sarah Riker."

Chance knew that meant she'd answered her phone without checking the caller ID. "Sarah, I know you're up to your ass in alligators. I need to know what these folks are overdosing on and if they're getting it from the same place. Are you finding any paraphernalia?"

"Plenty. Needles, spoons, lighters, you name it, we've got it."

"Any packaging? Something with a brand on it?" Chance wrote down notes on a pad she pulled from a cargo pocket. She looked up to see Khodi and Echo approaching.

"Honestly, Chance, I didn't have time to look too closely. Whatever this is, it's taking more than one Narcan to bring them around. I'm on my way to Garrett with one of them. I've got all three on-duty crews on these calls. My shift supervisor is rounding up another crew. If we get anything before that, we're going to have to call in mutual aid."

Their conversation stopped as another call dropped very close to where Jax's vet station was set up. A five-year-old male, unconscious and having a seizure after ingesting an unknown substance. This changed everything. If this proved to be an overdose and the child died, there would be hell to pay.

"I've got to go, Chance. Figure out what the hell is happening. I'll call you." Sarah disconnected the call.

Chance pushed the button on her mic after she'd rotated the channel selection to the main law enforcement channel. "SD-1 to Comm Center."

"SD-1, go ahead."

"Contact the Davis Fire Department for me and ask them to come up and handle traffic control. I'm responding to that last EMS call." Khodi and Echo jogged up to her vehicle, ready for duty. She was glad she'd taken the time a few days ago to have Echo introduced to the other K9 units.

"Received. SD-1 responding to Fairfax Ave."

"Khodi, no time to explain much. Let's get the dogs loaded and get to that call. Something's going on, and Sarah's out of crews."

Khodi opened the back door and loaded Echo inside beside Zeus. "What do you need me to do?" Khodi buckled his seatbelt.

"When we get there, look for anything drug related. That was the fourth call for an unconscious patient. We need to see if we can find anything in common with those other medical calls. We've got a problem, and I don't want it getting worse."

"This sounds like a bad batch of something. I'm betting heroin. I've been dealing with it for months over in Bridgeport. If it starts spreading here like it did over there, EMS will need to buy two things in bulk, Narcan and body bags."

Chance risked a look at Khodi. "Let's hope we can stop this before it gets to that point."

They pulled up to the large, Victorian-style home renovated into two apartments, one on each floor. They approached an entrance door where a piece of cardboard took the place of a missing pane of glass. The door was also sporting a boot print below the handle. Children's toys and faded paint chips littered the porch.

"Khodi, check the back. You know what I'm looking for, and I know Echo is trained in narcotics recognition."

"We're on it, Sheriff."

Chance announced herself as she stepped into the house while pulling on nitrile gloves. Zeus was ready at her side. "Sheriff's Department. Anyone in here?"

A woman came running from the back part of the house with a small child in her arms. "Help me. I don't think he's breathing!"

Chance grabbed the child from her and placed him on the floor to feel for a pulse. She checked his pupils and found them pinpoint. Shallow respirations and a weak pulse sent a shiver of fear up her spine. She heard the door bang open and looked up to see a sweating Jax barreling through with her jump bag. As she knelt beside her, Chance was beyond grateful for Jax's medic training. *She must have run here.*

Jax pulled up the boy's eyelid and spoke to the bedraggled woman who stood shaking, her hands over her mouth. "Tell me what happened."

The woman stood paralyzed and silent.

Chance yelled at her. "Dammit, he's in trouble. What the hell happened?"

The woman choked back a sob. "My boyfriend left his—"

She didn't get a chance to finish. Chance stood as Jax pulled items from her jump bag. "What did he get into? He could die if you don't tell us!"

"Drugs! I don't know what it was. He bought it down at the festival. He went to find his kit and left it on the table. Hunter must have thought it was candy." The woman dropped to her knees and screamed while she clasped her hands together. "Please, help him!"

Jax tipped the boy's head back and sprayed Narcan up his nostril before grabbing a stethoscope and placed it against his small chest. A prayer crossed Chance's lips that the boy would be all right. She'd heard an ambulance respond over the radio and heard the siren getting closer and closer. Khodi ran in with Echo.

Chance briefly looked away from the child and Jax. "See what you can find, Khodi. Zeus is hitting on something over there." She pointed to her K9 unit, barking sharply as he sat near a low table. "We need to know what we're dealing with."

"Echo, *zoek*." Khodi nodded and swept his hand across the room, and the dog went to work.

Chance ran to the door when she heard a siren outside. She held it open as a medic she didn't know pushed inside, followed by one of her search and rescue members, Ned Hauser.

"What have we got?" The medic dropped down beside Jax.

"He's stopped breathing. We've got to get him out of here." Jax scooped the child up in her arms and quickly moved to the door and out to the ambulance, the mother running behind them.

It took everything Chance had not to run after her. There was little she could do. Her job was to find the root of this problem and eliminate it. She turned to watch Echo, as he moved through the living room before he sat down beside Zeus. Khodi stepped to the dogs.

"Sheriff, I've got something." Khodi turned and pointed to several colorful paper tubes, the size of short drinking straws, that lay on the table. "I've seen these before. They call them pixie sticks like the candy, which is likely why the kid got into them."

"Fuck. How many more kids are going to get into this before we get it off the street?" Chance pulled off her hat and slammed it against her leg as she ran her other hand through her hair. "We've got to get someone on the mother." Chance grabbed her radio and called for Harley, as she watched the woman crawl into the front seat of the ambulance. When she answered, Chance got down to business.

"Harley, do you have any troopers who can head to Garrett and keep an eye on a subject from this emergency call? I need to know who the boyfriend is along with a dozen other things."

Harley answered quickly. "I can call one from Preston County. Can you give me a description?"

Chance relayed what unit the woman was traveling in and what the woman was wearing. "Dirty blonde, wearing a red, long-sleeved flannel shirt. Don't let her get out of their sight. I'm having the comm center call Child Protective Services as well."

"On it." Harley disconnected the call.

A glance around the room had Chance taking in the squalid conditions, including full ashtrays, empty beer cans, and food containers. She went to the kitchen where an overflowing trash can smelled of decomposing food, while the sink sat full of dirty dishes. Gnats swarmed around a rotting banana and flies dotted a fungus-covered plate on the table. *Dear God, that poor kid.* On her way back to the living room, she saw a burnt spoon and a piece of rubber tubing by the stove. "SD-1 to SD-2."

"Go ahead, Sheriff."

"Taylor, are you close to my location?"

"I can be there in five."

"Bring your ID kit with you." Chance wanted to test the items she'd found to give Jax and Sarah a heads-up as to what they were dealing with, specifically. "Khodi, look around for any pictures of the boyfriend. We need to figure out if he was the buyer or she was. He took off, which means I put my money on him."

"On it, Sheriff." Khodi and Echo started walking around the filthy apartment.

A few minutes later, Chance heard a vehicle pull up out front, as another overdose call went out in another part of the county. *How many more will there be?* Taylor came through the door with a small, black Pelican box in her hand. She opened it and pulled out a test kit. The system used colorimetric tubes inside a package, where a detection strip would be inserted after contact with a substance. A mobile app on a smartphone could scan a QR code and use an algorithm to identify a color match to a particular drug. Chance had done some extensive research and chose this system for the safety of her officers and the preservation of evidence.

She watched Taylor collecting samples and turned when Khodi came back in the room. He handed Chance a digital photo frame. As the pictures changed, she recognized several faces from arrests and law enforcement calls, including Leland Kurst and his brothers. The mother of the child was in several of the photos with her arm around Austin Langly, a twenty-three-year-old hoodlum Chance had arrested more than once for gas drive-offs, shoplifting, and petty theft.

"We've got heroin laced with fentanyl, Chance. This is bad." Taylor held up her phone with the display.

Chance knew this was a potent form of the narcotic that had caused numerous overdoses and deaths in other counties. She feared the epidemic would take root in the place she called home. The units transporting the patients needed this information. After rotating her radio to the medical channel, she grabbed the mic on her shoulder to call for Sarah's unit. A warbled tone from a radio signaled an emergency button had been activated. A voice followed, one she recognized.

"Emergency traffic, emergency traffic! This is Unit 5-2. I've got a medic down! I repeat. I have a medic down! I'm on Seneca Trail near the county line."

Chance needed no more information as to who was down. It could either be the other medic, or Jax. Chance had read recent articles that urged first responders to use extreme caution when treating overdoses related to the specific drugs they were dealing with from this incident. Accidental skin-to-skin contact had caused the narcotic to be absorbed by first responders treating a patient. Many law enforcement officers had gone down with accidental overdoses while collecting evidence.

Chance ran out of the house with Zeus on her heels. They flew into her vehicle. As she hit her lights and siren, her eyes scanned the street for any oncoming traffic. She needed to reach Jax. They were transporting the five-year-old from the house. With one critical patient on board, the conscious medic would be in an impossible position trying to resuscitate the child and determine what had happened to the other member of the crew.

Buildings blurred as she rushed past. The roadway ahead was littered with vehicles that had pulled out of her way. The city limits of Thomas came into view, as she watched one of the fire department's support vehicles pull out of a station bay. She blew past it, and then slowed as she entered the more populated area of the small town. With the bridge in sight, she floored the gas pedal and flew around the rolling curves of the highway, trees resembling fence posts. Most of the road curved gently until she reached the area near the stone quarry. Here the road was frequently covered with loose stone in the sharp turn. Many accidents occurred exactly at this point, and she had no intention of being the next.

Years ago, one of her mentors had told her, "You didn't make the patient sick. You didn't wreck the car, and you didn't start the fire. If you don't get there, you can't fix it." Chance took that message to heart and let off the gas. Once she'd cleared the turn, she accelerated toward the county line less than two miles away. Somewhere in that area, she'd find an ambulance and Jax. In the next turn, there was a pull off. To her relief, a box ambulance sat there with its lights on. She slammed her Suburban into park. With her keys in hand, she released Zeus and ran for the ambulance. Chance threw open the rear doors. Her heart stopped in her chest.

Jax lay on the bench seat, a bag-valve mask covering her face. Ned rhythmically squeezed. The child's mother sat in the front seat sobbing. Chance screamed, "It's heroin laced with fentanyl. Did you give Jax

Narcan? It's possible she came into contact with it at the scene."

Ned looked at Chance, and then at the medic. "Hanna, I'm not an EMT. I can't administer meds. If you two can handle this, I'll get us to the damn hospital." Chance took over bagging Jax, and Ned jumped out.

Chance looked out the windows of the ambulance. "The cavalry's here. A unit from Thomas just pulled up. Mike's an EMT. Get us on the road. Update the comm center and have them inform Sarah and the rest of the units."

A man in his thirties climbed in the ambulance. "What do you guys need me to do?"

Hanna, a tiny wisp of a medic with a shock of pink hair falling in her eyes, rushed out a list of instructions. "Mike, bag this kid for a few minutes and watch that heart monitor. If it changes, you let me know." She leaned up into the cab. "Ned, get us to the hospital yesterday."

Chance asked the fire department members to watch her Suburban until someone from her department could retrieve it. She told Zeus to jump into the open space between the bench seat and the side door.

When Hanna turned back to the patients, Chance saw a determination she was grateful for. "Hanna, I know we haven't met, but Jax is my fiancée. What do you want me to do?"

Hanna nodded. "Keep bagging her. Are her pupils still pinpoint?"

Chance lifted one eyelid, then the other. "Yeah, it has to be the fentanyl. That place had drugs everywhere."

Hanna administered a Narcan dose to Jax. She took a blood pressure reading, and when the dial dropped back to zero, she pulled the stethoscope out of her ears. "What's her pressure normally, do you know?"

Chance thought about it and tried to remember the day of the community blood drive a few weeks ago. "I don't know. We gave at the blood drive. The nurse told her it was perfect."

Hanna took a deep breath and grabbed supplies to start an intravenous line. "Until she can hold that pressure up, I'm going to push some fluids. That Narcan should start bringing her around."

Chance closed her eyes and said a silent prayer that the medical interventions would start bringing the most important person in her life around. Watching Jax lay so still and unresponsive made her blood run cold. She braced her feet wide apart to absorb the swaying of the ambulance, as it sped toward the hospital. Her hands shook as she squeezed the bag, and she nearly stumbled as she leaned down to whisper in Jax's ear. "Come on, baby. Wake up. I need you." Chance could only hope that Jax's narcotic muddled mind could hear her and fight back to the surface.

***

Lethargy and sludge were smothering Jax's fight for consciousness. She could hear Chance's voice in her ear and felt a pinprick of pain in her right arm. The Narcan smashed the sludge, and Jax jerked awake. After great effort, she focused on the gunmetal-blue eyes she stared into every morning and every night. With her left arm, she pushed the mask away. "Chance?" She saw relief wash over her lover's face.

Chance kissed her forehead. "Hey there, lay still. We'll be at the hospital soon."

Jax fought to remain alert. Waves of nausea compounded her headache. "I'm going to throw up." She rolled on her side and emptied the contents of her stomach on the floor.

"Jax, this is likely a side effect of the Narcan," Hanna spoke up. "It's okay."

Jax felt someone slip a nasal cannula into her nose, as Chance wiped her mouth. "Oh God, my head is killing me."

"It's okay, honey. We're about twenty minutes from the hospital. Hold on." Chance rubbed her cheek.

"What happened?"

"I think you touched some of the heroin-fentanyl mix with bare skin at some point."

Jax's memories of the house came flooding back. "The little boy!"

Hanna turned back to her. "We've got him, Jax. He's starting to come around."

Jax held Chance's hand and listened to Hanna talking to the boy.

The mother's angst-filled voice was littered with sobs. "He can't hear you. He's deaf. Can I come back there? He'll be scared if he doesn't see me."

Hanna held out her hand. "It's tight back here with four adults. You'll have to sit on the cot with him."

The woman crawled back. She signed to the little boy who had started wailing.

Jax looked at Chance. "He has to be terrified."

"So am I." Chance slid down beside her.

Jax cupped Chance's face. "I'm going to be okay. I promise." She watched a tear trickle down Chance's face. Jax physically ached from the pain etched in her fiancée's eyes.

The ambulance siren wound down and came to a stop. Jax knew they'd arrived at the hospital when she heard Ned report their location to the comm center. The back door opened, and Sarah's face appeared at her feet.

"Let's get them both inside. I have a gurney for Jax." Sarah reached for the release, as the child's mother got up off the cot.

Jax watched the woman sign to the little boy, whose wails had calmed to whimpers. The mother climbed out of the ambulance as Jax sat up. Everything in front of her swirled and tilted, until she felt Chance's hard body pressed against her back. She heard Zeus whimper at her side. "It's okay, boy."

The boy's cot was pulled from the ambulance, with Hanna, Ned, and Mike wheeling it through the ER doors. Sarah climbed in beside her.

"Let's see if we can get you out of here and checked out. Chance, you get one arm, I'll get under the other."

Ned reappeared and pulled the gurney into position as the three exited the ambulance.

"I think I'm gonna be sick again." Jax dry heaved as they got her in position. Chance put a cool palm to her forehead.

"Let's get her inside." Sarah nodded. Chance held Jax's hand, as they entered the ER.

Jax noticed a trooper she didn't recognize had detained the mother at the registration desk. Jax could hear the child screaming from beyond the treatment doors. "Find someone who can sign. That little guy is deaf and probably terrified."

"Let's worry about you first. I'll make sure they know." Sarah pushed her to a treatment bay, and Chance bent to slide a hand under her knees and behind her back, as she lifted her onto the bed. Zeus sat in a protective position near the head of the bed.

Sarah transferred her line and asked a few questions as Dr. Amy Halston and Bailey, the ER nurse, came around the corner.

"Well, well, you two. We've got to stop meeting like this. What happened?"

Chance explained the incident and the possible exposure to the heroin-fentanyl mixture. Sarah rattled off what Hanna had relayed to her about Jax's collapse and treatment.

"Bailey, let's draw some bloodwork and get supportive measures started. Once we get the test results, we'll know better how to counteract it completely. Let's get a health history and baseline vitals.

I'll be back in a little bit. I've got seven overdoses, and that little boy is my greatest concern right now. Do you have any questions for me, Jax?"

"No, go take care of him. I'm okay." Jax waved her off as Bailey came around and started the orders Amy had given her.

***

An hour later, Jax had a second bag of fluid and medications in her. She felt dizzy and irritable. Her body ached like she had the flu, and all she wanted was to go home. Lindsey had texted her that they had successfully closed down the free clinic and were headed to the office to put everything away. She and Megan offered to drive Uncle Marty over to Garrett. Jax advised them to take him home, and she'd call him as soon as she could. Chance had already stepped out to update him.

Hanna's voice came from outside the curtain surrounding Jax's treatment area. "Can I come in?"

"Please." Jax waved her in.

"We didn't have time for formal introductions. I'm Hanna Freeman. How're you feeling?"

Jax held a hand to her head. "Like I'm glad I never got into drugs. I feel horrible. How's the kid?"

"Hunter is up in pediatric ICU. He stopped breathing and his pressure crashed again and was intubated right after we got here. The amount of heroin in his system was nearly fatal. If you hadn't gotten there when you did with that first Narcan, he'd be dead. It's still going to be touch and go. The added complication of him being unable to communicate is a major issue. Fortunately, they've found someone who specializes in American Sign Language to work with him when he comes to, if his mother isn't available." Hanna cracked her knuckles.

"Sorry I went out on you, Hanna. I still haven't figured out when I came in contact with the drugs. I had gloves on." Jax wiped a shaky hand down her face.

Chance came back in the room just then. "I'm betting it was when you cradled him to your chest as you ran out to the ambulance. His face was against your neck."

Jax had been wearing a scrub top with a V neckline. "Or my arm, it was bare above the gloves. Why anyone would choose to feel this way is beyond me. Chance, this is Hanna Freeman, a recent hire to the emergency squad. Where's Hunter's mother?"

"Nice to meet you, Hanna. Thanks for taking care of Jax. Hunter's mother is with him for now. They're monitoring his progress. Child Protective Services is handling the case, pending a custody hearing. We haven't been able to come up with any family to notify. The mother isn't from this area. Right now, we have no idea if Austin is the father. She isn't talking."

Jax looked at Chance. "Who's handling the main investigation into all this? If it's you, then you need to go, I'll be fine. Megan and Lindsey can come after me when I'm released."

Chance came to sit beside her and took her hand in her own. She kissed the knuckles. "Harley is taking the lead. Taylor's working on it with her. I'm too personally involved, and the last thing we want to do is have anything I present to be brought up as questionable because of our relationship. I'm not even sure they're going to let you go yet. We'll have to wait until Amy makes a decision. If she tells me you can go home, that's what we're doing. Randy dropped my vehicle off a little while ago." Zeus jumped up and put his front paws on the bed. He licked Jax's face.

"Hey, boy. Thanks for watching over me." Jax rubbed her hand over his head.

Dr. Amy Halston walked to the bedside with a chart in her hands. "Jax, I'm going to send you home with orders to rest for a few days. We've pushed fluids to flush your system."

"I can tell. I've never peed so much in my life."

"No doubt. Since this was more of a contact overdose, whatever is left should be out of your bloodstream in the next twenty-four hours. That little guy you brought in...his skin was completely contaminated with that cocktail, beyond what he ingested. The rest of you were lucky it didn't happen to you. Chance, I understand you got to him first? If that's true, I'd wash anything that came in contact with him as soon as possible." She pointed to Jax, "Take it easy for a few days, okay?"

"I'll wash my jacket and make sure her ass stays put on the couch, Doc. Can I take her home now?" Chance clasped Jax's hand.

"Bailey has her discharge papers." Amy looked at Hanna and Jax. "Good work out there today. Chance, get this shit off the street. I'd like to avoid a repeat of an ER full of overdoses. There was something else cut in with the heroin and fentanyl. The lab is still trying to run tests."

"I'll have Sergeant Harley Kincaid get in touch with you. She's the lead investigator." Chance shook Amy's hand.

"Good deal. Goodnight everyone." Amy waved and left, as Bailey stepped up.

"Okay, let's get you signed off and out of here. I'll pull that line now."

Jax held up her arm. "Thank God, I was going to ask for some Depends if you were going to run another bag of fluids. I've put twenty miles on that wheelchair going to the restroom."

Hanna touched Jax's foot. "I'm going to go find Ned and head out of here. I wanted to check on you and give you the update on Hunter. Take care."

"Thanks again, Hanna."

In another fifteen minutes, Chance wheeled Jax out to the Suburban and helped her into the front seat. Zeus made his way into the back. Once Jax was settled, Chance joined her and started the engine.

Jax yawned. "Let's go home. I'm exhausted."

Chance leaned over and kissed her. "Your wish is my command."

Jax rested her head against the seat back. The sound of the tires vibrating against the pavement quickly lulled her to sleep and out of the nightmare of a day.

Chapter Twelve

SUNDAY MORNING CHANCE CLIMBED out of bed with extreme care to avoid waking Jax. She hoped that she could care for the horses and fix breakfast before the sleeping woman stirred. As she headed to the barn with Zeus, she noticed Kendra's vehicle sitting outside the corral. Quiet moans stopped her from opening the door. *You've got to be kidding me. Please let them not be having sex.* Chance tried to decide what noise she could make to break up whatever was going on in the barn. Zeus nudged her leg. *Perfect.* She whispered to her dog, "Zeus, *spreken.*"

The simple command sent the Belgian Malinois into a set of sharp barks. Chance cleared her throat and spoke loud enough she hoped her sister would hear. "Yes, Kendra's in there. I know you're excited. Come on, let's go see her." She waited a few more moments before she opened the barn door. Brandi was scooping feed into Mac's bucket, while Kendra used a pitchfork to muck out Kelly's stall. Chance noticed Kendra was sporting a fierce blush, while Brandi went about her business as cool as a cucumber. Kendra had several pieces of straw in the back of her hair.

"Morning, Chance. How's Jax?" Brandi filled Glenny's bucket next.

"Sleeping finally. Thanks guys, I appreciate the help. Want to take them out for a ride too? We didn't get to do that yesterday, and I want Jax to rest today."

Kendra stood the pitchfork against the door and moved the wheelbarrow to the next stall. "I was going to suggest that. I'd like to show Brandi the ridgeline on horseback."

"Great. Did you enjoy working at the stand-up clinic yesterday?" Chance took a water bucket from Brandi and headed to the sink.

"I did. Nothing like hands-on training. Whenever she's up to it, I'd appreciate if Jax could fill out some paperwork that would give me extra credit."

They worked in silence for a bit, mucking stalls and making sure everything was clean and fresh for the horses.

Brandi leaned on her pitchfork and spoke to Chance. "I'd like to come back and do some farm calls with her someday. Jax is a great teacher."

Chance smiled, knowing Brandi's flattery was sincere. "I'm sure she can work something out for you. I'm hoping she'll sleep in a bit."

Jax walked up beside Chance and slid her arms around her waist. "Not much chance of that when my heater crawled out of bed. Morning everyone."

"You're supposed to be resting." Chance kissed her softly.

"I've been in bed since four yesterday. Besides, I want to check on Hunter."

Chance sighed, though she understood. "Let's make some breakfast first. Then we can make some calls for updates. I asked the girls if they'd take the horses out for us."

Kendra came to stand behind Brandi, who leaned back into her. "We'll handle the horses and the stall clean up. You two take it easy this morning."

"Sounds like a plan. When are you headed back to Morgantown?" Chance took Jax's hand and wrapped it in hers.

"After lunch. We both have to study, and I want to be back before it's dark." Brandi stepped away, and Chance saw a furrow crease Jax's brow.

"Kendra, did you dress in the dark? Your shirt is on inside out. Come have breakfast with us. I'm starving." Jax leaned in and kissed Chance's cheek.

Chance smirked and shook her head, as Kendra grabbed at the hem of her shirt and cussed under her breath. Brandi was biting her lip and covering a smile with her hand.

"See you inside in fifteen. Maybe you can manage to dress yourself now that it's light. Like Jax said, you must have dressed in the dark." Chance barked a laugh at her sister only to be given the finger in return.

***

Chance watched, as Zeus lay near Jax as she worked at the stove. Since they'd come home, the dog had barely left her side. Chance knew that what was important to her was also important to her partner. She had no doubt Zeus would protect her Jax with his own life.

Chance pushed up her sleeves as she took in a deep breath, pulling in the smell of the spices in the cooking sausage. "What can I do to help?"

Jax smiled. "How about we do pancakes and dippy eggs?"

"Oh, I'm all over that. Are you going to do the eggs after the sausage?" Chance reached for the griddle and placed it on the stove as Jax nodded. After Maggie had taught her how to mix up pancake batter from scratch, she could do it in her sleep. Pancakes had always been one of Kendra's favorites, and Chance smiled knowing her many conversations with Jax had led her to take note of the things that mattered to her family. She'd seen Jax remember the kind of wine that Maggie liked or the seasoning from California that Dee had fallen in love with. It also meant the silver dollar pancakes and dippy eggs Kendra favored.

Jax poured Chance a cup of coffee and set it down at her elbow. "A dash of cream, just for you." She gently kissed Chance's lips as the door opened and the two college students stumbled through it hand in hand.

"Oh my God, that smells like heaven. What can I do to help?" Brandi went to the sink and washed her hands.

"How about putting the butter, maple syrup, and raspberry preserves on the table? If you want toast, there's a loaf of Italian bread on the counter over there."

"I'm on the toast." Kendra raised her hand and headed for the bread.

"Don't forget my mustard." Chance flipped four small pancakes and smiled at the women around her. She enjoyed time with family. She was missing Maggie and Dee. As if they'd been summoned, Zeus barked a greeting and the moms-squared walked in the door.

"It's so gross when you do that." Kendra shivered and made a face.

"My eggs, not yours." Chance stuck her tongue out at the younger version of herself.

Maggie stepped through the door and sniffed the air. "Thank God, you didn't pick up that habit from her, Kendra. Sausage?"

Jax hugged Maggie as she made her way to the stove. "Correct. You two made good time."

Dee scrubbed her hands together. "With an offer of free breakfast? That's better than a buy-one-get-one deal on cereal."

Jax winked at Maggie. "I've got turkey sausage cooking just for you."

Chance nearly spit coffee out her nose at the dejected look on Dee's face. She shook her head when Dee tried to be gracious.

"Thanks." Dee shot Chance a pleading look.

Chance nodded, knowing she'd slip her mother a piece of real sausage when Maggie was out of eyesight. She didn't defy Maggie very often, but some things were beyond salvage, like turkey sausage or bacon.

Maggie came and took the spatula from Chance. "Go sit and talk with your mother about aiding and abetting her next stroke with the links you'll slide onto her plate. Honestly, do you think I came by the eyes in the back of my head easily? Trying to keep ahead of you and Kendra granted them to me permanently."

Jax nearly doubled over laughing. "Honey, you are so busted." Jax kissed Chance as she passed her.

Chance eyed Kendra snickering behind her hand and sat quietly down between her and Dee. She leaned over and whispered in her sister's ear. "Good thing your shirt's on correctly now, or it would be you on the hot seat, Bullseye. I'd stop laughing at me if you know what's good for you."

Kendra turned ghost white and slumped down in her seat.

"It also gave me pretty good hearing, girls." Maggie looked at them both over her glasses.

Breakfast was a lively affair with each person telling their tales from the festival. Once the dishes were loaded in the dishwasher and the kitchen wiped down, Brandi and Kendra went to take the horses out. Maggie and Dee headed home. Jax and Chance made their update calls in their favorite room, the library. Jax reclined with her head in Chance's lap. They'd picked out comfortable, soft leather furniture for this room with the intention that this was where they would spend most of their indoor downtime. They didn't watch much TV and chose to occupy cool evenings by reading one of the books from the shelves or magazines from their respective professions.

Chance hit speed-dial number three to connect with Taylor and put the phone on speaker.

"Morning, Sheriff. How's the better half today?"

Chance ran her fingers through Jax's hair. "She's trying to be a good patient while she rests on the couch with me. How's our little mother?"

Taylor sighed with a small chuckle. "Restless and bugging the shit out of me to go back to work tomorrow."

"We did promise she could. I think there will be a revolt if we don't. If her doctor is agreeable and she feels up to it, let her come in. We'll keep her workday light. You can take her home after lunch and park her ass on the couch. I know what it's like to be forced into recuperation, it's maddening."

Taylor snickered. "And you were a terrible patient too, the worst if you ask Maggie. I can't help but worry. I've never been that scared."

Chance looked down at Jax and thought about the radio call that had alerted her to a medic down. When she'd heard it, her heart nearly stopped, and all the air left her lungs. The thought of Jax and a child being in danger was something that stopped her heart. "I can relate. You're going to be a good mom, Taylor, both of you are. Next subject. Have you talked with Harley?"

"Earlier this morning. The task force has a rush on the lab work to see if it's the same chemical makeup. At least if that comes back positive, we can try to tie them together and find the source. With the overdoses coming that close together, it has to be. Any thoughts as to who brought it in for sale?"

Chance remembered how quickly Leland Kurst and his brothers scattered to the wind as the calls started dropping. "I'm leaning toward our usual suspects. I know the task force has them under surveillance. Let's double our efforts. If Leland Kurst still has a direct connection to Baltimore, this won't be our last run. I'm going to make some calls to a few friends in the DEA, see if I can shake some assistance out of them. If I have to, I'll rattle a few chains on our high-profile politicians who sit on both the state and national level. They enjoy the protection and privacy they find here for their second homes, and we help make that happen. Let's see if they can help us with resources. Okay, I guess I'll see you both tomorrow."

Jax spoke up. "Give Penny my best, Taylor."

"That I will. Get some rest, Jax."

"Will do."

Chance hung up and smiled at the twinkling eyes looking up at her. "What do you say to some music and a lazy afternoon?"

"If we can talk weddings and you get me a glass of iced tea."

"Your wish is my command." Chance bent over and kissed Jax, knowing Jax could ask for anything and she'd do everything she could to fulfill her wish.

Chapter Thirteen

CHANCE CRITICALLY EXAMINED PENNY when she stepped up to the reception desk and set a travel cup of peppermint tea in front of her friend. "How are you?"

Penny narrowed her eyes and bit her lip. "Enough worrying. If you and Taylor had your way, I'd be in a glass box. Now, let's get on with what the people elected us to do. Go do sheriffy things, please?"

Chance squinted at her. "Sheriffy things? Is that even a word?"

Penny stood and put one hand on her hip while the other pointed directly to Chance's office. "If you don't get in your office right now, I will call for Midas and order him to chase you there. I may even ask Zeus to do the same if you don't quit worrying. Taylor is doing enough of it for the whole world." She came around the desk, one hand protectively on her abdomen. "I promise you, we're fine. Now, let's get to work."

Chance stuck out her hand. "Deal."

Penny pulled her into a hug before going back to her chair. Zeus followed Chance to her office. A text message buzzed her phone and she smiled at the display with Taylor's name on it.

Is she okay?

Chance typed back. *Kicked you out of the front office, didn't she?*

Yes, dammit. I'm relying on you to keep an eye on her.

Chance chuckled and typed her reply. *Use your access to the cameras, but don't obsess.*

Like you aren't obsessing about Jax at work? How often is Lindsey reporting in?

"She's got me there." Chance mumbled. *Busted. Every two hours.*

Chance shook her head and put her phone in her pocket, as she heard Taylor coming down the hall.

"Did you see that lab report yet?" She took a seat in front of Chance as Midas and Zeus greeted each other.

"I read it in my email this morning."

Taylor shook her head. "I printed it out and put it on your desk. The potency of that stuff was lethal. We're incredibly fortunate no one died. Jax saved that little boy; I hope she knows that."

Chance remembered Jax crying in her arms when they'd gone to bed that night, the weight of what could have happened tearing her apart. "It's hard for her to think about it that way. I know it, and you know it, making her see that will take some time. Hunter's conscious, but still on a ventilator. He's not out of the woods by any means. They're worried how much of the powder went into his lungs and whether the overdose caused any brain damage. Only time will reveal the depth. His mother's been allowed to stay with him for now."

Taylor smacked her fist into her palm. "Pisses me off. We still haven't found Austin Langly. He's in the wind."

Chance made a few notes on the report. "Keep watch on the Kurst place. From the pictures I saw, he's friends with Leland. I wouldn't be surprised if he's hiding out with them, or for that matter, selling for them."

Taylor nodded. "That mass overdose almost completely overwhelmed our resources. Then in the middle, it takes down one of our first responders. This is a mess. I've put out a warning to the department about overdose calls, making it mandatory for them to wear nitrile gloves when they touch anything or search any suspect. The last thing we need is to have one of our officers become incapacitated and left vulnerable. I'm worried about the dogs walking through it. I think we need to order Narcan for the K9s and investigate ways to protect them."

Chance rubbed her face. "I agree. Last night, I read that most departments are now keeping them on leads to better control what they get into. Knowing how easily Jax was exposed scares the shit out of me for both our human and our K9 officers."

Taylor stood. "I'm sure Jax can tell us what we need to do as far as the Narcan dosages for the dogs. I'll leave that part to you. I'm going to start working my connections to see if there are any leads as to who is dealing this locally and if it's anyone beyond our usual suspects."

"Good idea. I've got a stack of daily work I need to address before I find myself buried in an avalanche."

Taylor crooked her mouth. "Sucks to be you."

Chance glared at her, and then grinned. "You'll find out how badly in about six years. Now go do chief deputy things while I work on the sheriffy things your wife banished me to."

For the next few hours, Chance shoveled her way through the warrants, gun permits, and tax collection issues before her. When her stomach growled, she saw it as an opportune time to check on Jax without seeming overprotective. Lindsey had been sending her regular updates along with adorable photos of Jax and the animals that were passing through the clinic. After advising Penny of her plans, Chance picked up three orders of homemade chili with grilled cheese sandwiches and headed to the clinic.

The parking lot was empty when she and Zeus exited the vehicle and strode into the front door of Three Rivers Animal Clinic. Jax and Lindsey were standing at the front counter, looking at a computer screen.

"I come bearing gifts." Chance held the takeout bags high enough for the women to see, while Zeus went around the counter to greet them.

Lindsey put her nose in the air and sniffed. "If Megan wouldn't divorce me before we were married, I'd propose to you. You'd better set a date soon, Jax. If that's chili I smell, I might just steal that woman for myself."

Chance shook her head at Lindsey. "It is chili, but I am way too old for the likes of you. I will provide you with lunch even without the proposal." She leaned in and kissed Jax as Lindsey took one of the bags. "Can I tempt you into your office so we can sit down and eat lunch?"

Jax came around and slid her arms around Chance's neck. "Nice play, Sheriff. I'm fine, but yes, we can go eat in my office if Lindsey can handle things out here."

Chance looked over at Lindsey who waved them off with one half of the gooey sandwich in her mouth. Chance took Jax's hand and led her to the office. "I see you are on to me, so I'll come right out and ask. Any lingering effects?"

Jax took a seat on the couch in the office and cleared space on the low coffee table that sat in front of it. "Not one. No side effects, no dizziness, memory lapse, or irregular heartbeat. It was a contact absorption. With the amount of fluids they ran in, it was flushed from my system." Jax leaned over and kissed her again as Chance sat down and put the bag on the table. "Don't worry so much."

"I plan to do a lifetime of worrying too much, woman. That's what loving each other is all about. I seem to remember someone else worrying too much only a few months ago. Now, let's eat while the chili is hot."

For the next few minutes, they enjoyed lunch and talked about nothing of importance. Chance looked up and took note of the small black dome in the corner of the ceiling. After everything that had happened, she was grateful for the surveillance system with inconspicuous cameras in every room, including Jax's office. The area outside the building was also under camera surveillance with views looking out from the building as well as a Wi-Fi camera strategically positioned to view the clinic from a distance.

"Have you stopped noticing the cameras yet?" Chance took a bite of her sandwich.

Jax swallowed and wiped her mouth before speaking. "Sometimes it shocks me to see them, but after that first few days, they faded into the background, for the most part." Jax pulled the panic pendant out from her scrub shirt neckline. "This probably took getting used to the most, but it does make Lindsey feel more secure and in turn, Megan."

"I won't lie, I feel better knowing you have it. Sara said your self-defense classes start next week."

Jax nodded. "We're looking forward to it. Maggie and Dee are joining us. Sara told me she has about five others, including Kristi, signed up as well."

"Being prepared for a confrontation you pray will never happen can't hurt."

Jax nodded. "Did you make any headway on the drugs Hunter ingested?"

Chance closed her eyes and shook her head. "Not really. We do know that it all has the same chemical makeup, which strongly denotes a single source. We're breaking it down even farther to try and find the specifics, like what it was cut with and anything that might pinpoint it. People with a lot of letters after their name are making those determinations. What I can say is those pixie sticks were found in every overdose case that day, which also strengthens the case that they are a single source. The task force is tapping into some resources from our surrounding states to see if they've run into any cases with this type of packaging."

Jax took a drink of the Coke Chance had brought with the meal. "Well, that's more than you had at the beginning of this. It's like searching for a diagnosis. You use blood tests, X-rays, and physical examinations to lead you to an eventual conclusion. Each step takes time."

"Great analogy. I want it off the street before we start having to stock up on the body bags Khodi mentioned. Oh, by the way, put your thinking cap on about protection for our K9 units against accidental contact. I really don't like what I'm reading in the trade magazines and discussion boards."

"Hmm, I have a contact with the SWAT team out in California. They will be a good source of information. I'll call Gary later today."

"I assume Gary is a police officer you've worked with?"

"He was a lieutenant with the sheriff's department and the leader for the tactical team. He also headed up the K9 division. Let me call him and see what information they have. Treatment wise, I can write out a protocol for naloxone, but the best thing you could do is get them to me as soon as you see symptoms."

Chance finished her chili and leaned over to kiss the most important person in her life. "I love working with you." Zeus barked his agreement. "And apparently Zeus does too."

Jax scratched around Zeus' ears. "He also likes the peanut butter treats I keep for him in my pocket." She handed one to him and started gathering the trash. "Do we have plans for tonight?"

"I think a long horseback ride is in our plans. Oh, and maybe a trip over to Redemption's Road? Pastor Rhebekka is playing a set, if you're interested?"

"Only if you promise me a dance."

There was almost nothing Chance would deny her, despite having two left feet. "Deal. We need to talk to her soon, because if you're in agreement, I'd like to firm up that she'll officiate our wedding."

"I was thinking the same thing. I remember stopping in at Mountaineer Days to listen at the House of the Rising Son. I instantly liked her. There seems to be more to the woman than meets the eye."

Chance never held anything back from Jax, but Rhebekka's story wasn't hers to tell. When Rhebekka Deklan first came to town, Chance had recognized her by another name. Rhebekka had revealed that she was the former rock star, turned pastor. Pastor Rhebekka had followed her bodyguard, Tank Raines, to Thomas. Together, they built a microbrewery called Redemption's Road. "She's a pretty private person and a silent partner in the brewery. As far as anyone is concerned, Tank owns the bar and Rhebekka is just a local pastor who plays a mean guitar at the Confluence on the side."

"Sounds exactly like the kind of person we should ask to help us say I do, and maybe help us pick the beverages for the reception."

"Agreed." Chance stood. She adjusted her vest and gun belt before taking Jax into her arms for a long, lingering kiss. "Time to get back to work. I love you, and I'll see you tonight."

"You're on, Sheriff."

Chapter Fourteen

CHANCE WANTED TO CHECK in with Taylor. The plan had been to ease Penny back into the workday by going home at noon. Chance was well aware of how overwhelmed with worry her chief deputy was. Every time Chance thought about Brad Waters putting his hands on Penny, she could feel her blood pressure rise. She wasn't looking forward to the upcoming trial. Unconcerned about her legal footing, Chance was confident the evidence the special prosecutor was reviewing would justify his arrest. The reprimands Brad had received and the insubordination he was guilty of sealed his fate long before the assault on Penny. Her thoughts were interrupted with an incoming call from Taylor.

"Is my administrator relaxing on her couch?"

Taylor chuckled. "She is on the couch, but she's anything but relaxed. Fought me tooth and nail to finish a dozen things before I could get her to leave."

"I'm not even a bit surprised."

"I wanted to let you know the special prosecutor from Barbour County called the office. Marsha Abbott wanted to know if you could run over there and speak with her."

Chance glanced at the dash clock. "I can. I'm glad this is going to be handled by someone out of county. I sure as hell don't trust our prosecutor to do a good job of it, and I'm not letting him plead this down. He'll never wear a badge again, unless it's as a guard at one of the gated communities. His law enforcement credentials have been suspended, pending trial."

"I'm headed back to the office after I stop in at the stables. Khodi's coming in later to pick up his uniforms. We'll start him on shift tomorrow night, and he'll ride with Randy and Vader."

"Sounds good. I'll give you a call later tonight and update you on Brad's case."

"Watch your six."

"I'll watch my back, you watch yours."

They hung up, and Chance called the office and spoke with Carl, who was watching the front desk while Taylor took Penny home. The office was secure, so she headed across Mountaineer Highway to Philippi, where the county prosecutor was reviewing the evidence. The state police were also involved as a nonbiased agency to avoid the appearance of railroading Brad.

Philippi was another small town, like Parsons, that had seen better days when coal was king. Now the main employers were a small hospital and a private college that kept the businesses going. Half an hour after leaving Tucker County, Chance pulled into the courthouse parking lot and exited her vehicle with Zeus. She entered through the front doors and checked in with security before climbing the steps to the second floor. A young receptionist greeted her.

"Sheriff Fitzsimmons, nice to see you. I'll let Miss Abbott know you're here."

"Thank you."

"Never mind, Denise. I'm already notified." A petite woman in a sharp suit walked through the door carrying a legal folder in one hand and a briefcase in the other. "Come on back, Sheriff."

Chance followed her down the hall and entered the room with tall ceilings and a desk that dwarfed the prosecuting attorney. "Good to see you, Marsha."

Marsha put her briefcase on the corner of the massive, chestnut desk and threw the legal folder into a basket. "Wish we were meeting under better circumstances. What a shit storm." Marsha pointed to a set of leather chairs near a low coffee table. "Have a seat. Coffee?"

"That would be great. Thanks." Chance took a seat and brought Zeus to a resting position beside her. Marsha poured two cups of coffee from the service that sat on a sideboard at one wall of her office.

"Here you go. Let's talk about this case against your former employee."

Chance sipped at the strong, black coffee and collected her initial thoughts. "None of this was malicious or out of line. I'd just terminated him for a witnessed act of sexual harassment and insubordination, something that is specifically addressed in our county personnel policy as grounds for immediate dismissal. He was asked to collect his things and leave the premises. He came back into the building and tried to bypass my office administrator to get to me. In the process, Brad threw her down. Penny is well along in her pregnancy and had to receive medical care. I had him arrested. His actions toward my administrator were caught on tape by our office security system. Few people pay attention to the notices advising of the cameras. End of story."

Marsha tapped a long, crimson fingernail against a thin, gold band around the rim of her blue mug. "I've watched the video. I'm in complete agreement with those charges, and his attorney will have a hard time arguing that. What I didn't see was surveillance of the incident that led to his termination. Does that exist?"

Chance nodded. "It does. That's more of a civil service matter, and I've turned that over to the committee. I can get you a copy if you'd like?"

"I think it will help with the motivation for his actions. Anything I can review to determine whether to order him to trial or recommend dismissal of charges will be helpful. I have a report from Sergeant Kincaid as well."

Chance tried to regulate her breathing to not show anger at the thought of dismissal. "Marsha, I'll be honest with you on this one. He's fired one way or another. You'll know why when you review the office footage. All of that is a personnel issue that will be handled under civil service law. He could have cost Taylor and Penny their child. If Penny would have lost the baby, you can bet your life, I'd have charged him with homicide under West Virginia Code Chapter 61, Article 2. Brad Waters was well aware Penny is pregnant, and he chose to harm her in the performance of her duties. He put his hands on her, that's all I need to know."

"Simmer down there, Sheriff. I'm not saying I'm dismissing anything. Let's be grateful. Penny Lewis and her child are doing fine. It's my job to determine whether this goes to the grand jury or not. As with any other law enforcement case, I have to have my ducks in a row before I prosecute anyone. The whole point of bringing something to trial is to make sure the guilty party is punished for the offense within the confines of the law. That's what I intend to do, but only when I have an ironclad case to present. From everything I see now, I believe that's the direction we're headed."

Chance clenched her jaw. She knew Marsha was one of the good ones and a very tough prosecutor. She didn't envy her job at all. "Okay. Other than the office footage, what do you need from my staff and me?"

Marsha took another drink of her coffee and crossed her legs. "I assume that all of you are willing to testify in court?"

Chance nodded.

"I know Harley and her troopers did interviews, were they videotaped?"

"They were. Appointments were made to meet at their barracks across from the 9-1-1 center. Harley should have all that, along with our written statements."

"The report from where she sought medical treatment would bolster the harm done claim. I know I don't need to, but I'll subpoena the visit. Let Penny and Taylor know, so they don't feel like it's an invasion of their privacy, if you will?"

"Taylor would hand deliver it if you needed. Trust me on that."

Marsha set her coffee cup down and dropped her shoe off her heel and let it dangle. She leaned forward. "Off the record? I want to nail his balls to the witness stand. I read the testimony about how the whole thing started. I've been in this business a long time, and I've heard every misogynist comment about a woman in power. Brad Waters is a dinosaur who believes a woman should be barefoot and pregnant. Oh yes, Sheriff. I've had dealings with Brad Waters and his kind before."

Chance knew the woman's physical stature belied her tiger-shark reputation. "I have no doubt."

Marsha slipped her shoe back in place with a simple flex of her foot, firmly resetting the three-inch heel in place. "Somehow, I keep getting re-elected. I chalk that up to my conviction rate and the fact that no man, woman, or child—beyond my grandmother—scares me. We'll get a conviction, just let me go at this case the same way I always do, with attention to detail to make it bulletproof."

Chance finished her coffee and stood up as she put her hand out to Marsha.

Marsha stood as well and shook the proffered hand. "On the record, I'll look over the evidence and render a decision as soon as possible. In the meantime, give my best to everyone over there. I'll have Harley call in and give her more detail on what I need."

Chance squinted a bit, thinking about how comfortably Marsha let Harley's name roll off her tongue, the spark in her eyes when she said it. *Something to think about.* "Take care, Marsha. Thanks for your time."

***

Jax had dressed for a simple evening of good music and dancing at the Confluence. They rarely went out on a weeknight, but the crowds were thinner compared to the Friday and Saturday ones. Jax watched, as Chance pulled on a black, long-sleeve T-shirt and tucked it into her blue jeans. Once she'd slid into a comfortable pair of worn cowboy boots, she turned to Jax. "Good enough?"

Jax licked her lips and stalked over to her. "I think I'd rather stay right here and take that outfit back off of you. Your ass is superb in those jeans."

Chance kissed her nose. "You're biased."

"Maybe, but I speak the truth, and I can count on a dozen other people—men, and women—to check you out tonight."

"Likewise, I need to make sure I get my gun."

Jax felt Chance's biceps. "With these guns, the metal one can stay in your boot."

"You're good for my ego, you know that?"

"I hope I'm good for a lot more than that."

Chance picked her up and spun her around. "So much more. Now, finish getting ready so we can grab something to eat before Rhebekka goes on. I saw where Karmen's food is on the menu."

Jax slipped on a soft, green cashmere sweater that matched her eyes, and slid into a pair of tall riding boots. When she brushed through her long, black hair, she spied several more silver strands. *This getting old sucks.* "Good. I think she should cater the reception for us in the spare barn. We can stack the bales up against the walls and put round tables around the room. Mags and I've got some decorating ideas to make it simple but tasteful." She felt arms come around her waist from the back and leaned into the muscled body that drew her close. Jax looked in the mirror to see Chance's gaze devouring her.

Chance smirked and kissed her neck. "Scratch tonight's plans. We aren't going out."

Jax smacked her arm. She turned and kissed her. "Yes, we are. You promised to dance with me."

Chance bent and put their foreheads together. "It won't be good for the sheriff to get in an altercation defending your honor. My God, Jax, you're so sexy."

Jax kissed her fiancée. "You certainly make me feel that way. Now come on, I've got my dancing boots on and I want to do just that. Is Zeus set for the night?"

"Our boy is fed, walked, and napping on the couch. I'll go start the truck, it's a little nippy tonight. Make sure you wear your heavier coat."

Jax applied a little mascara and finished off with a little lipstick. "Yes, Mom."

She watched in the mirror, as Chance left the bedroom. She stopped for a moment and looked around the room. Chance's discarded uniform shirt lay over on the arm of the chair, her duty boots sitting below it where she'd taken them off. Jax picked up a photo of them Maggie had taken after they'd announced their engagement and ran her finger over the wide smile on Chance's face. Jax closed her eyes. She could still smell the sharp tang of the cologne the woman she loved wore, citrusy and crisp like winter. That's the best way she could describe it. How her life had changed. It wasn't just location, the 2600 plus miles and ten states between her past and future had little to do with the differences. It was her heart and the lightness of her spirit that had changed.

Chance came back into the room. "Come on, love, let's go. I say we go drink a beer and you let me step on those boots a few times. We have wedding plans to make. I'm looking forward to talking with Karmen about the reception plans."

Jax tilted her head up and kissed Chance with deep longing. She let her tongue glide along Chance's lower lip and groaned when she was granted entrance to explore the depths of Chance's warm mouth. She put her arms around the strong neck and ran her fingers into the dark locks. When she broke the kiss, Jax tugged at the silver shock in the front of Chance's hair. "I love you, Sheriff. Lead the way."

Chapter Fifteen

THE PARKING LOT AT Redemption's Road was sparse, typical for a Monday evening. Chance recognized a few of the vehicles and saw a few Maryland and Pennsylvania tags. As was her habit, she committed the description of the vehicles and licenses to memory. Rhebekka's fat-tire bicycle was chained to a post out front. Chance had driven through the parking lot many nights and witnessed the bright-green mode of transport sitting right there. *I've seen her ride that thing in the snow.*

Faint music emanated from the door as Chance pulled it open. Immediately, the warmth of the fireplace blocked the chill of the fall evening, drawing them inside.

Behind the bar stood Tank, with her hand in the air. "Evening, Chance. Nice to see you. This must be the lucky lady who stole your heart. I hear congratulations are in order."

Chance helped take Jax's coat off. The 'coat tree' had been stripped of its bark and real limbs served as the hooks. "Good to see you too, Tank. This is Jax St. Claire. Even a blind dog finds a bone once in a while. I was extremely lucky."

Jax stretched across the bar and shook Tank's hand. "Don't let her fool you; I'm the lucky one. I'm so ready for a beer. Can I get an Ascension Ale?"

"Very nice to meet you. Something for you, Chance?" Tank grabbed a mason jar and filled it before setting it in front of Jax.

"I think I'll start off with a Coke until I get something in my stomach. I'm driving."

"Karmen's got the Cubans tonight. They are to die for. Rhebekka's setting up in the Confluence. You can put your order in over at the food nook." Tank put the Coke down on the bar. "Want me to start a tab for you?"

Chance nodded as she took a sip. "That'd be great. Jax, why don't you go put in our order. I'll try to catch Rhebekka and arrange to talk with her on one of her set breaks."

"Divide and conquer. I knew I fell in love with you for more than your good looks. Tell her I want to hear something slow. You owe me a dance later."

"Fear not, I will put in the request."

Jax took her beer and walked over to the food nook as Chance made her way to the stage. "Light crowd tonight, Rhebekka. If they only knew who they had before them."

Rhebekka smiled and put her finger to her lips. "Shhh, I like it that way. Good to see you, Chance. I see you brought reinforcements."

Chance looked over her shoulder and couldn't hold back the grin. "I did, and I've been ordered to do two things." She held up her index finger. "The first is to request a few slow songs so that beauty can let me look like a fool on the dance floor, and"—she held up a second finger—"to join us on one of your breaks for a discussion about our upcoming nuptials."

"Ah, I did hear something about the most eligible lesbian in the county no longer being eligible."

"No, I hear you're still on the market." Chance chuckled. "Seriously, join us and I'll buy you a pint."

Rhebekka leaned in and cupped the side of her mouth. "You do remember I own this place, right?"

Chance leaned in and lowered her voice. "I'm helping you keep your cover."

Rhebekka let go a hearty laugh. "You're on. See you in about twenty minutes. Tell your lovely wife to be I've got her covered as well."

Chance tipped her nonexistent cap in Rhebekka's direction and found a small round table off to the side of the stage, just as Jax joined her.

"All set. Karmen said about ten minutes. I told her I wanted to stop in and talk to her about catering the wedding. She said she'd be happy to. I'll go to the shop later this week, when she'll have more time to talk."

"Rhebekka will be over in about twenty minutes. Until then, we'll enjoy the music."

The Confluence was named as a tribute to the rivers that came together nearby. A nice fire heated the room adorned with barn wood and decorated with everything from kayak oars to cross country skis. From the ceiling, an upside-down canoe and kayak hung above them. The place was comfortable. People must have carpooled, because there were nearly twenty wandering around between the bar and the music arena. Rhebekka didn't sing, but she played a variety of music acoustically.

They sat and enjoyed her first few songs before Karmen brought out their meals. Jax immediately put her pickle spears in Chance's basket and removed the ones from her sandwich.

"Why didn't you ask to leave them out?" Chance bit into her sandwich and rolled her eyes back in her head with pleasure. "Oh my God, this is so good."

"I love to watch you have a foodgasm. I didn't order them without because I know how much you love pickles. I also told her to put your coleslaw on my plate. I promise to wash it all out of my mouth before I kiss you." Jax took a bite of her food.

Chance screwed up her face at the mention of coleslaw. It was one of the few foods she refused to eat as an adult. "You know me so well. I'm going to grab a beer now. Do you want another one?"

Jax wiped some hot-pepper mustard off Chance's cheek with her thumb. "Please."

Chance wiped her mouth with a napkin and headed to the bar. The traffic there was light now that Rhebekka was playing and she returned to Jax's side quickly. She set a glass of Brimstone Stout by her plate as she made room for Rhebekka who was walking their way. Tank had already handed her a fresh pint, courtesy of Chance.

"Jax, nice to see you again. Are you enjoying the show?" Rhebekka turned a chair around, straddled the seat, and leaned on the backrest with her arms crossed.

Jax leaned up and hugged Rhebekka, who returned the gesture. "Very much. You play a slow one next, and I'll be eternally grateful."

Rhebekka grinned. "It might cost you a return visit on Sunday, to House of the Rising Son."

Jax laughed. "That could likely be arranged."

Rhebekka nodded. "Good enough. Now, what did you want to talk about?"

Chance sipped her beer. She licked the thick foam off her lip and laughed at Jax's shudder. "Well, I'm planning on making an honest woman out of her, and we'd like to talk to you about officiating the ceremony."

Rhebekka lit up. "Oh, I'd be honored. When's the big day?"

Jax scrunched up her face. "Christmas Day."

"Wow, go big or go home. What time do you want to do this?"

"We were thinking around three in the afternoon," Chance replied, "but that's not all."

"What, you want Santa to co-officiate?" Rhebekka dropped her head. "That's a tall order, you know. He's headed to the beach on

Christmas Day."

Chance shook her head. "No Santa requests. How are you on a horse?"

Rhebekka looked at them with her eyebrows reaching for her hairline. "You want to get married on horseback?"

Jax and Chance nodded. "We're talking a small wedding. Less than twenty people. Most won't be on horseback. If you don't want to be on a horse, you can stand in a wagon. That's how the majority of the guests will be arriving."

Chance nodded. "We have a spot on our property where we'd like to have the ceremony. Anyone who wants to come on horseback can. I've been cleaning up two wagons to transport the rest. Penny is in no condition to ride."

Rhebekka ran her hand through her shoulder-length hair. "Well, I've done some unique weddings, but this one will be a first. If it's at three, that gives me time to have my Christmas service at ten in the morning and make it to your place. I'm in. It would be my privilege."

"Can we also impose on you to play some for us at our reception, at least a few songs? The rest, we'll have a DJ for."

"Consider that my wedding gift. Okay, let's meet next week and hammer out the specifics. We've got a few months, but I've found the longer you wait to nail down the details, the more stressed you'll be before the big day." Rhebekka rose. "Time for me to play that slow song for you. I think I have something that you'll like, Jax."

"I can't wait. Chance keeps telling me she has two left feet, but I'm guessing she can follow my lead a bit."

Chance nearly spit beer out her nose. She coughed as she laughed. "A bit. Honey, I'd follow you to the ends of the earth."

Jax leaned in and nuzzled her neck, sending a shiver through Chance's body. Chance put an arm around her shoulder and held her, waiting for Rhebekka. Within seconds, Jax's smile grew wide. Rhebekka started playing *When You Say Nothing At All*. Chance stood and led Jax out onto the wide planked floor. "I'll follow your lead."

"I love you, Chance."

"Love you back."

They swayed together until the end of the song. Jax left her side to whisper in Rhebekka's ear. Chance watched the grin on the musician's face grow wide as she nodded. Rhebekka beckoned a young woman to come onto the stage and join her. Jax returned to her arms and Chance squinted at her. "What are you up to?"

"You'll see. Now dance with me, my love."

Immediately, the familiar melody of Etta James' "At Last," filled the room. The young woman on the stage began the iconic lyrics. Chance drew Jax close to her. *Amen to that.* "You never cease to amaze me. No matter how many times I think I couldn't love you more, I do."

"Just keep practicing those words, honey."

"Which ones? I love you?"

Jax kissed her softly. "Those, and the I do part."

"I'd say them tomorrow and every day after that if it means I get to spend the rest of my life with Jax Fitzsimmons."

Jax quirked her mouth. "And what if I want you to be Chance St. Claire?"

Chance rolled her head left and right. "Has a nice ring to it."

Jax cupped the side of Chance's face. "I've wanted to be Jax Fitzsimmons since I was nineteen years old. I've lost enough years."

Chance leaned down slightly and whispered in Jax's ear. "How about we go home and practice the wedding night."

Jax chuckled. "Let's finish this dance, then you can carry me across the threshold and straight to our bed."

"Deal."

They continued to sway as Rhebekka and her companion finished out the song. They bid their goodbyes and made their way to the truck. Chance immediately knew something was wrong. The Tundra dipped on the driver's side. As she made it around the truck, Chance diagnosed the problem. Something sharp had been driven into the sidewall of her front tire, and the back tire had been punctured as well. Chance fumed as she contemplated who might have perpetrated the vandalism. *Mighty long list.*

She pulled her phone out of her pocket, as Jax stood and gaped at the vehicle.

"Who the hell would do this?"

Chance shook her head as she spoke to the telecommunicator on duty. "Max, this is Sheriff Fitzsimmons. My personal vehicle has been damaged. I'll need a report and a tow truck at Redemption's Road on Appalachian Highway."

"State Police Unit 207 is on duty. Let me give her a call."

Chance could hear him dispatching Harley to the scene.

"Any tow preference?" Max asked.

"Someone with a flatbed, I have two flat tires on the driver's side, with punctures to the side walls."

"Damn, Sheriff, who'd you piss off this time? Okay, we've made the call. Sergeant Kincaid is on the way, and Ben Watson is bringing his flatbed. Anything else?"

"That'll do for now, unless you've got a pound of Advil in your pocket. Thanks, Max."

"No problem, Sheriff."

Chance hung up and pulled Jax under her arm, before using her phone to take several pictures. Let's go back inside for a minute. I need to check with Tank and see if they have surveillance cameras on the parking lot."

Jax wrapped an arm around Chance's waist. "Any ideas?"

Chance sighed as she opened the door. "A long list that will need to be sorted through."

Tank furrowed her brow at Chance. "Forget something?"

Chance shook her head. "No, unless you mean I should remember I'm not always liked everywhere I go."

Tank came out from behind the bar. "What's wrong?"

"Somebody popped two of my tires. A trooper is on the way here. Anyway, I know you're busy, but can we talk somewhere private?"

Tank waved her off. "Karmen, can you take over for a minute?"

Once Karmen had slid behind the copper bar top, Tank ushered Chance and Jax into her office. "What can I do to help?"

Chance led Jax to the couch and took a seat beside her. "I need to know if you have any surveillance cameras out in the parking lot. Someone stabbed my sidewalls. I've got a wrecker coming, but I need to find out if we have any photographic or video evidence of the culprit."

"That's one of the things I insisted on. I was part of Rhebekka's security team back in the day. I know how important it is to have clear evidence." Tank turned to a laptop on the desk and began tapping on the keyboard.

Chance's phone beeped with a text from Harley. "I need to step out. All right if Jax stays here for a moment?"

Tank nodded, as Jax leaned over and kissed Chance's cheek. "I'll see if I recognize anyone."

"Partners in all things." Chance rose and walked through the back door.

Her truck was about fifteen feet from the door, and Harley pointed to the tires. "You definitely peed in someone's Cheerios. They got you good. The bar have any surveillance?" Harley looked around for cameras.

"Tank's in there pulling up the footage with Jax. We've been here for a couple of hours. I didn't notice anyone with an ax to grind. My truck isn't marked with any stickers or indicators, but that doesn't mean it isn't known around the county as my personal vehicle."

"We've stirred a lot of shit lately with the mass overdose investigation. Hell, we've busted three small-time dealers in the last week. None with any heroin, but that doesn't mean they aren't in the chain." Harley walked over to her vehicle, retrieved a camera, and began taking pictures of the damage. "Tucker Comm tells me there's a wrecker on its way." Harley grabbed the metal clipboard from the hood of her vehicle. "Let's go see the footage."

They knocked on the door and Tank let them in, and they followed her back to the office.

"I've got a few things for you, but you're not going to like it." Tank clicked the mouse to start the video.

The quality of the video was excellent. The group watched a figure in a black, hooded sweatshirt, face covered with a skull balaclava, look in the direction of the front door, then drive a hay hook into the Tundra's rear tire. The individual pulled the hook free and walked forward to drive the hook into the front tire with greater force. The subject turned to the camera and flipped a gloved finger toward the lens, before turning and running off.

Chance studied the footage. "Well, white male, approximately six-foot, slender build." Chance continued to watch before she pointed. "Let's get back outside and look at that muddy area off to the side, see if we have a clear shoe impression. I wonder if the Sunoco has a camera pointed toward that alley?"

Tank spoke up. "It's possible. After that break-in they had last year, they installed more security. There's a back door that points to the alley, maybe they caught what direction that asshole went. Hell, if you're really lucky, maybe he stopped in and bought beer. It looks like there is some kind of design on his hoodie, there on the back." She pointed to the screen.

Harley squinted and studied the frame. "Looks like a skeleton hand giving the finger."

Chance closed her eyes and felt Jax squeeze her hand.

"What is it?" Jax asked.

"Trying to remember where I saw something like that." Chance searched her memory, knowing she'd seen that design. She just couldn't put her finger on it.

"It will come to you. Just think about all the assholes you've dealt with over the last month, and something will come to you. Tank, can you make me a copy of that footage?" Harley marked a few things on a report form attached to her clipboard.

Tank reached for a CD and slipped it into the laptop. "Can do, I'll email you a copy as well, Chance. I'm sorry your evening ended this way."

Jax rubbed across Chance's back. "It is a pretty rare occurrence for us to even go out."

"And now you know why." Chance drew Jax into her arms. "I texted Mom. She's on her way to pick us up after the tow truck takes off." She felt Jax nod against her chest and pulled her tighter. "You leave California and come back to this. I'm sorry, baby."

"None of it matters, we're together. Come on, let's get this done. I'm betting Harley needs some vehicle registration information."

Chance laughed and looked at Harley. "I might have to hire this one with all the procedural information she knows. I'll be right back." Chance squeezed Jax a little tighter, as much for herself as to reassure Jax.

Life was changing in her small community, and she didn't like it one bit.

Chapter Sixteen

JAX LOOKED UP FROM the examination table to make eye contact with Molly, a spitfire of a woman who was the local coffee hostess at the convenience store downtown. Jax was examining her dachshund, Doxy, who was as big around as she was long. "Molly, we've got to get some weight off Doxy. She's limping because of the stress on her joints."

Molly looked everywhere except at Jax. "I don't feed her that much dog food, she only gets a cup in the morning and one in the evening."

"And a hundred treats and bites from your plate." Jax smiled to lighten the chastising. "Doxy, your momma is going to love you to death." She scratched the red wiener dog behind her ears. "Okay, here's what we're going to do. No more treats except for an occasional apple slice or a carrot. Cut her food in half and add half a cup of cooked green beans in with it. Dogs like the taste of them, and they're a great filler. Twice a day, you and Doxy, are going on a walk. I want you to go down to the park and make a lap in the morning and one in the evening. Even if you have to stop several times. She needs the walks, every single day."

"Well," Molly patted her own belly. "I guess we're both going on a diet."

Jax chuckled as she listened to Doxy's heartbeat. "Just think how much longer you'll both be around to love each other. Okay, we'll have you go see Lindsey while I put some medications together for you."

Molly shook Jax's hand. "Thanks, Doc. I'll really try to do better."

Jax squeezed back. "I have all the faith in the world in you." She left the room and found Lindsey out front. She handed her the chart.

"Need me to do anything for them? Doxy okay?" Lindsey took the chart and opened up the program that allowed her to ring up Molly's bill.

"She's going on a diet, but otherwise, our Doxy's fine. I'm going to grab the meds Molly needs and be right back out. After that, we'll go take care of the barn call at Dogwood Flats."

Lindsey nodded and spoke to Molly as she rang her up. Jax stepped into the medicine dispensary and pulled out a three-month supply of flea, tick, and heartworm medicine before stepping back to the counter.

"See you in a few months for a checkup, Molly. Remember, no extras and a slow walk twice a day."

Molly gave her a thumbs up. "Thanks, Doc."

Jax walked back to her office and sent a quick text to Chance telling her where they would be going and making arrangements for a long horseback ride in the evening. They hadn't had near as much time to ride as Jax wanted. After the vandalism, she knew Chance's nerves were on edge. *A little moonlight ride is exactly what the doctor is ordering.*

***

Jax chuckled to herself. Trying to wrangle a small herd of goats was one of the most challenging jobs of being a farm vet. She'd been to Kidd'n Around Goat Farm a few times. The adorable Nigerian dwarfs were great milk goats, and the couple that owned the farm used the milk to make soaps, lotions, and other beauty products. Andrew and Kitt had moved to the area five years ago and now had almost a dozen goats. Four of which were young kids.

"The good thing is they already have headstands, which will help in the examinations. I want to check the adults' feet to make sure the Halsteads are taking enough off the hooves when they trim them, so they don't end up with problems. Sometimes people are timid about how much to take off, and it leads to issues. The four babies are about six weeks old, so we should have fun trying to catch and examine those little buggers."

"I love baby goats. Megan promised me we can have a few when we build. Dad said he'll help build their pens to keep the coyotes away, but I'm really going for a Great Pyrenees for the protection factor. With Meg's frequent night shifts, I'd feel better knowing there was a dog outside keeping the four and two legged predators away."

"I can't blame you there. Knowing Zeus can hear things we can't gives me a sense of security that I miss when Chance is out at night. Maybe I'd sleep better if there were still a dog in the house on those occasions. I don't know about a Great Pyrenees, though. Maybe something a little smaller than one of our horses."

"I don't sleep."

Jax wasn't sure she'd heard Lindsey right. "You don't sleep? Ever?"

Lindsey stared out the window, not turning to Jax. "No, not if Meg's not home. Not since Leland came back in town. It's been worse since that day at the office. Most of the time, I go to stay with Mom and Dad."

Jax's heart ached. She'd done everything she could to make Lindsey feel safer about being at work. More than once, she'd watched Lindsey reflexively reach for the panic alarm around her neck when she was startled by the office door chime.

"Anything I can do to help?"

"Not unless you can force Leland to leave the state and never come back."

That would be a relief but was unrealistic. Leland still had close family in the area, according to Chance. "I wish I could. Instead, we'll keep our security on and rely on the women we love to keep him in line, okay?"

Lindsey nodded.

Kidd'n Around Farm sat on a peak near the county line. A panoramic view of the mountains and valleys jutted up and dropped off into rolling tongues of fire, tipped in scarlet, burnt orange, and umber. The leaves rippled as the wind blew the ocean wave of color. Jax spoke out loud without even realizing. "There's nothing like autumn in the mountains."

"I agree." Lindsey pointed. "There's Kitt."

Jax pulled the mobile vet clinic up to the barn and shut off the engine. She marked the mileage down on her log before exiting. Immediately, four dogs surrounded the vehicle, tails wagging. Jax and Lindsey stepped out and joyfully greeted the pack of two Great Pyrenees, one border collie, and one Heinz-57.

"Hey, guys, how are ya?" Jax patted sides and stroked heads as she accepted wet dog kisses to her cheek and neck. "Okay, okay, I'm happy to see you too."

Kitt came over to the truck and started pulling the dogs off them. "Sorry. You know how much they adore you two." Kitt clapped her hands together and pointed. "Back to work, you guys." With the command, all four dogs went back inside the fence, where Andrew directed them into the field with the goats.

"I take it Heidi and Rex are working out well?" Jax stood with her hands on her hips, watching the dogs.

"Better than I could have imagined. We haven't lost a single kid to the coyotes since we got them. I never thought dogs would be happier being outside at night, but those two"—she pointed to the field—"take their job pretty damn seriously."

Lindsey raised her hand to shade her eyes. "They were bred as protection dogs to watch the flock and deter predators. So many people see this fluffy, white puppy and have no clue they'll turn into a hundred-plus-pound dog, whose back might be taller than some people's hips."

Jax smiled with pride; Lindsey was going to make a great vet someday. Lindsey had helped Kitt and Andrew find the dogs through a rescue group.

They meandered to the enclosure to watch the hysterical group of little goats running around. The babies were bouncing off the adults and jumping sideways as they played. "The babies look good. Anyone showing any issues?" Jax leaned against the fence and eyed each of the little ones, looking for anything that seemed amiss.

Andrew put his arm around his wife. "Nope, everyone looks healthy and seems fine. We've got the head harness set up at the milking stand."

Jax stepped back. "All right, let me get my bag and we'll get this show on the road." Once at her truck, she donned her coveralls and Lindsey did the same. Jax pulled her long hair into a high ponytail and tucked it into the back of her coverall. She slipped on her boots and put a set of disposable covers over the top. Jax made it a priority to take every precaution against bringing some parasite or disease to the goats that she might have picked up from another farm.

"Ready, Jax?" Lindsey met her at the front with a bag full of equipment to trim the goats' hooves.

"Let's do it."

***

An hour and a half later, they were on their way back to the clinic on a backroad. They'd decided to take in some scenery to soak in a few more minutes of fall's beauty. It was after four, and the temperatures in mid-October dropped off quickly.

Jax rested her arm on the edge of the driver-side window. "Did you text Meg that we are on our way back to the office?"

Lindsey nodded. "She's going to pick up dinner and meet me at home. She had court today and is off for the next two days, before she moves to day shift for a week."

"I'll bet you're looking forward to that. You have less than a month until your wedding." Jax caught a quick glance in Lindsey's direction and saw the smile.

"I know. I can't wait. We've been dating since high school. Meg wouldn't even consider us getting married until she was a trooper." She waved a hand around. "She said something about being old-fashioned and wanting to be able to take care of me. I never needed her to do more than to love me. Meg wanted my dad to know she could support me. Pissed me off for a long time, but that's just Meg."

"It's in their DNA to protect, and that means in all ways. You can't change them." The sky grew darker, and Jax could hear the faint whine of an off-road vehicle or maybe a dirt bike. She glanced in the rearview mirror and saw headlights approaching quickly. The sight wasn't unusual in a rural county. Much of the population enjoyed off-road activities and frequently used ATVs for farm chores. What worried Jax was the speed with which these vehicles were traveling. The narrow, blacktop road wasn't very forgiving, and one side dropped off sharply, with guardrail only in the most dangerous spots.

Lindsey agreed. "No, you can't. I don't think we'd want to. Admit it...it's kinda hot."

Their laughter filled the truck. "Oh, yeah, in an annoying kind of way. It's nice being able to talk with someone who understands." Jax heard the rider getting closer, and it was obvious there was more than one.

Lindsey pushed her hair behind her ear and looked at the side mirror. "Do you hear that?"

"Yeah, it's been coming up on us for a bit. I've seen lights but not the bikes."

Jax concentrated on her driving. They still had a few miles to go on the narrow, winding road, before reaching the main route. She caught glimpses of Lindsey fidgeting and watching the side mirror. *Relax, dirt bikes out here are normal.* She needed to calm Lindsey's apprehension. "So, how are the wedding plans coming? Did you settle on the reception meal?"

"We're bringing in Hog Wild to do a pig roast and Karmen's catering the rest of the meal."

Jax nodded. "We're having Karmen do our catering as well. She's so good. I don't think I've ever had anything from her I didn't like."

The bikes were close enough that Jax could finally see them clearly. Both riders were in all black.

"Lindsey, see if you have cell service. Send Chance a text with our location, please."

Lindsey picked up her phone and started tapping the screen with her thumbs. "Anything else you want me to tell her?"

"Yes, tell her to come and find us. When you're done, I want you to tighten your seatbelt."

Lindsey whipped her head at Jax, her face full of alarm. "What's going on, Jax?"

"I'm not sure, Lindsey. Whoever these individuals are on the bikes, they don't seem to be trying to get past me, even though I'm giving them plenty of room to do so. I might be wrong, but I think the one on your side has a hay hook in his left hand."

"Isn't that what you said someone used to flatten Chance's truck tires the other night?"

"And that's why I need you to make sure you're fastened in good and tight." Jax saw Lindsey's phone light up. "I'm assuming you don't have enough service to make a call, if my dash display is any indication. If that's Chance, give her a description of the bikes and landmarks where we are."

Lindsey tapped quickly on the screen as the bike pulled up alongside. They heard a screech of metal. Jax looked in the mirror to see the rider dragging the hay hook along the side of the truck as it went past. Jax's blood ran cold. The back of the sweatshirt was imprinted with the same skeletal hand with the middle finger extended. An incoming call rang over the integrated system, and Jax hoped there was enough service to complete the call.

"Chance, we've got trouble. Same sweatshirt from the vandalism the other night, and they've got a hay hook. Two riders."

Jax strained to make out anything Chance said, but she was dropping in and out of service. All she could make out was "coming." The call disconnected. "Siri, call 9-1-1." Jax hoped that at least in attempting the call, the communication center could pinpoint their location if anything happened. She could hear the ring, but the call dropped off again before she could make voice contact. "Lindsey, keep trying 9-1-1."

Jax moved more to the center of the roadway that had widened out to nearly a lane and a half. They were approaching a blind spot, and she prayed no vehicle was coming in the other direction. When she rounded the curve, she jerked the wheel in reaction to the bike driving straight at her. The rear wheels broke loose in the gravel and her attempts to correct the slide were ineffective. The edge of the roadway came closer with shocking speed, and Jax could do nothing more than yell to Lindsey to brace herself.

"Hold on!"

The vehicle tilted sharply to the right as the tires dropped off the edge, sending them into a roll over the embankment. Darkness claimed the last of the light from the sky. The truck's headlights illuminated the trees, as they rolled in a dizzying kaleidoscope. Side airbags deployed. The inertia of the truck continued to roll them, metal screeching then yielding to the solid objects around them. Finally, they stopped. Jax was disoriented and tried to clear her head as small glass pebbles from the busted rear window plinked off the vehicle's interior and showered them both. Pain seared Jax's body. She dangled upside down against the seatbelt.

"Lindsey? Lindsey, can you hear me?" Jax felt around the darkened cab, trying to check on Lindsey. Her hand found the warm flesh of a dangling arm, and she followed it down until she had the wrist. A strong pulse bounded under her fingers, though Lindsey still hadn't answered.

I've got to get out of this seatbelt. Jax stopped moving and took several deep breaths, trying to clear the disorientation from her head as blood rushed into it from the inversion. *Solve one problem at a time, Jax.* She tried to release the buckle on her seatbelt, but the weight of her body seemed to bind the clip. *Where's your knife? Cargo pocket on your right leg.* That would require her to pull up with her core muscles to get to the knife. *Thank God for all these years holding myself up in the saddle.* Using her abdominal muscles, she used her left hand to push against the roof while she located the Gerber tool and pulled out the blade.

Jax realized the only way to control her fall was to try and brace herself with her left hand on the truck's roof. It wasn't going to help much, but she hoped it would keep her from causing Lindsey more injury. The second the blade sliced through the webbing, Jax dropped from the seat into an incredibly awkward position that bent her neck painfully. It wasn't until she went to push with her legs that she realized something was wrong. Apparently, the adrenaline running through her veins had masked the pain. Her left leg, below the knee, screamed in protest as she tried to push off with it. The pain was so excruciating, her mouth felt like it was filling with hot water, alerting her that she was about to throw up. Jax forced it back down, when she heard Lindsey moan. She focused all her attention on checking on Lindsey.

Think Jax, you need to see what's going on. "Flashlight, find the flashlight." Jax felt around for the edge of the bucket seat, knowing she had a Maglite jammed in between. Gratitude flooded over her when she felt the cool cylinder and found the button. A bright beam illuminated the cab, and she got her first look at the trouble they were in. The roof was bent into the cab, and part of Lindsey's door protruded in and against Lindsey's body. She moved the beam around to be able to see her assistant's face. Her eyes were closed, her face partially covered in blood. Her arms were stretched above her head and lay on the roof.

"Lindsey! Lindsey, talk to me. Wake up, Lindsey! Come on, wake up, honey." Jax tried several times to get a response from Lindsey. She watched her chest press tight against the seatbelt, relieved to see she was still breathing. "Lindsey, wake up."

Jax was trying to maneuver closer to Lindsey when she heard a siren off in the distance. Unsure as to whether emergency services would be able to tell where they went over the embankment, she did the only thing she could do to get their attention. She blew the horn.

Chapter Seventeen

CHANCE RACED UP LIMESTONE Mountain Road with Zeus, praying she would find Jax's truck. There was only one thing on her mind, getting to Jax. Someone was threatening her happiness, and she wouldn't let anyone take what she'd just gotten back. There had been no more texts from Lindsey pinpointing their location. All she knew was that they were on their way down the mountain, and someone was chasing them. Not just someone, possibly the same individuals who had vandalized her personal vehicle at the brewery.

"Comm Center to SD-1."

Chance gripped the steering wheel with one hand and grabbed the mic. "This is SD-1, go ahead."

"We had a 9-1-1 call from your half unit. We couldn't make a connection, but we've triangulated the signal to Limestone Mountain Road."

"I'm headed up the road now, I'll advise as soon as I find them. What other units do you have coming this way?"

"State Police Unit 207 is en route from the Clover Run area."

Zeus started to bark, and Chance squinted as she rounded a corner. Lights showing where there shouldn't be any. *Over the hill!* She saw yaw marks on the blacktop and disturbed gravel at the roadway edge. Silencing the siren, she watched Zeus' head turn in the direction of the embankment and heard him whine. She rolled down the window and heard a car horn. Short bursts followed by a long one, repeating over and over. "That's our girl, Zeus." She grabbed the mic and relayed information to the comm center to alert fire and EMS to her location. "Put the helicopter on standby, the vehicle is over the hill and is going to take some effort to reach." Chance flipped her radio to act as a portable repeater for herself and incoming units. Communications in this area could be sketchy.

Zeus jumped across her and headed over the hill the second she opened his door. "Find Jax, Zeus. I'm right behind you." She pulled on a rescue helmet and clicked on its bright headlamp before grabbing her trauma bag out of the back.

The horn continued to blast in intermediate bursts as she

clambered down over the hill through brambles, laurel bushes, and trees. She could see the headlights below her and could smell gasoline and hot brakes. Heart pounding, she stumbled and felt her pants snag on the briars that impaled her knees and hands. Righting herself, she continued over the hill, making her way to the overturned vehicle. Zeus was already there and barking. The horn stopped.

"Chance!"

"I'm coming, Jax! Hang on!"

Chance fell again and felt the scrape of rough bark against her cheek. The overwhelming drive to get to Jax pushed her forward, as she gained her footing again and turned sideways to control her descent. *Twenty more feet.*

"Chance, Lindsey's out cold!"

"I'm coming, baby. Almost there." She climbed over several saplings that had been bent over as the truck rolled. Pieces and parts of the vehicle were strewn from the top to where the truck rested on its roof. Chance stumbled the last few feet and dropped to her knees at the side of the truck. She grabbed her knife from her side and cut away the airbag hanging limply in the doorframe, obstructing her view. Zeus was half in the vehicle and she gently pushed him aside. "Let me in, boy." He whined but backed out and lay at the entrance. Her headlamp illuminated a terrifying sight. Jax's left leg below the knee lay at an odd angle. When Jax's face turned to her, there were tiny rivulets of blood on her face. "Your leg's broken, Jax. Try not to move around. You could be more seriously injured. I'm coming around to Lindsey's side to check on her. Sit still. Help is on the way."

"Help Lindsey. I'm fine." Jax grimaced as she tried to readjust her position.

"Like hell, you are. Sit still." Chance scrambled around the vehicle and tried to work her way around the tree the truck was pinned against to get to Lindsey. She cut away the airbag but still couldn't get access to Lindsey. The rear window was completely gone. The missing glass gave Chance ample room to scramble inside. She threw her bag inside and felt small pieces of the shattered window cutting through her uniform pants as she followed it in. Chance ordered Zeus not to follow her. "*Blijf.*" He whined, as she disappeared inside the cab.

"Chance, how are we going to get her down? She hasn't done more than moan since we came to a stop."

Chance could hear approaching sirens and prayed they'd get there soon. Her Suburban would mark the location for those incoming units.

I've got to try and cradle her head and protect her spinal integrity. Let me grab a cervical collar out of my bag." Chance felt around on the floor and found the light attached to the vehicle's headliner. She also pushed the overheads near the windshield to illuminate the cab. Now that she could see, she could better assess both women and give a report. She felt for Lindsey's carotid pulse, pounding but steady. There was a gash on the side of her face, along with a significant cut to her right arm.

Chance pulled the cervical collar from her trauma bag, deftly fitting it around Lindsey's neck, as she assessed her breathing for rate and quality. "Lindsey, can you hear me?" Chance listened, as the young woman groaned but did not offer a response. With the collar in place, Chance looked over Lindsey's body, trying to locate any other injuries. It was possible they were internal. Zeus barked, and Chance turned to see Harley in her olive-green uniform, the agony on her face clear.

"Chance, is she okay?" Harley clambered in beside Chance.

"Head wound, unresponsive to anything other than painful or verbal stimuli. If you think you can support her head and neck, I'll cut her seatbelt so we can get her on the ground back here. Being upside down with a concussion has to be causing her pain."

Tears streaked down Jax's face. "Harley, I'm so sorry. I don't know who ran us off the road."

"Jax, this isn't your fault. Whoever did this will be held accountable. Let's concentrate on getting you two out of here and to the hospital. After that, Katy bar the door."

Chance found a way to squeeze into the front cab between the bucket seats. She stopped for a few seconds to kiss Jax on the forehead. "It's going to be okay. I'm going to get you out of here."

Harley put her hands on Lindsey's shoulders while using her forearms to cradle Lindsey's head and the cervical collar. "I'm ready."

Chance braced her shoulders up against Lindsey's thighs and wrapped one arm around them in preparation to control her descent. "Here we go." Chance used her knife to slice through the seatbelt that held Lindsey in the air. Once they'd guided Lindsey down, they used the lever to lay the seat back and maneuver her into the back seat. "Harley, you're going to have to stay where you are and keep her neck in line. I need to give an update."

Harley nodded. "I'm not going anywhere. I may not have given birth to her, but she's as much my daughter as Meg is."

"She knows that too. Keep talking to her." Chance keyed her radio. "SD-1 to Comm Center."

"SD-1, go ahead."

"I've made access to the patients. There are two cruisers where the vehicle went over. Two patients, one with an obvious tib-fib fracture. Second victim has a facial laceration and is unconscious. Advise the incoming units they will need to set up a haul system to bring them up over the hill. Both patients will need to be carried up out of here in rescue baskets."

"10-4, Sheriff. You have units from Thomas and Parsons coming your way along with SR-5 and an ambulance out of Thomas."

"Thanks, Willa."

"SR-5 to SD-1."

A wash of relief flooded over Chance as Sarah's voice came across the radio. Chance was so very grateful her best friend was coming on the rescue unit.

"Sarah, I'm probably thirty feet down a steep embankment. The terrain is rough. They aren't trapped but getting them out of here is going to be a bear. Who do you have with you?"

Sarah rattled off names, further relieving Chance's building anxiety. "Okay, bleeding is controlled on patient one. I'm going to splint patient two now." Chance could hear sirens a bit closer. "Jax, can you describe anything about the bikes or riders?"

Jax gritted her teeth and nodded. "Dirt bikes. One of the guys had the same sweatshirt from the other night. I can't give you much detail other than one of them had a hay hook."

Chance leaned in and kissed her softly. "Hang in there. I'm going to get you out of here. Then cocoon you in bubble wrap and put you in my pocket until we get married."

Jax somehow managed a smile. "I might just take you up on that. I was so scared I'd never see you again."

Chance ran her fingertips over Jax's jaw. "Not ever going to happen. Let's get that leg stabilized. Sarah and the rest of the gang will be here soon." Chance watched, as Jax closed her eyes.

***

Chance paced the hallway, Zeus at her heel. She tapped her cellphone against her chin, willing it to vibrate with a text from Taylor. Her deputies and several state troopers were out searching the area of the scene for the bike and riders that Jax described. Lindsey had regained consciousness in the emergency room, with Meg at her side.

Harley had gone back out to lead the search with a promise to both her and Meg to find who did it.

Dr. Amy Halston stepped to her side. "Chance, we're spending too much time together lately."

"I really wish it was under different circumstances, though I am extremely grateful you are on duty. How is she?"

Amy put her hands in her lab coat. "The orthopedist is looking at the MRI now. If it's a simple break, he'll set it and put a cast on it. If it's more complicated, it may require surgery. Fingers crossed." She pulled her hand from her pocket and crossed her middle finger over her index.

"From your lips to God's ears. I'm going to go check in with Marty and the moms-squared. How about the next time we catch a beer over in my neck of the woods instead? Redemption's Road has great beer and music."

Amy squinted and pointed at her. "Deal. I hope she's okay; you guys have been through enough."

"Thanks again, Amy."

Chance made her way to the waiting room, Zeus following closely. Marty sat, rubbing his hands back and forth through what was left of his hair. Maggie patted the seat beside her, and Chance sat down between her mother and Marty. Dee leaned against the wall.

Maggie leaned in. "Did they tell you anything yet?"

Chance let out a slow breath. "Amy said the orthopedic doctor is taking a look now."

Marty grinned at her. "Her mother and father are on their way, should be here in a few hours. I'd leave that bulletproof vest on if I were you."

Chance groaned. "Let's hope her dad is a little more understanding."

"Mike St. Claire is a good man. The fact that he's put up with my sister all these years is a testament to his character. I've never been a fan of the way he let Jacqueline treat Jax. It was one of the things that drove her to California."

Chance ran her hands over her face. She was sure Mrs. St. Claire would put the blame squarely on her for Jax's injuries. She wasn't looking forward to seeing her after all these years. "Well, I'm certainly glad Jax didn't let it stop her from coming back."

Marty put a hand on Chance's shoulder. "It wasn't just my offer that brought her back, you know?"

Chance let a smile sneak through. "Thank God for that."

Maggie pulled Chance's hand into her own. "You let me head Jacqueline off. You concentrate on Jax and figuring out who did this. Have you gone down and talked with Megan?"

"Briefly, when she first got here. She's a wreck. Whoever did this better hope Harley gets to them before Meg or I do. They're already jumpy about the threats Leland Kur_." Chance stopped abruptly and stood, grabbing her phone and scrolling her contacts.

Dee stood up and followed her. "What is it?"

"Leland Kurst. He used to race motocross. Something has been niggling at my brain since my tires got flattened. It was a long time ago, but he won some big championship up in Pennsylvania. He was almost disqualified because his backplate had something the officials considered vulgar, a skeletal hand with fire engulfing an extended middle finger, one that closely resembles the one that assailant from the brewery was wearing. Jax said the guy that ran her over the hill was wearing that same sweatshirt as the guy from the bar. It's a longshot, but if Rick and Tess can pull up the old photo, I might have enough to get a warrant to go search their place. With the paperwork Lindsey and Jax filed, it would be one more piece of ammo to take to the judge." She found the number she was looking for and called her friends who owned the newspaper.

Rick answered the phone. "Sheriff, what can I do for you?"

"Rick, I need a favor from you and Tess. Can you check your archives and find a story about Leland Kurst? It's a motocross story and a near disqualification."

Tess had joined the conversation. "I remember that. Something about an obscene sticker. We didn't have anyone cover it, but I got some untouched photos from one of the freelance photographers from the area. It might take a while to look through the files, but we'll start searching. We'll send you anything we find. What's this about?"

Chance rubbed her eyes. On one hand, she was asking them for help, on the other, they were the media. The good thing was they were media she trusted, and in the end, she'd give them the story. "Jax and her assistant were run off the road and over the hill tonight. Both were seriously injured. I have reason to believe Leland might be involved, and heaven help him if he is. That's why I need those pictures. I can't tell you how important this is, but if it plays out, I'll have one hell of an exclusive for you."

"We'd help you even without that, Chance. We've been friends for a long time. Tess and I are so happy to see you settle down with Jax.

Give us some time and we'll find everything we can and email it to you."

"Thank you, both of you. I appreciate it. Jax's doctor is coming. I'll check in with you later."

They disconnected the call, as a tall doctor in scrubs and a lab coat walked up to her.

"Are you the family with Jax St. Claire?"

Chance nodded. "I'm her fiancée, and this is her uncle, Marty Hendricks. How is she?"

"I'm Dr. Mason. She's being prepped for surgery."

Chance clenched her fist. "Her leg is that bad?"

"We're going to set and cast the fracture. The surgery is to repair a meniscus tear discovered when we did the MRI. It's bad enough it wouldn't have healed on its own. She'll require therapy afterward, and she'll have a cast on that lower leg for at least three months."

"Are there any other major injuries?" Chance knew there was a distinct possibility serious complications might exist.

"She has some severe bruising across her chest and lower abdomen from the seat belt. When we catheterized her for surgery, we noticed some blood in the urine, likely caused by the seatbelt and the rollover. She'll be here for the next few days, so we can watch her for any other delayed injury presentations. She has a slight concussion, and we stitched up a laceration in her hairline. She's very lucky. I'll come back out after the surgery and give you an update."

Chance felt as if her heart was suspended in time. The center of her world was undergoing surgery for injuries sustained by someone with a grudge. "Thank you, doctor. We'll be here." She needed to go down to Lindsey's room and see if she felt up to answering a few questions. When Dr. Mason left, Chance felt incredibly antsy, near consumed with blinding anger. *This is my fault.* Zeus whined at her side. "I'm okay, boy. Jax is going to be fine. Mom, I need to go check in on Lindsey. Call me if they come back or Jax's parents show up. I have to do something."

Maggie placed her hands on the sides of Chance's face. "You listen to me for one minute. I know you, and no matter what's going through that thick skull of yours, this is not your fault. You will find who did this and bring them in. Jax needs you, don't go off half-cocked. You hear me?"

Dee put a hand on Chance's back. "She's right. Jax needs you to be strong. Don't make her worry about you while she's trying to get better."

"Thanks, moms-squared. You've always been the voice of reason for me."

Maggie grinned and shook her head. "Not one you've always listened to, but you've come a long way, honey. Deep breath in before you charge out of here. Give Lindsey and Meg my love."

Chance kissed both her mothers before leaving the waiting room with Zeus at her heels. With the phone in her hand, she pushed open the door to the stairs, she was too full of nervous energy to endure the elevator. She punched one of the contacts and spoke when the call was picked up. "Anything, Harley?"

"I've got a piece of plastic up on the road at what looks like a point of impact. It didn't come from the truck. It's flexible, something like a part of a motorcycle fender. It took two wreckers to get Jax's truck up. Thank God it was a newer model, my friend, that's all I'm going to say."

"I was literally sick when my headlamp hit the scene. Jax ordered all the safety equipment she could on that truck. I'm guessing we'll be going shopping again. Look, I'm on my way down to check in on Lindsey, but something that's been tapping at the back of my brain finally made its way to the front."

Chance proceeded to fill Harley in on the logo that she had her friends looking into. "We need enough evidence to get a warrant. If we can get it, the warrant will have to be pretty inclusive. The main things we're looking for is a bike that's missing a piece of its fender, a hay hook, and a black hoodie with that logo. I know in my gut it's Leland, Harley. He threatened both of them, and I'll bet my ass he's dealing the drugs that have flooded our area. He moved back home from Baltimore and has ties to a gang there. I've got a few contacts I want to get in touch with, see if they have any footage or photos of him wearing a hoodie like that."

"Damn, if we could deliver the news to Jax and Lindsey that we've nailed his ass, I couldn't think of a better get-well present. How's Jax doing?"

Chance relayed an update and pushed through a door, running directly into Faith. "I've got to go, Harley, if I hear anything from my sources, I'll call. Stay safe." Chance disconnected and pointed a finger at her ex. "I don't have the time or patience, Faith. I'm not kidding, step out of the way."

Faith crossed her arms and scowled. "I didn't think you could be a bigger ass, but you surprise me all the time. I was coming to tell you they've moved Lindsey to room 307."

Chance turned and started back through the stairway door when

Faith spoke again.

"How's Jax?"

Chance turned slowly, trying to determine the sincerity of the question or an underlying mask of intention. "She's headed to surgery. Don't try to act like you give a damn about Jax."

"My God, Chance. Drop the hostility. I'm a doctor, you know, it's part of my job to give a damn. Is there anything I can do?" Faith reached out a hand and placed it on Chance's forearm.

Chance looked down at the chilly fingers encircling her arm. "No but thank you. I've got to go."

"Chance, dammit."

"Faith, I mean it. We have nothing to talk about. I appreciate your concern, but we aren't friends or anything else. Period. You burned that bridge. You deal with being stuck on the wrong side." Chance turned and took the stairs two at a time, Zeus bounding in front of her as if it required no effort at all, until they both reached the third floor. Her phone rang, and the display indicated an incoming call from FBI Agent John Harris.

"Agent, this is Sheriff Fitzsimmons. To what do I owe the pleasure?"

"I wanted to pass on some information in reference to your inquiry about a Leland Kurst."

Chance stopped in the stairwell before opening the door, wanting privacy for the conversation. "Thanks. Anything I can use to nail this jackass would be appreciated."

"We've had him on our radar for a few years, as part of the government corruption case and RICO investigation into the Murdaland group. I'm aware that you've spoken with DEA Agent Andy Treeland. We know Leland is neck deep in midlevel trafficking and racketeering for the gang and had been watching him when he was in this area. If we can nail him on what I assume will be attempted homicide charges, then we might be able to leverage information out of him on the Murdaland gang."

Chance's frustration nearly boiled over. "He's not walking on these charges as a bargaining chip."

"Not what I meant, Sheriff. He can bargain to be closer to home for his incarceration, better facilities, visitation and the like. He'll also need protection if he rolls. Those are the carrots on the stick that we can use. Even if he doesn't talk, Murdaland will assume he did when we put him somewhere a little too nice for his convictions. So, you can see why it would be beneficial for him to cut a deal without us ever giving anything up."

"Leland Kurst has been harassing my fiancée's assistant since they were in high school together. Less than a month ago, he showed up at the clinic and verbally harassed both of them in the presence of my chief deputy. Tonight, he nearly killed both of them. He's going to jail if it takes my last breath to make it happen. What I need now is enough solid evidence to get a search warrant issued."

Zeus shuffled nervously at Chance's feet at her raised voice. Chance knew she was a jumble of nerves and needed to find the inner strength to calm herself. She stroked his head and made a conscious effort to bring it down a notch.

"Sheriff, I'm willing to give you as much information as I can so that we can both accomplish our goals. Leland isn't high enough in the chain to have intricate details. What he will have is names and small pieces of information that help us fill in the blanks leading us to the next string to pull."

"Anything that you can provide will be appreciated. I'm sorry if I'm short-tempered. I think he's connected to several overdoses we had recently, one of which was a small child who accidentally got into a stash. I want this trash out of my county."

"Then let's work together. I'll email you a link to any of our unclassified information."

"Thank you, John. I'll get back to you with anything we come across."

After disconnecting the call, she pushed through the large, steel door leading out of the stairwell and into the hallway of the third floor. Chance and Zeus strode into Lindsey's room, where Megan lay in the hospital bed holding her. Meg started to sit up, and Chance waved her back down.

"Stay where you are. If Lindsey's anything like Jax, she's freezing and scared. You are exactly where you're supposed to be. Has she remembered anything else about what happened?"

Megan ran a hand through her hair. "The only other thing else she said was that whoever they were, they busted out Jax's taillights with the hay hook. She couldn't see their faces through the motorcycle helmets they wore. You and I both suspect we know who did this."

"As a police officer, you know we have to have more than just a suspicion. That's why we are gathering evidence. Your mom is out on the scene doing just that, and I'm working sources to corroborate the suspicions we have. We'll get them, Meg, it's just going to take time. How's she doing?"

"She got sick from the head injury, they gave her some meds to settle her stomach and manage the pain. She was shivering so bad, I couldn't stand it, so I crawled in bed to hold her. She finally settled down about ten minutes ago. I wish I could be out there looking for that asshole. It's taking all I have not to go after him."

Chance put a hand on Megan's arm. "I'm right there with you, but remember this, you're getting ready to start a life together. Don't let blind rage jeopardize that. I'm trying to remember to take my own advice, and it's hard as hell. Let's do this the right way and give that slimy bastard nowhere to run and no loophole to slither out of. Deal?"

Megan lay there for a moment, and Chance watched as Lindsey snuggled closer, tightening the hold she had on Megan's shirt.

"You've got a deal, Sheriff. I make no promises if he comes after either of them again before we make that happen."

Chance nodded. "You won't be alone. Now, the two of you get some rest."

Chapter Eighteen

JAX WOKE TO THE feeling of a warm hand rubbing her arm and another holding her hand. She knew that touch and fought through the haze to squeeze back. Her eyelids felt heavy, and her throat felt like dry pine needles. She managed a croak. "Hey."

Chance kissed her hand as a tear rolled down her cheek. "Hey there. About time you woke up. I've been missing you."

"How bad am I? I don't remember much after they brought me in."

Chance ran down her list of injuries and told her the doctor would be in sometime in the morning.

"What time is it?"

"It's two in the morning. Now, do you want the bad news?"

Jax tried to clear her eyes with her other hand and cursed at the IV lines. "Great, more bad news?"

"Your mom and dad are coming. They started here last night but hit a bad thunderstorm and had to turn back. They'll be here sometime today. We'll deal with that later. How are you feeling?"

"Like I went over Blackwater Falls in a barrel. I hurt all over, and my back is killing me."

"If you could roll over, I'd rub your back, but they have your leg immobilized for tonight. The doctors were able to do a repair job on your knee and set your tib-fib fracture. You'll be wearing pink for our wedding."

Jax tried to sit up a little to see her foot. "You did not let them put a pink cast on me."

Chance chuckled. "No, you told them black, because it would end up being filthy. You have no recollection of that do you?"

Jax lay back. "None. The last time I was under anesthesia, I didn't wake up for hours. It affects me funny."

"They were pretty worried when you weren't coming out of it. You have a concussion and five stitches along your hairline as well. Before you ask, Lindsey is fine. They admitted her for observation, since she was knocked out. She's pretty bruised up and has a cut above her eye. I still can't believe you cut yourself down."

"Desperate times called for desperate measures. I needed to be able to defend us if those jackasses came over the hill. Did you catch them?"

"No, but I have a good idea who it was." Chance held up her phone and zoomed in on a photo.

Jax pointed to the screen and nearly jerked her line out. "That was on the hoodie!"

"It is, and we're getting a warrant. Mr. Leland Kurst apparently doesn't know about cameras set up at the cell tower. We've got a video of two people loading the bikes up in the back of a truck near the tower base on Backbone Mountain. We were able to pull a plate. I couldn't see his face in the video, but it's him, I know it. A security company called the 9-1-1 center about suspicious activity they saw on the cameras. Taylor caught the call and asked them to send video surveillance. You can definitely make out the logo on the sweatshirt. With the video evidence from the bar and some corroborating testimony from you both, we'll get a warrant. Once we put him behind bars, he won't ever be able to threaten either of you again."

"What if he runs?"

"Harley has officers sitting on his house, and he hasn't left. He's cocky and will believe he's too good to get caught. As soon as we get the paperwork, we'll get everyone in position before they even get out of bed."

Jax felt Chance's lips on her arm. "You promise me to be careful, all of you. No more hospital visits, we've spent too much time here lately."

"Agreed. Now, how about you go back to sleep? I'll wake you if I have to leave."

Jax yawned. "I'd rather have you in bed with me. I'm cold, and you're always like a furnace."

Chance leaned over the rail and kissed her forehead. "I'll go get you a heated blanket. Rest now."

Jax drifted and let the lingering anesthesia quiet her mind as she fell back asleep.

***

Chance stood at three thirty in the morning and stretched her neck from one side to the other in an attempt to relieve the kinks that had developed while sleeping in an awkward position. Even with a small couch provided, Chance chose to stay in the chair at Jax's side in case she needed anything. She remembered Jax doing the same for her not long ago. Twice, Jax had been forced to seek medical treatment for things that never should have happened. *I'm going to take better care of her if it's the last thing I do.* She leaned over and kissed Jax's lips softly and whispered in her ear. "I've got to go baby. I'll be back as soon as I can. Mom's coming to sit with you." She looked up to see Maggie, standing in the door with Zeus. Chance had sent him home with her earlier to be fed. "I love you, Jax, with all my heart and soul."

Jax stirred and reached up to pull her down for another kiss. "I love you, too. You and Zeus come home to me. Don't you dare leave me alone to face my mother. I mean it. I expect to see the whites of your eyes soon."

"I wouldn't dream of missing my reunion with her. Now I mean it, rest." She kissed her again and then walked to her mother.

Maggie put her hand over Chance's badge. "I'll just repeat what she said, you be safe and come home. I'll be right here. She won't be alone. Now you two get out of here. Zeus, you're in charge."

Zeus wagged his tail but didn't bark. He walked over to the bed and nuzzled Jax's hand, while Chance watched her mother check on the woman who meant a great deal to them both. Chance kissed her mother on the cheek. "Thanks, Mom. I'll be back as soon as I can. Let's go, Zeus." The dog gave Jax's hand a small lick then joined her at the door.

As soon as she'd cleared the hospital, she was on the phone with Harley. "Are we good to go as far as the warrant?"

"We are. The paperwork says we can search all areas of the barn, the house, and the three detached garages on the property. We're looking for the clothing that both Lindsey and Jax described, any hay hooks, the motorcycles, and the truck they used to transport the bikes from the area."

Chance nodded with satisfaction. "Which judge did you get to sign off?"

"The honorable Judge Arnold. It was a bit of a tough sell, even with the information from Rick and Tess. If there hadn't been bodily injuries, I'm not sure we'd have gotten it. The good thing is, we did. I've had my trooper and Taylor watching the house and all roads leading in and out of their place. All indications are that he's there. Are you on your way?"

Chance sat at a light in downtown Oakland. "I've got to stop by the house for my tactical gear. Where are we mustering?"

"I'm trying to keep this off the radar, so everyone is meeting out by the airstrip off Cortland Road. There is a maintenance garage I have access to, where we can get everyone on the same page. I've got seven officers: three of mine, plus Taylor, Khodi, Randy, and Carl with their K9s from your department, and Quade Peters and one other US Fish and Wildlife officer. With you and me, that gives us eleven."

Chance glanced at her dash clock. "It will take me another forty minutes to get to my place and get suited up. I'll send a text when I'm on my way to your location."

"We'll put an end to this, Chance."

"Let's hope we do it without any bloodshed."

***

Chance stood with Harley, leaning against the bucket of a front-end loader. They were looking over the warrant. Harley called for everyone's attention.

"Listen up. We've watched the house all night. The truck that transported the motorcycles is in the driveway, and all indications are that Leland Kurst, his father, and two brothers are there. We have no way of knowing who else might be there. All of you have had dealings with the Kursts and know they likely have some heavy-duty firearms in there. Our plan is to catch them sleeping. We've located a bench warrant on Ronny Kurst, for driving on a suspended license in Marion County. He failed to show up for court. If they located him, he'd be taken immediately into custody. A warrant search on the rest came up clean."

Chance stepped forward. "How many of you have never been inside the Kurst house?"

Only Khodi and the second US Fish and Wildlife officer raised their hands. Chance used a whiteboard to draw out the basic layout of the house. "Single story with a basement. There are three doors, one at the front, one at the back, and one that leads out of the basement. This back door leads directly into the kitchen, and there are four bedrooms back in this hallway, right off the kitchen. The front door opens into an entryway to the living room. I suggest we put a K9 at each door. Zeus and I will be on the entry team. Taylor, I want you on that back door with Midas. Randy and Vader will follow the entry team in. Carl, you and Petra take that basement door with Khodi and Echo."

Harley went through the rest of the plan and assigned entry personnel. Everyone went through a safety check on equipment and weaponry.

Harley held up the warrant. "These are the things we're looking for once we have everyone in the house secured." She passed around photos from the vandalism scene that showed the hay hook and the individual wearing the hooded sweatshirt with the logo. There were also some slightly grainy photographs from the cell tower, showing the individuals loading the bikes up. "Let's not miss anything. I don't need to tell you how serious this is. They nearly killed Jax St. Claire and Lindsey Hawthorne tonight. I don't want them to have another opportunity to finish the job. Are there any questions?"

Chance watched around the room. Officers huddled in their assigned groups, discussing plans and making sure they knew exactly what they would be doing. They wanted to conduct the warrant search before the sun came up. She wanted nothing more than to go back to the hospital with news that Leland Kurst would no longer be a threat to anyone. She was pulled from her musing by Harley telling everyone to head to their cruisers.

Harley stepped to Chance's side. "Your head on right?"

Chance grinned. "On a swivel. Let's take care of business, so you can get back to planning a wedding for your daughters, and I can go meet the in-laws to be."

"Deal." Harley patted her on the back as Taylor stepped to her side.

"Sheriff, I have orders from your mothers that you are not to come home with any broken bones, any knife wounds, any bullet holes, or concussions. You going to help me keep the promises I made?"

Chance rolled her shoulders and clenched her fists. "As long as they cooperate, it shouldn't be any problem at all."

"How's Jax?"

Chance rubbed the back of her neck. "Sore and beat up. I don't know how many times they rolled, but the truck is destroyed. What I could see of it will haunt me for years. I could have lost her, Taylor. I want his harassment to end tonight. If we can prove what I suspect, he's going to spend a very long time in federal prison. I'm positive he's involved with those overdoses, and I'm praying we find evidence of it tonight. Once we get them subdued, it's time to find those articles we're looking for. If, in the course of our search, we find evidence of narcotics, we hold the scene until we can obtain further warrants. The FBI and the DEA are both looking at him."

Taylor put her hand out and took Chance's in hers. "Good hunting, Sheriff."

***

Chance looked at the military-style tactical watch Jax had given her as a birthday present. She enjoyed the fact that Jax had taken the time to talk to Taylor and Sarah about what would be important functions, one of which she used now. The low light feature helped her maintain her cover, as they amassed around the Kurst property at two minutes before five a.m. The single-story farmhouse was unimpressive and in desperate need of repair. She watched the windows, a few of which were covered with cardboard. Shingles from the roof littered the yard and lay among the broken-down lawn equipment and disabled vehicles. Randy and Vader stood at her side as one trooper held a large shield and another a heavy battering ram. Harley stepped to her right.

"You ready to shake things up a bit?"

Chance nodded and thought of Jax lying in a hospital bed. "More than ready. Everyone is in position. This is your call."

Harley touched her throat mic. "We're a go."

The front entry team moved to the door, and exactly at five, Harley announced their presence.

"Search Warrant!"

The next few moments were total chaos as they stormed in the front and back door. Lanny Kurst was easily subdued, while Ronny made a run for the basement and was apprehended by a waiting team. Leland and Danny Kurst put up the greatest struggle. Chance chose to concentrate on Danny and leave Leland to Randy and one of the troopers, to prevent any of her personal feelings from giving Leland any cause to claim brutality. She heard Randy calling out Dutch commands for Vader and felt confident Leland would soon be in custody.

"Danny, stop fighting me! You're making this harder than it has to be. Submit, or I'll engage the dog!" Danny continued to kick and strike at her and left her no choice. "Zeus, *stellen!*"

The second Zeus sunk his teeth into Danny's arm, he screamed out in pain. "You fucking bitch! Get this dog off me!"

"Comply! Put your hands behind your back! Get on your knees!" Chance watched Danny fall to the ground and try to put his arms behind his back. He was hindered by the sixty-two-pound attack dog with his teeth sunk into his arm. Zeus, *houden!*" She told the other member of her team to subdue Danny while she found a light switch and turned it on. She could see Harley and Randy struggling with Leland, who was swinging a baseball bat with great force. Vader had gone in for a grab at

Leland's leg with the bite command that Randy gave him.

Chance leveled her Glock at Leland. "Leland, drop the bat! Drop the bat!" She felt Harley move to her side with her own gun drawn on Leland yelling the same command. It was important for them to stay out of the danger of crossfire if they were left no choice but to use deadly force.

Quade Peters came up to Chance's side with his taser gun in hand. "Drop it, Leland, or I'm going to hit you with the taser!"

Everyone watched as Vader continued to hold onto Leland, who took a swing at the dog. Randy disengaged Vader, and Quade announced the taser warning again. Leland looked directly at Chance and flipped her off. Quade pulled the trigger and shot the taser directly at his target, who dropped the bat and jerked as he fell to the floor.

Randy held onto Vader's collar, and Chance turned back to see Zeus still holding Danny in place with the sheer ferocity of his snarl and display of his teeth. Her adrenaline was running high and her heart was pounding. They needed to call EMS to have Leland checked after he was secured.

Harley grabbed her radio and called for all the officers on scene to sound off with their status. One by one, each officer advised of their status, condition, and position. Harley nodded at Chance and they bumped fists. "Well done, Sheriff."

"Job's just started. Let's find what we came for so we can give some good news to my fiancée and your daughters."

The house had been swept for anyone else present during the initial entrance and again after all four individuals were moved to the living room and cuffed. Randy and Vader, along with two very large troopers, guarded the individuals in custody. They began to systematically search the house, room by room. Every drawer and cabinet that might hold a hay hook was opened, and every article of clothing examined for the distinctive sweatshirt. Other officers were busy conducting a search out in the garage and storage shed.

Taylor moved a chair to the closet and began pulling items from the top. She turned and handed a leather saddlebag to Chance. "Odd spot for a motorcycle bag, don't you think?"

Chance slid the strap out of the buckle. "With these guys, nothing would surprise me." When she opened the flap, her blood boiled. "Pay dirt, at least on one item." She held a hay hook in her gloved right hand, praying to find chips of paint from Jax's truck on the end. "Now, if I find the bike and the fucking sweatshirt, I'll bury him under the jail."

Taylor jumped down. "We can dig two spots, one for him and one for Brad."

"I'm with you there as well. Okay, let's find the rest." Chance and Zeus continued to search the room.

Khodi called from the basement. "Sheriff?"

"On my way, Khodi. Keep looking, Taylor." Chance walked through the living room on the way to the basement stairs. Sarah was walking in with her Lifepack 10 to take an electrocardiogram on Leland.

Sarah pointed at Chance. "You okay?"

"I'm good, make sure he'll live to see the judge."

"You got it."

Chance hurried down the steps to find Khodi back in a corner of the basement with Quade.

"Sheriff, I don't know what's behind this panel, but Echo is giving a passive alert to drugs." Khodi pointed to Echo, who was making the same indications he'd done when they'd been at the overdose in Davis. Zeus had joined him in the alert position, indicating narcotics.

Chance looked around the room, noting the dimensions. The basement seemed like it didn't span the entire length of the upstairs structure. It seemed to be at least a third smaller. She needed to proceed with caution as the warrant they'd obtained did not mention the search for any drugs. She nodded to Zeus, who swished his tail at her and let out a sharp bark. "Good boy, Zeus. Good boy, *blijven*." She gave him the command to stay and pointed to a wall of junk and scuff marks on the floor in front of it.

"You know, in my grandmother's house, she had a cold storage area that was little more than an area dug into the soil to put potatoes, onions, and her home-canned goods. She called it her root cellar, and it had some outside ventilation from a pipe. This house is about the same age. Wanna make a bet there's one of those behind that junk somewhere?" Chance looked at Carl, who had just come down the stairs with his dog Petra.

"Sheriff, you know what that means." Carl pointed to his K9, who was trained in explosive recognition.

"I do. Let's get everyone out of here. We may need to call out some specialized troops. Unless I miss my bet, behind all of it is some kind of door. Don't use your radios. I need to find Harley."

Carl nodded. "You got it, Sheriff."

Chance made it upstairs and located the supervising trooper. "Harley, we need to get everyone out of here. Petra hit on some kind of explosives in the basement.

"Shit. Everyone out." Harley waved her arms toward the door.

Chance agreed. "I've got two dogs in the basement alerting on narcotics, and Petra alerting for explosives. I told them to leave everything in place, not to move anything. We still haven't found the sweatshirt or the second hay hook. Can you call your bomb squad guys in to check this out, before we start digging around and trigger something?"

Harley wiped a hand over her face. "Good Lord. Yeah, I can do that. It shouldn't take Micah that long to get over here. Get everyone out to the property edge. I need to check on a few things."

Once they were all outside, Chance checked with Sarah. She was just removing the pads from Leland's chest. "Sarah, tell me he's well enough that he doesn't need to go to the hospital."

"His vitals are stable, and his EKG is normal. Jax okay?" Sarah continued to pack up her gear.

"She will be now. Harley, I need to talk to you. Can you step over here with me a second?" They stepped away from the group in custody. "Sarah said Leland is fine for now, but I think we should run him by the ER to be checked. That way he can't come back and say we didn't give him medical attention. I don't think it's worth a trip in an ambulance, so someone needs to drag his sorry ass over there in a cruiser."

Harley nodded her agreement. "With these guys, you can't be too cautious. Once we get that done, we can question him. Don't be surprised if he lawyers up."

"I'd say count on it. If he's in as deep as I think he is, his buddies in Baltimore aren't going to be very happy about his recent activities. We need to be able to tie the bike to him directly. Let's make sure whatever we charge him with, it's ironclad."

"And welded."

Harley started punching in a number on her cellphone, as Chance sent a text to her mother.

Raid is over, suspects in custody. No injuries. Tell Jax I love her and will be back as soon as I can.

"My bomb tech will get his equipment and be here in thirty minutes. I need to call the judge and make sure we don't screw anything up. If we find drugs, I want the charges to stick. Two dogs trained in separate facilities showing indicators of narcotics is pretty strong evidence. If that is a root cellar, it could be big enough to hold a bike and the drugs. The law says we can enter or open anything large enough to hold what we're searching for. I need to make sure the judge agrees on the basement. On the bright side, take a look at this." Harley held out the camera. The display showed a motorcycle missing a piece of its fender. "They found it behind a stack of hay bales, under a tarp in the garage."

"You don't say." Chance turned to Leland and narrowed her eyes. "I'm not leaving until we get in that space. The icing on the cake, for me, would be finding that sweatshirt with his DNA on it and flecks of paint from a demolished Toyota. I want nothing more than to be able to hand his ass over to Huttonsville on a silver platter."

Harley held up the warrant. "Then let's make sure we do this right."

Chapter Nineteen

FORTY MINUTES PASSED BEFORE Trooper Micah Livingston showed up. He swept the basement with sensors and looked for any trip wires or booby traps. The junk in front of the door was carefully removed. All that was left was to cut the lock and open the door. They didn't know what was behind the peeling paint but were concerned enough with Petra's signal of explosives that they were taking extraordinary precautions. Chance and Khodi helped Micah dress in his 'turtle' suit, while Harley worked the phones and confirmed their right to pursue their current course of action. The bomb protection suit could absorb a great deal of concussive force but offered no guarantee of survival. Micah was a tall, quiet, lion of confidence who'd done two tours in Iraq on an explosive ordnance disposal squad. He brought those EOD skills with him when he left the army to pursue his law enforcement dreams. Chance helped him put on the heavy Kevlar arm protectors.

"We've got the go-ahead from Judge Arnold." Harley held Micah's helmet in her hands. "Okay, get everyone out of here. Is the fire department on scene?"

Chance nodded. "They are. We've got everyone inside individual cruisers."

Harley placed Micah's helmet on and tapped his head. "You good to go?"

"I am, Sergeant. You guys get clear. I've got the throat mic on, so you'll hear everything. This camera is set up so you watch too. Let's see what's behind door number one."

They left Micah and made their way outside the house and a safe distance away. Harley's commander from Elkins had joined the group, and they were using Micah's bomb truck as a command post to see the monitors. "All his radio and video equipment is intrinsically safe, meaning it won't set anything off. A second technician is on standby if, after entry, Micah needs assistance."

They watched. Micah cut the padlock and removed it from the hasp.

Chance had put Zeus back in her cruiser for his safety and stood beside Harley with her arms crossed, staring intently at the screen. "This is freaking nerve-wracking."

Harley nodded her agreement. "That's why it takes a steady hand like Micah has. Guy's got nerves of steel. I've stared down madmen with guns, but I couldn't do what he's doing."

They watched Micah stand to the side and use a long, fiberglass pole to open the door and push it out of the way. The helmet cam and light he used clearly illuminated the four-by-ten room. One side was lined with shelves of canned goods. The other side held the pay dirt.

"Sergeant, are you seeing what I'm seeing?"

Harley clicked her mic. "Are those pipe bombs?"

The camera view shifted up and down. "If they aren't, they certainly look like it. That's not all, check this out." They saw brightly colored spools. "Pretty sure that's primer cord, and these are certainly blast caps. I think I've found what you were looking for when you stumbled on this." Micah pointed his camera to two black sweatshirts, with the skeleton-hand logo. Motorcycle helmets, gloves, and a red hay hook sat at the end of a table.

Chance grabbed the mic. "Are you finding anything that looks like narcotics?"

The camera angle changed again. "I've got a set of scales, cutting material, and some kind of short straws. There are a ton of handguns. I'm looking at two AK-47s, with hundreds of rounds."

Chance grabbed her cellphone and called her newest deputy. "Khodi, can you come over to the command vehicle for a minute?" She hung up and began to fume. *I've got you, you son of a bitch.*

Khodi appeared, his hands holding the neckline of his bulletproof vest. "What do you need me to do, Sheriff?"

Chance pointed to the screen. "See anything familiar?"

Khodi leaned in and closely examined the images being shown on the computer screen. "Mother fucker. Those look like those pixie stick straws we found up on Fairfax Avenue, where that little boy overdosed."

"That was my observation as well. I think we just found our dealer. Harley, this thing just blew up."

Harley winced. "Bad choice of words, my friend, given my trooper is in there with a bunch of what we assume are illegal explosives."

"Shit. Sorry."

Micah called over the radio. "I'm going to put these pipe bombs in a blast bucket. That will let you guys get down here and collect some evidence. I don't want you guys moving around in here until I render them safe. Can someone grab the other can and bring it to the bottom of the stairs? I don't want to put them all in one."

Khodi spoke up. "I'll take it."

Harley moved up in the truck and handed Khodi the can. They watched him enter the house and eventually heard Micah tell him to leave it and get back outside before he started. For the next twenty minutes, they watched him delicately move materials off the shelves and into combustion chambers.

"Okay, I think we're safe to look at everything. You guys can come back in." Micah called to them.

Chance let out a long sigh. There were genuine reasons to be concerned for Micah's safety. Within minutes, they'd reached him and helped him take off the heavy and stifling suit.

Harley handed him a large Gatorade and a towel soaked in ice water. "Nice job, Micah."

"Thanks, Sarge."

Chance moved into the room and used her flashlight to illuminate the bench. A trooper entered with her and began cataloging evidence. She watched, as he held up the sweatshirt with the skeletal hand graphic. "No, Leland, fuck you."

Harley leaned in the door. "I couldn't have said it better myself."

Chance stepped out of the small space and allowed Randy to enter with his test kit. He swiped the scale and inserted the detection strip in the box where the chemical reaction would help them identify the substances. Within a few minutes, he held the screen over in front of Chance.

"It's heroin laced with fentanyl. Looks pretty similar to what we found with those multiple overdoses during Leaf Peepers."

Rage bubbled through Chance. On two separate occasions, Leland's actions had endangered the woman she loved. She needed to remove herself now, before there could be any question of compromised evidence. Quade stood with a digital video camera in hand.

Harley placed a hand on her back. "Get out of here, Chance. I've got this. Jax is waiting on you, and if I remember right, you said you're meeting the in-laws. It's eight in the morning. I don't know what time they'll get there, but you might want to shower and clean up. First impressions are important."

Chance sighed. "I can't argue, but a shower isn't likely to make a difference. Her mother has disliked me since I was eighteen. I doubt smelling good will change that, but I'll feel better. Thanks for everything,

Harley. I mean it."

Harley looked at Chance long and hard. "No thanks needed. We did this for both of them. I'm hoping this will be the end of it, and they can have some peace."

Chance shook Harley's hand. "From your lips to God's ears."

***

Once Chance made it home, she tended the horses and Zeus, showered, and put on a clean uniform. It was likely she'd need to attend to official business later in the day. She loaded a travel mug with coffee and sent her mother a text asking her to let Jax know she was on her way.

"*Laden*, Zeus." Her K9 partner assumed his position and the two headed back in the direction of Garrett Memorial. A million things were going through Chance's mind as she sipped her coffee. She'd broken down in the shower, allowing herself the realization of how close she'd come to losing Jax again. It reminded her of how Jax must have felt when she'd been in the shootout. *Christmas can't come soon enough.* The wedding they were planning seemed like eons away. In reality, it was only a few months. Maybe they were waiting too long. Maybe they shouldn't wait another day. *No, Jax wants this wedding, and moms-squared would kill me.* Their plans were simple but meaningful. Chance couldn't imagine a better Christmas present. They had no plans to go away for a honeymoon, needing only the finality of their commitment and their first night at home as a married couple.

Chance listened to traffic over her radio as the miles of blacktop that separated her and Jax receded with every minute. Chance wasn't looking forward to seeing Jax's mother again. She'd never met Mr. St. Claire, though Jax spoke of him fondly. When she pulled into the parking lot, she was relieved to see Momma D's vehicle parked beside Maggie's. She'd known three incredible parents, first her father, then the two women who had made her who she was today. Some might not think so, but Chance counted herself incredibly blessed.

Chance left Zeus in the air-conditioned and monitored vehicle. He needed some rest, and she wanted to remove some of the intimidation factors for this first adult meeting with Jax's parents. There would be enough tension, and Zeus tended to ramp that up just with his presence. She pushed through the doors of the hospital and ran into the last person she truly needed to see, Faith. She closed her eyes for a moment. "Lord, give me strength. And patience, buckets of patience, please."

Faith held her hands up. "Truce, I promise. They're releasing Lindsey. I promised Megan I'd check in with her later this evening after I get off shift. Their place is only about a mile from mine. I looked in on Jax and she's resting comfortably. All her tests look good, Chance. She's going to be okay."

"Thank you, Faith. I'm on my way up to her now."

"I know, I just saw Maggie and she told me you were on your way in. That's why I waited here. I wanted to talk to you for a few minutes if you'll grant me that."

Chance squeezed her temples with her right hand. "Faith, it's been a long night. I just got off a pretty tense situation, and I really need to see Jax. If what you want to talk with me about is a single word about us getting back together, then no, I don't have a spare minute. Honestly, this isn't the best time at all. Jax's parents are coming this morning, and I need to be there for her."

Faith let out a long sigh and looked up. Chance saw tears forming in her eyes. "I just want a little of your time. I understand not today, but sometime this week. Can we have lunch? No expectations, I promise. We used to be friends. I could really use one of those right now."

Chance gritted her teeth and clenched her jaw. "I'll call you later this week when I see what's going on with Jax. No promises to the lunch, but I will call. Jax is going to be immobile for a bit. Have no doubt that she's my first priority."

Faith nodded, then turned and walked down a hallway. "She always has been."

Chance shook her head in frustration and walked over to the stairwell, too impatient to wait for the elevator and needing the physical exertion to calm herself some before seeing Jax. By the time she'd reached Jax's floor, she'd cleared her mind of the encounter. Her boots squeaked on the tile when she passed the janitor mopping. "Sorry, I'll try not to mess up your clean floor."

"It's all right ma'am. Twenty minutes from now, a herd of people will come through here after you. We just try to keep it as clean as we can. Have a good day."

"You do a great job. Thank you." Chance offered the man a handshake. He beamed and wiped his palm over his uniform before accepting.

"You're welcome. Stay safe, Sheriff."

Chance knew that the service personnel were rarely thanked, and she took it upon herself to let them know that they were an important part of what made being here a little better for everyone. At the door to Jax's room, she paused and settled herself. Once inside, she observed the three women she loved. Maggie sat on the couch, with Dee asleep against her. Jax lay in the bed. Her face was slightly bruised and swollen. Her leg was elevated. Chance sat down beside Jax and took her left hand. She kissed her finger beside the ring she'd placed there.

Jax stirred beside her. "Hey. I'm so glad to see you."

Chance sat back and pointed to her chest. "No holes."

Jax chuckled. "Good to know. Zeus okay?"

"He is. I left him in the SUV to take a nap. How are you feeling?"

Jax sighed. "You want an honest answer?"

"Humor me with the truth, though I'm betting I know the answer."

"I hurt everywhere." Jax pointed to the IV pump beside her. "They gave me a pain pump, but all it does is make me sleep."

Maggie spoke softly. "That's because sleeping right now isn't a bad thing. You should try it every once in a while. It does wonders for this one's disposition." She pointed to Dee, who snuffled and moved closer into her shoulder.

Jax tipped her head. "You know that's us in twenty years."

Chance shook her head. "I don't drool like that."

"I do not drool," Dee grumbled.

"You do dear, but it's only one of the things I love about you." Maggie kissed Dee's head.

"Good thing, the paperwork says you're stuck with me." Dee drew Maggie's arm around her tighter.

Jax squeezed Chance's hand tighter. "How'd it go? Any luck?"

Chance put her forehead against Jax's hand. "We found what we were looking for, and a whole lot more. Harley's handling it. Nothing for you or Lindsey to worry about. Oh, by the way, I heard she's going to be released."

Jax sighed. "I'm so relieved. I don't know if I could have survived if something happened to her. This whole thing is so surreal. One minute we are inoculating goats, and the next we're in the tumble cycle of a Toyota clothes dryer. I'm just relieved we both survived."

The door pushed open, and someone entered the room behind Chance.

"Yes, that is comforting to know, though how you got yourself in this condition is still a question to me."

Chance turned at the new voice. An older version of Jax moved to the foot of the bed with a man two inches taller right behind her. Jacqueline looked at her daughter with more than just concern in her eye. There was an air of disgust that angered Chance. She stood to take exception to the tone of Mrs. Jacqueline St. Claire. "She didn't do this to herself."

Jax tugged at Chance's hand, pulling her closer.

Jacqueline glared at Chance. "I see you are still getting my daughter into things she shouldn't be in. Typical."

Chance felt Jax tighten her grip. "Understand one thing, Mrs. St. Claire, nothing you say or do will change how I feel about your daughter. For once, how about you see her for who she is, not who you wanted her to be. I do, and that's permanent. This time we're old enough to not need your approval."

Chapter Twenty

JAX TRIED TO CLEAR her mind of the lingering drugs. The woman who held her heart was defending her to the woman who'd given birth to her. "Mom, if this is what you came here to do, you could have saved the trip and left me a voicemail. Chance is no more responsible for my injuries than you are. The man who did this is in custody, thanks to the woman I love. My God, you drove three hours, walked in, and I already wish you were gone."

"Jacqueline Elizabeth St. Claire, how dare you talk to me like this."

Jax chuckled. "Oh, just wait, I'm still doped up. When I have a clear head, I'll have plenty more to say."

Jax watched as a large hand grabbed her mother's shoulder and turned her around. Her father's normally tan and shiny forehead was beet red.

"I'm only going to say this once. Jacqueline St. Claire, if you can't be civil to our only daughter, then you can wait outside. Not one more word. I mean it. Don't test me on this."

Jax was stunned. In her entire life, she'd never heard her father raise his voice to her mother. She saw Chance relax slightly and was relieved when Maggie stood.

"Jackie, it's good to see you. It's been too long. Seems like only yesterday we were running around in my Belaire." Maggie placed a hand on Jax's arm.

Jax saw her mother visibly blanch. There was more to this story, and eventually, she'd find it out.

"Margarette, thank you for being here for my daughter. I'm sure she appreciates your concern. I'm here now, and I'll make sure she has what she needs."

Jax watched the exchange between the two women. Two forces of nature, one destructive, one a confident diplomat.

Maggie smiled. "I'm sure Jax is glad to have all of us with her during this time. If Jax needs anything, I have no doubt my daughter will make sure she has it. They're completely capable of caring for one another without us. Mike, it's good to see you as well."

"Maggie, it's been a very long time. Nice to see you too, Dee."

Dee stretched and stood to come by Chance's side with a hand on her shoulder. Mike reached out to shake Dee's free hand. "Far too long. How's retirement treating you?"

Jax took in the conversation. There was something far too familiar about the group's dynamics. She hadn't put a finger on it yet, but Dee and her mother had yet to speak.

"Jackie, seems you haven't changed a bit in fifty years. Still carrying the weight of the world and refusing to bend." There was something in Dee's deep voice.

"Dee Ann."

Jax's pulse raced, and the monitor she was hooked to showed it. Jax's mother stared at her, and it took everything Jax had not to laugh. She could see it as plain as day. Something had happened between the three women years ago. The other thing that was plainly evident was that her mother still wasn't over it.

Chance stared at the monitor and creased her brow at Jax. "Are you okay?"

Jax let a small smile cross her face for her lover. "Oh yeah, I'm just fine." Jax watched her mother fiddle with her pearls and fidget uncomfortably. "Uncle Marty will be here around ten. I told him not to jump up this morning. How was your drive? I heard you had a storm last night."

Jax's father put a hand on her uninjured foot. "We had hail the size of golf balls and were under a tornado watch for a while. I wanted to get to you, but the weather was just too bad."

Jax smiled at her father, as she watched her mother fuss with things on her bed table. "I'd rather you have started out in the daylight. I was out for most of the night after surgery anyway. I'm fine, though a little hobbled."

Her father smiled, though stress lines worried his forehead. "How bad was the break?"

"She broke the tibia and fibula," Chance answered. "The doctor said she'll heal with time but will need therapy."

Mike St. Claire held out his hand. "Chance, it's nice to finally meet you. I've said it before, but congratulations. I'll be proud to call you my daughter-in-law soon. It will be good to talk shop someday."

"Thank you, sir, and I agree. I promise to make her happy and take care of her." Chance blushed.

Jacqueline slapped the table. "Yes, and you've done a stellar job of that so far. In the last two months, she's been in the hospital for an accidental overdose and now a car wreck where someone ran her off the road. And let's not even mention the kidnapping of my brother. Yes, you're doing an outstanding job of protecting and serving," Jacqueline St. Claire quipped.

Jax could not believe her mother's callous nature. Blaming Chance for everything that had happened was out of line. "Mother!"

Dee took two steps toward Jax's mother. "Jackie, you will not talk to my daughter like that. Chance would die for Jax and go to the ends of the earth for her happiness. You've spent your life trying to keep them apart and for what? A vendetta against me?"

"Oh yes, Dee Ann, this is all about you. Jax is my daughter, and I'll never be happy to see her tied to your dysfunctional family."

Maggie stepped directly into Jacqueline's sight. "This isn't about Dee or Chance, is it Jackie? If you have something to say about my family, you address it to the person you really have the issue with, me. Now, everyone else can keep walking on eggshells to kiss your ass, but I won't do it a single second more. Despite your best efforts, Jax and Chance found their way back to each other. They'll soon be married, and there isn't a damn thing you can do about it. Both of them are adults, capable of making their own decisions. This is a long time to carry a torch, Jackie. You've run out of oil, and the wood has burnt down to your fingers. Let it go and be proud of the family you made. My God, you're an obstinate woman. Always trying to make things into what you wanted them to be, even when life chose another path. You have a wonderful husband and daughter, and yet, you insist on making them feel inadequate. To what end? For what, Jackie?" Maggie covered her mouth with her hand, and walked over to Dee, burying her face in her wife's neck.

Dee wrapped her arms around Maggie. "Come on, honey. Let's go take a walk."

Jax sat stunned by the scene before her. Without her mother explaining any of the exchange, everything made sense. The adamancy that she stay away from Chance, the hesitancy to allow her to visit her aunt and uncle where her mother grew up, and the constant frown that came over her mother's face whenever the Fitzsimmons name was brought up. It all had a reason. There was a history there, one long ago hidden, buried beneath years of animosity. Jax would find out the truth, if not from her mother, from Maggie.

"Mother, care to explain?"

Jacqueline St. Claire huffed as she straightened the covers on Jax's bed. "I'll do no such thing."

Jax looked to Chance, whose wide eyes told her she didn't have a clue either. Jax sighed and looked to her dad. "Pretty obvious you aren't a casual observer in this. How about you telling me what the hell is going on?"

"It's not my story to tell, honey. How long did the doctors say you'd be in here?"

Jax was becoming more agitated by the moment, with her family's insistence on keeping her in the dark. "I'm not sure. I'm hoping I'll be out at least by tomorrow. Are you going back today or staying?"

Her mother stepped closer to the head of the bed. "We'll be staying at Martin's. I wouldn't presume to stay at a house I haven't been invited into."

The man who'd always acquiesced to his wife's every mood and wish stood up straight as he walked over to her mother. "That is enough. I will take you home and leave you there if you don't start acting like a mother that puts her child first."

Rage showed all over the older woman's face. "How dare you talk to me like that, Michael? I am your wife."

Jax watched with rapt fascination at the conversation. Her father was not one to stand up to her mother.

Mike St. Claire nodded. "Yes, you are, and this is our only child."

"We have Jackie and—"

"Those are our grandchildren." Mike moved his finger between the two of them. "We brought Jax into this world. I've always been grateful we were still in good enough shape to keep up with the two children we tragically had to raise. Our son and daughter-in-law should have been here to do that. I'm beyond proud of Jax and the woman she's become, despite being our daughter. It's about damn time you were too. Now, if you persist in being opposed to those she's chosen to have in her life, then keep your mouth shut about it. I lost decades with her when she was in California."

Tears ran out of Jax's eyes, listening to her father and mother argue. On the one hand, she'd never been so happy to hear how proud her father was of her, and then there was her mother. She was incredibly tired of being a disappointment and of feeling like it should still matter.

"Dad, it's okay. I'm the great disappointment in her life. That will never change. I didn't act the way she wanted, become who she wanted me to be, and I won't be spending the rest of my life with someone she approves of. It's completely exhausting feeling like she would have been happier if I'd not been born. I'm always going to fall short, and it's time I stopped giving a damn about it."

Chance leaned down and held her face close to Jax's. She whispered to her, "You matter to me. My parents love you, and so do yours. They just have a strange way of showing it, though it seems your dad is done being a doormat. Maybe change is on the horizon."

Jacqueline faced the window with her back to Jax. "I approved of Lacey. She was from a family of refinement. Once you made a life with her, I never questioned your choices. That is until you left her."

Jax laughed so hard, she felt pain in her ribs and clutched at the bedsheets. "Oh, that hurts. Don't make me laugh. Refinement, that's a joke. You were happy with their social status and money. The fact that Lacey regularly had affairs with other women meant nothing to you. Fidelity apparently isn't listed in the Montgomery family creed. I was never so alone in my life than when I was married to her. By the way, to most of her family, I didn't make the grade, and neither did you. My family didn't come from old money, and the daughter of a blue-collar worker was beneath what they expected for Lacey. Face it, Mother, for once you weren't good enough for someone. Spare me the adoration for the Montgomerys. I'm tired, and my leg hurts like someone is sawing through it with a dull knife." She reached for her pain pump and pushed the button.

Her mother took a seat on the couch across the room. "Yes, I suggest you rest. I've called Lacey, and she wants to come and see you. Why she still cares is beyond me."

Jax sat straight up, horror and anger bubbling to the surface. The morphine was quickly taking effect, and Jax squeezed Chance's hand as she screamed at her mother. "Get out! Get out and don't come back. Adopt Lacey if you want, but she is no longer part of my life. I never want to see her again!" Drowsiness forced her to lay back, as tears flowed down her cheeks. "Chance, make her leave, please. Daddy, please." Sleep overtook her as she heard her father address her mother.

"Only you would bring even more pain to our daughter, only you."

***

Chance closed her eyes in pure shock at Jax's mother. Many things over the years had caused her agony. The burns paled in comparison to what she felt watching Jax's distress. Jax had asked her to get her mother out of there, and that is what she'd do. Chance leaned over and kissed Jax's temple. "Sleep, love. I'll take care of it."

Mike walked over and grabbed his wife's hand. "I knew bringing you would be a mistake. I just didn't know how much. You called Lacey? That woman broke our daughter's heart by sleeping with other people, including their staff. Your logic escapes me, Jacqueline. Get up."

Chance watched Jax's mother pull her hand from her husband's grasp. "You will not manhandle me, Michael. She's my daughter, and I'll leave when I'm ready to go. Not a minute before."

Chance walked closer to where Jax's mother sat. "That's where you're wrong, Mrs. St. Claire. I can, and will, have you removed."

Jacqueline looked at her, indignation written all over her face. "You might be the sheriff of Tucker County, but unless I'm mistaken, we are in Maryland. I doubt you have any authority."

"Oh, I have plenty of ways of making you leave. The first of which is to call Jax's doctor and advise her that your presence is causing her patient stress. Secondly, I can contact security, and have you escorted out of here on Jax's request made to a sworn officer of the law. If all that fails, I'll personally pick you up and place you outside this door as her fiancée and medical power of attorney. So which authority would you like me to use to accomplish what Jax asked? Which, in case you missed it, was to get you out of here."

Mike walked over to Jax and kissed the top of her head. "I'm sorry, Jibber Jack." He held up a hand in Chance's direction. "None of that will be necessary. My wife's leaving now and not coming back. I'm sorry, Chance. Tell her I love her and will be back later." Mike walked over and put a hand under his wife's elbow and pulled her up. "We are going now. I'm taking you to Martin's, and you're going to stay there. I'll be coming back to try and fix your meddling. I suggest you use that phone of yours to make another call to Jax's ex-wife and tell her she isn't welcome here so save the trip. If you choose not to do that or not to stay at Martin's, you can also find your own way home. I'm done with this, Jacqueline. Now move, before I let Chance exercise one of those options."

Chance stood by in stunned silence, as Mike escorted the shocked woman out the door. Something told her that life had irrevocably shifted for the unhappy woman. Chance had another problem to solve, an unwanted visitor who would also likely cause her lover pain. *Not a chance in hell I'm letting that happen.* She followed the couple out into the hall and turned to watch them make their way toward the elevators.

Chance caught sight of her parents. "You guys need to go home, get some rest. I'm fine, and I'll call with a progress report later. Thanks for being here. You've never let me down."

Maggie wrapped her arms around Chance and squeezed as she spoke softly in her ear. "I know you have questions. When things settle down, Dee and I will answer them. Until then, take care of our girl. Do you want me to take Zeus? He can't sit in the car all day."

Chance nodded. "Here's the spare key. Just lock it up after you get him."

Dee hugged her next. "All in good time, Five Points, all in good time."

As Chance watched them walk away, she saw Mike take Jacqueline's arm. Jacqueline tried to break Mike's hold, but he grabbed her hand again and began tugging her down the hall. She turned and glared at Chance.

"This isn't over, Chance Fitzsimmons, not by a longshot."

"This is the last thing she needs." Chance pushed open the door to Jax's room and returned to her side. "Not on my watch."

***

Jax lay in the hospital bed, once again fighting through the drugs. She had no idea how long she'd been out. The dull thumping in her leg told her long enough for her last shot of morphine to start waning. A thumb brushed over the top of her hand. She cautiously opened her eyes, anxious as to who she would see in the chair beside her bed. Chance's concerned blue eyes brought a rush of relief.

"Hi."

Chance rose and kissed her lightly. "Hey there. I missed you."

Jax smiled. "I was having a wonderful dream. We were riding out to the bluff, snow all around us."

"Sounds like our wedding."

"Might have been."

Chance smiled. "We've still got some planning to do. Kendra's coming in tonight. She wants to drop by with Brandi and see you."

Nodding, Jax tried to adjust herself in the bed and grimaced at the pain.

Chance stood and helped adjust the pillows. "Do you need to hit your pain pump again?"

"Not unless my mother or ex is walking through that door." Jax glance at Chance. "They aren't, are they?"

Chance tilted her head from side to side. "Not walking through the door, but not far from it. I have no idea if your mother called your ex and told her not to come."

"With Mother, I thought nothing could surprise me. This did. The last time I checked, I'm an adult who can see or refuse to see whomever I want. I have no desire to be around either of them ever again. I'm still in shock over Dad. It's so unlike him to overrule Mother."

"He did and in a big way."

Jax sat stunned while Chance relayed what happened outside her room. She wasn't shocked at her mother's arrogance. The last thing she wanted to do was argue with anyone in her weakened condition.

"And don't worry. If either comes through that door, they'll promptly be escorted back out until you tell me differently. Consider me your personal protection detail."

"Never felt safer in my life. Now, tell me what happened on the raid this morning."

For the next ten minutes, Chance caught her up on the particulars. Currently, the entire Kurst family, minus the grandfather who was in a nursing home, were residents of Huttonsville Correctional Facility.

"We also found packaging material and heroin that appears to be of similar makeup to the drugs from our mass overdose calls during the festival. It will take more testing at the state crime lab to see if it's an exact match. I got a text from Harley, twenty minutes ago, with the latest update. I don't think we are going to be worrying about the Kursts for a long time."

Jax sighed in audible relief. She'd been so worried about what Leland would try next. She didn't want Lindsey to go through one more minute of the man's harassment. "Lindsey and Megan have to be relieved. They've suffered enough with him."

"Harley was more than happy to give them that news. Lindsey is doing fine. She's at home resting. She said to get better soon."

Jax stiffened at a knock on the door. She moved her gaze to the thick wooden barrier. Chance got up to see who it was and let in Uncle Marty. He approached the bed, still limping a bit from his ordeal earlier in the summer.

He leaned over the bed rail and kissed her temple. "Hey, kitten. It's good to see you awake. I've been busy hog-tying your mother, or I'd have been here sooner."

Jax looked at the man she was extremely fond of. "You shouldn't have to do that, but if you can keep her away from me, I'll feed you for a month of Sundays."

"It's a deal, even without the meals. She's none too happy with me or your daddy right now. Came into my house and kept wiping her hands every time she touched anything."

"Doc, you need me to remove her from your place?" Chance shifted from her position and came to stand beside him.

Marty waved his hand. "No need. Ten minutes after she got there, she made a reservation for herself at Canaan Valley Lodge. Your daddy is staying at my place."

Jax held his hand, her head swimming with regret and anger. "I'm so sorry, Uncle Marty. When I get out of here, my mother and I are having a little talk. If Lacey shows up, she can get back on a plane and fly west. I've said all I need to when it comes to her."

Marty patted her hand. "You concentrate on getting out of here. The rest will keep. I'm not going to stay long. I'm covering the clinic for emergencies. Before you fuss at me, I know what I'm doing. I've asked Dr. Kester from over in Elkins to help out if it's something I can't handle. Get some rest, and I'll be back later tonight. I love you, kitten. Stop scaring an old man, will ya?"

Jax kissed his hand. "I will if you will?"

He stood and kissed her cheek. "Deal."

Uncle Marty left, and Chance took her seat beside Jax again.

"It's making him feel useful."

Jax sighed. "I know, but he retired for a reason. Lindsey isn't there to help him."

"He called his former secretary. She agreed to come in and help keep track of what they do. He can't use your computer system, but together they'll cover the emergencies. Anything else can wait."

Chance's cellphone rang. "It's Mom."

Jax nodded and listened as Chance told her that Jax was awake. Chance looked to her and asked if it was okay if Maggie and Dee came to visit. Jax nodded, and Chance hung up. A few seconds later, there was another knock on the door. Chance got up to admit Maggie and Dee. Jax could see the distress on Maggie's face. Jax held a hand up to beckon the woman she cared deeply about to come closer.

"Come over here for a minute. I promise, I don't bite."

Maggie chuckled as she sat down. Dee stood behind her, with her hands resting on her wife's shoulders. Maggie tilted her head. "I imagine you have questions."

"More than I likely have the stamina to stay awake for. How about you give me the CliffsNotes version now, and we fill in the finer details later?"

Chance put a hand on her mother's arm. "Mom, are you all right?"

Maggie looked at Chance and nodded. "This should have come out a long time ago. Dee and I always felt that, without Jacqueline's consent, it wasn't right for us to speak for her."

Jax furrowed her brow. "I don't understand."

"Jax, you know that Dee and I went to school together. Jacqueline was older than us. We all used to be very good friends and spent a great deal of time together. Your Uncle Martin was a few years older still. I've always known I was a lesbian, even when it wasn't accepted the way it is now. It was difficult in those days. I was harassed, because I wouldn't go out with the captain of the basketball team, or at least not the captain of the men's team."

Dee grinned and pulled on the chain around Maggie's neck, revealing a vintage, high school pendant. "She was too busy dating the captain of the women's team."

Jax couldn't help but smile. Maggie and Dee had been together since high school, and the love between the two of them was clearly evident. Part of her realized that she and Chance could have done the same if not for her mother's meddling. "And my mom was in this mix how?"

"My sophomore year, I started to see jealousy from your mother. I thought it was because Frank, the aforementioned basketball captain, was trying to get me to go to the prom with him. Your mother always seemed to have her eyes on him. A group of us girls decided we weren't going with any boys. Five of us were going to go and enjoy the evening together."

Dee clasped Maggie's hand. "It was one way I could take Maggie, and no one think twice about it."

Chance cleared her throat. "A few years ago, Kendra took that Morris girl to the prom. It still rattled people."

Maggie nodded. "So many things have changed for the better, though we aren't where we need to be yet. We had to be terribly discreet. If you think about it, what we were doing by being together was illegal, and we were underage. Anyway, I'd turned Frank down and he wasn't happy about it. No one turned down the star. Your mother eventually went with Leonard Hall. Every time Dee and I went somewhere together, your mother tagged along. She had a tendency to snub Dee whenever she got the opportunity—little smug remarks, or a jab whenever she could. You know how teenagers are. We all believe we can only have one best friend. The thing is, we realized later that your mother didn't just want to be my best friend. She wanted to be my girlfriend." Maggie looked up at Jax with tears in her eyes.

Dee stroked Maggie's hand. "It's okay, honey, tell her."

"Dee was working one night at her father's convenience store, and your mother came over to my house. We were listening to records, or vinyl, as I've heard Kendra call it. That was a big thing back in our day. Of course, we called them records." Maggie stopped and wagged a finger between Chance and Jax. "No old jokes, you two. Anyway, we were in my room listening and singing along. When your mother sang along to "Unchained Melody," she wasn't looking at me the way a friend would. She surprised me by kissing me. I sat there in shock and had no idea what to say."

Jax tried with all her might not to laugh, but she couldn't stop herself. The thought of her mother having even a single lesbian thought in her mind went beyond amusing Jax. It also angered her. All the hell she'd put Jax through. The number of times Jacqueline St. Claire had spewed disdain for Jax's life, and here the object of her mother's own desire sat in front of her telling her a story Jax could barely believe. "It all makes sense now."

Maggie nodded. "Your mother laid out her feelings with her heart on her sleeve. I tried desperately to not hurt her, but I had my heart set on a tall redhead with a laugh that reminded me of warm honey. When I told her I was in love with Dee, your mother went into a rage. She demanded to know why not her. Why wasn't she good enough for me? Nothing I said, no amount of explanation, could appease your mother. After calling Dee and me every vile name she could think of, she stormed out of my room and started a course of vindictive actions that caused the two of us a great deal of grief. Years later, that same vindictiveness sent you running for California, away from Chance and what you two could have had. Your Uncle Martin was livid at the way she treated us. I think he always knew about me and had suspicions about your mother. I tried to talk to her when you left for California, imploring her to stop. She vowed that you would never spend one more minute with Chance if she could help it."

Jax pushed up in the bed, trying to relieve the pain in her back that had developed from lying there for hours on end. "She made good on that threat, trust me. That first year I met Chance, she grounded me after I got back. Informed me she was not going to let me defile myself. I knew I was a lesbian before I met Chance. I'd never acted on it. I turned my attention to my studies. I had to have a scholarship to be able to attend vet school. My original plan was Virginia Tech. After meeting Chance, I started exploring West Virginia's program. The minute Mom saw paperwork from the school, she went ballistic. She informed me she wouldn't pay a dime for my education if I went there. Scholarships pay for a good bit, but there are expenses I'm sure you remember paying for Chance and now Kendra."

Dee chuckled. "We do. We were fortunate with Kendra's scholarship. With Chance, we tried to put away money from any of our real-estate sales to make sure she had what she needed. She had to work for her fun money. College isn't cheap, and I imagine veterinary school had to be even more expensive with the length."

Chance shook her head. "I had to pay for my own truck too. Dad didn't leave much when he passed away, I'm sure. I've always been grateful to have landed where I did with you two. I know it wasn't easy."

Maggie stood and put a hand on Chance's cheek. "We were young, barely out of college ourselves. I worshiped my big brother. He was seven years older than I was. The day he met your mother, there was no going back for him. Ray wanted a family. Losing your mother so young was his greatest sorrow, but raising you was his greatest joy. When he died, I couldn't think of any better way to honor him than raising you to be the woman you've become."

Jax watched the love between the women standing near her. How she wished she'd have made different choices back then and avoided missing so many years with Chance.

Dee turned to Jax. "You've always been a part of this family, Jax, even when you weren't here. Not a year went by when your Uncle Marty didn't give us an update on how you were doing."

Jax wiped a tear away. "He and Aunt Mary were the only ones to ever fight for me. He used to send me money for school. I can't tell you how many books or pizzas he bought. It wasn't easy, but I got through. I thought I found love in California, a reason to stay out there and the life I'd always wanted. What a mistake that was. I was so very wrong."

Chance leaned down and kissed her. "Not mistakes, only lessons learned. I wish more than anything to have those years back, but I won't let it hinder the years ahead I have with you. It sounds like your dad is having a change of heart about a few things as well."

Jax sighed and reached for a cup. She took a small swallow and placed it back on her table. "I hope so. It would be nice to believe at least one of my parents is glad I'm still around. It's like I said, Mom got her do-over family with Jennings' kids. The perfect family that she could mold into what she wanted. At least Jackie didn't take after her personality. She's a great deal like my brother, kindhearted, sensitive, and loving. Her brother, Jessie, reminds me of Dad, duty bound. He's also as gay as I am."

Chance's eyebrows shot up. "Does your mom know?"

"Why do you think he went into the Air Force? He's a technology geek and is happily living with his boyfriend of six years. He doesn't come home often. If he does, he stays with his sister on the premise of visiting with his niece and nephew."

Maggie paced across the room. "I wish I could go back and help your mother find her way. She might have ended up exactly where she is with an entirely different mindset. I tried to be kind, I truly did, Jax."

Jax waved Maggie to her. "Come here." When Maggie came to sit in the chair beside her, she took Maggie's hand. "None of this is your fault. The only difference between then and now is that I have control over my life. I say where I live and who I love. It's my decision who I let into my life. When I called home to tell Mom I was engaged to Lacey, she refused to speak to me for over a month. What she didn't know was a great deal of my decision to stay out there was based on the desire to keep her far from my life. Once she found out Lacey came from a wealthy family with power and influence, it suddenly didn't matter that I was a lesbian. All had been forgiven, because I wasn't marrying Chance. As long as I had nothing to do with a Fitzsimmons, life went on. The problem is, she was the only one happy about that."

Maggie grimaced and shook her head. "Such a sad way to live life. I honestly don't think your mother would have stayed in a same-sex relationship. She was far too boy crazy. Back then, you didn't discuss being bisexual, even in our circles. I have no idea what she even saw in me."

Dee came around and knelt before her. "Oh, I don't know. Beauty, brains, and a personality that lights up a room even on the darkest of days. I know exactly what she saw in you, because I was lucky enough to see it first."

Maggie leaned over and kissed Dee softly. Jax looked up at Chance, who smiled lovingly at her parents. So many things Jax had missed. *Not one more. I will not miss one more minute.*

Chapter Twenty-one

THE NEXT DAY, CHANCE ran into Rhebekka Deklan in the hallway. She'd left Kendra and Brandi chatting with Jax so she could run home to shower and pick up Zeus. Kendra and Brandi had volunteered to care for the horses before arriving. The hope was they would release Jax on Friday.

"Rhebekka, nice to see you. Are you stopping in for yourself or to see someone?"

Rhebekka was an interesting woman Chance had worked with several times over the last few years. On more than one occasion, Chance had called for her support on a death notification or to counsel a young person bordering on the edge of trouble.

"Good to see you too. Actually, I was coming to check on Jax. I went out to see Megan and Lindsey. I'm so glad to know they're both all right. How are you doing?"

Chance shuffled her feet. "I've never been that scared."

"I have no doubt she felt that same way when you were hurt. I hope to be able to sit down with both of you soon, so we can lay down some solid plans for this wedding. It gives me great pleasure to know that I'll be performing Megan and Lindsey's wedding, then yours and Jax's. It's always one of my favorite parts of this job."

"If I haven't told you this lately, I'm glad you landed here. You've made difficult situations much easier to handle. I've got to run home. Kendra is in with her. Go on up to see her."

"Excellent idea. Will you be back soon?"

"I need to run home, then take care of a few work things. The job never stops, even when personal things come up. My sister and her girlfriend will be here for a while. I'm sure Kendra would enjoy seeing you."

"I've missed her in my youth group. She always was killer at ArchAngel. I also heard about the big bust. Think it's going to stop some of the drugs coming in?"

"We certainly hope so. Time will tell. Someone will always try to bring it in, there's too much money in it. We can only stop what we know about."

Rhebekka patted Chance on the shoulder. "I have every confidence in you. Now, get out of here. I'm going to go check on one of my favorite brides."

Chance tipped her hat and headed to her vehicle. "Thanks, see you soon."

***

Chance had made the drive on this winding road so many times she could do it in her sleep. Her mind wandered while she drove to the home she shared with Jax. She wanted to make sure everything would be ready when Jax came home. It was also time to check in with Harley. Chance used the voice activation to make the call.

"Hey, Harley."

"How's Jax?"

"Getting antsy."

Jacqueline had returned to the hospital Wednesday evening. Jax still refused to see her. Chance had spoken with security, who stepped in to escort the woman back out of the hospital on Jax's request.

"I heard she had an unwanted visitor."

Chance sighed and growled in frustration. "I am extremely grateful to have been brought up in a home with parents who accepted me exactly as I was. Maggie and Dee never tried to change how I was or who I wanted to be with."

"That's how I felt about Megan. I wouldn't choose the road my child has walked, but she was free to follow her heart. I'm grateful to be gaining another daughter, but I'd have been just as grateful to gain a son if that's what Meg had wanted. Let's talk about something we can do something about. The preliminary report on those drugs is coming back with the same chemical makeup as the overdose calls. The packaging is the same, colored straws with melted ends to hold the product. We found the clothing we were looking for and another hay hook. Both appear to have paint scrapes the same color as Jax's truck. The lab will confirm. The second bike was in the outbuilding. Prints all over them belong to Leland and Danny."

"All good news, my friend. Anything else?"

Chance could hear Harley flipping through something.

"Get this, we found a ledger book with a few interesting things."

"Like?"

"The names of those guys who had Doc Hendricks. The dates of the entries fall in with what appears to be a delivery on the day they shot Kenny and kidnapped Doc. Connect the dots, and I think we've found our link."

"Harley, that is the best news I've heard since they said Jax was going to be fine. I need to check in with Taylor before I head back to the hospital. I'll pass that info on to her. Lindsey doing okay?"

"She's extremely sore, and you know the concussion side effects. Megan is having a hard time keeping her down. Lindsey swears she needs to get to the clinic and feed the animals."

Chance turned up the gravel road to the farm and hit a pothole she'd meant to fix. "Damn."

"What's wrong?"

"Just a reminder of the million non-law-enforcement-related things I'm behind on. Tell Lindsey we've got the clinic covered. Doc is going in, and he called Maddie and Allie from Doggy Sodds to help with the feeding and walks. Kendra and Brandi have volunteered to help as well. Tell her to relax; we've got this. You can also tell Megan I'm having the same trouble with Jax. Give them both my love. I'm going to get showered and changed. I didn't want to leave, but Jax insisted I bring her a few things. She hates those hospital gowns. I have orders for track pants that snap up the side and a soft T-shirt. Her wish is my command."

"That's the spirit. Give her my best. I'll keep digging on this new angle. I'm going to call the federal prosecutor and get her up to speed. Oh, before I forget, Taylor might not say anything, and I want you to know. I was in your office yesterday, and Brad walked through the door."

Chance hit the steering wheel as she put the vehicle in park. "That son of a bitch better not have said a single word to—"

"Simmer down. I escorted him back outside before he could. Taylor was there with Penny at the desk, so nothing happened. It shook Penny up pretty good. Before you ask, she's fine. Taylor wasn't going to say anything, because you have enough on your plate. I asked Brad what he wanted. He gave some lame excuse of something in his locker. I informed him that any personal items still there would be mailed to him."

Chance unclenched her jaw and took a deep breath. "Thanks for handling that. Penny doesn't need any more stress. She's past seven months along now. It's going to be a race to see whether Jax and I get married before that baby comes into this world."

"Let's just hope it's not at the same time. I'll keep you updated. Hug Jax for me."

"Will do." Chance hung up and shut the Suburban off. She looked out over their home. More than four walls and a roof, it was a sanctuary Chance couldn't wait to bring Jax home to. She was going to wrap her in all the love she could show her. *With my dying breath, I vow that no one will ever hurt her again.*

***

Jax held her side, as Brandi described the first time Kendra found the courage to look her in the eye.

"I swear, I couldn't tell if she was shy or staring at my, well you know." Brandi pointed both her index fingers toward her chest.

Kendra groaned. "I was not staring at your chest! My mothers would have smacked the back of my head for doing that to someone. I was nervous!"

"I'd been trying for weeks to get you to talk to me. I even bribed Holly to switch seats with me in that lab so you would talk to me. I bought her lunch for a week."

Jax hugged a pillow tightly. "Oh God, Brandi, take it easy on me. My ribs are so sore."

Kendra shook her head. "I swear, Jax. I wasn't that bad. I've never been forward, and well, she's so damn beautiful."

Jax smiled at Kendra with love and affection. "You know, your sister was pretty shy too. Even though you aren't blood related, I'm betting she rubbed off on you a bit. The first time I ever met her, she couldn't say three words to me. Maggie said it was like she went mute. Of course, I thought she was the most gorgeous creature I'd ever met. I made sure Uncle Marty took me back. Eventually, they had a backyard barbeque, and Maggie invited me. After that, I was taken in by the way Chance made me smile and laugh. There was a protective side of her as well. One of the guys she and Sarah went to school with asked me out. Chance told him we already had plans. Up until that point, our conversations had been casual without a great deal of substance. From that moment, I knew she was someone I wanted to know better. We enjoyed one more amazing summer followed by thirty years of wasted time."

Kendra stood. "I'm going to grab us something to drink. Do you want anything, Jax?"

Jax nodded. "I'd kill for a hot chocolate."

Kendra leaned over and kissed Brandi on the top of the head. "I'll be right back."

Jax watched Brandi's eyes follow the younger Fitzsimmons to the door, never breaking the line of sight until she was gone. "She's so much like Chance. It's funny how two people born in completely different families can be so similar. Kendra is the product of powerful role models telling her she could be whoever she wanted to be."

Brandi pulled on a charm attached to a bracelet on her wrist. "Chance is her hero in every sense of the word. If I've heard it once, I've heard it a thousand times. Her goal in life is to make them proud, to be like Chance, and have a love that lasts as long as Maggie and Dee's."

"That admiration goes both ways. Chance knows how hard Kendra's life was before she came to live with the Fitzsimmons. The sun rises and sets in Kendra for all of them. I always wanted a little sister. From what I see, I'm pretty lucky to have two."

Brandi wrinkled her forehead in confusion. "Two?"

Jax nodded. "Unless I miss my guess, you don't have any plans of going anywhere, anytime soon. When the Fitzsimmons girls love someone, they love with their whole being. That's rare, Brandi, and something you don't throw away. I never meant to, but that's what I did. I wanted to be away from my mother so badly, I walked away from Chance and ended up in a relationship that made me question if true love existed."

As Jax said those words, her mother pushed through the door. "It's about time I get to visit you without interference. I need to speak to my daughter alone. Leave please."

"Mother, you've been told not to come back."

Kendra walked in with a carryout tray of drinks. "When my sister gets back, you're likely to find yourself enjoying the Garrett County lockup. You aren't wanted here. If you decide that's not something you can do on your own, I can find security. They will help you find the exit sign."

Jacqueline St. Claire stepped closer to Jax's bed and set down her handbag. "No Fitzsimmons will ever tell me what to do, even an adopted one. Like all the rest, you're just another piece of trash."

Jax shot up in bed, grabbed her mother's purse, and launched it across the room. "That's enough! Nurse! Nurse!" Jax screamed for help, and her mother moved closer to her, attempting to put her hand over Jax's mouth as she fought. "Get your hands off me! How dare you!"

Kendra grabbed Jax's mother and spun her around, pulling one arm up behind her back and pushing her into the wall. "Brandi, get security! Now!"

"No need, Kendra. All the security she'll ever need is present. *Blijven*, Zeus."

Everyone turned at the low growl emanating from the Belgian Malinois along with the show of teeth he was exhibiting. Chance stood with her hand on her service weapon, and two security guards stepped in with her.

"Chance!" Tears ran down Jax's face. "Thank, God."

Indignation thick in her voice, Jacqueline confronted Chance. "If he bites me, I'll sue you."

Chance stepped closer and took over the hold from Kendra. "If he bites you, it will be because he's been ordered to. That only happens if someone fails to comply. My suggestion is you do exactly what these security officers tell you to." Chance leaned in but didn't drop her voice. "And if you ever put a hand on Jax again, it won't be Zeus you have to worry about. Now, I suggest you follow orders and get out. Don't turn around, and don't ever come near her again. Am I making myself clear?"

"This isn't over!"

Chance laughed. "Oh, it is. If we have to put a restraining order on you, we will."

Jax watched it all play out in front of her. The exertion of throwing her mother's purse and struggling to get free of the hand over her mouth had left her in nearly blinding pain. "Chance please, make her go away. Make her go away. I don't ever want to see her as long as I live. I'll do whatever I have to, sign any papers, testify in court, but please get her away from me!"

At that moment, Jax's father pushed through the melee to Jax's side. "Jibber Jack, I'm here. It's okay. Calm down. It's going to be okay."

"Daddy please!"

Jacqueline walked near the window and began picking up the items from the purse Jax had thrown. "Your father has no say in whether I see you or not. He is not my keeper, nor a person who orders me around. I will not leave, and I will not be thrown out of here."

Jax watched as her father walked to her mother. He towered over her. He bent and began picking up the strewn items. He handed them to Jacqueline. Jax had never seen her father's head so red. She detected a tremble in his hands. She actually worried for her mother's safety. "Daddy, come over here. I need you."

Jacqueline turned to Jax, fire glinting from her eyes. "You are a grown woman. Calling him your daddy is so juvenile."

Jax's father stepped between her mother's line of sight and her bed. "In all my life, I've never known a woman so hell-bent on the destruction of her family. I *am* her daddy and always will be. Why are you so determined to cause our family the amount of pain you have? Do you know why Jennings and Lynn decided to hike that trail? Lynn was going to take the kids and leave Jennings because of your interference. Our son thought that some time away from you would help them find each other again. That's what he confided in me. They were on that trail because of you! I lost my son and daughter-in-law because of you. I'll be damned if I'm going to lose my daughter."

Mike St. Claire clenched his fists, then wiped a hand down his face before pointing to the door. "I want you to get the hell out of here. Get in the car out front and drive your ass back to Richmond. When you get there, find yourself a good lawyer. You're going to need one to handle your side of our affairs. This is the last time I will let you speak to my daughter this way. Consider yourself on notice, Jacqueline. I'm done. My attorney will send the papers as soon as you advise the name of your lawyer. Don't try to use Sam, he's already drawing up my side of the decree."

Jax winced through her pain. Listening to her father dress her mother down would have been music to her ears years ago. This pronouncement rang with a pang of regret for years that could never be retrieved. The words about Jennings and Lynn hurt more than anything her mother had ever done to her.

Jax cleared her throat. "I'm going to make myself perfectly clear to you. I want you out of here."

One of the security guards waved an arm toward the door. "Please don't make me physically remove you. I'd appreciate it if you'd vacate the area."

Physically hurting and emotionally exhausted, Jax pressed her head back into her pillow. She put a hand over her eyes, as the pounding in her head grew sharper. She felt warm breath near her ear.

"You okay? I'm getting them out of here, now."

Jax opened her eyes and looked into the gunmetal-blue eyes she trusted more than any other. Chance, the woman she was choosing a life with, was all she'd ever need. "Please."

"Enough. Everyone out!" Chance stepped toward the group in the small room and opened her arms wide as she walked forward. "No arguments. Out!"

Jacqueline St. Claire huffed indignantly and walked out the door. For the first time in the last fifteen minutes, Jax breathed easy. Her leg ached, and all she wanted to do was go home so she could be wrapped up in Chance's arms. The lasts few days had been a complete nightmare. *I always liked rollercoasters, but this is one I want to get off.*

Chance was back at her side, protectively leaning in and holding her hand. "It's going to be okay. I promise you. She won't get back in here. My hope is they are going to release you. That's why I was held up. I called and talked to Kristi, who's offered to come and check in on you if Dr. Mason agrees to let you go home. There is too much access to you here, and you're certainly not resting."

Jax pulled on the back of Chance's neck until their lips were a breath apart. "Have I told you how much I love you? Take me home."

Chapter Twenty-two

CHANCE PEERED AROUND THE bedroom door to see Jax. *Good, she's sleeping.* She'd been home for two days, and Kristi was due to check on her around two in the afternoon. Chance was trying to juggle work with caring for Jax. She was grateful to her mothers, and to Kendra and Brandi, who'd stayed with her while Chance went and took care of some things at the office she couldn't put off. Mike was still in town and had taken his turns sitting with Jax. Fortunately, Jacqueline had returned to her home in Virginia.

Chance was more than grateful that she hadn't seen Jacqueline since the last scene at the hospital, and she hadn't heard from Lacey at all. She knew Mike and Jacqueline's impending divorce was on Jax's mind, though Chance wasn't sure she was upset by it. On her way to the kitchen, she let Zeus out the back door into the yard. They really needed a run, but the thought of leaving Jax held no appeal. She was scheduled to work the midnight shift with Khodi. Thankfully, next weekend was Daniel's graduation from the academy. With Khodi on board and Daniel working the court duty, she would be back up to full staff. At least until Daniel left for his K9 training. She planned to step back into her administrative duties that would allow her to be home more. Her phone buzzed, and the display screen let her know it was Sarah calling.

"Hey, what's up?"

"Kristi and I are on our way over. Can we pick anything up for you? She's bringing a lasagna with her, so we've got dinner covered for later."

Chance smiled. She really did have the best friends in the world. "No, that's perfect. She's resting right now. I'll be glad to have Kristi take a look at her injuries and reassure me we did the right thing bringing her home."

"On our way. See you in twenty minutes."

Chance juggled the phone, cursing herself that she hadn't put it on speaker, as she made lunch for Jax and herself. "We'll be here." She hung up and continued making the turkey sandwich and stirring the chicken soup her mother had made the day before. It wasn't that Chance couldn't cook, she just preferred to do her cooking on the grill. She placed everything on a tray and carried it upstairs to Jax. When she pushed open the door with her foot, she was grateful to see two bright eyes looking back at her. "Hungry?"

Jax adjusted her position. "Starving actually. Tell me that's Maggie's soup?"

"It is, and half a sandwich. That way, you can take your pain medicine."

Jax sighed. "I really want to stop taking it altogether. It makes me feel like I have oatmeal between my ears."

Chance nearly dropped the tray chuckling. "Don't make me laugh or you'll be wearing the soup instead of eating it."

After arranging everything for Jax, she grabbed her own portion, and the two of them dug in. Chance swallowed a bite. "Sarah and Kristi are on their way."

"Good. I need a good progress report from her if I'm going to Daniel's graduation."

This was a discussion they'd had more than once over the last few days. "Jax, we've talked about this. You don't have to go."

"I know I don't have to. I want to." Jax sipped soup from the oversized mug.

"I'm worried about a trip that long, then coming back after. If you go, will you agree to stay overnight in Charleston and start home the next day? The graduation will wear you out after that drive."

Jax nodded. "That I'll agree to. I'm not delusional enough to believe it won't exhaust me, but it's important."

Chance couldn't stop the smirk that made its way across her face. "And you have no plans of letting Faith have an opportunity to be alone with me."

Jax grinned over the rim of the soup bowl. "Nope."

"And this is why I love you."

"I love you too."

They finished lunch, and Chance took the dishes to the kitchen. Zeus barked, drawing Chance's attention to the door as she wiped her hands on a dishcloth. Sarah and Kristi stepped out of the vehicle. Chance came down the steps and took the large pan from Kristi.

"Let me help you."

Kristi leaned in and kissed Chance's cheek. "You just want to make sure you get the biggest piece."

Chance tilted her head toward the house. "Not going to lie, that's probably true. She's awake."

Kristi patted her on the back. "I'll go check on her."

Sarah stood at Chance's side. "How are you doing with all this?"

"Scared shitless."

Sarah patted Chance's back. "I figured."

"We've spent a lifetime apart. Almost losing Jax was worse than being shot at. It got even more complicated when her mother piled on with some shitty things, including calling her ex-wife. I swear, Sarah, you know I'm a patient person. I've made it part of how I respond as an officer, but that woman brought me right to the edge. I can't understand wanting to hurt someone like she does."

"I can. Look at my parents. For that matter, look at Faith."

They made it inside, where Chance put away the food as Sarah let Zeus back in the house. Chance gestured to the library, where they sat down.

Chance put her face in her hands and took a deep breath. "Speaking of Faith, she wants to have lunch."

"You're kidding."

Chance held up her right hand as if she were swearing an oath.

"Some days I wish she'd move away." Sarah paused and shook her head. "I'm a terrible sister."

It was sad for Chance to hear Sarah talk about her sister that way, even though Faith had always been less than supportive of Sarah's career and partner choices. "No, you aren't. It breaks my heart for you and Kristi. Those years I was with Faith, I tried to be the voice of reason. I don't know if you've noticed, but she's one of the most stubborn people I've ever met." Chance was glad she could make Sarah break out into a full-blown laugh.

"Ya think? She's really my only family. That's why it hurts so damn much that she can't just be proud of the life I've made for my wife and child. It hasn't been easy; you know that. The thing is, I wouldn't change one single second of it. Faith has the education, the looks, and the money, but I have true love and a son who's going to work for my best friend. A best friend who's always been more of a sister to me."

Chance knew that the Ryker family had always had high expectations for both their daughters. Sarah's parents had basically disowned her when she came out. Dating men through medical school gave Faith a few years reprieve. When she started dating women exclusively, their parents had washed their hands of both of them.

"I've always considered you like a sister, too. Hell, you spent as much time at my house as you did your own. moms-squared adopted you a long time ago. You know they consider Daniel like a grandchild."

Sarah dropped her eyes. "I don't know how I'd have gotten through high school and college without your family. I know I didn't become a doctor, but I take care of my fair share of patients to make sure they get to those highly trained doctors."

Chance turned and looked Sarah directly in the eyes. "Sarah, don't let Faith into your head like that. You make a difference in this community every day. You've raised an incredible kid who will soon be protecting this community from harm. You have a great deal to be proud about and nothing to feel like a failure over."

Sarah nodded slowly. "He is something. Hard to believe next weekend he'll graduate from the academy. I can't tell you how much it relieves my mind to know he'll be under your watchful eye."

"Daniel is a special young man, and he's got a long career in front of him. God help us when Kendra graduates from college. Our worry factor will be times two then. For now, how about we go check on our girls?" Chance wrapped an arm around Sarah's shoulders as they headed upstairs.

***

"Well, what's the verdict?" Jax shifted in the bed as much as she could without causing herself pain.

Kristi pulled the blood pressure cuff off Jax's arm. "All your vitals are good. You seem to be managing your pain level, and the incision looks good. I'll call Dr. Mason and give a full report. Are you sure you want to make that ride to Charleston?"

Jax brushed her hair back behind her ears. "If he thinks it will be a problem, then we'll figure out what we need to do to mitigate it. I'm going, one way or another."

Kristi put a hand over her mouth, stifling a chuckle. "With Faith going, I had money on you dragging yourself there if you had to."

"These last few months, she's been so persistent. Poor Theresa, my heart breaks for her."

"I've known Theresa for years, and I don't know that I've ever seen anything that could make her pull back from her kids at school. I've tried to talk to her. There just doesn't seem to be a good ending to this."

Jax adjusted a pillow behind her back. "And if it's not Chance's ex, it's mine. I still can't believe my mother called her."

"Your mom is something else. She hates the Fitzsimmons family so badly, she's willing to hurt you to get back at them for some perceived wrong. Bizarre."

"That's one way to describe her. Dad says he's going forward with the divorce no matter what. It's certainly not what I was expecting. They've been together a very long time. He always bent to whatever she wanted. That included never standing up to her for me, until now."

"We think differently the older we get. Some things become more important when we realize we're closer to the end of our life than the beginning."

Jax squeezed Kristi's hand. "Very true. So, I have a favor to ask. I know Sarah will be standing with Chance, will you stand with me?"

"Do you know how many times I've been on a horse in the last few years? I can count them on one hand." She laughed and nodded. "For you, anything." Kristi vowed.

Two new voices floated a conversation to the doorway. Sarah and Chance stood side by side, both with smirks on their faces.

"How's the patient?" Chance leaned on the door frame.

Jax pointed to Kristi. "I've been told by my highly qualified nurse that I'm doing well."

Chance moved farther into the room and came to sit on the wide footboard of their bed. "Is that so?"

Kristi nodded. "Everything looks good. I'll call Dr. Mason and confirm everything. If all stays the course, I think she can make the journey with some light pain meds."

"Something that won't make her feel like she has oatmeal between her ears?"

Kristi looked at Chance. "Do what?"

Chance shrugged. "Don't look at me, I just quoted the patient."

Kristi packed up her small medical kit. "I think we can work on that." She turned to Jax. "You up for some cards if we get you to the couch? I brought lasagna for dinner."

Jax nodded and let the simplicity of an afternoon with friends bring a smile to her face. "Sounds like a perfect afternoon. Thank you, Kristi. You and Sarah are a godsend."

Chapter Twenty-three

CHANCE SMILED FOR PICTURES as she stood to the right of Daniel with Taylor on his left, Zeus and Midas right beside them. His graduation from the police academy gave Chance a great deal of pride. She'd watched Daniel experience all the traditions she'd experienced when she went through the academy. Daniel graduated at the top of his class with honors. He had represented both his department and his family well. Faith stood beside Sarah taking pictures with her cellphone as Daniel's girlfriend Dezi did the same.

Daniel groaned as he pulled off his Stetson and held it in front of his face. "Enough pictures. You'd think they didn't have any of me."

Chance laughed and patted him on the back. "They're proud of you, and so am I. Hard to believe you work for me now, as a duly appointed deputy."

"Watch out, Daniel, she's buttering you up." Taylor wrapped a one-armed embrace around a very pregnant Penny.

Daniel grinned as he bent to pet Zeus. "No doubt. So, I start to work Monday morning at the courthouse?"

Chance nodded. "You leave for K9 training next month. Enjoy the time at home."

He stood and smiled. "I'm looking forward to seeing what K9 I'm assigned. I have no problem saying I've missed Mom's cooking. Not that it's bad here, just not hers."

Kristi stood on her tiptoes and kissed her son's cheek. "I've promised him an early Thanksgiving since he'll be gone."

Taylor extended her hand. "Daniel, I'm proud of you too, but we're going to head out. I want to get these two home." She put her hand on her wife's swollen belly.

Daniel shook Taylor's hand, and then took Dezi's hand in his. "I'll see you Monday morning."

Faith stepped forward, and Chance watched as she wrapped Daniel in a hug. "Seems like yesterday, I was meeting you for the first time as a tiny little bundle at the hospital. You've grown into an incredible young man."

Daniel blushed. "Thanks, Aunt Faith."

"He's turned out to be more than I could have ever dreamed of in a son." Sarah hugged him next.

Chance wheeled Jax close to him. From her chair, Jax shook his hand. "I feel better knowing men like you are on the job, Daniel."

"You guys are getting all mushy on me." Daniel pulled his mothers into a tight group hug.

When they stepped away, Kendra slugged him in the arm. "Not me. Deputy or not, I can still stomp your ass with the bow."

Chance watched the two friends banter and leaned down to Jax. "How are you holding up?"

Jax squeezed her hand. "I'm fine. Wouldn't have missed this for the world. Watching you look at him makes me think about what it would have been like to have a son with you."

Chance stepped around and stooped in front of Jax. "It would have been one of the great joys of my life." She reached up and wiped away a tear that had escaped Jax's eye. "I think it's time we get you to the hotel. I'd really like to hold you."

Jax cupped Chance's jaw. "Let's say goodbye to everyone first."

They worked through the group and were about to take off, when Faith stopped them. "Can I talk to you two for a second?"

Chance looked down at Jax with some trepidation. She was unsure about what Faith was going to say and that put her on edge. They moved to a spot at the perimeter of the parade ground. The broad limbs of the ancient oak tree still defiantly held its leaves against the chill of the coming winter.

Faith wrung her hands before putting them in her coat pockets. "I wanted to tell both of you something. I told Sarah and Kristi earlier. I'm leaving two weeks from now. I've taken a job offering in South Carolina. I think I need a new start, and you both could use less interference from me. I've signed the house over to Theresa and agreed not to contest anything she wants in the divorce."

Chance looked at her former lover and tried to summon compassion. "I wish things with Theresa could have been different for you, Faith."

Jax reached out a hand and placed it on Faith's forearm. "Sometimes, a change of scenery is exactly what we need to put everything into perspective." She slipped her other hand into Chance's. "I can personally attest to that."

Faith nodded. Chance had once cared deeply for Faith. Seeing her look so defeated was difficult. She couldn't bring herself to be remorseful that things had turned out the way they had. Once Faith left Chance for Theresa, she'd unwittingly put Chance on an intersecting path with Jax. Soon, they would be married. Faith needed to find her way, and no one could point that out on a map for her.

"I'm not going to stand here and say I regret trying to get back what you and I had, Chance. I regret the pain it's caused everyone. I'm still trying to wrap my head around the fact you won't be in my life. For that matter, my head is kicking my ass for hurting Theresa the way I have. I hope she finds happiness with someone someday. She deserves that."

Chance looked at the deep sorrow on Faith's face. "Everyone deserves to find love and be happy. I'm sure you'll find it when you least expect it."

Faith rocked back on her high-heeled boots. "We'll see. I think maybe what I need is to figure out who I am first. I'm accepting an ER Chief position near the beach. Plenty of sun and tourists should keep me occupied. Well, anyway, I just wanted you to know I'll be leaving."

Jax spoke up. "We wish you all the best, Faith, really, we do."

Chance echoed that sentiment but refused to make any physical contact with Faith. In her mind, the less connection they had, the better. In less than two months, the woman sitting in the wheelchair would become her wife. That was something she'd been waiting a lifetime for. *I won't allow anything, not Faith and not Jax's mother, to stand in our way.*

***

The next three weeks flew by with court appearances for Chance and follow-up doctor appointments for Jax. Chance had given a deposition in the case against Leland Kurst and his family. The federal prosecutor had stepped in once the link between Leland and the men who'd kidnapped Marty Hendricks had been established.

Her phone rang. "Yes, Penny?"

"Taya Chapel on line one for you."

"Thanks, are you going home soon?" Chance shifted papers on her desk and pulled out a stack of tax collection reports.

Penny sighed across the line. "Yes, mother hen, Taylor is taking me home after lunch. I'm all right. Stop worrying. It's just normal swelling."

"Don't care why...just go home, I mean it. Thank you, Penny." She worried about Penny and her recent diagnosis of gestational diabetes.

"You're welcome, Sheriff."

Chance clicked over on the line where her call was waiting. "Taya, good to hear from you. What can I do for you?"

"I have a bit of good news to share. With the additional evidence, we were able to push the case against the Kurst family. They will stand trial for the drug charges and the case involving your fiancée. I will warn you, his attorney is trying to plead down the charges for attempted murder of both Jax and Lindsey."

Chance took a deep breath and clenched the phone tightly in her hand. "Taya, I—"

"Before you get wound up, I'm not doing it. We have enough on the others that we don't need him to turn state's evidence. He's low on the food chain. The guys who took Dr. Hendricks are a better bet for us to get information on the Murdaland gang over in Baltimore."

Chance released the breath she'd been holding. "Thank you. That piece of shit nearly killed the woman I love and Lindsey. To see him cut a deal on that would have sent me over the edge. I've had about enough of people getting off for the crimes they commit. That's nothing against you, Taya."

"Rest easy, Sheriff. We've got this."

"Thank you. I appreciate it. I'm sure there are more things you'll need from me closer to trial. Don't hesitate to ask."

"Oh trust me, I will."

They ended the call and Chance looked at the doodle she'd scratched on the legal pad. She'd traced the infinity symbol over and over. It's how she thought about her love for Jax, a continuous path that wound back on itself over and over, never finding its end. *Now, if I can just tie up all these loose ends, I can get my happily ever after.*

There had been one bright spot recently. Last weekend, Megan and Lindsey's wedding had gone off without a hitch. The only regret of the day was that she and Jax couldn't take advantage of the dance floor. Jax's leg was healing, though it still caused her some pain. She'd still be wearing the cast for their own wedding. Chance dialed a number on her cell and waited for the one voice she wanted to hear.

"Hey there, I was just thinking about you."

Jax had returned to work under the watchful eye of her uncle. Lindsey and Megan were on a short honeymoon and would be back next Monday.

Chance felt her face break into a smile. "That's funny, I was just thinking about you too. I needed to hear your voice."

There were still times when the one thing Chance needed to turn her day around was hearing Jax say how much she loved her. Currently, Chance was stressed about Brad Waters' upcoming trial for his assault against Penny and expected a call from Marsha Abbott, the special prosecutor for the case against the former deputy. His attorney had asked for a pretrial meeting.

Jax brought her out of her musings. "Well, I'm happy to fulfill that need. I have a few of my own, you know. Some of which you did an amazing job fulfilling last night."

Chance began to trace the infinity symbol again. "Last night took care of more than a need, that was a fantasy come true."

"Still no word from Marsha? I know you're waiting to hear from her."

"Nothing yet. Even after all this, we'll still have the civil service hearings to go through. Depending on how this works out, we'll either have stronger footing against Brad or lose ground. We've got him on video, that's going to be difficult for him to dispute. It still scares me to think what might have happened. If Penny had lost the baby, I don't..." She stopped, unable to continue that line of thinking.

"Thinking about what could have happened serves no purpose."

Chance was always grateful that Jax could walk her off the ledge when her mind spiraled out of control with the what ifs. "Let's talk about something else. Moms-squared is planning Thanksgiving for noonish. Your dad and Uncle Marty are joining us. Around seven, we'll go out to Sarah and Kristi's for pie."

Jax chuckled. "I'll be in a tryptophan coma by the time we get home. I'm thankful Maggie and Dee invited Dad. I think he's feeling a little lost."

"I'm sure. Mike and your mother were together for a long time. Has he heard from her?" Chance looked up to see Marsha Abbott standing in her door and gestured for her to have a seat.

"She called him last week, demanding he come home and work out their differences. Dad told her that if she insisted on being so obstinate and hateful toward his future daughter-in-law and her family that they had nothing to talk about. Anyway, I've got a cantankerous dachshund who needs his anal glands expressed."

"Now there is one reason I'm glad I'm a police officer and not a vet. I love you."

"I love you, too. Talk to you later."

Chance hung up the phone and studied Marsha's face. Her

expression gave nothing away. "I'm hoping that look doesn't mean we've dropped the case."

Marsha unbuttoned her jacket as she sat down and reached into her briefcase. "Not on your life. They presented an offer that I need to discuss with Penny and Taylor. Personally, I say we reject it. I think our case is strong enough to win, especially with the video evidence. You can lie about a lot of things, but the video clearly shows what he did."

"I'm sure they haven't left yet, want to use our conference room?"

Marsha nodded, and Chance picked up her phone to call Taylor to the front office.

Minutes later, the four of them were seated around an oval table. Marsha passed out a set of papers with what Brad's attorney had presented as an alternative plea. As the three of them read, Chance could barely contain her rage.

Taylor threw the papers she'd been holding back on the table. "This is horseshit, Marsha." She reached over and clasped Penny's hand in hers. "He could have killed my child."

Penny put a protective hand over her abdomen. "Do we have to accept this?"

Marsha shook her head. "No, we don't. I wanted you to see it, because when we go to trial, this is what we will be combating. He's not going to make this easy."

"What's the timetable on this trial?" Chance asked.

Marsha looked at each of them. "Right after Thanksgiving."

Penny closed her eyes. "I want this over before this baby is born. I can't have this hanging over me going into delivery. This stress is not good for either of us."

Taylor pulled her into her arms. "Do you want to take his deal and just be done with it?"

Chance watched, as Penny eyed the paper in front of her. Maybe there was something she could do. "I have a feeling one of the reasons he's trying to plead this down to a misdemeanor is to save his pension. With a felony on his record, he'd lose the percentage the county puts in and only get back out what he's paid in. That would be a significant loss."

Taylor pounded her fist on the table. "What about what he almost cost us? If we'd have lost our child, it would have been murder!"

Penny reached out and cupped Taylor's cheek. "We didn't. Our child is alive and growing right here." She pulled Taylor's hand over her belly.

Chance watched as both women smiled. She understood Taylor's frustration. "Penny, what do you want to do? As much as this has angered and frustrated both of us"—Chance waved a finger between Taylor and herself—"it was you that he assaulted."

Penny nodded and read over the proposal again. She took a deep breath and looked up to Marsha, who sat quietly at the end of the table. "I want this over. The thing about this agreement is it leaves it open for him to seek active employment as a law enforcement officer again. I'm sorry, but he abused his authority with his actions. He would have arrested anyone else for what he did to me, if he wasn't so damn incompetent. I couldn't care less about him doing any more time. I don't think that will serve as anything more than increasing his anger against these two." She looked up at Chance. "If he puts his retirement paperwork in, can you fast track it?"

Chance thought about the request and realized what Penny wanted her to do. "I can. He'll still have to go through the state process. That'll take a few weeks."

Penny looked at Marsha. "Then, here's what I want. He drops the civil service case and puts in for retirement. He pleads guilty to the highest misdemeanor charges, not felonies that will cost him his pension, but things that will show up in any employment background check. He agrees to never seek employment as a law enforcement officer. Brad also agrees to counseling and community service at the 4H camp, doing whatever they want him to. If he agrees to all that, I'll sign off."

Marsha was making notes. "You're generous Penny. I'll go talk to them and see if this is agreeable. If he doesn't agree to the conditions, we go to trial. I hope he listens to reason. If not, then we go both barrels. I'll make sure I lay out all the evidence we have and advise him I'll be going for the maximum sentencing because you are an extension of the sheriff herself." Marsha looked at Chance.

Chance's blood raged, as she thought of the scene she'd walked in on, Penny on the floor, and Brad being restrained and held at bay by one of her K9 units. What Penny was asking for was far less than what Chance wanted, though she hadn't been looking forward to the civil service proceedings. The fact that Penny was taking that into consideration tempered her anger. She silently recited her mantra. *Steel is tempered by fire, and gold is refined by it.* This was one more thermal cycle she would use to strengthen her conviction to be the absolute best she could be. There were times when she was reminded that her position required restraint to achieve their ultimate goal, order in chaos.

Penny reached for Chance's hand. "This, too, will pass. You have a wedding to focus on." She cupped Taylor's cheek. "And we have a baby to bring into this world. Let's do both with less stress from someone who has caused us far too much grief."

Chance saw Taylor's eyes soften. She looked at the relationship the two women had built. They'd been through a great deal in their marriage, things Penny had revealed to her over hours of paperwork together. She knew that the child they were bringing into the world would be loved and cherished. She was glad that she and Jax would be there to see it all.

Chapter Twenty-four

A FEW DAYS LATER, Jax helped Maggie in the kitchen on Thanksgiving morning. Cinnamon and allspice floated over the aroma of turkey roasting in the oven. Her first true family holiday with the Fitzsimmons family was turning out to be one of a blended family. Her dad and Uncle Marty were in the living room playing cards. Chance and Dee were outside splitting logs for the fireplace, while Kendra and Brandi were cuddled up on the couch watching the Macy's Thanksgiving Day Parade. This was what family was supposed to be, and she was grateful to be a part of it. She wondered what her mother was doing. *Likely spending the holiday with Jackie and the kids.*

"Penny for your thoughts?" Maggie put a hand on Jax's shoulder.

Jax shrugged. "They aren't worth that much. I was thinking about Mom. This will be the first holiday she and Dad have been apart other than when he was doing shift work. He hasn't said much about what's going on, but I get the odd feeling he's not that upset."

"What were the holidays like when you were young?"

Jax sighed and shifted on the stool she'd been ordered to park herself on. It wasn't hard to conjure up the memories, they just weren't that pleasant to share. "Mom would cook dinner and have me help with preparations. Unfortunately, no matter how hard I tried to follow her instructions, I never seemed to measure up. I could be doing something as mundane as stirring the ingredients for something, and within minutes, she'd take it from me. Jacqueline St. Claire never had more than three seconds worth of patience for me with anything. I'd try to do something else. She'd eventually kick me out of the kitchen, only to complain I didn't help enough. It was a no-win situation. That's one of the reasons I went so far away from home for school."

"I'm so sorry."

"It's okay, Maggie. We never had the money for me to fly back and forth. I took summer jobs to pay the bills for the small apartment I shared with two other girls. That wasn't what kept me from coming home. I missed my brother and my dad, but life without her constant scrutiny allowed me to breathe."

Maggie wrapped Jax in a hug. "No child should ever feel that way. I know things got rough after you met Chance."

Jax nodded. "That's putting it mildly. She put the vice grips on me after that. I never understood why until you told us about what happened. I'm not going to say I wish things had turned out differently for her. When I try to imagine you with her, it looks like a puzzle piece that someone tried to line up but couldn't fit well. Hell, for that matter, like an entirely different puzzle."

Maggie walked back to the stove and stirred one of the pots. "Jackie was always complicated. Nothing ever fit, as you say. She was never content with anything. It was like she was always searching. For what, none of us knew, just that she'd never stay here in what she considered the backwoods. Whatever she was searching for didn't exist here. I always assumed that was why she changed her plans about where she was going to school and ended up at James Madison. In the end, she met your father, and they moved to Richmond. She never came back here much, not even for holidays."

Jax shook her head. "No, I can't even remember her coming to visit Grandma and Grandpa. Uncle Marty used to come and pick us up when we stayed with them. Always strange."

Maggie turned to her. "Well, you always have a family here. I know I'm not your mom, but you can always think of us as your moms-squared too."

Jax wiped away a tear. "That means more to me than you will ever know."

They continued to work on the meal preparation. By one o'clock, everyone had gathered around Maggie and Dee's large family table. A second table butted up against the first to make room for all those gathered. Dee sat at the head of the table and tapped her glass with her knife. "It's a tradition in this family that we start the meal by saying at least one thing that we are thankful for. I'll go first, and we'll go around the table to my left. I'm thankful that both of my children have found wonderful people to add to our family. I want to say welcome to both Jax and Brandi. I'd also like to extend a warm welcome to Mike and Marty as you join this circus."

Everyone continued around the table until Jax was the last person to speak. She'd listened to Chance say how grateful she was to have her back in her life and that soon they'd be married. She leaned over and kissed Chance softly. "Sweet talker." She turned to the rest of the table. "I spent a lifetime in California, surrounded by people and things that never meant as much to me as the people at this table. I've been given a second chance at a life I always dreamed about. I'm grateful that I wake up every day knowing what true love is and understanding that family is more than just our DNA, it's a group of people who love and treasure the bonds they share. All of you are what I am grateful for." She looked at her father and uncle before she let her gaze visit the rest of those gathered. She raised her glass. "A family both of blood and of choice."

***

That evening, as they got ready for bed, Jax heard Chance groan. "Too much turkey? Maybe it was that second piece of pumpkin pie I saw you shovel away."

Chance turned with a glance that was pure sheepishness. "How'd you see that?"

"Eyes in the back of my head, my love. Plus, I know how much you love Kristi's pie."

"She should have been a baker. That woman kept me in cookies long after Mom stopped making them for me." Chance stepped closer to Jax and wrapped her arms around her. "How's your leg?"

Jax sighed. "I was on it more than I should have been. Despite therapy, it tires quickly. I just wish I wasn't going to be in a cast for our wedding."

"It's going to be fine. Don't worry, we'll get you in the saddle on Glenny. If we have to, we'll skip the horseback part altogether."

Jax planted her hands on her hips. "No, that's the wedding we wanted and the wedding we are going to have."

Chance pulled her shirt over her head. "You know the other thing I'm thankful for?"

"That you can run off that pie tomorrow morning?" Jax slid down her loose track pants and sat on the bed to pull them over the walking cast.

Chance laughed. "That too. No, I'm thankful Brad accepted the plea deal. Marsha gave him two days to decide, and I wasn't sure how it was going to go. If he hadn't taken the deal, we'd be going to court on Monday."

Jax unbuttoned her blouse. "I know Penny is relieved. Taylor is livid, but that's because she wanted to bury Brad under the jail. Thank God for small miracles. That puts it to rest, right?"

"Yes. No civil service hearing. Brad retires, and we move forward to a better department without him. What's really bothering you?" Chance kissed her temple.

Jax sighed and leaned into her lover. "Mom. She emailed me a news link from California about Lacey expanding the clinic and hiring two new veterinarians. Why she thinks I would give a shit, I'll never know. If she thinks she's making me jealous or trying to show me what I'm missing out on, she's wrong. I'll take my practice any day over that rat race."

"Honey, I've come to believe that your mother is a deeply unhappy woman. That isn't going to change, any more than you're going to suddenly agree with her. There's a prayer that talks about being granted serenity to accept the things we can't change, the courage to change the things we can, and the wisdom to know the difference. You dared to change your life and come back here to start a new one. Now you need to accept that your mother is never going to approve of me or be happy for us. Ask yourself what about our life will change if she never accepts us."

"Nothing, nothing would change."

Chance nodded. "Exactly. We're going to get married with or without her blessing. We're going to spend the rest of our lives together, with or without her blessing. I'm happy your dad will be there. Time may eventually change her, but I won't hold my breath, and neither should you. If you think it would help, I'd gladly go have another conversation with her."

Jax finished undressing and slid into bed, beckoning Chance to join her. "No, if anyone needs to have a conversation with her, it should be me. Maybe someday, but not now. Right now, what I want is to feel your body up against mine."

"I like that plan."

"The truth is, I have other plans for you well before that." Jax held her lover tight to her own body and brushed her fingers between Chance's legs.

"Tell me those plans include making love?"

Jax pressed her lips to the side of Chance's neck. "Repeatedly." She ran her tongue around the rim of the ear closest to her. "And so much more, Sheriff."

"You silver-tongued devil." Chance settled between Jax's legs. Passionate kisses, followed by a warm hand that cupped her cheek, instantly transformed Jax into a boneless shell. She relaxed into the touch and brought her hands to Chance's face. "I love you so much, Chance."

"Good thing, because I refuse to live one more moment without that love. Nothing has ever freed me from everything like your kiss."

Jax watched as Chance lowered her head and kissed her again before she felt a calloused finger trace her lower lip. She tentatively touched it with her tongue before drawing it into her mouth. Chance's moan of pleasure let her know she was having a definite effect on her fiancée. Gunmetal-blue eyes bore a hole straight into Jax's soul. As the pupils dilated, the color was replaced with a reflection of pure desire. When the finger was withdrawn, Jax uttered four simple words that were a request she knew Chance would be happy to fulfill. "Make love to me."

"With pleasure."

Jax felt her center clench, as Chance placed a line of soft, wet kisses from the corner of her mouth down her jaw, until she stopped at the juncture of her neck and shoulder. The sensation of teeth grazing her pulse point caused a gasp to escape from her lips. "Oh God, Chance."

The kisses started again. Seconds later, Chance hovered over her breast. Jax put her hands on the sides of Chance's face and guided her exactly where she needed those lips. When soft lips closed around her nipple, her back arched in pleasure. The sensual assault continued, as teeth grazed the untouched nipples until both were in stiff peaks. Jax burrowed her hands in Chance's hair and traveled with her while kisses rained down on her abdomen and landed on each hip bone and the small hollows beside them. Chance nestled between Jax's legs and looked up.

"I love you, Chance." Jax stared intently at her lover.

"I love you back, and I'm about to show you how much. You'll tell me if I hurt your leg, right?"

Jax gently pushed Chance's head where she wanted her. Hot breath wafted across her center, causing Jax to shiver with desire seconds before Chance's tongue touched her most sensitive areas. Every nerve ending fired off, as fingers slid inside her and made her clit pulse. Conscious thought was completely absorbed by the feeling of soft suckles and flat licks. Jax found and locked on her lover's eyes, driven higher and higher by Chance's deep strokes. In moments like this, Jax found safety for her heart and a solid resolve in the love that would survive any storm. Seconds later, she felt the telltale tremors start as her body yielded to a bone-melting climax. "Chance!"

The next thing Jax became aware of were strong arms that gathered her in and held her close. They rarely spoke in those few moments after making love, preferring to enjoy the quiet with nothing between them. Chance's fingers gently stroked up and down her back, and soft kisses fell on her forehead. Jax tilted her head up to capture those lips in a sweet kiss.

"Welcome back."

Jax chuckled. "You do have a knack for completely exhausting me in the best way possible."

"I prefer to think of relaxing you rather than exhausting you." Chance shifted a bit in the bed until their eyes met. "Consider me your personal relaxation therapist."

"I like the sound of that. Although, on the way to the relaxation part, you have a unique ability to cause my pulse to race." Jax kissed the nipple that lay close to her lips and felt Chance jerk slightly.

"You don't say."

"I do say. I think it's time for me to return the favor." Jax urged Chance on top of her again and leaned up to deliver a searing kiss. "I want you, Chance Fitzsimmons, and I intend to show you exactly how much." Jax slid her hands down Chance's sides and urged her up over her mouth. She vowed to never take a single day with Chance for granted. As she savored the taste of the woman she loved, Jax knew she would do anything to wake up beside this woman for the rest of her days. Christmas couldn't come soon enough, as far as she was concerned.

Chapter Twenty-five

THE NEXT FEW WEEKS flew by, and before they realized it, they were in the throes of Christmas preparations. The busy holiday season should have given Chance a sense of relief with the Brad and Leland dramas out of the way. She still felt a bit edgy. The end of the year always brought a slew of reports that needed to be filed and last-minute court appearances to close cases before the holiday break. To shake the feeling, Chance invited Taylor to go Christmas shopping one afternoon.

Taylor asked Jax if she would come over and spend the day with Penny. She'd confided that she was terrified of something happening to her wife and child so close to delivery. Jax had readily agreed and the two were going to spend the day putting the final touches on the nursery.

Chance snuck a glance at Taylor whose leg was bouncing in the passenger seat. "Stop worrying, Jax is with her."

Taylor rubbed the back of her neck. "I can't help it. If she breathes too slowly, I panic. If I ask to check her blood sugar one more time, she's likely to punch holes in the ends of my fingers."

"The last few months haven't been easy for either of us. Love has made us nervous wrecks."

"You can say that again. I'd rather face ten Leland Kursts than think about Penny going into labor. I'm afraid I'm going to faceplant right in the delivery room."

Chance put a hand on Taylor's shoulder. "You're going to be a terrific mom. Don't worry so much. You'll be there for her when she needs you most; I know it."

"Easy for you to say."

"True, but I believe in you. It's why I trust you with my life and that of my family without worry. Remember that."

They drove on to the mall in silence, until Taylor changed the subject. "How about you? Starting to get nervous about the wedding?"

Chance chuckled. "Only about getting Jax and her cast in the saddle."

"You guys are still planning horseback?"

"Yeah, but not as far from the house as we'd originally planned.

You'll be able to drive there in your Cherokee. Putting Penny in a wagon at this point isn't happening. We have that little bluff that looks over the field. I'm just hoping for snow."

"Either way, it's about damn time you get hitched. You're like a different person with Jax around. I've never seen you enjoy life more."

Chance parked the Tundra. "My friend, you hit it on the head. For the first time in my life, I have no doubts. I missed years with her. I just hate that she and her mother are at odds. The woman hates my family and is none too happy her daughter is about to become a Fitzsimmons."

They exited the vehicle and walked into the mall's entrance.

"So Jax is going to take your last name?" Taylor checked her phone.

Chance nodded. "She is. I think it's one more way of separating herself from Jacqueline. She never took her ex-wife's last name. Something about professional issues with licenses and such. Now, she just doesn't care about the paperwork a name change is going to create. Jax wants to be my wife in every sense of the word. She's still her own person, but she wants to be a Fitzsimmons now."

Taylor put a hand on Chance's back. "I think she already is, in everything but name. Come on, according to my phone, it's going to take six hours of face time with my wife to pick out things for the baby. The doctor doesn't want her traveling unnecessarily. The UPS driver has been getting a workout delivering all those Amazon boxes to my house daily. These are things she wants me to look at in person today. How about your shopping list?"

Chance pointed to her head. "Got it all right here. The only thing I might have trouble finding is a particular brand of Scotch Jax's dad enjoys. I don't think we can get that here at the mall, but I know a liquor store in this area we can try." Chance looked at her watch. "Let's meet back here in an hour, then I'll help you with your list. Here's an extra key to my truck if you have things you want to go ahead and put out there before we meet up. May the force be with you."

***

It was a week before Christmas, and more importantly, her wedding. Jax sat at her desk at the animal hospital, looking over the mound of charts she needed to work on. *As fast as this place is growing, I'm going to have to hire more staff. A receptionist for sure.* She and Lindsey were working five days a week, and there was a need for late evening and weekend hours. Brandi offered to come and help during

Christmas break.

Jax had been surprised when Brandi remarked that she wasn't going home. Brandi wanted to be with Kendra for both the wedding and Christmas. The opportunity to enjoy a white Christmas and some ski time was a definite draw for a native of California's North Coast. *Pretty sure the opportunity for a romantic Christmas also has its own appeal. Well Jax, this isn't getting those charts done.* She picked up the first one and had just put pen to paper when Lindsey knocked on the door.

"You need a break."

Jax threw down her pen and pushed her long hair back. She gathered it up and pulled the hairband from around her wrist to tie the strands back. "I know, but I need to finish these charts so you can enter them. I've come to a conclusion. It's time to hire someone to do the secretary's position." Jax held up a hand, stifling Lindsey's protest. "It's not that I don't think you can do it; it's that I need you for other things. I also need to start thinking about what will happen when you accept that scholarship to go to vet school."

Lindsey crossed her arms. "I'm still planning on working. I have to. Meg's salary alone won't carry us while I go to school."

"Don't worry. Your position here is safe with as many hours as you want. That's why I'm thinking of bringing on another vet who can handle evenings and weekends. Your classes will be during the day, so you'll be able to keep your full-time position by working what days, evenings, and weekends you want. That scholarship comes with a stipend for living expenses as well."

"You're really ready for someone else to step in here?"

Jax put her head back on her chair and put up her thumping leg on the edge of the desk. "I am. Honestly, at this point in my life, it can't all be about work. I did that in California, and I lost sight of the things I loved riding my horses and even a nice candlelight dinner at home. Not that I really wanted that with Lacey, but you get the idea. Now, I have someone I do want those things with, and she's about to be my wife. That's something I don't ever want to take for granted."

Lindsey nodded. "I get that. Meg and I don't get to spend nearly enough time together, even though we're now married. With her shift work, sometimes it seems like we just pass each other at the door with coffee. The difference is, I know she's always there for me, no matter where she is. I also know I sleep better knowing Leland Kurst is locked behind bars."

"That makes two of us. How are you doing with what happened to us?"

Lindsey came in and sat down in the chair in front of Jax's desk. "The nightmares are better. Mom had to come and stay with me for a while, when Meg was on shift. Physically, I'm fine. Mentally, I get better every day. I know his trial will be coming up and we'll have to drag it all up again. He could have killed both of us, and for what? Because we didn't want anything to do with him. This constant harassment from these idiots who think we just haven't met the right man drives me crazy. Why can't they just accept we aren't interested?"

"I wish I had a good answer to that. For far too long, women were considered property, unable to decide who or what they wanted in life. Somehow, when we aren't interested, it's considered a personal affront. The fact that we love another woman somehow demeans their manhood. The reality is, our life has nothing to do with them at all. It's none of their business who we decide to build our lives with. Men like Leland Kurst take that a step further."

"If I can't have you, no one will."

Jax pointed at her. "Bingo. No matter what happens during that trial, I want you to feel safe here. I hope you do. The security and panic system Chance had installed offers us a modicum of insurance. We changed our procedures, and now, we'll add staff."

"I hope, when I graduate, you'll have a vet position for me. I never want to work anywhere else."

Jax stood and hobbled around her desk, extending her hand to Lindsey and pulling her up for a hug. "You're family, Lindsey, both you and Meg. You will always have a place here. I'm going to retire to my farm's front porch someday. I hope that you'll be interested in keeping the legacy of this place going."

Jax could see the tears well up in Lindsey's eyes before the younger woman tipped her head and nodded against her shoulder.

Lindsey wiped the tears away. "I used to think I loved working over in Elkins. I enjoyed it, but I didn't love it like I do this place and working with you. You've given me more than a job. I hope I can make you proud."

"Lindsey, you already do. You already do."

Jax squeezed her, and then looked back at her desk. "Those charts aren't going to finish themselves. Best get at it."

Lindsey nodded and walked out the door, as Jax returned to her desk.

"Oh, Chance called and said you have a dinner meeting with Pastor

Rhebekka at six. She'll pick you up. Don't forget."

"I've got a reminder on my phone and a sticky note on my computer. Go on, get out of here. I know Meg is on day shift and will be home not long after you. I'm going to finish these, then get out of this lab coat and fur-covered scrubs. See you tomorrow."

"Have a good evening."

Jax picked up her pen again and thanked the stars for Lindsey and their friendship. "Get on it Jax, the rock 'n' roll pastor is waiting."

***

Chance pulled up to the clinic. She stepped out and opened the door to let Zeus join her. "Let's go get Momma." Zeus yipped and headed to the side door. The front office lights were off, as the clinic had closed two hours ago. Chance used her key fob to activate the door lock that led to the lit back office area. Zeus immediately bounded to Jax's office. *Traitor. Though, I'd abandon me for her too.* Chance knew that the minute they entered the clinic, it was like being home. Zeus had grown very fond and protective of Jax. Chance could hear her lover cooing over Zeus.

"Oh, I've missed you. Does that feel good? So handsome."

Chance leaned in the doorway. "If I didn't know you were talking to my partner, I might get jealous."

Jax was bent over, scratching Zeus behind the ears and patting his side. "Well, he is handsome."

"That he is." Chance walked over to Jax. "And you are beautiful. You about ready to go?"

Jax took off Chance's Stetson and kissed her. Chance wrapped her arms around Jax's waist and melted into the kiss. Arms came around her neck, and a hand was threaded into her hair. She loved the feeling of the fingers tightening there, pulling her deeper into the kiss. Chance felt her center clench. A few more minutes of this and they'd miss their appointment. Jax slowly pulled away from the kiss, lightly pulling Chance's bottom lip with her teeth before releasing it.

"Now that was a hello. Damn, woman. Have I mentioned how much I love you?"

Jax squinted slightly and tipped her head as if in contemplation. "Not in the last hour, no." She put Chance's hat back on and pushed it up off her forehead, as she leaned in for another kiss.

"Well, that won't do. I must rectify this unfortunate situation. I love you with all my heart. Now we need to get going. We're meeting at Rhebekka's place. Karmen will be there to discuss last-minute menu things along with providing us a meal. I'm starving."

Jax poked her where her vest met the top of her gun belt. "You are a bottomless pit."

Chance raised a hand. "Guilty as charged. It's why I run almost every morning. That way, I can eat more of your cooking."

"Let's get going then."

Chance followed Jax down the hall, making sure each room was open so that no one could hide behind any door. When she was satisfied that everything was as it should be, she stepped in front of Jax, looked around and held the door for her. "All good."

"When I get this boot off will you still be driving me to work?"

Chance blushed a bit. She enjoyed bringing Jax to work and relished the fact that she could check the office in the morning for her and make sure it was secure when she picked Jax up. "Maybe. It's as much for me as it is for you. Any idea on when the new truck you ordered will be in? I know our dually is a bit big for Lindsey to drive you around for barn calls."

"I called the other day, no word yet."

Chance opened the back door of the Suburban. Zeus, *laden.*" Zeus loaded upon command, and Chance climbed in beside Jax and buckled her seatbelt. Her eyes constantly searched the area around them.

Jax clasped her hand. "You'll never be able to let it go, will you?"

Chance took a deep breath and faced her. "It could have been you they took. It could have been you they forced into that truck and out to that cabin. When I think about that, I..." Chance couldn't finish the thought.

"But it wasn't me, love. I'm fine."

"And Leland Kurst nearly took you from me, twice."

Jax sighed. "But he didn't. A few days from now, we're going to be on horseback in front of Rhebekka and our friends and family, promising our lives to each other. I could have lost you to that guy who shot Zeus, or those drug dealers, or the man who had his wife at gunpoint, or—"

Chance leaned over and stopped Jax's sentence with a kiss. "I get it."

Jax kissed her lightly again. "Good. The point is that things happen, and anything could take us from each other. What matters is that we make every minute in between count. So onward, Sheriff. I'm starved, and Karmen is cooking."

Chance laughed and nodded. "Let's go then."

Jax's stomach rumbled. "See, even my stomach agrees. I love you, Chance."

"And I love you. Let's go find us a preacher woman."

Chapter Twenty-six

CHANCE AND JAX SAT around a small table in Pastor Rhebekka Deklan's kitchen. Karmen served them a savory beef stew, swimming with carrots and potatoes. Thick slices of warm, homemade bread lay slathered with Amish butter at the side of each crusty bread bowl filled with stew.

"I'm going to need to move a slot on this gun belt. Holy smokes this looks good. Thank you, Karmen." Chance's mouth was watering. The urge to gorge herself was nearly overwhelming, but she politely waited for Rhebekka to say a short blessing.

Jax picked up a spoon and blew across the hot stew. "As long as you still fit into that long, leather duster for our wedding, eat as much as you want, my love."

"Karmen, if I devour the entire pot, do you have anything for the rest of you to eat?" Chance bit into the buttery bread. She couldn't stop the groan that escaped.

"I'm sure I can find something." Karmen shook her head. "But if you eat that much, Jax is going to have to roll you down Rhebekka's stairs to your vehicle. While we're eating, let's go over the menu again."

For the next fifteen minutes, Chance and Jax talked about the food that would be served at their reception that was to be held at the Confluence, inside Redemption's Road. They had changed venues on Rhebekka's suggestion.

"Christmas Day was a good choice for your wedding because the bar is normally closed anyway. Your friends and family, along with Tank, are serving as bartenders. According to Karmen, the food will be buffet style. Since the service is just before sunset, everyone will have had their Christmas festivities over and be ready to party." Rhebekka sipped her beer.

"I know it likely wasn't the most convenient, but we wanted to be able to celebrate this with a few family and friends who are coming back to Tucker County for the holidays. Most everyone has Christmas off, so no one needed to take any extra time. We want this ceremony to be meaningful but short and sweet."

Rhebekka nodded. "Short, sweet, and meaningful are my three

middle names. Now is there anything specific you want? I know you're writing your own vows."

Jax set down her mug of hot coffee. "The vows are the easy part."

"Easy for you," Chance quipped while she shoved another piece of brownie in her mouth.

Jax lightly smacked her on the arm. "Come on, you've spoken in public hundreds of times."

Rhebekka laughed as the two bantered back and forth. "Look, Karmen, already arguing like an old married couple, and I haven't even pronounced them yet. Oh, that brings up another question. How do you want to handle that, Mrs. and Mrs....Wedded Spouses?"

Jax looked to Chance who shrugged. "Well, I like Mrs. and Mrs. Chance Fitzsimmons."

Chance leaned over and kissed Jax lightly. "Whatever you want."

Rhebekka wrote in a leather-bound book. "Okay, that's settled. Any particular reading or scripture you'd like to have?"

Chance turned to Rhebekka. "We'll leave the scripture to you. My job is to enforce the law, hers is to care for animals, Karmen's is to cook amazing food, and yours, Pastor, is to find the scripture that ties it all together."

Rhebekka smiled. "I can do that."

They finished dessert and finalized the elements of the ceremony. The wedding would begin at four thirty and come to a close right around sunset. While Karmen and Jax continued to talk food, Chance took the opportunity to speak to Rhebekka.

"I just wanted to say thank you for coming to visit Jax at the hospital and at home. It meant a great deal to her. She's even more comfortable with you preforming our ceremony."

Rhebekka put a hand on Chance's shoulder. "That's all part of being a pastor, caring for those who need comfort and reassurance. I'm glad I could provide that and ease her mind. I know I'm an unconventional pastor. Sometimes that puts people off."

Chance noticed when Rhebekka dropped her eyes a bit. "I want you to know something. Jax has never been comfortable with any kind of organized religion. The few services we've been able to attend and the times we've listened to you play have shown us both a different side of what we know as grace. That's all because of you. I know you didn't conventionally come by this calling, but you're very good at it. My father used to say part of being a law enforcement officer was being able to have empathy. He told me that it was actually the most difficult part of the job. You, Rhebekka, for who you were and the life experiences you've had, bring a unique ability to show not only sympathy but deep, true empathy. You can put yourself in the shoes of others, because you've walked that path. Few pastors can boast of gold and platinum records on the walls or a career that was as successful as yours. One that you left while you were on top, I might add."

Rhebekka grinned at her. "I forgot what a fangirl you are."

"Look, Regal Crimson has and always will be in my top five bands. Your sister is killing it, but I'll be honest; I miss you wailing on that Strat."

Rhebekka lifted her head and laughed outright. "Thanks, you're good for my ego."

Chance patted Rhebekka on the back. "And you're good for my wedded bliss. Now let's go see what those two have cooked up for this shindig."

***

Christmas Eve, Jax and Chance sat in front of the fire at the Fitzsimmons' homeplace. Kendra and Brandi were toasting marshmallows in the fireplace and passing around smores. They'd decided to do their Christmas celebration on the twenty-fourth, knowing that Christmas Day would be jam packed with all the last-minute things related to the ceremony.

Jax snuggled in close, wrapping Chance's arms around her. "I'm so comfortable. I could go to sleep right here."

Chance kissed the top of Jax's head. "We could stay. I fed the horses before we came, and Zeus is with us. I'm sure Brandi wouldn't mind giving up her guest room and bunking in with Kendra."

Kendra turned around and grinned at Chance, which sent Jax into a fit of giggles. Maggie threw a pillow and hit Chance in the head.

The room smelled of pine and cherry wood. The lights on the Christmas tree danced with the shadows the firelight threw off, creating the perfect Christmas Eve. Maggie stood up and walked toward the tree.

"Okay, girls, last present of the night before Santa comes."

Kendra groaned. "Mom, you're not going to make me wear them, are you?"

"Bullseye, it's a tradition. You have to wear them." Chance completely lost it.

Dee pointed a finger. "Don't be so smug, Chance, you know your mother bought a set for each and every one of us. It's time for the annual Fitzsimmons family Christmas photo."

"What's going on?" Jax furrowed her brow.

Chance shook her head. "You'll see."

Maggie returned and handed each of them a flat box wrapped in colorful foil paper. She smacked Kendra on the head with hers. "Someday, when you have kids of your own, this will matter. Now quit griping."

"Should I be afraid?" Jax looked at Chance again.

"Depends."

"Depends on what?"

Chance tugged her ear. "On a lot."

"What she means," Dee explained, "is that it depends on how many Maggie could find in the correct size and matching pattern."

"Oh, this is going to be good." Jax put her finger under the ribbon and waited for further instructions.

"You have no idea how bad this can be." Kendra scoffed.

Maggie stood with her hands on her hips. "Now look, Scrooge, this is a Fitzsimmons tradition started by my great-grandmother, who made them by hand back then. You want to talk about bad, I can tell you about bad. We said thank you just the same. Be very careful, or your stocking will be empty tomorrow morning. Okay everyone, open them."

Kendra rolled her eyes, as she slid her finger under the wrapping paper. "Get ready to die, Brandi."

Brandi raised her eyebrows and opened her eyes wide in mock fear.

Chance pulled off her paper and shook off the box top. "Just open it, Bullseye. Make our mother happy."

Jax did the same and started laughing so hard she snorted. She put a hand over her face. "Oh my God, where did you find these?" She pulled out the blue pajama top and displayed the Star Wars characters stacked up on top of each other to form a Christmas tree. There was even a matching shirt for Zeus in her box. She called him over and pulled it on over his head. He licked her face, and then turned in a circle.

"There you go, Zeus approves."

Dee held up her matching fleece pants that displayed the heads of Darth Vader, Yoda, and Princess Leia. "Oh, your mom's got your number, Five Points. This year is all about you. I remember taking you to see the original when you were little. You were Star Wars nuts for the next two years."

Jax felt tears forming when she saw her pants had been slightly altered to accommodate her walking cast. Maggie sat down beside Jax and wrapped her in a hug. "I'm so glad to be buying two extra pair this year." She looked over to Brandi who was holding her shirt up to her chest. "Having both of you with us makes me feel like we now have six times the love." Zeus barked. "Sorry Zeus, seven times the love. Now everyone go change, time for pictures."

Chance helped Jax get up off the couch. They made their way to Chance's old room that Brandi was occupying, while the other two changed in Kendra's room.

"Need help?" Chance pulled off her shirt and slipped on the Star Wars top.

"You're just trying to get me naked." Jax grinned.

"Would I be trying to do that before making an honest woman of you?"

"I certainly hope so." Jax worked her way into the pajama shirt and unbuttoned her track pants. Chance helped Jax into her pajama bottoms and snapped the pants leg over her cast.

"Just wait until we get home."

They rejoined the family and saw that Dee had the camera set up on a tripod. She looked through the lens. "Okay everyone, in front of the tree. Closer together. I've got the remote in my hand. That's good, now stand still." Dee moved into her place by Maggie's side.

Zeus sat in front of Chance and Jax, who stood in an embrace. Kendra wrapped her arm around Brandi's shoulder and her girlfriend returned the hug by snuggling into Kendra's side.

"Okay everyone, say Merry Christmas!" Dee gave them the key phrase.

As the flash went off, Jax thought how grateful she was to become part of this amazing family.

Chapter Twenty-seven

CHRISTMAS MORNING, CHANCE WOKE to the smell of bacon frying. Her arms were empty, and she could hear muted conversation in the kitchen. She and Jax had finally left her parents' around nine and made their way home. *My guess is Maggie Fitzsimmons is in there with Jax, fixing Christmas breakfast for everyone. Guess I'd better jump in the shower while I can.* She couldn't wait to have the most incredible gift she'd ever been given in Jax's love. *All wrapped up in the most beautiful package ever.*

Chance climbed from the shower fifteen minutes later and stood in front of the mirror. She rubbed the cocoa butter into her scars, each a reminder of how much she'd gone through before reaching this day. *Steel is tempered by fire, and gold is refined by it.* "Today, I'll put a gold band on her hand and promise myself to love no other. That's a promise I'll keep until my dying day."

Jax slid in behind her and wrapped arms around her chest. Soft kisses rained down on Chance's bare skin. "Good morning."

Chance turned and pulled Jax to her, focusing on the frost-green eyes that reminded her of pulling in a breath on a crisp morning. "Good morning to you and Merry Christmas."

"Ah yes, it's Christmas morning, isn't it?"

"Indeed, it is. Were you a good girl?"

"What do you think? Naughty or nice?" Jax kissed her. Chance felt the heat of their bodies and melted into the soft lips that met her own.

"If my mom weren't in the kitchen, I'd show you just how naughty. That is her in there cooking, right?" Chance kissed her again.

Breathless, Jax answered with a groan. "Yes."

"Well then, we'll just have to wait until you are Mrs. Chance Fitzsimmons to continue this. If I hadn't been so exhausted last night, you would know exactly which list you're on."

"Ah, an old married couple already, too tired for sex."

"Easy now, or I'll show you that list with my mom right in the next room."

Jax laughed and reached behind her for the coffee mug that sat on a small table. "I think I want to wait for the full show. In the meantime, I bring gifts of black liquid gold. Hurry up, Kendra and Brandi will be here with Dee in fifteen minutes." Jax smacked her on the ass and strode away. "And before you think about drinking one too many tonight at the reception, remember, I want a full accounting of that list."

The blood rushed to Chance's center and she closed her eyes in an attempt to drop her heart rate and calm her libido. When she could no longer hear the cadence of Jax's walking cast, she opened her eyes. "That woman is trying to kill me."

***

The family sat around the massive farm table laden with breakfast food. Maggie Fitzsimmons stood at the head of the table with a clipboard in one hand and a cup of coffee in the other. Jax smiled, as her future mother-in-law assigned tasks to the troops like a well-trained general. Jax had been given the task of making sure the rings and the flowers she and Chance would wear on their dusters were present and accounted for. Dee was to use the truck and plow a path out to the field for the vehicles that would be driven to the site. Six inches of fresh powder had fallen the night before. Jax had prayed for a fresh layer to brighten the wedding. It was a crisp seventeen degrees and would likely raise only another seven to ten in the heat of the day. The pictures would be breathtaking. They'd hired a local photographer who would be at the farm around one in order to document the entire day. He'd promised to fade into the background and only ask for them to pose or remain still if absolutely necessary.

Jax sat tucked under Chance's arm, enjoying the morning with this family of choice. "Oh, we need the horses brushed out."

Kendra had her hand up in an instant. "Brandi and I are on that, first thing after breakfast. We'll curry their coats and polish the saddles."

Chance punched her younger sister in the arm. "Don't make them too slick. I'd like to stay on my horse for the wedding."

Kendra snapped her fingers like any good smartass would.

"Don't worry, Chance, I'll keep her in line." Brandi leaned over and softly kissed Kendra's cheek before smacking her in the back of the head. "Right?"

Kendra feigned a mortal wound and whimpered. "Yes, dear."

Maggie checked an item off her clipboard and pointed to Kendra again. "After that, take those straw bales and blankets up to the site for the guests and cover them with tarps until this evening."

"Aye, Aye, Captain!" Kendra saluted, soliciting smacks on the back of her head from Dee and Brandi. "Ow. Okay, okay."

Jax put her hand up and waited for Maggie to look at her. "I know I'm a bit hampered, but I can do more than you're giving me."

Maggie scowled. "I'm not through with my list. Hold your horses."

The bantering went back and forth for the next thirty minutes, as everyone was assigned several tasks. Jax was also put in charge of making sure Chance's and her own outfits were ready, and that Zeus had his own boutonnière that would be affixed to his collar. She loved the family she was marrying into. She heard a truck pull up and watched her father and Uncle Marty climb out. She met them at the door. "Morning, you two. I have breakfast plates in the oven from Maggie and your assignments."

Each man hugged Jax. Her father lingered a little longer in the embrace before kissing her temple. "Morning, Jibber Jack, how are you?"

"Really good, Daddy. You?"

"Thankful to be sharing this day with you." He looked at her, then hugged her again. "Wouldn't miss this for the world. I know I won't be walking you down any aisle this time, but to tell you the truth, you're not mine to give away. You're a beautiful woman your mother and I somehow managed to have a very small part in bringing into this world. I'm proud of who you've become all on your own."

Tears welled up in Jax's eyes and she snuggled into her father's embrace. "Thank you, Daddy."

"No tears, it's your wedding day and Christmas to boot. I brought you something. You're supposed to have something old and something new, something borrowed, and something blue. This was Jennings', and I'm sure he'd want you to have it with you today. He handed her a small box. Jessie said he wished he could be here, but he's deployed."

Jax wiped her eyes and opened the small, hinged box. A royal blue ribbon held the medal Jennings had received for bravery as a police officer. The sight of it completely took her breath, as she remembered the circumstances. Jennings had rushed onto the train tracks as the long line of cars barreled down on them with screeching brakes. He scooped up the small boy in a dirty diaper and dove for the other side of the tracks. Both received minor injuries, but the boy lived and was placed in foster care. They'd found his overdosed parents in a van, several blocks away. Jennings had always been Jax's hero, right along with their decorated father. She put a hand to her mouth and stifled a cry.

Mike St. Claire held his daughter close. "He's watching over you, Jax, and he's so proud that you've always taken your own path. I know it."

They stayed like that for a few minutes, until the clang of dishes from the kitchen drew Jax out of the moment. "We'd better get you fed. Maggie has a list a mile long that needs to be done before one. I love you, Daddy.

"I love you, too. Now, show me to breakfast."

Jax did just that, knowing that her father was right. *You'll be right with me, Jennings. I love you, and I miss you more than I can say.*

***

Chance fidgeted with her shirt, trying to fit the studs through the buttonholes. She struggled with the top button, before Sarah slapped her hands away.

"You're going to make that shirt a grubby mess. Bend down here." Sarah deftly slotted the last stud through the buttonhole and adjusted the collar.

Chance scowled. "My hands aren't grubby. I've showered three times today! Give me a little credit."

"Easy there. Tell me your palms aren't sweating like crazy right now?"

Chance wiped her palms down her jeans. "Yeah well?"

Sarah laughed and shook her head. "Oh, my God. Was I like this when our roles were reversed? I don't remember yelling at you." She reached for the small bow tie; the beautiful grouse feathers matched the colors of Chance's vest.

Chance closed her eyes as Sarah threaded the bow tie around her neck. "Fuck, Sarah. I'm sorry."

"It's all right. You're nervous, I get that. The woman loves you. It's not like you have to impress her or anything. She's gut hooked, just like you are. There, you look great."

Chanced turned to stare in the mirror. She looked so different in something other than a uniform. Jax had chosen her outfit to complement her own, something Chance had yet to see. "Have you seen her yet?"

Sarah nodded. "I have, and you are going to fall off Kelly when you see her. I'd hold on to the saddle horn if I were you."

Chance had been banished to Maggie's house while Jax got ready with the assistance of Kristi, Brandi, and Penny. "I don't want to rush this, but I want it over with. It feels like today will erase so many empty years."

"You can't erase them, but you can make up for them. You've always been like a sister to me, and I couldn't be happier for the choices you've made."

Chance knew she was talking about Faith, the one subject she wouldn't bring up today. *Not today.* "Thank you for always standing by me. I don't know how I'd have ever made it this far without your friendship."

"You can pay me back by keeping my son as safe as possible. I've only got one kid, Chance. Someday, I'd like to be a grandmother, as odd as that sounds."

Chance put her hands on Sarah's shoulders. "You know I'd jump in front of a bullet or a train for him. I'll keep him as safe as I know how to. He's doing great at K9 training. I'm glad he's home for this. It wouldn't be right without him here."

"You're his hero, you know?"

"I think he has many of those, starting with the two women who brought him into this world. Sarah, don't ever think he doesn't look on you with the same admiration. Trust me on that."

"Well, don't get me all sappy now. We've got a hitchin' to go to. I brushed your Stetson. God, you're a femme's wet dream, you know that?"

Chance shook her head in laughter. "I only want to be one femme's wet dream, the one who's about to wear my ring." Chance straightened Sarah's jacket lapels. "You look pretty spiffy yourself."

"Kristi thought so. As she was dressing me, all I could think of was undressing her. She's smoking today."

"We are two lucky fucks, you know that?"

Sarah slapped Chance on the back. "I know we don't usually say this to each other, but I can't imagine you don't know it. I love you, Chance. Let's go get you married off."

"Love you too. Would never have made it this far without you." Chance looked at her watch. "It's about that time." She and Zeus made their way to the door, and she turned back to the house that she'd grown up in. "Way past time." She patted her breast pocket and felt her dad's badge there. *I wish you were here, but I know you have the best seat in the house. Thanks for thinking, back all those years ago, to make the moms-squared my guardians. They did well, Dad, raised me like you would have.*

***

Jax sat in front of the mirror while Kristi and Penny worked on her hair. Penny frequently stopped to sit down, as she was very uncomfortable. Taylor hovered outside the master suite door.

"Penny, are you doing okay?"

The very pregnant woman rubbed a spot on her side. "I would be if this baby would stop trying to kick its way out. Wee one wants to come out and play one minute, then takes a nap directly on my bladder in the next. Which reminds me, I have to pee."

Penny practically waddled to the master bathroom.

"I'm glad you're here for more than doing my hair," Jax said to Kristi. "I'm half afraid she's going to go into labor any second. Taylor is near frantic." Jax applied her waterproof mascara.

"I'm keeping a close eye on her." Kristi nodded. "I've already checked her sugar once today. It's not going to be long. I think she's going to go early. Don't worry, she's got a dozen people watching her."

Jax clasped Kristi's hand. "Thank you for doing this."

"It's my pleasure. I haven't seen Chance this complete since you left all those years ago. You've made her so damn happy by coming back."

"I sure as hell took my time doing it, out of pure stupidity. Running from something never solves anything."

Brandi walked in, awkwardly fumbling with something in her hands. She handed it to Jax. "This is from your mother. Maggie says you shouldn't read this. She took the message and promised she'd have it brought to you, but she says you should trash it."

Jax rolled her eyes. *Not today, devil, not today.* She tucked the note into a drawer, determined to not let a single spiteful word from her mother ruin her day.

From the bathroom, they heard Penny yell for them. "Uh, can someone go get Taylor, please?"

Jax jumped up and went to the door. Penny was holding her abdomen. "What's wrong?"

Penny looked mortified. "I think my water broke."

Kristi rushed to her side, as Taylor pushed past everyone and stood shaking in front of Penny. "I knew this was a bad idea. Are you okay?"

Penny patted her cheek before doubling over a bit. "I'm pregnant, Taylor, not dying. My water broke. We need to go."

Taylor pulled at the front of her shirt. "Oh shit, are you sure? It's too soon."

Penny groaned, while Jax held her hand. "Taylor, I'm only going to say this one more time. We need to go. Get the Jeep, and the girls will help me out to the vehicle. My contractions aren't close together, but with the problems we had earlier on in this pregnancy, I'm not taking any chances. Let's go to the hospital."

Taylor fumbled in her pocket to find the keys. She dropped them on the floor, twice, before she ran out the door. Maggie saw her and ran to Penny. The others jumped into action. Kristi got on one side of Penny and Maggie on the other.

"Penny, I'm not sure if Taylor will survive this. You'll have two babies to deal with." Maggie held one hand and put her other on the small of Penny's back. "Don't worry about anything here, you just go have a healthy baby. That will be the best present for the married couple."

Taylor rushed back in. "I've got the Jeep right outside the door. Let me help." She took the hand that Maggie was holding and walked Penny out the door.

They helped get her situated and buckled in. Kristi whispered something in Taylor's ear, and Jax watched her take several deep breaths before climbing in. Penny waved. "I'll call and let you know. First babies take a while. Don't worry if you don't hear anything. I promise we'll keep you updated. Be happy Jax and save me some cake! Even if you have to freeze it so I can eat it later, I want a piece!"

Jax waved. "You've got it. Drive carefully."

The bridal party watched the Jeep Cherokee drive away. *Watch over them Jennings, they've been through enough. A new life coming in is exactly what we need to start this life off.*

Maggie stepped forward and clapped her hands together. "Okay, show's over. We have less than an hour to finish getting ready for a wedding. Let's go girls."

Jax wrapped an arm around her soon to be mother-in-law's waist. "Thanks for the warning on that note. I didn't open it. I'll deal with all that another day. She won't get a shot at putting a single cloud over this day. I love you, Maggie. I'm grateful I can call you Mom after today."

"Honey, you could have been calling me Mom all along. Dee and I love you like one of our own. You've given Chance her smile back and let her believe in love again. That's all these two mothers can ask for."

Jax kissed the silver-haired woman's temple. "She's my forever chance, and I'm holding on for the rest of my life. Count on that."

***

Chance stood at the door to the barn, holding Glenny. They'd rigged up a wagon with steps that Jax could walk up and easily step into the saddle. They'd practiced over the last few days and had it nearly down to a science. Chance stood there in her dark leather duster, Stetson in place, with Zeus at her side. Kendra held Kelly for her.

"You nervous?" Kendra rubbed Kelly's nose as she spoke to her sister.

"Damn skippy. I just want to see her." Glenny nickered beside Chance, and she turned to soothe her. "Easy girl, she's coming."

Kendra pointed to the pathway coming from the house to the barn. "And there she is. Remember to breathe."

Chance lifted her eyes to see Jax coming toward her with her slowed gait. The path had been cleared to make it easier for Jax to trek the distance out to the barn. "My God," she whispered, incapable of putting any power behind her voice. Her strength had been stolen, along with her ability to think about anything beyond how beautiful Jax looked. She wore a pair of tan denim jeans and a thick, cream-colored sweater in an Aran honeycomb pattern. A tawny duster just brushed her shins. "Stunning."

Kendra stepped forward with Kelly. "I agree, Chance. Let's get you two saddled up and hitched up."

"I'm all for that." Chance moved toward Jax and took her hand, kissing it lightly. "Be still my beating heart."

"You look dashing, yourself. I love the tie." Jax leaned in and kissed Chance lightly.

"You look good enough to eat, and later, I will," Chance whispered in her ear.

Jax slapped her lightly on the arm. "First things first. Make an honest woman of me, and I'll see what we can do about that hunger. I do need to tell you, Taylor and Penny had to leave." She put a hand on Chance's shoulder. "Settle down. Penny's water broke, and she's having contractions. She told me to tell you to get on with this wedding, because apparently, we'll be having a christening soon."

Chance stood there in shock. "Was Penny doing all right?"

"Better than Taylor. She's fine. She's going to text Maggie updates. What do you say we get married?"

Chance held out her arm and allowed Jax to crook her hand inside. "It would be my greatest honor." She handed Kendra the reins and helped Jax up the steps. Jax was able to swing her good leg over the saddle, allowing her walking cast to rest on a special stirrup Chance had designed. When she was seated and comfortable, Chance leaned over and kissed her. "Let's go do this. I can't wait to call you Mrs. Fitzsimmons."

Jax took the reins from Kendra in one hand and cupped Chance's cheek in the other. "I've waited a long time for this."

Chance nodded and walked back down the steps to climb into Kelly's saddle. She and Jax waited for Kendra and the rest of the wedding party to make their way to the bluff. The sky was just turning that dusky blue, and millions of snowflakes floated in the air. Large torches lined the procession to the final spot overlooking the fields. Rhebekka would meet them on an elevated platform that would allow her to be at eye level with the couple. The song in their hearts was the only music they needed for their processional.

The last car door shut, and Chance looked to Jax with one final reassuring glance. They waited another five minutes, then slowly made their way out through the snow-covered field. Their photographer was also on horseback, slightly up and out of the way of the pristine snow they would ride through. As Chance watched Glenny carry Jax, she marveled at the beauty of the woman atop the gorgeous snow-white Arabian. Jax was every bit the horsewoman she was, and Chance looked forward to many long trail rides together.

Sprigs of holly and pine adorned Glenny's and Kelly's manes, to match the small flowers each woman wore pinned to their dusters. Zeus bounded through the snow beside them. When they reached the gathering, their friends and family stood to the outside of the platform. Both Sarah and Kristi had ridden out on their own horses and were waiting for them.

When the couple made it to the platform, they joined hands and held their horses as still as possible. The snow continued to fall softly around them. The torch lights warmed the area with a golden halo in the fading sunlight. The silence gently held the breathing and soft rumbles of the horses.

Rhebekka stepped forward. "We are gathered to join these women, Chance Raylynn Fitzsimmons and Jax Elizabeth St. Claire, together in matrimony. Their road has not been an easy one. Together, they've overcome tragedy and hardship to be here before us now. These two hearts were once separated, yet they found their way back to love once more. When I spoke to them about a favorite scripture, they told me that I would know better what could offer the greatest gift of wisdom." She stopped for a second. "Chance also said it was my jurisdiction."

The assembly joined her in the moment of levity with soft laughter.

"There were many I could choose, some that would be expected, but the 'Song of Solomon,' the eighth chapter, says this. 'Place me like a seal over your heart, like a seal on your arm; for love is as strong as death, its jealousy unyielding as the grave. It burns like blazing fire, like a mighty flame. Many waters cannot quench love; rivers cannot sweep it away.'" She paused. "Given our area, this felt like the right one to me. Both Chance and Jax dedicate their lives to the service of others in different ways, yet in the end, they both serve as a reminder that God loves all his creatures, great and small. The couple has chosen to say their own vows. Jax, would you like to start?"

Jax nodded and turned slightly in her saddle. "Chance, I fell in love with you as a teenager. Today, as a woman, I will marry you and take your name as my own. The road back to you was winding and full of tears. That same road led me to your door once again. I didn't know if you would even want to see me. The minute I laid eyes on you at that rescue, my heart knew the love in yours. You've accepted me with all my flaws, all my baggage, and all the love I have to give, for better or worse, in sickness and in health. You opened your family to me and saved me when I called for you. You've been my shining star and my soft place to rest." Jax took the ring from Kristi. "With this ring, I pledge my heart and soul to you." Jax slipped the gold band, adorned with mountains and rivers, on the ring finger of Chance's left hand.

Chance choked back a tear and cleared her throat. "Jax, over thirty years ago, you swept into my life and showed me what love at first sight truly was. We were kids then, but now we're two fully grown women completely in love and free to be together for the rest of our lives. When I was burned, I lay in that sterile hospital bed, searching for anything to take away the pain. A single memory let me escape into a place where there was nothing but joy. I held on to the memory of floating on the Cheat River with the most beautiful woman I'd ever met. You helped me through. The memory of your touch, the depth of that teenage love, and the prayers of my parents compelled me to stay in the land of the living, when all I really wanted to do was die. In a very visceral way, you saved me then, and you save me now." Sarah handed her Jax's matching band. "With this ring, I pledge my heart and soul to you."

The couple clasped hands and looked back to Rhebekka. "As these two have signified their desire to be married and faithful to one another, let no one and nothing come between them. You may each kiss your bride."

Chance leaned over and pressed her lips to Jax's. She felt a soft hand snake around the back of her neck, drawing her in. She whispered through the steam from their shared breath. "I love you, Jax, now and forever."

"And I love you right back." Jax kissed her again before releasing her. They pulled on their horses' reins, until they faced outward toward those gathered.

Rhebekka gave her final pronouncement. "It's my pleasure to present to you, Mrs. and Mrs. Chance Fitzsimmons."

Their friends and family erupted in loud whistles and clapping. Chance held their joined hands aloft and smiled from ear to ear from under her Stetson, as the setting sun painted the sky as if it had been specially ordered just for them. The photographer circled the group, as Chance leaned in again and kissed the woman who was now her wife. When their lips parted, she whispered. "Ready?" When Jax nodded, the two riders urged their horses forward and took off across the field, breaking fresh snow in their path. They were married and bound by more than a band of gold.

Chapter Twenty-eight

REDEMPTION'S ROAD WAS DECORATED in a Christmas theme. Tiny white lights were twined around the pine boughs strung from the wooden beams in the ceiling. Guests were still picking at the buffet along the back wall and at tables strewn around the room in no particular order. Jax sat beside Chance and forked up a bite of their wedding cake.

Karmen stopped by their table. "Well, did it meet expectations?"

Jax grabbed her hand. "Exceeded anything I could have imagined." She pointed to the white confection with strawberry filling. "This is the best cake I've ever had."

"One of my specialties. How about you, Chance? Happy with everything?" Karmen pointed to the buffet.

Jax watched, as Chance looked directly at her. "Karmen, you could've served shoe leather, and all I would have needed was this woman by my side. With that being said, the food was spectacular. Thank you for everything."

Karmen nodded. "It was my pleasure, and I never serve shoe leather on Christmas. That's for Thanksgiving. I need to go check on my staff. I'm so happy for you."

"Thank you again." Jax smiled.

Chance leaned over and kissed her again. "How are you, Mrs. Fitzsimmons?"

"Fabulous, Mrs. Fitzsimmons. I love you." Jax stroked her cheek.

"I love you, too."

Rhebekka had started to play twenty minutes ago, and the room was filled with the soulful sounds of her guitar. Jax felt a hand on her shoulder and turned to see her father kneeling beside her. "I think it's time for the father daughter dance. May I?" He held out his hand to her.

Jax grinned and looked at Chance.

"Go on, he loved you first." Chance waved her on.

Rhebekka waited until they'd risen from the table, and then began Carole King's "Child of Mine." A local singer provided vocals.

"I'm so glad you were there, Dad. I can assure you this will be the last wedding you ever have to attend for me."

They swayed around the room. "I'd attend a hundred if that's what it took to make you happy, but I am rooting for this to be the last one. I think Chance is your one true love. If I'd just stood up to your mother, we'd have been doing this three decades ago."

"Daddy, no more room for regret. Life is too short to look back. I hope there's a happy ending in your future too."

"Oh, baby girl. I think I want to spend the rest of my life fishing and enjoying my daughter's happiness. As much as I like being with Marty, I'm looking for my own space. I want a little bachelor place that doesn't have a huge yard to mow or a long driveway to plow. I plan to check out every trout stream in three counties and watch the leaves turn."

"I love you, Daddy."

"Love you too, Jibber Jack. Be happy, it's all that matters from here on out. Promise me?"

"That is one promise I can easily make."

***

When the song ended, Chance walked over and grabbed the hands of her mothers. "Come on, this dance is ours."

Dee balked. "Go dance with Maggie, Five Points. I'm good right here."

Chance grabbed Dee's hand and bent down to look her directly in the eye. "I was blessed with three mothers in this life. One I never knew, and two who raised me when they didn't have to. Not one of you is more important to me than any other. I want to dance with my mothers. Both of you."

Tears filled Dee's eyes as she rose. The three of them circle hugged as Rhebekka began a special version of "Holes in The Floor of Heaven." She'd rewritten the lyrics to more accurately reflect Chance's life. Chance hugged them both closely. "I love you both so very much. Thank you for making me who I am today. I can't imagine where, or who, I'd be without you."

Maggie leaned back. "It's been one of the greatest privileges of my life raising you and watching you grow into who you are now. You and Kendra were the daughters we always dreamed of."

Dee laughed. "After you, Kendra was a breeze."

"Nice, Momma D."

Maggie pinched Dee, making her squirm. "I'm so happy for you and very happy to have a third daughter now."

Dee grinned. "I won't be surprised if we already have another daughter-in-waiting with Brandi."

Maggie smacked her arm. "Let her graduate before you go marrying her off, though I don't think you're wrong."

The song ended, and Maggie and Dee kissed her cheeks, before Chance went over and held out her hand to her bride. "I think this one's ours."

Rhebekka's vocalist broke into Jim Brickman's 'The Gift.'

For the next few minutes, the couple danced, holding each other close. Chance's mind lingered on the lyrics. She knew what a gift Jax's love was, and it was one she'd do everything in her power to keep every day. Her phone vibrated in her pocket, just as the song ended. With Jax's permission, she'd been checking for updates on Penny. When she saw who the text was from, she opened the message and showed the phone to Jax, who covered her mouth and wiped tears away. Chance walked over to the mic. "Can I have your attention? I have some greatly anticipated news. At 19:24, that's seven twenty-four for those who don't speak military time, Jackson Chance Lewis..." Jax rubbed Chance's back when words failed her at the combination of names for the newest member of the family. Chance wiped a tear. "Jackson Chance Lewis came into the world on Christmas Day, nineteen inches long and weighing in at a whopping seven pounds, three ounces. Penny and baby are doing fine, and Taylor is recovering nicely."

Everyone cheered and hugged the person nearest to them. Jax grabbed the mic from Chance. "I say we tear this dance floor up to celebrate the newest Tucker County resident."

Rhebekka began to play the Isley Brothers' "Shout" as the dance floor filled up. Chance took the opportunity to collect herself. "I can't believe they did that."

Jax rubbed away a falling tear with her thumb. "I can. The two of them love and adore you. Penny told me that without your financial help with that last round of in-vitro cycles and letting them move into your old place practically rent-free, their lives would have been financially precarious. Beyond that, Taylor looks up to you. We are going to be that little guy's godparents, so why not?"

Chance nodded. She still had no words for the incredible gift the couple had given them. "You knew, didn't you?"

Jax shrugged. "Girls talk, you know. Penny mentioned it. If the baby had been a girl, the names would have been reversed with a tad different version of my name. As Penny got in the car, she told me to tell you, Merry Christmas. Now, I'm suggesting that you take your wife out on the floor. Let's show them how it's done."

Chance grabbed Jax's hands in hers. "Thank you, my love, for giving me that gold star chance my dad used to talk about. From this day forward, you are my wife and the woman I will always love."

"I like the sound of that, Mrs. Fitzsimmons, now let's dance!"

Chance led her wife into the crowd of revelers. She hoped all those who were watching them from those holes in heaven were enjoying the show. She'd been given a second chance at love and a life with Jax. No matter what tomorrow brought them, Jax would be by her side, as her wife, until her final breath. Their love was more than she felt worthy of. One thing she did know for sure, she'd spend the rest of her life trying to live in the moment with Jax's hand in hers, walking into whatever tomorrow would bring them.

Redemption's Road-

(Five Points Series Book 3)

Chapter One

MY NAME IS RHEBEKKA Deklan, Pastor Rhebekka to most, and tonight, I'm sitting here at the bar, applying one of my unconventional ideas about how to be what Jesus referred to as a "fisher of men." I've learned that casting your net in the right water is important. My world revolves around being the spiritual leader of a non-denominational church in Thomas, West Virginia. Tonight, I'm doing my fishing in this little brewpub, the perfect place to spread a little grace in the pint glasses of the patrons as spiritual bait. You have to understand, this isn't just any brewpub. Redemption's Road was secretly purchased with proceeds from my music career. The woman with the blonde dreadlocks sitting beside me was giving me a curious look.

"So, Rhebekka, you're really a preacher?"

A small sigh left my body. If I had a nickel for every time I'd heard the question Senna had just asked, I could be retired. With that kind of money, I'd be enjoying a sandy beach in the Caribbean with a tan that would be sure to mute the colors of my many tattoos.

"I prefer pastor compared to preacher, but yes, I am. One with more than just an online ordination to be able to marry people."

My current conversation with the newcomer took a sharp right turn, as the word pastor fell from my lips. The shocking revelation that someone wearing a Metallica T-shirt—whose tattooed arms were adorned with an angel's wing down one and a demon's down the other—could be a minister had obviously sent Senna into a contemplative trip down the proverbial rabbit hole. The reality is, all five foot eight, one hundred and sixty pounds of me is, in fact, a minister. I watched as she shook her head.

"No, shit?"

I held up my right hand as if giving an oath. "I actually have a degree in theology."

Senna's pint jar traveled back to her lips, as I watched her try to wrap her head around that latest tidbit. The taproom area was small and dimly lit. I picked up my mason jar and took a pull off tonight's poison of choice, a stout as black as coal dust and flavored with hints of coffee and chocolate. Most patrons sat in front of the hand-hammered, copper bar top on stools that resembled sawhorses with a wider top board.

Her eyebrows went up. "Definitely a different kind of preacher. That's so fucking cool." Senna slapped her hand over her mouth as her face turned crimson. "Sorry."

The woman standing beside me in a flannel shirt with baggie jeans tucked into Doc Martins, washed her warm gaze over me. Something about her screamed crunchy granola and had my gaydar needle pegged. As a pastor, I was always observant for subtleties in body language and demeanor.

"Don't worry about it. The word fucking is merely a present participle adjective, unless you mean the verb, then that is something totally different." I decided it was time for a subject change. "Karmen over there tells me you're new in town."

Senna took another drink and nodded. "I am. I'm a chef at her fresh food grocery store, three days a week." She pointed to her glass. "This beer is so good."

Karmen was the unofficial welcome wagon, as well as being one of my best friends. An invitation to one of my beer and Bible gatherings was on the tip of my tongue. Instead, I opted for a bit more introductory conversation. "Total agreement there. Let me personally welcome you to our little piece of heaven. I'm sure, by now, you know most of the entertainment spots and places to eat?"

Senna nodded as she lit up and a wide grin graced her face. "I've devoured pizza at Sirianni's, had the best guac I've ever eaten from Hellbenders, and inhaled a mouthwatering corned beef sandwich from Big Belly Deli. Haven't I seen you play at the Purple Fiddle?" Senna finished the rest of her pint and looked toward the bartender.

I raised my hand and caught Tank's eye, motioning for her to get Senna a fresh beer on my tab. "I do a set once in a while, around town. You've already found the best beer."

"I can't believe how many craft breweries are in this one little area."

There was my proverbial crack in the door I'd been waiting for. "A small group of us do a tasting of the latest offerings, twice a month, at my place." My place, meaning The House of the Rising Son, the church I created where saint and sinner are welcome as equals.

It was obvious that Tank heard my lead-in, when she set the fresh pint in front of Senna. "She's telling the truth. I provide our latest beers for the event. The reverend here provides the Bible trivia. A little bread with the wine, so to speak." Tank wiped at a water ring on the bar top and winked at me, before she moved back to serve another customer.

Senna turned to look directly at me. "When do these epic beer and Bible soirées take place?"

God bless Tank. "The second Tues and the third Thursday of each month, six in the evening right down the street from where you work with Karmen. It's in the old community theater. Look for the sign on the door that says—"

Senna laughed and nearly spit out her beer. "The place that says House of The Rising Son, the one with the big Jesus?"

I'd had a lightning strike of clever irony the day I'd decided on the official name of my church. The double entendre played to my advantage as much as it was tongue in cheek. "That's the place. The giant Jesus was accidentally created when I placed a small fountain of Christ with outstretched arms in the courtyard. Once it got dark and the floodlight came on, it cast a large shadow of the Messiah on the side of the building. It would have felt sacrilegious to take it down after that."

I'd endured a good bit of ribbing for it over the last few years, but it'd become something of an iconic place for tourists to visit. With one last drink, I finished up my beer and put the mason jar back down on the counter. As my tongue snaked out to remove the froth off my lips,

Senna's eyes were drawn to me like a moth to a flame. *Oh, yes, very gay.* "Senna, I've got to roll. It was nice talking with you this evening. Again, welcome to town. Feel free to stop in if you're interested in the beer and trivia night."

Senna nodded her head. "Shouldn't you be working on a sermon for tomorrow morning or something?"

It was close to ten o'clock. I laughed and was about to throw out one of my best lines, when Tank came to retrieve my glass. The former Marine, built like a brick wall, winked at me again. She knew my shtick so well; she could repeat it with flattering imitation.

"The Lord can't do no saving on Sunday without sinners from Saturday night. Be careful on that bike, Reverend. See you in the morning." Tank saluted.

Senna's eyes got wide. "You rode a motorcycle in this weather?"

"Not a motorcycle. Tonight, my ride home is a Salsa Mukluk fat bike."

"That lime green one chained to the post out there?"

I nodded my head. "The very one."

She shook her head and laughed. "Radical. Shiny side up, Pastor."

I pointed up to the ceiling. "God willing."

I grabbed my helmet from the shelf before pulling on my leather jacket and gloves and waved to everyone before I took a step out the door. The frigid night air stole my breath. I fastened my helmet in place. Eyes heavenward while muttering a small prayer, I expressed my gratitude that home was less than a mile away and that the snow wasn't too deep. After pulling my neck warmer up over my face, I unchained Marvin. I'd named my trusty steed after the Looney Toon character, Marvin the Martian. I even ordered a sticker and placed it on the frame right after I'd bought it. As I slung my leg over the bike and settled my right foot on the pedal, the wide expanse of midnight sky and stars that twinkled from a million miles away took me aback.

"'Lift up your eyes on high and see: who created these? He who brings out their host by number, calling them all by name, by the greatness of His might, and because He is strong in power, not one is missing.' Isaiah, chapter forty, verse twenty-six."

I pedaled my way down a back street to avoid the snowplows on the main road. The ill-prepared tourists had mostly arrived on Friday night to take on the slopes. The streetlights illuminated the high, dirt-streaked snow piles packed with rocks and grime left by the plows as they cleared the roads. This January, we'd had exceedingly low temperatures and steady snowfall, both good news for the tiny mountain communities full of small businesses. They'd be able to pay their bills this month from the tourism dollars. I avoided a section of ice and used a small snowbank as a ramp, launching myself slightly into the air before landing in softer snow that led into my courtyard. Jesus' shadow welcomed me home with open arms.

With my bike on my shoulder, the three icy steps into the back door of the church weren't easy to manage. After a struggle with the door, Marvin was hung vertically on the hooks I'd positioned with a tray underneath to catch the melting snow. My favorite low-top Chuck Taylor's without laces replaced my snowy boots. The stairs that led to my loft were dull and lacked finish from thousands of footfalls.

"God, my fingers are freezing." I blew on my hands and sprinted up into my private sanctuary that sat above my spiritual one.

Senna was partially right, I had a sermon tomorrow, but my preparation was already done. With the flick of the switch, the loft's interior was bathed in soft white light. Each step on the hardwood floor produced the creaks and snaps that had become part of my everyday world. Like a song stuck between the individual boards, they sang out with each footstep. A strong aroma of cinnamon drifted to me, a sure sign that Karmen had visited before stopping by the bar. There on the counter, covered in glorious white icing, sat a plate of freshly baked sweet rolls. She left a note. *Bite me.*

Joyous laughter bubbled up from my belly, along with a hungry growl. Karmen had a wicked sense of humor that you either loved or hated. I poured a cup of coffee into a small metal pan on the stove to warm it, exactly as I'd seen my MaMaw do a thousand times. In fact, I was still using that exact pan that held no more than a cup or two. My parents bought her a microwave one year, and they never heard the end of it. I'd watched MaMaw use the pan every day of my childhood until the day she died. It had been one of the few things I'd asked for when the other grandkids were asking for money or her 1988 Oldsmobile. I'd also ended up with her recipe box filled with scraps of paper covered with barely legible handwriting. It was decipherable only by those who had spent years having birthday and Christmas cards sent to them. It was amazing that I could read them at all, as I'd never celebrated my birthday or Christmas until I was nearly twenty-one.

Jehovah's Witnesses believed those occasions were for 'the others.' Always *us* versus *them*. I nearly scorched my coffee reliving that feeling of separation. For the first twenty years, the God I prayed to was very different than the one in my life now. With a full cup, I pinched out one of the rolls and went to my small, soundproof studio in the corner of my loft.

Heather-gray acoustic tiles lined the walls and ceilings. I'd hired a professional to come in and build it for me. Writing songs and making music is like a drug to my system, the only kind I indulge in. I chewed off a giant bite of the roll and let my eyes flit back in my head as the sweet sugar rush met my taste buds. *Bless you, Karmen.* Karmen might be self-taught, but she is the most incredible chef I've ever run across. In my travels with the band around the globe, I've eaten in the finest restaurants staffed by French chefs and still had never found anything as decadent as Karmen's creations.

The steaming cup of coffee drew me in with its aroma. I'm not a coffee snob by any means. I know what I like, and for me, Maxwell House beats a thirty-dollar bag of organic beans any day. I washed down the rest of the sweet roll with another swallow and pulled my grandfather's 1956 Gibson L7C Sunburst off its stand. The story goes that when the organ at their Baptist church died, he decided to learn how to play for the choir. MaMaw had a voice like butterfly wings that would land on your ears so gently, you weren't sure you'd actually heard it. They were quite the pair.

I strummed a few cords of Grandpa's favorite hymn, *It Is Well, With My Soul.* The melody poured from my fingers and transported me right back to that rickety wooden porch, where he taught me to play the instrument I held in my hands.

"Grandpa, when will my fingers stop being sore?"
"When the music is something more than what you're playing."
"Huh?" My twelve-year-old brain couldn't understand.
"When the music reaches here"—he poked a finger over my heart—
"and not just here." He touched my forehead before urging me to
continue.

It'd taken years for enough callouses to build up on my fingertips while I learned to play at grandpa's knee. My sister and I were proud of where we'd gotten our musical talents. None of our other cousins had inherited the gift, but grandpa sat on the porch with us on hundreds of occasions. He taught us the verses to every hymn he knew, much to my mother's angst. Dad, on the other hand, couldn't have cared less. His conversion as a Jehovah's Witness was merely a ruse to get my mother to remarry him after he'd strayed one too many times. He was my own personal version of the devil.

I sipped my coffee before strumming through *Here I Am Lord*. I was feeling introspective tonight. Senna's innocent question hadn't shocked me, only pointed out the obvious that I was anything but a typical pastor. My phone rang, and as if I'd conjured her up with the notes, the name of the woman who'd changed my life appeared on the screen. I answered the call in a way I knew would make her smile.

"Peace be with you, Pastor."

"And also, with you. How are you, Rhebekka?"

I pictured the woman on the other end of the line, all five foot five of her. "I'm good, Naomi. How's the weather out there?"

"Freezing, how about your neck of the woods?"

"The same. Fresh layer came down last night, a good eight inches." She was beautiful no matter what time of day it was, and if I tried hard enough, I could smell her perfume.

"Ha, not more than a skiff then. Try seventeen here."

Reverend Naomi Layman lived in Colorado and was the spiritual leader of Open Door Ministries, an unconventional church. Like my own, she accepted saint and sinner to join her in worship. That's how I'd ended up sitting in the back row, hungover and watching a very sexy woman drop wicked riffs on a Fender, as she espoused the grace of God. At that point, I didn't think it existed and certainly not for someone like me. Her voice pulled me out of that memory.

"Dusting the cobwebs?"

"Huh?" Apparently, I'd missed something with my thoughts of a woman in a short leather skirt, boots, and a leather jacket.

"I asked if you have your sermon done."

"Sorry, got lost in a moment there. I do. Tomorrow, we're examining the issue between love and lust."

"Ah, as if you aren't lusting right now."

The loft filled with the sound of my laughter bouncing off my plaster walls. She knows me far too well. "Guilty as charged. I was thinking about the first time I saw you in those boots."

The returned laughter over the line was like water in the desert. It'd been far too long since I'd held her, something I'd likely never do again.

"Wow, you really did step into the way back machine. I'm way past the miniskirt."

"You could still rock it. I've seen you, remember?" Oh, the

memories I have.

"I'm almost old enough to be your mother."

"Given my mother was sixteen when I was born, that's not saying much."

Naomi grew far too quiet for my liking, and I knew the thoughts running through her mind. "I'll behave. Now, to what do I owe this honor?"

"I'm coming to Pittsburgh. I know you got an invitation as well, so don't bullshit me."

Eyes closed, I focused on her voice, smooth like aged bourbon, with a burn at the end that left my nerve endings raw and exposed. At fifty-six, she was still the sexiest woman I'd ever met.

"I did, I looked at the schedule, and I can't make it. I didn't know you'd be there. I'm playing that evening."

"At your own bar. Find someone else. Put your ass in that rust bucket you own and drive north."

God, how this woman knew me and how to work the internet. The little shit had checked the entertainment schedule on the Tucker County live music web page. I was sure of it.

"It's not that easy." I strummed the chorus to Eric Clapton's, *You Look Wonderful Tonight*, our song.

"It is that easy. You're making it difficult."

I heard her join in on the Fender I knew she still played during her services. I could feel her long fingers stroke my skin, as I visualized them strumming the harmony. I more than lusted after this woman, I still loved her with all my heart.

"I probably am. It doesn't mean it's going to change."

"Not until you're ready for it to."

There was silence between us, only the notes of the melody drawing out in a long cry. We reached the point of the song that epitomized the crux of our relationship, the lesson we'd learned the hard way. The chords we played blended like honey melting into hot tea. They became one, inseparably joined. As the final note drifted off, we sat silently with thousands of miles between us. "I need to go to bed." My jaw ached from holding back what I really wanted to say.

"You're a terrible liar, Rhebekka. You forget, I know that you never go to bed before four in the morning. Peace be with you."

"And also, with you."

I heard the click, and then the endless silence that indicated she'd disconnected. I raked my pick across the strings angrily, frustrated at my inability to forgive. I'm a minister who speaks of God's grace, the forgiveness of sins paid for by Christ. Yet, with all of that, I have been unable to forgive—myself. My mood was on a downward spiral. If I didn't reverse course, the morning's sermon was headed for an iceberg bigger than the one that had sunk the Titanic.

I stripped down to my black jog bra and jeans, then carried my guitar back to the stand. I stepped into my recording room. After I chugged the rest of my now cold coffee, I picked up my Strat and plugged in the amp.

Sometimes, I would sweat out my frustration in the gym or on a long trail ride. Not that night. My exorcism of this demon would come in the form of the vibrating strings on the black and white electric guitar. At heart, I am a musician, and right then, I was going to channel Stevie Ray Vaughn, Jimmie Hendricks, and Joan Jett until I could cast it out. I launched into *Voodoo Child* and prayed to the God of peace and mercy.

Available in 2020

About CJ Murphy

I began to create lesbian fiction after my wife suggested I write her a story as a personalized gift. I was privileged to be mentored by another published author who helped turn a raw manuscript, into an actual novel. Upon completion, she encouraged me to submit to Desert Palm Press. DPP offered me a contract for my first novel, 'frame by frame' in 2017. My second novel, The Bucket List, was published in late 2018. I credit my story telling ability to being an avid reader and having an adventure filled occupation for twenty-five years as a career firefighter.

Connect with CJ:

Email: cptcjldypyro@gmail.com

Facebook: CJ Murphy (Murphy's Law)

Blog: Murphy's Law Ink

Note to Readers:

Thank you for reading a book from Desert Palm Press. We have made every effort to edit this book. However, typos do slip in. If you find an error in the text, please email lee@desertpalmpress.com so the issue can be corrected.

We appreciate you as a reader and want to ensure you enjoy the reading process. We would like you to consider posting a review on your preferred media sites and/or your blog or website.

For more information on upcoming releases, author interviews, contest, giveaways and more, please sign up for our newsletter and visit us as at Desert Palm Press: www.desertpalmpress.com and "Like" us on Facebook: Desert Palm Press.

Bright Blessings

Made in the USA
Lexington, KY
06 December 2019